Jade
The Secret Begins

By: Janet Racciato

Copyright © 2014, 2015 Janet Racciato

All rights reserved.

Available through Amazon.com

Cover photography done by Christine Feiner-Grossman

ISBN: 1495488209
ISBN-13: 9781495488207

DEDICATION

I would like to dedicate this story to my two wonderful daughters, my biggest fans.

ACKNOWLEDGMENTS

I would like to thank my Aunt Millie who encouraged me to write, even when I was just learning to put together a coherent story.

I would also like to thank my toughest critic, my husband, whose editing helped put the final polishes on this story.

Finally I would like to thank all of my family and friends who read my many drafts.

CHAPTER 1

Mary gasped. She looked around her small living room. The air was filled with smoke that had the spicy smell of a local brush fire. Rushing to the window, she expected to see a column of dark smoke nearby, marking another brush fire. *Where is the smoke coming from?* she asked herself. Mary watched as the smoke in the room drifted out through the windows over their front yard. Looking back into the room, she saw that some ash had already drifted onto the two brown leather couches and the trophy case holding her daughter's old track and field awards from high school. Mary's gaze landed on her daughter Julie, whose blue eyes were wide with shock. She had a black smudge on her now even more pale cheek, ash had also settled onto her daughter's sun-bleached blonde hair. What was even more unusual was, she was standing in the center of the room holding a bewildered and slightly singed Rottweiler puppy that Mary had never seen before.

    Her husband Frank came bursting in the front door. He had been working in the yard, and came in with the hose in hand. His face was red with the beginnings of a sunburn, his thinning, dark-brown hair stuck up wildly around his head, and his gray eyes were wide in fear.

"Where's the fire?" he shouted as he looked around the room in an attempt to find the threat.

"I don't know," Mary answered bewildered, she turned to her daughter. "Julie what's going on. Where's all this smoke coming from, and where did you get that puppy?"

"I don't know what happened, Mom," Julie said. "I was just watching the news," she said motioning to the large flat screen TV on the wall behind her. Mary saw the news footage that showed a small house surrounded by flames. The camera zoomed in on the back yard of the house and you could just make out a chain lying on the ground.

"It appears that the puppy has broken lose from its chain," the news reporter was remarking on the TV. "Hopefully it will be able to escape the oncoming flames."

After a quick look around the living room to make sure there was no fire, Frank ordered Julie to the kitchen table to explain what had happened. As Mary followed behind her daughter, she saw neighbors approaching their front yard. "I'll be right back," her husband reassured them. "I'll tell them we had a baking accident."

A few minutes later they were all sitting around the kitchen table, while Julie tried to explain. "Like I said, I don't know how it happened. I was watching the fire on the news. They zoomed in on a little Rottweiler. That one," and she pointed to the sleeping dog, "chained to a post in his backyard. When they panned away to the fire that was rushing toward him, they were talking about how they didn't think rescuers would get there in time. All of a sudden I was there with him, behind that house. I didn't know what else to do so I grabbed him. When I looked up I saw the fire coming. It was so hot, and I was so scared I wished that I was back at home. Then I was in the living room again."

Mary held what was left of the chain the puppy had been tethered to. The last link ended smoothly. *It doesn't have any tool marks or crimping, like it was made to just end mid link*, she thought fascinated. She was having a hard time believing what had just happened, but one look into the living room and the still clearing smoke and she couldn't doubt that it had really happened… somehow.

"Let's keep this to ourselves," Frank suggested after they had time to think about what happened. "We'll sound like lunatics if we try and tell people, and our lives will be turned into a media circus."

"Besides, we don't even know how it happened, we have no proof," Mary was nodding as she agreed with her husband. Her blue eyes, a match to Julie's, held a look of worry. "Or even if it will happen again," she said coming to a decision, and nodded her head again decisively. "Yes, it probably won't happen again." The worry faded from her eyes. It had just got back to normal this last month. Julie had nearly died in an accident a few months ago. She didn't want their lives turned upside down again.

"What're we going to do with the dog?" Frank asked, interrupting her train of thought.

"Can I keep him?" Julie begged, coming back to the present.

"Shouldn't we try to return him?" Mary asked.

"How would we explain how we got him?" Julie asked doubtfully.

"I don't know… Will you have time to train him with all of your classes?" Frank asked frowning. This was their daughter's first semester back to classes at California State University at San Marcos after her accident, and he still worried about her overdoing it.

"No problem dad, besides it'll be like having my own therapy dog." Julie assured him, giving her dad an impish grin.

Mary groaned to herself. *He never could resist that overly innocent look.*

Julie's life went back to normal after that weekend. In the end they had decided to alert the local animal shelter that they had found the puppy by the side of the road while they were driving near the fires. The animal control agent had asked them if they could keep it because their shelter was full of pets that had been displaced by the fire. The man took their information hurriedly and told them that they would be contacted if anyone came forward looking for the young dog. When they called the animal shelter again a few weeks later to check, they found out that no one had been looking for him and were told they could keep him if they wanted. Since then Julie had named him Cinder, for obvious reasons.

That had been two weeks ago and fall semester had started. California State University, San Marcos was built on a hillside. The large granite-faced buildings were bright in the Southern California sun. Julie's college classes were all going well, but she was kept busy studying and taking Cinder to obedience classes at the local pet store. Luckily he was slowly learning that the study floor was not his personal potty spot.

At that moment Julie was sprinting up a long flight of stairs between the Administration Building and the College of Business. She was breathing heavily from the effort, but it was the fastest way to her next class, and she had to hurry. She had a math midterm today and she was running late. Her professor's tests were always really long and she needed as much time as she could get. So now, she was taking the steps two at a time desperately trying to get to class on time. The bell on the school's clock tower started chiming the hour, and she knew she was losing precious time. Julie started up another set of steps and the next thing she knew, her foot kicked the classroom door open. The door slammed open and hit the wall behind it with a harsh bang as she stumbled through it. The entire class stared at her as she struggled to recover her balance.

"Oh! …. Oh, I'm sorry," Julie looked up at the class

and tried to compose herself, "I tripped," she said lamely. When she walked up to her professor, he handed her the exam with an annoyed look for her interruption. She blushed in embarrassment and ducked her head self-consciously as she searched for an empty seat. The other students went back to concentrating on their tests. *I can't think about what just happened*, Julie thought. *I need to pass this test first.*

Later, back in her car, she sat thinking about what had happened when she had 'tripped'. *I was hurrying, wishing I was at the door to the class already, wishing so hard I had pictured it in my head…. Maybe that's it, maybe I have to want to go and then picture the place in my mind.* She started her car, resolving to try her theory later.

CHAPTER 2

"This is a Channel 12 Special Alert. The Oceanside Police Department is asking for assistance in finding this man," the news commentator announced.

Julie was doing her homework in front of the TV, and her attention was drawn to the pretty, blonde reporter and the picture of an elderly man on the screen next to her.

"His name is William B. Chesterfield and he was last seen in the old business area of town," the reporter explained. "He was wearing a Hawaiian print shirt and tan pants. Mr. Chesterfield suffers from Alzheimer's and could be a danger to himself. His family is very worried about him, because he is in need his of heart medication. If you have any information regarding the whereabouts of this man please contact the Oceanside Police Department."

Behind the woman, Julie could see the local police station. She knew the area well. It was next to the pet store where Cinder was taking his obedience classes. The news was now showing the picture of the man with his basic description of height, weight and age. The next screen had the contact information for the task force the police department had set up. Julie looked at the picture; the man had a white beard and his white hair was short but unkempt. His nose was bulbous and his cheeks were flushed and his brown eyes were slightly rheumy.

Julie had been practicing 'zapping' over the last few weeks. She could not think of a better word for it, *besides teleporting sounded too stuffy*, she thought. She had used her puppy Cinder and different places in her house as destinations. She had found that if she thought about a person, or in this case Cinder, she could tell if they were alone and sort of where they were. Then she could teleport to them. Also, if she knew a place and could picture it in her mind well enough, she could will herself there. She had never told her parents what she was doing because she did not want them to worry. Ever since her accident a few months ago, her parents had been a bit on the over-protective side.

Now Julie concentrated on the picture of the elderly man that was still on the screen. She could feel him, but her head felt fuzzy when she tried to get a sense of where he was. Instead she just used him as a beacon and tried to zap herself right next to him.

"Yuck," Julie exclaimed when she realized that she was sitting in trash. Standing up quickly she looked around at the rundown alley; debris from several overturned trashcans littered the ground around her and it smelled like rancid milk and urine. Holding her breath she looked around and found the man a few feet away, slumped against a grimy wall, passed out. His hair, which had looked unkempt in the picture, looked even worse now. She knelt down next to him and tried to rouse him. Slowly he opened his eyes and looked up at her.

"Oh Donna, isn't it a wonderful day?" he asked, obviously not really aware of where he was.

"Yeah, it is," Julie agreed with him as she helped him to his feet, belatedly remembering that she was supposed to keep her identity secret. *I'll have to take him somewhere where I won't be seen.* Julie thought. *I really didn't plan this very well.* Then she remembered there was a narrow parking lot between the police station and the pet store, *maybe I could zap in there without being seen.* Julie concentrated on the area she had in mind. *Okay,* she thought she remembered enough details about that side of the building. She held onto the elderly man tightly and willed herself to teleport to that spot. The next instant they were there and she steadied her passenger.

"What just happened?" he asked, looking around bewildered. "Where are we?"

"It's okay, you're safe," Julie reassured him as she started leading him around the corner of the police station. She stopped abruptly at the sight of the news crew. *I don't want to deal with answering questions,* she groaned, *not just from the reporters but also my parents when they find out.* Julie looked around and noticed a couple walking toward them on the sidewalk. They had not noticed Julie yet, so she faced the man in the direction of the police station entrance. "Go in there and ask for help," she instructed him and then quickly ducked back around the building. As soon as she was out of sight she zapped herself home.

Julie settled herself in front of the TV again to finish her homework. A few minutes later the same reporter came on with Breaking News emblazoned across the bottom of the screen. Next to the reporter stood the couple that Julie had seen walking in front of the police station. "I have an update on the missing person. Mr. Chesterfield has been found. With me are the two people credited with finding him." The reporter turned to address the couple standing next to her. "Were you aware that there was an ongoing search for this gentleman?"

"No, we'd just finished eating lunch at the sushi place nearby," explained the woman.

"Then how did you know the man needed help?" the reporter asked the couple.

"He just seemed really lost," the man answered, a bit bewildered by the camera. "He almost walked in front of a car, so we thought we should take him into the station."

"There you have it folks," the reporter spoke to her audience turning to face the camera. "This story will have a happy ending, thanks to a pair of good Samaritans. In conclusion, Mr. Chesterfield has been found and is being transported to a local hospital for observation, but appears to be in good condition." The report ended with a short video clip of the man being loaded into the back of an ambulance.

Julie chuckled ruefully to herself. There was no way she was going to tell anyone what had really happened. Now that she thought about it, she had not been ready when she had so quickly gone to help that man. She realized she needed to think about places in the community where she could zap without being seen. For a moment she hesitated, *what am I doing? Am I really going to do this again?* She thought about her parents and how they did not deserve to worry about her again. *All those weeks they had spent at her bedside not knowing if she was going to live.* She also thought about what she wanted to do with this power of hers. *But I want to help people*, she realized. After all, that was the reason she was becoming a nurse. She had always felt helpless when the news reported on missing people. Now she could do something about it, but she knew she needed to keep it a secret too.

Then it hit her, *a costume!* She needed a disguise. Grabbing her books she headed to her room and threw them on her twin-sized bed. Then she turned to survey her closet. She had seen enough investigative documentaries to know she needed to cover up anything that could be used to identify her. Her eyes scanned through her clothes. Mostly she wore jeans and T-shirts with catchy or cool slogans emblazoned across them. *No, those won't work*, she thought disappointed. She kept looking, starting to think that she would have to go shopping. Then she spotted one of her Renaissance Faire costumes. The costume was based on an old Elizabethan style that went with the old world theme of the fair. Part of the costume was a dark green, velvet, hooded cloak with a black satin liner. Of course it would not be practical for her to wear the matching green dress, but it was a good start. She thought about her options. If she wore all black under the cloak with a black ski mask and black gloves, no one would be able to distinguish any of her features. Then an idea hit her, she had seen the black Army style uniforms the police SWAT team wore, that uniform and dull black boots would work. *A black ski mask will be way too hot*, she thought critically, *especially under the hood of the cloak. I'll have to find some other option.*

Julie came up with an idea a week later as she was on her way home. When she stopped at a light, she looked over and saw a motorcycle rider in the lane next to her. Where his face should have been was a skull and the man's eyes looking through two holes. *It must be a mask*, she thought, but it was so tight fitting it looked like it might be painted on. After studying it longer she decided it must be some kind of full face mask. A skull face was not what she was looking for exactly, but maybe she could find a plain one.

That night she found it online, on a motorcycle supply site. The black, tight fitting, lightweight mask was meant to protect motorcycle riders from wind burn, but she could use it to hide her identity. It only took a few days for it to arrive in the mail. When it was finally there, Julie worked on designing her costume a little more. In the end she attached the top of the face mask to the hood of the cloak in order to hold the hood in place. At last, she had the costume ready to try on.

It'll work, she thought as she looked in the mirror critically, *it'll hide my identity*. Her eyes were barely visible in the shadow of the hood and it was very hard to tell where her body ended and the cloak began. Suddenly Julie giggled and grinned to herself self-consciously. *I look like a Saturday morning cartoon character.*

Hassan stood in the long line to go through customs. There were several lines that he could have chosen, but he had noticed that the agent in this line was not asking the airline passengers as many questions as some of the other customs agents. The man had a bored expression on his pale, gaunt face and his eyes appeared a bit sunken as well. As Hassan watched, the agent paused to blow his nose. *He's sick*, Hassan thought to himself pleased, knowing the man would be even less likely to spot a fake passport. He waited patiently, maintaining a pleasant expression on his face no matter how long he had to wait.

"Next," the sickly agent called as he motioned Hassan forward.

Finally, he thought impatiently, even as he smiled broadly at the customs agent. "How're you doing today?" Hassan asked cheerfully as he placed his passport on the small counter.

"What is the purpose of your visit to the United States?" the agent asked in a raspy voice ignoring Hassan's question. The man sniffled loudly and blew his nose again.

"Business," Hassan said helpfully.

The man looked over Hassan's passport. "How long do you plan to stay?" he asked disinterested.

"A week," Hassan explained. In reality he had no idea how long it would take to accomplish his mission. He thought about the encrypted thumb drive in his briefcase.

CHAPTER 3

Julie sat at her computer desk doing her homework. Glancing over at her costume, which was draped over her chair, she snorted. It had sat there for weeks and she had not had any opportunity to use it. *The comic books never talked about how boring a superhero's life was* between *saving the world*, she thought ruefully.

"Dinner's ready," Julie heard her mom call from downstairs. *Good*, she thought with a sigh of relief, *I need a break from my chemistry lab write-up*. She finished the sentence she was working on and then headed downstairs.

Julie settled into her seat at the table. Her dad was already sitting at his place on her left, reading one of his favorite tech journals. *Engineers and their idea of recreational reading*, she thought with disgust.

The TV was on in the background as it usually was during dinner. She ignored it as she started eating the pasta her mom had served her.

"Oh, that poor boy. His mother must be so worried," her mom commented, watching the news report over Julie's shoulder.

Julie turned around to look at the television; the crawl along the bottom of the screen said a boy had been lost in the mountains in Oregon while hiking. The sheriff was standing in front of the police station, a squat, white stucco building. The reporters and onlookers crowded around the podium waiting. The sheriff raised his hands to quiet the gathered crowd, preparing to make his announcement.

"From what we have learned, Tommy was hiking with his Cub Scout group when he somehow got separated. He knows some basic survival skills so we are very hopeful for his safe return," The sheriff reported. "However, weather forecasts are predicting an early fall snowstorm tonight. We are hoping to find him before the worst of the weather hits. There are close to a hundred volunteers helping us search for him at this hour and the local National Guard unit has already offered the use of one of their reconnaissance helicopters equipped with a thermal imaging device to continue the search after dark. I'd like to thank all of the volunteers who have come out to help. We will keep you informed of any further developments after we have alerted his parents," the sheriff concluded as he prepared to take questions.

The camera shifted from the podium to the field reporter. "Well, it seems the sheriff is very confident that they will find this boy safely. One big concern however is the storm moving in from the northwest that could drop the temperatures on the mountain down to near freezing tonight. Snow is also possible at the higher elevations. Reportedly the boy was only wearing shorts and his Cub Scout shirt. He should have a backpack with emergency gear, but even with an emergency blanket he'll get awfully cold tonight. This is John Takahashi, reporting from Crater Lake National Park, near Roseburg, Oregon."

Julie thought about the boy all through dinner, but she could not leave too quickly or her parents would get suspicious. The news had only shown a picture of Tommy for a moment, not long enough for her to try to get a fix on him. She was sure the internet would have a picture. *The poor kid is probably scared and cold by now*, she thought. Julie finished eating and excused herself from dinner with a comment about a lab report she was working on. She headed upstairs to her bedroom and locked her door.

It only took a moment for her to find the news report about the missing boy. They had a picture of him that had been supplied by his parents that was only a few months old and showed him at the beach. Julie concentrated on it as she closed her eyes. She focused on picturing his thick curly hair and green eyes, his small chin and his round face. *I've never tried to zap so far before, I wonder if I'll be able to find him.* After a few minutes, she was about to give up when she 'saw' something in her mind. It was like a small spark in a dark room, one you are almost not sure you saw. She concentrated on where the spark had been, she felt like she was getting closer to it. It was like floating through complete blackness with only a single shining star to guide her. She slowly became aware of the sensation of cold and fear. Not her fear. It was not inside her. This felt like it was… the best way she could describe it was outside of her. *It's the boy, I've found him!*

Julie opened her eyes, breaking her concentration. Quickly she put on her costume before she went back to her computer and looked up Roseburg, Oregon. *I need a place I can take him after I find him.* This time she wanted to have a plan; she had lucked out the last time because she had known the area, *but I can't always drop off people in front of the Oceanside Police Station.* She found a picture of the Roseburg town hospital. It looked like a modern facility, with mostly concrete gray walls and very sharp corners. She printed the picture, just in case, and tucked it into her pocket. Then she went back to the picture of the little boy that was still up on her computer screen. She concentrated again; this time it seemed like she found him faster. Once she was ready, she shifted her concentration the way she had learned, to zap her to the boy.

She had often tried to find the words to describe the

sensation she felt when she zapped to a place. The best she had come up with was that it was like she suddenly moved forward without walking, like she had stepped onto a fast moving sidewalk, or like the world moved under her, and she would be at the new place. It always left her slightly dizzy, but the feeling cleared quickly after she arrived.

When Julie got to the boy, the cold and dark hit her with an almost physical force that made her gasp. It was not all that cold but coming from a warm fall night in Southern California to the side of a mountain in Oregon was a bit of a shock. She looked around as her eyes adjusted to the dark and saw that she was in the middle of a forest of large pine trees. There was a light rain falling and the ground was covered in wet pine needles. A little in front of her, where she had expected to see the boy, was a particularly large tree. She focused her mind to find the boy, to find his spark. That was where he was, she was sure, but she could not see him. She got down on her hands and knees and peered under the branches. He was tucked under the low hanging branches in a sort of tree made tent. He had an emergency blanket wrapped around himself tightly. It was completely dry under the tree and a bit warmer. *Smart kid*, she thought briefly. The boy's eyes were closed, and his head was tucked a little inside the silver blanket. He was sitting too tensely to be asleep, but he had obviously not noticed her arrival.

"Tommy," she called his name but he did not respond. "Hey Tommy," she said a bit louder. *I don't want to scare the boy by touching him unexpectedly*. This time he did look up into the surrounding darkness.

"Who... What are you?" the boy asked, his voice quavered in fear. He had a scared expression on his face. "I can barely see you."

Julie saw him try to focus on her face that was hidden by the darkness of her hood. "It's Okay. I'm here to help," she said reassuringly. *Great, my cloak blends in too much*, she thought as she realized that she would be just a darker form in the gloom around him.

"Where's the others? You wouldn't be out here searching for me all by yourself in the dark," he pointed out, definitely not believing her yet.

Julie cursed; *I really should've brought a flashlight.* "My name's J...," she stopped abruptly. She had almost said her name! She stopped herself mid letter, and thought frantically for a name she could use. Then the thought of her image in the mirror flashed in her mind. "Jade. My name's Jade, and I've come to take you home."

With a little more coaxing the boy crawled out from under the tree. The hope of seeing his parents again was stronger than his fear of her. Julie helped him to his feet and tucked him under her cloak for warmth. The emergency blanket helped keep him warm but it was not enough. Now that he was out from under the tree he started shivering from cold and exhaustion. "You don't happen to have a match, or a flashlight, do you?" she asked as she reached for the picture of the hospital, again wishing she had thought to bring a flashlight.

"No I don't, sorry. So how are you going to find our way back?" The boy was obviously starting to doubt her promise to rescue him.

"It's Okay, just let me think for a moment," she said reassuringly. Frantically, cursing herself under her breath, Julie thought back to the picture she had found of the town hospital. Then she concentrated on the image in her memory. After a few moments she had it. Julie squeezed the boy's shoulders, "Don't be afraid, here we go."

Julie zapped them both to the entrance of the building. They arrived just outside the main lobby, under an overhang. Warm light glowed around them and it was sheltered from the rain. There were a few people leaving the hospital. One woman shrieked at their sudden appearance. Julie ignored them and turned the boy to face toward her. The boy tried to look at Julie's face as she said, "You'll be safe now," and then she let go of his shoulders, took a step back, and was gone.

The man was frustrated. He sat in the cheery living room; a stark figure perched on the edge of the couch, as if afraid of the flowery print fabric. His Ivy League black hair had some gray at the temples and his skin was so pale it seemed like he must never go outside. His black suit and tie clashed with the Get Well Soon bouquets that filled every flat table space available. He was frustrated because he had just spent half an hour trying to get even a single piece of useful information from the Cub Scout who had been rescued mysteriously. All he had learned from the boy about the woman who had rescued him was that her name was 'Jade'. The man in the black suit was sure 'Jade' was as much her name as 'Mr. Smith' was his.

"Thank you for your time," Mr. Smith said curtly. "If you think of anything *useful*, please call me."

"Tommy, go play upstairs," Tommy's mother suggested firmly as they all stood up. She waited until the boy had left the room. "I don't think we'll have anything else to say to you, Mr. Smith," Tommy's mom said coldly. "You act as if what Jade did was somehow wrong. She saved our son's life!"

"I'm sure your son's life is very important to you, but I have to worry about our country," Mr. Smith said evenly walking toward the front door.

"How can you think Jade is a threat to our country?" Tommy's father exclaimed. He had had just about enough of this pompous ass and his attitude. "We need more people in this country who help others. She just saved our son. There's nothing wrong with that."

"Pardon me if I disagree," Mr. Smith said coldly. By now they had reached the door and Tommy's parents did not bother to say goodbye; they simply shut the door on the dark man who had interrogated their son and insinuated that his hero, Jade, was some kind of threat.

CHAPTER 4

The next month went by quickly as Julie spent her free time hanging out with friends and surfing when she was not studying. She had spent that morning studying for midterms at the college's library. On her way home she had heard about the terrorist video on the radio. The news had reported that a terrorist group had released a video of a group of US soldiers that they had captured in a battle in Iraq. In the video the terrorists had demanded the release of several of their leaders from prison. They had threatened to start killing the soldiers if their demands were not met. Unfortunately, this had happened the year before. That time it had been a civilian contractor. The man's body had been found a few days later in a river, decapitated. Later the terrorists had released a video of the beheading. The memory still made her sick with anger when she thought about it.

This time I can do something about it, she thought, determined to help. A part of her thought about how dangerous this could be. She argued with herself all the way home, by the time she got there, she had made up her mind. *I can't let those guys suffer the same fate as the contractor; not when I might be able to get even a couple of them out to safety.*

When she finally got home, Julie headed to her room. She knew her next step was to get pictures of them and their base. The news report had said they were from San Diego, but that left several options as far as possible bases. *Strange, none of the news reports online say which base they are from either*, she thought skimming another news report. In the end, she decided to use Pendleton since she was familiar with it and it was as good a choice as any.

Then Julie started searching for a copy of the terrorist's video. She paused the video at a spot that showed all of the men in detail. There were six of them, all wearing desert camouflage. Several of them had bruises or cuts on their faces, evidence of battle and of being beaten.

Julie chose one of the captives to concentrate on first. *He's cute, even battered and bruised as he is. I hope he's still alright*, she worried. The terrorists hadn't put a time line on their threats. *Don't think about that now, concentrate!* she told herself sternly. Julie focused on the picture of the man she had picked to try first; he had short black hair, and fair skin. The last thing she focused on were his bright blue eyes. Closing her eyes, she concentrated. She stretched with her powers farther and farther. Like before, she was near the edge of her reach when she felt the spark of the man she was looking for. She focused harder on that spark and slowly became aware of his condition and surroundings.

He was in pain; it was a dull throb on his arm. She could feel hints of his emotions too, a deep but controlled fear. But he was alright for the most part. He was sitting alone in the corner of a small room with no furniture. *Okay, I've found him. Now for the others.*

Julie repeated this process five more times. She found each one and got a lock on them. But this time, maybe because there was more than one person she was concentrating on, she was able to picture the layout of that part of the building. It was like she could see a ghost image of a blueprint in her mind. She could sense that they were in small rooms all in a row off the same hallway. Each of them had been in various conditions of pain, fear, and anger, but they had all been alive. At one end of the hallway there seemed to be more people close by. She was guessing that they were the terrorists. She figured she should get the soldiers starting from the end farthest from the terrorists and hope they did not notice before she could zap in and get the one closest to them. She printed out the picture of the hostages in case she needed it. Next she found a picture of Pendleton's back gate. She wanted to be sure she would be able to get them back, and she might not have a chance to concentrate like she had when she rescued Tommy. She practiced focusing in on each of them and the back gate. Each time she looked for them it was easier. *I guess practice does make perfect*, Julie thought to herself.

When she was ready, she put on her disguise. In the weeks since rescuing Tommy she had improved it a little. Now she had a utility belt (*her fellow superheroes would be so proud* she thought) with a few essentials like a flashlight. She tucked the pictures into a pocket of the belt and closed her eyes. Concentrating on the man that was at the far end of the hallway, she focused on 'being there'.

Julie found herself in a dimly lit room. The cinderblock walls had probably been white at one time, but they were now streaked with dirt and blood. There was a single light bulb hanging from the ceiling. The air was stale and smelled of things Julie did not want to think about. In front of her the first soldier looked up at her, his dark brown eyes wide and disbelieving. It was early morning in Afghanistan but the man looked weary, like he had not been able to rest at all the night before. Even sitting on the floor, Julie could tell he was a fairly tall man. He had a lean build and dark brown skin. From the faintly visible dark line on his shaved scalp she could tell he would have been mostly bald anyway. He had a cut above his hairline that still glistened with wet blood and he stood with obvious pain from an injury to his leg.

"I'm here to save you," she said and realized after she said it how cliché that sounded, *the other comic book heroes would be so proud.*

"What do you mean you're 'here to save me'? How?" he demanded. Now that he was standing Julie realized he was several inches taller than her, and she had to look up at him.

"I'm going to take you to Pendleton," she said with a hint of impatience.

"Pendleton, that's insane. Did you bring a pair of bolt cutters too?" the man asked pointing to the shackle and chain attached to his ankle and bolted to the floor. He moved his foot and the chain rasped along the floor.

"That's not a problem," she said with a hidden smile as she remembered Cinder's chain. She did not bother with any further explanations, she knew that she needed to work faster. She stepped up to the man and put her hand out. "COME ON! We need to hurry," she said in a low tight voice.

"Better you than them," the man said and took her hand. Instantly she shifted them to outside of the back gate of Pendleton. The man wobbled slightly as they arrived. Julie looked around as he recovered from the shock. They were standing in a field of low weeds. Not wanting to be shot, she had chosen a spot a little ways off from the gates. About fifty yards away she could see the two guard posts with a larger building nearby. On either side of it were lanes for traffic to enter and leave Pendleton. She knew from the times she had visited friends on base that there would be at least one guard in each of the smaller buildings and more in the larger one. By now it was after rush hour and there was very little traffic going through the gate and the guards were out of sight for now.

Julie let go of the man's large hand and zapped to the next hostage. The next room looked the same as the last one, but this soldier was lying on his side on the concrete floor, vomit pooled around his face. They had not bothered to chain his ankle because they did not need to. His skin was very pale and the brown hair on his forehead was plastered with old blood, but he was still breathing. She went up to him and knelt down. He moaned in pain as she placed her hand on his side. Quickly she zapped him to the same spot as the first. By now the first soldier had summoned the gate guards who were running over.

Julie looked toward the gate and shouted at the top of her lungs, "Medic! Trauma STAT!" like she had been taught in her rotation through an ER. The tall black man turned when he heard her cry and started back toward them. She left the second soldier unconscious on the ground and before the first man had reached them she had already zapped herself to the third cell.

The third soldier had been moving around the room when she zapped and he spun around into a fighting crouch at her arrival, his ankle chain scraping the floor loudly. This man looked like a Vietnamese friend of hers from high school. The difference was his dark skin was marked with dirt and bruises and his eyes were sharp and dangerous.

"It's alright, I'm here to help," Julie whispered, hoping the terrorists could not hear her, and held her arms out with her palms up trying to calm him. The man relaxed slightly if for no other reason than she probably did not look like much of a threat. "Let's go, we might not have much time," she stepped forward and held out her hand.

"Like hell I'm going with you!" the man said as he stepped away from her grasp. "This is some kind of sick trick," he said harshly. "If you think I'll just walk out with you, you're mistaken." He lunged forward trying to grab her. Reflexively, she zapped a few feet away avoiding his reach.

"Look. We don't have time for this," Julie said and waited a moment. Her disappearance out of his grasp must have shaken him from his anger because he stood with his mouth visibly hanging open. "Fine, I'll leave you here then," and she dropped her hand to her side, as she began concentrating on the next soldier.

"Wait," the man said with a hint of desperation. "I don't know what you have in mind but it has to be better than here." He hesitated another moment, then took her hand which she had offered again.

This time, when they arrived at the back gate the tall soldier was ready. He started over when he caught sight of them. Julie could hear the sound of approaching sirens. *Three down and three to go, but I've got to hurry*, she thought as she focused on the next man and zapped away. She wanted to be done before too many people gathered.

Julie found the fourth soldier sitting against the wall cradling his arm. This was the cute one she had searched for first. It looked like he had tried putting his arm in a make shift sling using a part of his uniform. He was also chained, but like the others that did not worry her. She was running out of time so she just stepped forward as he sat, staring at her in disbelief. Without explanation she touched his shoulder and zapped them to safety.

The field was now teeming with activity. An ambulance from the base hospital and its EMS crew were tending to the rescued men. She saw a figure on a gurney being loaded onto another ambulance nearby.

What happens if I zap in on top of someone, Julie worried. Again the first soldier was quick to react to their arrival and she caught his attention. "Keep these people back! I don't want to land on them," she called out to him. She had always tried to use large open areas when she zapped because she did not know what would happen if she zapped into the same space that something else was in, and she did not want to try it. *I only have two more left*, she thought, but she knew they were also going to be the most risky. *They're the closest to the terrorists.*

As she zapped into the fifth soldier's cell she

stumbled from a wave of dizziness that hit her. She was breathing fast and she felt like she had been running sprints. She had never zapped this many times, this quickly, in a row before.

A small, lanky man stepped out of the corner at her arrival, his ankle chain dragging on the concrete. He was only a little taller than she was, kind of short for a guy. He had a narrow face, with a nose that spoke of his Italian heritage. His brown eyes narrowed as he looked at her.

"Who are you? Where'd you come from?" the man asked with a slight Chicago accent.

"We don't have time, come on," Julie said slightly breathless.

"Not without some explanations," the man insisted. "You just popped in out of thin air, like some freaking fairy godmother."

Julie laughed quietly at the image, but answered him seriously, "Fine, I'm your fairy godmother, but we have to go NOW."

"Where?" he asked suspiciously.

"Pendleton," she answered him with impatience plain in her voice. She heard shouting from somewhere nearby. Without any further explanation Julie took him by the arm while he was distracted by the shout and zapped them out of there.

The area at the back gate was clear of people. Obviously the black soldier had understood her fears. They were arranged outside of a perimeter that had been hastily assembled. Now several Oceanside police cruisers had gathered along the street, officers and armed marines stood assembled around the edges of the clearing to keep onlookers back.

Julie hesitated. The cry she had heard meant that the terrorists knew their prisoners were disappearing. Without further thought she zapped to the last cell. She tried to arrive as close to the man as she could; she ended up standing right in front of him. She quickly took him by the shoulders. Just as she zapped them out, she felt a hand clutch her right arm.

After Doc had checked his arm, Matt sat down to one side of the cleared area. He needed to think. Everything had happened so quickly and his head was still foggy from confusion. He watched as the cloaked figure popped into the center of the clearing with Demetrio and then popped out again. Demetrio had caught sight of the others and was yelling at them urgently, Matt heard something about "they know." *Oh crap,* thought Matt, *they're going to run into trouble.* The next instant Green Cloak was back with Simmons, the only one left to save. But this time they were not alone.

Matt recognized the second man. He wore the usual dirty white, man jammies that most Taliban wore, but it was his face that was most remarkable. The terrorist's cheeks were covered in small pits, like scars from chicken pox. But it was his eyes that Matt remembered most. *He's the bastard who broke my arm,* he thought. *The look in his eyes as he did it had been so cold.*

As Matt watched, the cloaked figure slumped where he stood, and Matt could see the terrorist behind Simmons reaching for his weapon. Simmons reacted first; leaping over his fallen rescuer, struggling to get control of the gun. As Matt rushed forward to help, he saw several other people reacting too. Deciding to get the strange cloaked figure out of the middle of the brawl, Matt let his buddies and the MP's take care of the bastard. Green Cloak was trying to rise, so Matt grabbed his closest arm with his one good one and half lifted, half dragged him to the side of the clearing where Matt had just been sitting. As he supported the figure to drag him to the side, he changed his assessment of the person. The cloaked figure had been lighter than Matt had expected and was very slim. *A woman*, his instincts supplied him with the answer.

After they reached the spot Matt had chosen, he took a defensive position between her and the fight, but soon saw that it was not needed. The others had already overwhelmed the terrorist and had him on the ground. Matt saw with some satisfaction that they might have given him a few extra kicks than were entirely necessary. A sound drew his attention back to the woman. He turned and knelt in front of their rescuer. "Are you alright?"

"Yes," she said nodding. Her voice confirmed his suspicions, but it also seemed young.

"Good," Matt said. "Now, who are you, what are you, and how the hell did you do that?"

The girl was chuckling softly even before she answered, "You can call me Jade, and I thought it'd be pretty obvious I'm a girl," she said sarcastically.

"Very funny, but you have a lot of questions to answer," he said seriously.

"No way," the woman said shaking her head tiredly. "I'll end up on someone's hit list. After all, I didn't just make a bunch of friends with those terrorists now, did I?"

Matt realized she had a point and he could not blame her for being cautious. In his line of work he understood all too well, that keeping secrets could mean life and death. He reluctantly stopped questioning her, realizing he probably would not get any more answers anyway. "Well thank you, for saving me and my team," as he said it the girl rose to her feet shakily. "Are you alright?" he asked again as he offered his hand to steady her and she accepted the help. He noticed as he steadied her that she was a bit shorter than he was, so he guessed she was a little under five and half feet tall. When he tried to look under her hood to study her face all he could see were her eyes. They were an intense blue color.

"Yeah, I'm Okay. I'm just tired. I feel like I just sprinted ten miles."

"Sit down. Rest," Matt suggested, but he knew what

her answer would be even before she started shaking her head again.

"I've got to go," she motioned to the growing crowd, "there's too much attention."

Again Matt held her arm, but this time to stop her for a moment. "If you ever need anything, just let me know. I owe you for this," and he waved in the direction of his team. She nodded and he let her go. The next moment she was gone.

CHAPTER 5

Matt and his team sat in a classroom on the Marine Base. It was normally used by the Marines for training, but tonight they were sitting in the small desk-chairs. They had arrived at the back gate around sunset, and it was now well after dark. They had just finished their debriefing, well, all of them except Lieutenant Cooper. He had a concussion and multiple broken bones from the beating the terrorists had given him. He had been rushed to Pendleton's base hospital. *The docs said he would make it*, Matt reminded himself. His CT scan had come back clean, but he would be unable to answer questions for a while.

The rest of them had been on their way to the base hospital for treatment too when they had been ordered to this debriefing. *This is the strangest one I've ever had*, Matt thought for the hundredth time since the meeting had started. Most debriefings included personnel from the Joint Special Operations Command, and sometimes even lawyers and psychologists. This one had started with just one man, a Marine general who did not even identify himself completely. Not only that, but most debriefings were lengthy step-by-step accounts of what happened from start to finish, but this one was only about their rescue. Finally, trying to explain how you just appeared halfway around the world is a bit difficult.

The general paced angrily in front of the men. He was wearing a nondescript Marine officer uniform, with no name, just rank insignia. What hair he had was dark with gray at the temples, but the most suspicious thing about the man was his haircut. The man's black hair had a very businesslike haircut, not Marine regulation.

Matt thought the whole situation was wrong and he did not trust this general, so he had decided to withhold the physical descriptions of the girl that he had gathered. He was pretty sure the others were doing the same. They had been trained to assess people and normally they would have been able to gather more details about her than they had. But most of their answers had consisted of "Don't know," or "I have no idea." That was definitely not what their superior had wanted to hear. In fact, General Smith was very angry at their lack of answers. He was even more upset that Matt had 'let her go' instead of trying to subdue her along with the terrorist.

Normally after a team has been debriefed about a mission they are allowed to go. However, because this general was so upset they were still being held. "You WILL remember more details about this 'Jade' woman! One way or another you will tell me what I need to know!" General Smith fumed.

"These men need to go back to the infirmary for further care. They are in no condition to be held longer for your questioning," Admiral Huntington asserted. The admiral had come up from Coronado when he had learned that his mean were being held in this debriefing. It was obvious that their base commander did not think too highly of this 'general' either, and was trying to provide interference for his men.

"Nonsense! There are tests we need to run on them to find out the effects of their being teleported. They'll also have to have psych evaluations to ensure that their minds haven't been altered," the general was explaining. The man's brown eyes were taking on a maniacal gleam. "They need to remain under armed guard until we are sure they don't pose a security threat as well. Who knows what else she did to them besides teleportation."

"I will not let you treat my men like guinea pigs or criminals," the admiral stated, raising his voice. He was not a huge man, but he obviously worked out more than the general. The two of them glared at each other. Breaking the stalemate, Admiral Hutchinson turned to the team. "Report to the base hospital," the admiral barked. Gratefully, his men began to leave.

"You don't have the authority to override my orders!" the general shouted, his nostrils flaring in anger.

"Until I get orders to the contrary I am still the commanding officer for these men. What they do and where they go is my decision," Admiral Huntington stated coldly. Again the two men locked gazes with an added threat of violence, but this time it was the general who backed down and shifted his gaze first. With that the admiral turned to them and barked, "Dismissed!"

The five men hurried to get out of the room. They had escaped the general for now, but Matt guessed they would see him again.

Julie zapped herself back to her room and locked the door. She hung up her costume and crawled into bed. She slept the night through, only briefly waking when her mom called for dinner. She told her mom that she was did not want dinner because she was starting to feel sick.

The next day Julie decided that she needed to confide in someone. The terrorist hitchhiking on her last return trip had really scared her. She knew she was getting in over her head. It did not take her long to decide who she should talk to; her Uncle Mark was the obvious choice. He was not really her uncle, but an old friend of her dad's. Mark had a slightly... different outlook on life. He was not exactly a criminal, he did not do anything technically illegal but, well...he was the type that always lived in the gray area of the law. He would know what she needed to do to protect herself in case she was grabbed again.

Mark lived a couple of hours away in Long Beach, so she gave him a call. After the usual greetings she asked if she could talk to him about something.

"Sure, what's up?" he asked on the other end.

"I need your advice. I almost got in big trouble last night," Julie admitted. "Can I come over?"

"Sure, you know you're welcome to come over anytime."

Without warning Julie zapped herself to Mark's condo. He stood holding the phone, dressed in his customary long sleeve black shirt and black denim pants. His brown hair was braided tightly back and hung past his shoulders. Some of his many tattoos were just visible past the end of his rolled up sleeves, and at his neck where a few buttons were undone.

Mark took a few steps back in shock at her sudden arrival, and then got a hold of himself. He calmly set the unnecessary phone back on its cradle. "I see. I'm guessing that's part of what caused you trouble last night?"

Julie proceeded to tell him everything that had happened since she had rescued Cinder up until the night before. He asked her several questions, and asked her to zap around the room so he could see it again. Finally he seemed to come to terms with this new part of his niece. "So what do you need me for exactly?"

"Last night when I rescued the soldiers that the terrorists had captured, a terrorist grabbed onto me as I zapped out with the last hostage," she explained. "I didn't think someone could do that. I need to know what to do if I get grabbed again. I won't always have a squad of soldiers there to help me the next time I come back with a hitchhiker."

"Oh, I can teach you what to do if someone tries to grab you again," Mark said with an evil gleam in his eyes. "That's not a problem," he said quietly.

Mark had black belts in several martial arts and enjoyed the thought of pummeling any bastard who touched his niece. He did not really have close family of his own. After being bounced around the foster system for most of his life, he had joined the Marines as soon as he had turned eighteen. Then he had used the GI Bill to go to college. That was when he had met Julie's father, Frank. Even though Frank was several years younger than him, he had become like a brother to Mark, and Julie was the closest thing he would have to a real niece. He was very protective of his adopted family, so the thought of anyone hurting her made him feel like punching someone.

Consciously calming himself down, he considered what she should do next. "One thing that I think you are going to need is a safe place where you can hide out if you need to. It should also be where you keep your gear. Someone is bound to find your costume in your bedroom closet eventually. Also, if you ever can't go home, you will need a safe place where you can live for a while," he said listing off his reasons.

"Why wouldn't I be able to go home?" Julie asked surprised.

"If our government or a foreign enemy is trying to capture you, your house would be the best place to ambush you."

"You're just being paranoid, Uncle Mark."

"I'm serious. They'd try to take you when you least expect it. So if you ever think you're being followed or watched you should plan to stay at your hideout for a while."

Julie laughed at the irony. "I'm going to have a secret lair to go along with my superhero costume," she remarked ruefully.

"You laugh, but it could be the thing that saves your

life someday. You also need a hideout because you said that you need to be able to visualize the places you go to. If there is a time that you need to zap quickly out of trouble, without thinking, your hideout would be there for you."

"Okay, okay... I get your point. Let's do it," Julie agreed. She realized she might really need a place to go, and Mark had come up with possible problems she had not even thought of yet. Now she was really glad she had confided in him. "I guess the first thing we have to do is decide where to put it."

"That's easy, the Chocolate Mountains out by the Anza Borrego Desert. No one will look there."

"The Chocolate Mountains? Now you are teasing me. At least you could come up with a better comic book name like the Mountains of Loneliness."

"I'm being serious," Mark objected. "The Chocolate Mountains are a real mountain range. No one ever gets close to them and they are very well protected."

"How are they protected?" Julie asked. She trusted Mark, but she was curious what would make a place that inaccessible to rate so high on her Uncle Mark's paranoia meter.

"It's in the middle of an active artillery range used by the Navy. Even if they guess your hideout's there, they won't be able to get there very easily. The area around it is littered with unexploded shells. They'd have to go slowly and you'd see them coming long before they could try to grab you."

"And how do you have access to it?"

"Remember the company who just hired me? They own the mineral rights for that area."

"And how does that help us? I need a picture of a place up close for me to zap there."

"I am their new 'Military Liaison'," he said smugly. "An old friend of mine who used to be in the Corps with me hooked me up. Since I used to be in the military they use me to handle all of their communication with the base located there. I go out there periodically to check that the company's interests are being looked after."

"You mean you actually have a job that's aboveboard?" Julie asked with mock surprise. "Is that allowed?"

"Yeah, I know what you mean; earning an honest dollar is really mundane. At least I get to watch things blow up," Mark remarked grinning. "Now let's start planning your hideout. We won't be able to get much done today; I need to get that picture before we can start building it. I'll be going out there next week, so I'll try to find a few likely spots."

"Don't get yourself blown up trying to hike around."

"Don't worry; you know I'm really good at keeping my butt out of danger."

They spent the rest of the day deciding exactly what equipment she would need in the hideout. In true Mark fashion he went overboard in what he wanted stocked in her hideout. His biggest concern was having food and water supplies to last her several days, preferably a few weeks. He insisted that she also needed a power source, and the first aid kit he proposed would make any trauma ward jealous. He wanted her to not only be able to hide there in case they found out who she was, but also hold off a major attack. Mark also insisted that she needed to start shooting lessons with him. Of course her hideout had to have a full arsenal of weapons including, but not limited to, at least one rifle, one shotgun and one handgun, so she needed to know how to use them. They finished that day's planning and Julie left after promising to call him to set up her shooting lessons that week.

Two weeks later they had the pictures of possible locations he had found in the Chocolate Mountains. "What are these for?" she asked as Mark handed her a desert camouflaged combat uniform.

"They're just in case someone's in the area. You'll be less likely to be seen in those, than in your bright green cloak," he pointed out.

"I didn't know you owned anything that wasn't black," Julie joked heading up to his bathroom to change.

When she was ready, Julie zapped them both to the first location, then the second, then the third. At each location they carefully considered its pros and cons, but they had not found one that worked really well. They needed a place that she could hide inside. A cave would be best. The fourth picture was of a steep, narrow crevasse on the side of the mountain. It was so steep, that they had to zap to a place nearby and climb up to it. The hillside was covered in loose gravel and the only plant life that could survive was a few ocotillo cactus and teddy bear cholla. There was no place to stand easily and Julie kept slipping as she looked into the shadowed depths of the deep gulley.

"No sign of a cave. Not even a place we could set up a small camouflaged tent. I guess this won't do either," Mark said obviously very disappointed.

"Hang on, I have an idea," Julie said as she knelt down and placed her hands on the ground in front of her. She closed her eyes and zapped back to the ledge they had climbed up from a moment ago. In her hands was a chunk of rock. The rock's surface was smooth, except for where her hands were, but it was not round, it looked like a bumpy blob.

"What the…" Mark looked down at where Julie had been standing next to him. There was a hole in the rock that matched the chunk Julie was holding. "I'll be damned. How much can you take at a time?"

"I don't know. Let me try again," Julie said as she climbed back up to where she had removed the chunk. Then she started climbing down into the crevasse. She made it into a hidden gap behind a boulder. This time she placed her hands on the rock face in front of her and closed her eyes. She stretched her mind, trying to 'hold' a larger piece of rock. Then she zapped back to the lower ledge. The mass of rock and dirt that she moved this time was so big there was no way she could hold it. She had to dodge to the side as it fell at her feet, several chunks continued to roll the rest of the way down the mountain. Then she zapped back up to where she was working behind the boulder. Meanwhile Mark had climbed into the crevasse and was examining the hole she had made. It was about the size and shape of a ball two foot in diameter. It was in the back of the crevasse and would be hidden from sight unless you looked straight at it.

"This is great! I think you should carve a tunnel here, just like you did. Make it just big enough at the entrance for you to crawl in, then you can make it bigger. You don't want it to fill with runoff in the rainy season so angle it upward for a little ways. Then go straight into the mountain," Mark explained enthusiastically. Julie could practically see the gears turning in Mark's head as he planned the layout of the hideout.

"That'll take forever," Julie groaned. "And where do I dump all of the rock? Someone is bound to notice a large pile of rocks at the base of the mountain."

"I have an idea," Mark said after thinking for a moment. "Take us back to the first site."

Back at the first place they had tried, Mark led her sideways around the mountain. It curved imperceptibly, and then suddenly they were at the edge of a large rock slide.

"No one will notice a little more rock added to that rock pile," he said motioning to the debris at the bottom of the cliff.

"You're right. That'll work," Julie agreed. "Now can we go home? I'm exhausted."

Julie spent all of her free time over the next few weeks slowly burrowing into the side of the mountain. As she worked she found she could take larger and larger chunks with her as she zapped, and she could work at it longer each time before she got tired out. Mark went with her on many of the days she was tunneling and had her change direction a few times for no apparent reason. Finally she had made a tunnel that was about sixty feet long and about six feet tall and wide.

Today they planned on starting on the hideout's main living area, and Julie zapped to her Uncle Mark's condo. She found him sitting at his kitchen table.

"Hey Uncle Mark," Julie called cheerfully when she got there. Since they were working there today she had not bothered to wear her cloak.

"Hey kiddo," Mark said. He looked up from the diagram he was working on, and frowned. "I hadn't noticed how skinny you're getting. Have you been sick?"

"No, and I've been eating a ton, but I'm still losing weight. I don't know what's going on," Julie confided in him. "I've lost two pant sizes since I started working on the hideout."

"You didn't have any extra weight to begin with and now you're wasting away," Mark scolded her. "You must be using a lot of energy moving all of that rock. I want you to eat higher calorie foods and more of them."

"You're right," Julie agreed with a nod. "I'll try."

"Okay, so let's get to this layout. I think it should be set up with a living area in the center. Then you can have a storage room and a holding cell going off from it."

After another couple weeks of work they finally finished the basic rooms. Then for the final touches she and her Uncle Mark installed a generator in the supply room, and a hatch from an old abandoned ship for her holding cell. They had also scrounged some lighting and several outlets from a camper and wired it all up to a bank of marine batteries. The trickiest part was digging the ventilation shafts. Mark wanted them as narrow as possible to prevent someone from sneaking in that way. Julie had to learn how to shape the mass that she zapped out. In the end she was able to take sections of rock that were six inches in diameter and about fifty feet long out at one time. Her skill at shaping the space of the rock that she took enabled her to make spaces for cabinets and a bed in the main living area.

After her hideout was complete they started with her martial arts training, which included firearms. She never thought she would like guns, but she found it was kind of fun. She liked shotguns the best and after the first day on the trap range she even found shooting relaxing. It turned out that she was a decent shot. She tried several of her uncle's shotguns, but her favorite one was a semi-automatic 12 gauge. It was the easiest for her to use, and it was as accurate as a shotgun could be.

CHAPTER 6

Julie saw the Amber Alert about the missing girl on her way home. She had been hanging out with friends at the mall and it was on a digital traffic alert sign over the freeway. When she got home she looked it up online.

The girl's name was Gabriela, and she was just twelve years old with black hair, brown eyes and dark skin. She was last seen being forced into a car as she walked home from school in the City Heights area.

Julie focused on the girl's features and found her quickly. *She's still alive*, Julie sighed in relief. Julie had just finished the final touches to her hideout and had already moved her disguise to its closet. Zapping to her hideout to get her disguise and the pistol her uncle had given her, she was ready in a few a minutes. *What do I do now?* she thought. *If I just zap the girl out of there, the police won't be able to catch the slime ball.* Julie studied as much of the area around the girl as she could and realized that the girl was alone. *Maybe I can help the girl escape to call the police.*

Making up her mind, Julie focused on the girl again. The area she was in was too small for Julie to zap into so she shifted her focus a little ways away. *There, that was a clear area*, Julie thought and zapped to the place. The room was very dark. All of the windows were covered by cardboard. The room was lit by the little bit of light that seeped around the edges of the window frame where the cardboard did not fit exactly. The room was a bedroom, if you could call it that. It's only piece of furniture was a bed, with just a fitted sheet covering it. There were two doors in the room. One led to where Gabriela was, the other must lead to the hallway.

Julie turned to where she knew the girl was. It was a closet with a heavy lock holding it closed. Julie looked at the lock, and paused. *I didn't planned for this,* then she realized she could just zap it away like she had the tons of rock of her hideout. She took hold of it, and then zapped two feet away, dropping the now useless lock on the floor.

"Gabriela," Julie called her name, before she opened the door. "I'm here to help." As she opened the closet she found Gabriela huddled in a ball at the back corner of the closet. She was looking at Julie, terror plain in her eyes.

"Gabriela, it's Okay, I'm here to get you out. He's not here, don't worry," Julie said reassuringly. But the girl was still terrified and refused to come out of the closet. She sat huddled in a ball staring at Julie. *She's scared of me*, Julie thought sadly and made up her mind to remove her hood and mask. She was taking a chance, but she figured the girl was so scared she would not remember what she looked like anyway. She tried talking to her again. "See, I'm not scary, I'm here to save you."

"Who, who are you?" stammered the girl.

"Jade."

"Are you an angel?" the girl asked. She seemed stunned at seeing Julie's face.

"No, far from it," Julie scoffed. "I just want to help you. Come out of there," she encouraged the girl.

The girl crawled out of the closet, and clung to Julie, looking around and trembling from fear. Now that Julie could see her clothes she noticed that they were torn in a few places and were in disarray like they had been put on in a rush. *That bastard will pay*, thought Julie, *if the cops don't put him away then I'll take care of him somehow.*

Julie resisted the urge to just whisk the girl out of there, and instead guided her to the room's door. It was locked from the outside. Julie eased out of Gabriela's terrified embrace and stepped away from the traumatized girl, who startled at the slightest sound. Again Julie took hold of the door's handle and zapped herself a few feet away. Then she gathered up Gabriela again and together they entered a hallway. At the end of the short hallway they could see that it opened onto a very normal looking living room. On a side table Julie spotted a phone. *Should I have the girl call 911 from here? No,* she thought, *then they'd have to wait for the police, and the girl looks like a nervous wreck.* Instead they headed to the front door.

Julie reassured the girl before putting her hood and mask on again. Then she opened the door and looked outside. They were in a normal looking suburban neighborhood. The houses lining the street had the cookie cutter look of a typical southern California development. Each one had a red tile roof and off white, stucco walls. A few houses away she saw kids playing in their front yard.

Julie turned to Gabriela, "Do you see that house, the one with the kids out front?"

"Yeah," Gabriela's voice held a wistful note of hope and longing in it.

"Do you think you can make it down there? Just knock on the door and ask for help. They have kids, so I'm sure they'll help you," Julie explained. After a moment's thought Julie grabbed a throw blanket from the couch and wrapped it around the girl's shoulders. "Ready?"

"Yeah," she said dazed and the girl started walking toward the house as if she was in a trance. Then she started walking faster as if she felt an urgency. By the time she reached the house's yard she was running, and she dropped the blanket in her panic. She made it to the front door and pounded on it frantically. The kids had stopped playing and were watching her curiously. A moment later an older woman answered the door. After a quick exchange the woman exclaimed in dismay and quickly led the girl into the house, calling to her grandchildren to come inside. Julie was sure that the girl would be safe.

As the girl went inside the woman's house a car pulled up next to Julie. "What the hell are you doing on my property!" the driver yelled as he got out.

Julie felt her barely contained anger growing inside her when she spotted the girl's attacker. In one practiced motion Jade pulled her pistol, tapped the button turning on the laser designator and placed it squarely between his eyes. "I think WE are waiting for the police," she informed him coldly. She could hear sirens in the distance. As they drew closer, the man started to get back in his car, and Jade zapped beside him to put the barrel to his ear. "Do it!" she hissed. "Please, give me an excuse to shoot you." She had never wanted anyone dead so badly in her life.

As the squad car arrived the officers jumped out of their vehicle, and drew their weapons. "Hands up!" one of them yelled.

In the silence that followed Julie noticed a thumping sound come from the car's trunk. The police surrounded them both, confused as to who to arrest. Before they could act; Jade holstered her pistol, zapped to the rear of the car, put her hands on the trunk and zapped six feet away. In the trunk was another young girl. Satisfied that the cops would arrest the man, she decided it was time to leave, and zapped back to her hideout.

The man sat at his large, oak desk. In front of him he held the police reports from the girls who had been kidnapped. The first girl had reported to the police that a woman dressed in a green cape had freed her from the house where she had been held. She had not seen the woman arrive and she had not seen her leave. When asked what the woman had looked like, she had replied, "Like an angel."

The man threw the report down on his desk. *Stupid girls*. He did not even bother with the idea of going to interview them himself. The one had been raped by her kidnapper and was so traumatized that she would not be a credible witness anyway, and the other one had not seen anything more than the police officers.

His search for Jade was running into dead ends. He had questioned that SEAL team for two months. He knew they were holding information back, but he could not prove it. Especially the one with the broken arm, Burke, he had to know more. They had been tested for mind control, drugs and radiation. Nothing. Everything came back clean and none of the men had remembered any more details of their escape. They had not given him any more answers than he had before.

The man rose from his massive leather chair and began pacing his office. He wanted this girl, he *needed* to control her. That was the only way the country would be safe from someone with her abilities. Even if she did not turn to a life of crime, a foreign government could get a hold of her and force her to do assassinations or espionage for them. *No, there's no other way*, he reminded himself, *I have to catch her and control her*. If that wasn't possible then she would need to be eliminated for the good of the country. She could be a valuable tool, but one that was too dangerous to leave lying around.

CHAPTER 7

Matt walked down the hall of his friend's house. He was spending the day with a bunch of his friends and they planned on watching football all afternoon. He heard excited shouts coming from the living room, and hurried to get there. He found his buddies gathered around the large flat screen TV watching the news.

"What's going on?" Matt asked. "Did the Chargers actually score?"

"Hey Matt! It's that girl that saved you guys. She's at it again," Rob said excitedly, pointing at the screen.

Matt looked more closely at the news story that they were watching. The crawl along the bottom of the screen read: Severe Floods.

"Where's this happening?" Matt asked.

"Colorado. A dam broke and this town is being hit by a flash flood," Nate supplied. "Jade's already rescued one man."

Matt watched as the camera panned along the rushing water. The news commentator's voice came on over the video. "We are getting a report from our Channel 8, Eye in the Sky. They've heard from the local fire department that Jade has personally requested that our helicopter look for more stranded survivors." It took a moment for the helicopter to find another group of people trapped by the rushing water. Again the commentator's voice could be heard, "Jade, we hope you are getting this. It looks like our Eye in the Sky helicopter has spotted a mother and child." Matt saw a woman clutching a small child in one arm and hanging onto the lower branches of a tree with the other. Along the shore rescue workers could be seen frantically struggling to reach them before the woman lost her grip.

The next second Jade was in the branches of the tree over the woman's position, she fell a few feet before she was able to grab on. Matt held his breath as the green cloaked figure reached down to the woman below her. *She isn't going to be able to reach her*, he thought.

Jade must have decided the same thing because she started to climb farther down the tree. Meanwhile the woman was trying to lift her son higher out of the water for Jade to grab, but she was not ready yet. Before Jade could reach him, the boy slipped from his mother's grip and plunged into the water. Jade jumped in after him; their heads disappearing under the waves. The camera crew panned over the rushing water trying to spot them. Matt caught glimpses of Jade's green cloak as she was swept down river. Then she seemed to disappear entirely.

She's drowned, Matt thought sadly. *That cloak must have dragged her down.*

"Chopper 8 is trying to find the child and Jade in the river," the reported said tensely. "Wait, we're receiving word that they are with the rescue crews."

The camera swung around back to the side of the river. Behind the assembled rescuers, farther back from the river, Matt saw a muddy skid mark that swept over ten feet through the wet grass. Jade was sitting at the end, covered in mud, the boy cradled in her arms. Rescuers rushed over to them, and Jade handed the boy to the first one to reach them. She shifted her position to kneeling and it looked like she was coughing up water. One paramedic approached her and Matt could see Jade pushing him away with a shake of her head. After she caught her breath a few moments later she vanished and the camera swung back to the river.

The woman could still be seen clinging to the tree branch, but now she was hanging there limply, with her head down. "Hopefully Jade gets there soon," the commentator said urgently. "It doesn't look like she can hang on much longer."

Suddenly Jade was in the tree above the woman again. This time she had arrived much lower and she easily reached the woman's arm. The next moment they were gone. When the camera caught up with them in the field, there was a puddle of water spreading away from the prone form of the woman. Jade was sitting a few feet away, her shoulders slumped as she sat, looking exhausted. Emergency personnel ran toward them, carrying blankets and gear. Matt saw Jade look up at the oncoming men and then she vanished. He remembered her comment about not wanting too much attention.

"Damn, that girl's got guts, I'll give her that," another one of Matt's friends piped in as they all collectively let out the breaths they were holding.

"She's either brave or nuts," Matt agreed.

"Hey look, the chopper's found another group," Rob said bringing their attention back to the screen.

"It looks like our Eye in the Sky has found a stranded car," Now the news anchor addressed Jade directly, "Jade, if you're still watching; we've found some more for you."

It did not take long for Jade to appear. The guys watched as she made several trips between the car and the waiting people along the shore. There were three kids, plus the driver, an older man, who were trapped this time. Jade took them two at a time. As soon as she had dropped off the last set she disappeared again, and the news helicopter returned to searching the river for more trapped survivors.

They followed the rushing water and found a person trapped farther downstream. Matt studied the scene in the video. The man was clinging to debris under a thick canopy of vegetation. Matt could not see anywhere that Jade would be able to get close to him.

The camera view widened as they heard the news commentator explaining. "Jade is on the shore, talking with the rescuers. It looks like she's trying to coordinate with them to rescue the victim. Let's hope together they'll be able to reach him in time."

Matt and his friends watched as one of the emergency personnel headed away from the group talking with Jade. He returned a few minutes later wearing a life jacket and carrying another one along with a coil of rope. Jade was shaking her head, evidently she did not like the idea they had come up with. She gestured toward the trapped victim and then at something upstream. This time it was the rescue personnel who were shaking their heads. They planned for a little longer before they seemed to come to a decision. Jade took the vest and disappeared for a minute. When she returned she was wearing the life jacket. She had removed her cloak, but still wore her black outfit and mask covering. Somewhere she had picked up a helmet and wore that over her mask. Reaching over, she held onto the rescue swimmer and they vanished.

"Hang on folks, we are trying to find them," the reporter assured the viewers. First the camera zoomed in on the man clinging desperately against the strong current. When they widened their angle, Matt spotted Jade and the rescue swimmer upstream standing on another pile of debris. Their perch was barely big enough for the two of them to stand. The man began securing his rope to a large branch that was jutting out of the debris, and then he clipped the end of the rope to Jade's rigging. Once she was secure she lowered herself into the rushing water.

"It looks like Jade is planning on letting herself get washed down to the victim's position," the reporter stated the obvious as Jade sort of swam, but was mostly dragged down river to the trapped man. Luckily the rescue swimmer was able to use the rope to try to guide her into position.

"She's insane," Matt decided. "It looks like she barely knows how to swim, and she's jumping into a raging river," Matt stated in dismay.

"Shhh…!" one of his buddies silenced him. "I want to see what she's going to do next."

Jade was able to grab onto some debris close to the stranded victim. Then she climbed her way through the current over to the exhausted man. It took her several minutes to negotiate around the obstacle, and her rope was constantly getting hung up.

"Come on girl, you can do it," Rob encouraged her through the TV.

Finally Jade reached the man and grabbed onto his shoulder. A moment later they disappeared, to arrive next to the waiting paramedics. This time she did not bother standing up before she disappeared again to retrieve the rescue swimmer who had helped her. Once she had returned with him, she disappeared one last time.

Julie sat on the soggy carpet, soaking wet.

"You owe me a carpet cleaning," Mark said teasingly.

Julie looked around at the mess she had created. "Sorry, Uncle Mark, I'll get someone to come clean it for you."

"Don't worry about it, kiddo. I was just joking." Mark wrapped a towel around his niece. "You look wiped out," he said when she removed her mask. He noticed her shivering. "Head upstairs and take a hot shower, I'll find you some dry clothes."

"What if there're more people that need rescuing?" Julie objected.

"I'll watch the news, and let you know if they find anyone else. You need to at least warm up again before you try another rescue," he told her and pointed upstairs. "GO!" he ordered.

Mark watched the news like he had promised. The rest of the victims that were found were already being rescued by firefighters. Julie came down about half an hour later; dressed in the set of black sweats he had supplied her. He noticed approvingly that her skin was a more normal color, not nearly blue from the cold like it had been. She seemed a little less tired too.

"Come on, I've made you some soup to help warm you up," Mark told her gently.

Hassan sat on the park bench. It was a cool, overcast day. He was bundled in an overcoat, as the chilly weather threatened to start drizzling. It had been a month since he had arrived in Seattle, and he had not seen the sun the entire time. He hated this city, but this is where his contacts had led him.

"Are you Hassan?" a voice said as the man sat down next to him.

"Don't ever use my name," Hassan hissed. He looked over at the man he had been trying to get in touch with since he had arrived in the states. The man was the leader of the North American Islamic Jihad, an upstart terrorist group comprised of real jihadists and any loser who felt they had been oppressed by the government. Nidal was their leader. *Nidal, even his name's a joke*, Hassan thought disdainfully. Nidal's real name was Hank Douglas; he had changed his name when he had converted to Islam a few years ago.

"I was told you wanted to help us," Nidal said accusingly.

"If you can do what I need," Hassan confirmed. "It needs to be big, and it needs to all happen on the same day."

CHAPTER 8

It was about three months later that Julie heard the news of another hostage crisis, this time in the Philippines. The militants had grabbed several exchange students from the United States and Europe. Julie had been packing up her stuff to spend the day at the beach when she heard the news. Since her parents already knew she was going to be gone all day, this was the perfect cover. So instead of packing her beach stuff she packed some supplies for her cave. Before she left she went online and downloaded all of the pictures she would need. Then she drove her car to a local mall and found an inconspicuous parking spot far away from any of the buildings. After checking to be sure no one was watching, she zapped herself to her hideout.

Once Julie was there, she turned on the simple light that hung in the middle of the ceiling. Then she headed over to sit on the bed she had carved out of the rock wall. The mattress she had put there was soft and she made herself comfortable as she pulled out the picture of the hostages that she had downloaded. She studied the picture in front of her. It showed a group of five college-aged kids, four boys and one girl. Choosing the girl first, Julie noticed that the girl's long brown hair had been pulled back in a ponytail, but the sides had come loose in the kidnapping, and now hung down limply. Her light brown face was smeared with dirt now. Julie concentrated, and quickly found the girl. To her surprise the hostages were being kept all together. *Evidently the kidnappers aren't worried about them fighting back*, she thought. Having them all together made it almost impossible for her to rescue them though. She did not know if she could take all of them at once, and the ones she would have to leave were bound to make noise. *Someone will get killed for sure,* she thought as she let the mental image fade... *I need a new plan.*

After a few minutes of consideration she came up with a new idea. She closed her eyes again, but this time she concentrated on the cute soldier's image. It was easier to find him this time. Not only did he seem much closer than before, but it was as if once she had zapped with someone she had a kind of link with them. She found him, but he was not alone, and she did not want to risk appearing in front of strangers. So she got up and did some organizing around the cave. She was still getting it all set up.

Julie tried again a little while later. He was alone this time, so she put on her costume and zapped to the small room where he was. When she got there she heard a shower running. She had arrived in a small bathroom.

"Oops," she said out loud and giggled embarrassed. The sound alerted the man who was currently taking the shower. He jerked back the curtain to see what the noise was. "What the... Shit!" he cursed when he spotted her and quickly closed the curtain enough to cover himself.

"I guess this means you need my help?" the man asked grumpily. "Can you at least wait until I'm dressed?"

Stifling another laugh, Julie headed out of the bathroom and found herself in a plain, painted cinder block room with two beds and some simple furniture. One of the beds was neatly made in true military fashion, the other one was bare. She guessed he lived here alone, so she found a chair and sat down to wait. A few minutes later the man came out of the bathroom, mostly dressed, rubbing the last of the water from his hair with his towel.

"What's your name anyway?" Julie asked. She felt silly thinking of him as 'the cute one'. In all of the news reports about the rescue, none of them had mentioned the names of the men.

"Matt, Matt Burke."

"You're right, I need your help, Matt." Julie said getting straight to the point.

"Wait, let me guess, the captured students?" Matt asked, remembering a briefing his team had received that morning.

"Yeah, how'd you guess?"

"Personal experience," he said with a grin. "By the way, thanks to your rescue we were all poked, prodded and questioned for weeks. They're still trying to figure out how you did what you did."

"If they figure it out, let me know would you?" Julie said with a laugh. "I don't know how I do it either."

"Sure," Matt said chuckling, "So tell me, why do you need my help? Can't you just pop in there and pop them out again?"

"I can't… they're all being held in the same room, and there are at least a dozen men in rooms close to them."

Matt paced the room as she spoke. He was surprised by how much she knew about how they were being held. *She knows more details than our best intelligence sources do*, he realized.

"I'm not sure I can zap five people out at once," Julie continued. "And if I don't, the ones I leave behind might make noise."

"How do you know all this? Never mind, I know you won't tell me," he said dismissively. Matt paced the floor for a moment longer. "What do you want me to do? Go in and stand guard for you, and shoot anyone who opens the door while you shuttle them all out one by one?"

"Yeah, that sounds like a good idea to me. A quick jump in, you provide defense, and I zap us all out one at a time."

Matt shook his head. "No, that won't work. Besides, I think we could come up with a much better plan for those bastards," he paused thinking. "My squad needs to hear this too. Here's my cell phone," he said as he picked up a phone off of the bedside table. "When I call, you can find me again, right?"

Julie hesitated. She really did need their help, *but what if it's a trap?*

"Don't worry," Matt said, seeming to sense her fear. "No one will hurt you. I swear."

"Alright, I guess I have no choice but to trust you," Julie said as she took his phone and zapped to a secluded mountain meadow to wait. *No sense giving them a chance to track his phone to her house, or her hideout.*

About an hour later the phone rang. It was Matt. "Can you find me? Great... we're ready for you."

There were four of them sitting around a conference table, the chairs and table looked like an executive's meeting room. They matched the room itself which had nicely painted walls which were very businesslike and were bare of any of the normal wall decorations. The only things that interrupted the beige walls were the large dry erase board along the front and a clock by the door. She arrived in front of the white board next to Matt. She recognized each one of the soldiers she had rescued from the terrorists, but one was missing, the one that had been seriously beaten. Now Matt took the time to introduce them to her.

The one she had rescued first was Petty Officer Paul Miller, or 'Doc', to his friends. He was the medic for the group. He stood a little less than six feet tall, with a medium build.

The soldier who had reminded her of her Vietnamese

friends in high school was Chief Steve Nguyen, their second in command even though he seemed only a few years older than she was. His black hair was cut very short on the sides, and the top was short and spiked up. He was average height and now that he was cleaned up he looked even more like her friends.

Petty Officer Jack Demetrio was their explosives expert. He was much smaller than the others with a thin, lanky build. His thick Chicago accent made her think of the old Godfather movies.

The last one, Petty Officer Simmons, had been the first to react to the terrorist who had hitchhiked back with them. He looked like a blonde-haired, blue-eyed surfer, except his eyes had an intense gleam in them, not the normal dreamy gaze of surfer boys. He was introduced as their radio man.

"So what are you?" Julie asked Matt.

"He's the new kid," Simmons joked, and Matt looked embarrassed.

"I'm the point man," he told her with an embarrassed smile. "I go in first, when we enter a target."

After the introductions were done, Julie explained what she knew. "They're all sitting huddled together by a wall."

"Where are the closest kidnappers?" Chief Nguyen asked.

"They're about fifteen feet away maybe. Here let me show you," Julie offered as she started drawing a picture on the white board. They noticed that she occasionally would stop and close her eyes before drawing another detail. "I think the door is here," she said and pointed to a portion of her sketch.

"How do you know?" Doc asked.

"I can just tell," Julie answered with a shrug. When she was done she stood back and watched them plan their 'entrance' as they called it. She realized these were probably not your usual group of soldiers. At one point she saw Matt standing away from the others and she went over to him. "So what are you guys, some kind of Special Forces?"

"I can't tell you," he grinned slyly. "I have to protect my family," and then walked back to the others.

"Ha, ha very funny," Julie called after him, laughing.

In the end they planned an all-out attack on the terrorist group. They knew details that Julie had not given them, and she decided that this group of terrorists had already been on their hit list. They wanted to put them out of business and this was a great way to get in. It took them another hour to get their gear assembled and ready. While they were getting geared up, Matt came over to where Julie was sitting, carrying a vest.

"I want you to put this on. It's body armor. You can put it on under your…" and he waved at her costume, "other clothes."

Julie agreed and zapped herself back to the cave to change. When she returned they were ready. They had even moved all of the furniture to the edges of the room to give them a big enough area to zap back to. "We want you to take us in one at a time," Matt explained. "We'll keep the hostages as quiet as we can. Once we're all there, if everything goes well you can start zapping the hostages to Pendleton's back gate."

"Why Pendleton again?" she asked.

"You used it before," Chief Nguyen said with a shrug. "The most important thing is that the guards there will be witnesses to say that they only saw you," he added seriously.

"Yeah, we don't want that general finding out that we had contact with you again," Simmons said, his blue eyes serious for once.

"What general?" Julie asked.

"There's a general who wants to get his hands on you real bad," Chief Nguyen answered her.

"There's one thing we haven't figured out," Demetrio

pointed out. "How are we going to contact you when we're done?"

"What if one of you stood in the center of the cell alone?" Julie asked. "Would that work for you?"

"You'll be able to tell?" Matt asked.

"Sure, no problem," Julie assured him dismissively.

The rescue went without a hitch. The students had been blind folded and tied up when they got there so the hardest part was getting them to hold still long enough for her to touch them. After she was done dropping them at Pendleton she zapped back to her hideout. It seemed like an eternity while she waited for the signal. She sat, using all of her concentration, and watched for the signal with her powers. At last she sensed Matt standing still in the center of the cell alone, and she immediately zapped to his side.

He jumped a little at her sudden appearance and cursed quietly under his breath. Julie snickered at startling him. Matt called to the others that it was time to 'head out', and she was able to get them all back to their briefing room without anyone noticing.

CHAPTER 9

General Jian of the People's Liberation Army sat in his office at the National University of Defense Technology. It was a very luxurious office. The bookshelves along one wall were filled with leather bound texts. He sat behind his large wooden desk with its intricate carvings. But none of those things mattered to him right now. He had just received a very interesting intelligence report. It was on the mysterious American woman named 'Jade'. She was apparently able to teleport great distances and he was very interested in everything he could learn about her. He had seen the first video of her several weeks ago. It had been the hospital surveillance video of her rescuing the missing boy, and he had been intrigued. Since then he had instructed his spies to learn as much as possible about her.

"Do you want me to order our spies to watch the base's gate?" General Jian looked up at the man who had spoken. He had forgotten his assistant was still standing in his office. The man had just brought him the intelligence report of her rescuing the hostages from the Philippines. The report had included a cell phone video of her appearance at the Marine Base.

"No, that would be too risky. Instead, order them to

concentrate on the area around there. Maybe she lives close by," he instructed his assistant. He thought again about the woman they were looking for. Her talents were amazing and unheard of; they could be used by his government to do so many marvelous things. "When they find her, have them watch her. I want to know everything about her, and her family," he added. "We need to be able to control her," he explained to his assistant. *I'm sure she wouldn't let any harm come to her family. With any luck she has kids we can use*, he thought with satisfaction. "Notify me when they find her. I want to be there when we bring her in," he stated with a brief smile at the thought.

"Yes, sir," the man said and bowed before he left.

General Jian sat and looked at the image of Jade with one of the hostages. *If I can control her I will become one of China's greatest generals*, the thought excited him. He had to concentrate to calm himself. *I can wait*, he thought, *my spies will find her, and soon enough she will be working for the People's Republic of China, whether she wants to, or not.*

The next few weeks went by uneventfully. Julie went to her classes and hung out with friends like any normal college student. While she had been building her hideout her friends had complained about not seeing her enough and now she took time to make it up to them. The news of the hostage rescue had finally died down. Their plan had actually worked better than they could have hoped. The hostages had been blindfolded when they had found them in the cell and they had been so terrified that they all remembered different details about their rescue. The general consensus of the media was that they obviously were too traumatized to remember what had really happened. The only hard evidence were the witnesses who had seen Jade at the back gate to Pendleton, and Julie knew that suited the guys just fine. They had not wanted to be identified, even vaguely.

One interesting thing that had come up in the news was the debate about whether the government should have control of Jade and her powers. Most of the commentators agreed that it would be great if she did work for the government, but that the government had no right to force her. However, there was one official, who gave a particularly troubling interview with a national news reporter. The reporter questioned him about his view that she was dangerous to the country unless she was controlled by the government. But Julie put any worries about him out of her mind; they would never be able to find her and if they did, they could not make her do anything she did not want to do. She would just tell the government to go take a flying leap.

There was one person she could not get out of her mind though, that was Matt. She had thought about him a lot over the past few weeks. She was constantly tempted to check on him to make sure he was alright, and the urge to try to meet him as herself had been nagging at her.

Tonight Julie was headed home after a long week of mid-terms. It was Friday night and she had the next week off for spring break. She got home and settled her books on her messy bed and sat down heavily next to them. Curious, she focused on Matt and found him easily. She had expected to find him far away, in combat or something, but from how quickly she found him she could tell he was still in town. He was in a busy area surrounded by people. She stretched her senses as far from him as she could, looking for a secluded area. She found one nearby. With a sudden burst of daring, she stood up, grabbed her wallet, and zapped herself to the empty room.

When she got there, she looked around surprised. The floor had black and white tile that continued halfway up the walls. There were sinks along one wall that were set in a fake black granite counter top. From the looks of the urinals mounted on the walls, she had zapped herself into a men's restroom. Luckily it was empty, but she hurried to get out before anyone came in and noticed her. She bumped into a man on her way out; embarrassed, she mumbled something about "oops, wrong turn," then headed away from the restroom to looked around. The place was huge, with a garish chandelier in the center of the room and neon lighting decorating the walls. The bright gold and red wallpaper matched the red patterned carpet. The huge posters of the current movies playing and ones coming soon told her that she was in a movie theatre.

As Julie scanned the lobby, she saw Matt waiting at the back of the line for snacks in front of the large concession area. He was with a group of young military guys she had never seen before. They were joking with each other like they were all good friends. She walked over and got in line behind them, wondering what she should do next. Luckily the line was not moving very fast, and it gave her a chance to try to talk to him. She caught his eye a few moments after getting in line and coyly smiled and turned away. The next time he was the one to catch her eye and she smiled and said "hi" shyly.

Julie saw his friends laughing and one hit him in the shoulder. Matt laughed and smiled with his friends. A few moments later he hesitantly came up to her. "Hi, I'm Matt, what's your name?"

"Julie," she replied, suddenly shy for real. Now that she was actually talking to him, her courage left her. For a moment, she wished she had her costume on to hide behind.

"Are you here all alone?" he asked.

"Yeah, some friends of mine were going to come too, but they flaked on me last minute," she explained improvising the story quickly. Thinking fast she asked, "What movie are you guys going to go see?"

"Zombie Dawn, it looks like it should be good for a few laughs."

"Laughs? It's a horror movie!"

"Yeah, like I said, it should be hilarious. How about you? What movie are you going to see?"

"Actually, I'm going to the same one, but I'm worried I might be too scared by myself," Julie lied, trying to give him an idea.

"Hey, would you want to sit with us?" he offered.

"Sounds like fun, I won't get so scared with you guys there," she said coyly. Matt smiled and started introducing her to his friends. Julie chuckled to herself; *guys could be fooled so easily*.

The movie was actually pretty funny when you had a bunch of guys making sarcastic remarks and adding silly dialog to scenes throughout the entire film. It was like an episode of Mystery Science Theatre 3000 she'd seen once. Julie had not laughed so hard in a long time.

After the movie, they all went to an ice cream shop that was right outside the theater. Julie even let Matt buy her the ice cream. They were all great guys and she had a lot of fun. She was disappointed when it was time for them to head home. On their way out of the ice cream shop Matt offered to walk her to her car.

"Nah, that's Okay, it's just right over there. I'll be fine," Julie said, motioning vaguely in the opposite direction from the way the other guys were headed.

"Are you sure? It's pretty late and I'd feel better making sure you were safe."

"No, really, I'll be fine," Julie said. She knew she could not let him walk her to her car; he would find out she did not have one here. Desperately she tried to think of something to distract him. "Here's my phone number," she said as she quickly wrote her cell number on the receipt from the ice cream shop. "Call me if you want to go out again, see ya…," and she turned to go, barely waiting for his response. She had spotted a likely side street nearby and headed for it.

"Okay…, see ya later," Matt replied weakly, as he watched her leave. Her sudden departure left him stunned.

Did I do something to upset her? He stood there for a moment, not sure what he should do next. It really bothered him leaving her alone in this neighborhood at night. *I'll just follow her to make sure she's alright*, he thought. *If I stay out of sight I won't make her even more upset with me.* He saw her turn the corner around the building at the end of the block and he hurried to catch sight of her again. As he came around the corner he looked for her. The street was littered with trash and the street light was burned out leaving the near side of the street in almost total darkness. He was barely able to spot her where she had stopped on the sidewalk, leaning against the brick wall. She turned to see if anyone was around. He ducked behind the building in time for her to miss seeing him, and then he looked again. He saw her close her eyes and then she just disappeared.

"Damn! No way!" Matt was shocked to realize he had just spent the evening with the girl who had saved them from the terrorists. "Ah hell," Matt grumbled as he turned to walk back, deep in thought.

Matt's friends were now calling him to hurry up. He did not want to miss his ride back to the barracks, but now Matt had to decide how much, if anything he was going to tell the rest of his team. He looked down at the paper she had hastily written her number on. A thought hit him; *had she even given him her real phone number?* It would not be the first time a girl had pulled that trick on a guy. He pulled out his cell phone, and dialed the number.

"Hello?" she answered after the second ring.

"It's me, Matt; I just wanted to make sure you'd gotten to your car alright."

"Oh yeah, no problem, thanks for worrying."

"Sure, hey I had a great time." Matt told her.

"Yeah, me too."

"Could I see you again sometime?" Matt asked, holding his breath.

"I'd like that," Julie replied.

"Great, I'll call you later."

"Okay, bye."

So she had given me her real cell number, he thought surprised. Matt knew what kind of questions and testing he and his team had gone through. If that nut ball general got a hold of her, she would face much worse. He made up his mind. He could not tell anyone what he knew for now, for her own safety, if nothing else.

Matt could not stop thinking about Julie the next day. He decided to give her a call when he got off work for the day. "I was wondering if you wanted to go to dinner and a movie tonight?" Matt asked when she answered her phone.

"Sure, where do you have in mind?"

"How about someplace like Friday's Sports Bar in La Jolla?" Matt suggested.

"Sounds great, I'll meet you there, say seven o'clock?"

That night Matt made sure he arrived well before seven so he could see her car and get its license plate number. He had been thinking about how he could get more information about her without arousing her suspicions. He had picked a restaurant with TVs for a reason. He planned on using them to bring up the topic of 'Jade'.

Julie arrived in a new, yellow Volkswagen bug. Matt could hear her radio blaring with the latest in pop music. She smiled shyly as she saw him waiting in front of the restaurant. *She seems so sweet and innocent*; he thought as he wondered what made a young woman like her want to risk her life to save them. That was part of what he wanted to find out tonight.

After quick, nervous greetings they headed inside for dinner. They spent the first few minutes at the table looking over the menu. But after they had ordered they sat in an awkward silence for a few minutes.

"So what do you do?" Matt decided to start the conversation innocently.

"I'm a college student at Cal State University at San Marcos."

"Really? What degree?" Matt asked.

"I'm working on getting my bachelor's as an RN."

"Nursing huh? That's cool. What kind of nursing, pediatrics, geriatrics, …trauma?" he asked trying not to sound too interested.

"I'm not sure yet, maybe trauma. I had fun on my rotation at Palomar Hospital's ER." Julie admitted.

On the TV a news commentator's voice could be heard over the security video from a shopping mall. "A calm morning at an Idaho mall today turned into a siege of terror for unsuspecting shoppers in this Boise area shopping mall. A man armed with an AK-47 opened fire today in the mall's food court, killing three people and wounding a dozen others."

"That's terrible!" Julie exclaimed as she watched the video. "I heard he had ties to a Muslim terrorist group," she said as she turned back to Matt.

Matt had seen even more graphic videos from that mall shooting earlier in the day. From what they knew the guy was part of a home grown terrorist network that had been growing for years called the North American Islamic Jihad. Officially the government had decided not to reveal that information to the public. "Yeah, can you believe that? Why would anyone who grew up here turn to terrorism?" He said feigning ignorance.

"What about you?" Julie resumed their original conversation. "What do you do?"

"I'm in the Navy," Matt answered vaguely.

"Navy? I thought you were a Marine," Julie told him looking embarrassed. "Sorry, I know one doesn't like to be mistaken for the other."

So that was why she had dropped us off at Pendleton, she thought we were Marines, Matt smiled at the thought. "Nope, I'm based at Coronado." Matt noticed a teaser for the upcoming nightly news. It mentioned an analysis of Jade's last rescue and debate about the limits of her powers. He used this as the excuse he was looking for to move the conversation away from him and back the way he wanted it to go.

"Hey, have you heard about that 'Jade' character?" Matt asked innocently, pointing to the TV headline.

"Yeah, I think she's pretty cool," Julie stated as she turned to look at the older video. It had been taken by the patrol car's dash cam. It showed her with a gun pointed at the kidnapper's head. She felt a little ill, she wasn't proud of herself for losing control and almost shooting him.

"I think she should've just shot that guy who kidnapped those two girls," Matt suggested when he noticed her discomfort. He tried to use it to get more information.

"It was,…I mean, I'm sure it was tempting, but I don't think she could really do something like that," Julie said awkwardly. She felt weird talking to him about herself in the third person.

Matt noticed her slip up, but didn't let on. *So she's upset because she almost shot him*, he thought, *interesting*. He kept asking her questions. "Yeah, but he deserved it. What I think is amazing is she had the courage to go save me and my buddies in Iraq," Matt said. "She could've been killed."

"What? Really? That was you? Cool," Julie pretended to not know. "What was it like meeting her?"

"I didn't really meet her. We said a few words, that's all," Matt said pretending to be disappointed. "What I want to know is why would a civilian risk herself like that?"

"Why are you surprised about that? If she had a chance to get you out of there before the terrorists could kill you, why wouldn't she?" Julie pointed out.

"Why wouldn't she? Because most people would be scared of getting killed that's why. She put herself in a lot of danger doing what she did," Matt said more forcefully than he had meant to. He had meant to keep the conversation strictly matter of fact, but he couldn't help showing his frustration with her attitude.

"I think she can take care of herself. With that power of hers she'd be really hard to catch."

"She's not invincible. You have no idea what it's like in combat," he argued.

"A year ago a friend of mine was killed by a sniper in Iraq. He died before medics could get to him. It was worth the risk to get them to safety," Julie said, admitting her real feelings. "Honestly, it's really frustrating when our military guys are tortured or killed and there's nothing I can do about it."

So that's what made her rescue us. But her sense of invulnerability could get her killed next time, Matt thought considering her answer. "What about the talk that she could be a threat to national security, or might start robbing banks?"

"That's nonsense, if she was going to do that she would've already!" Julie answered impatiently. "Why would she start by saving people and risk being seen, and then turn to a life of crime?"

"Then why do you think she hides her identity?" Matt asked.

"I think she just wants to help people without her life being turned into a three ring circus. Movie stars can't live without the paparazzi bugging them constantly. It'd be even worse for her. Can you imagine?" Julie shivered dramatically. "Besides not everyone likes her powers. I heard the stupidest interview the other day with some military guy. He kept saying, 'she needs to be controlled'. Yeah like that's going to happen." Julie rolled her eyes.

Matt nodded in agreement, but he was remembering the general and he worried about what he had in mind to 'control' Jade. He completely understood why Julie wanted to keep her identity secret.

Their dinner arrived, and he decided to change the subject, he'd already gotten answers to most of his questions for now. During the rest of dinner he only found out a little more about her. She told him that she had a dog named Cinder that she had found. But her story about how she found him seemed made up. He suspected it had something to do with her powers. He also learned that she lived with her parents in Oceanside. They sounded like a normal enough family, so normal he wondered even more where she had gotten her powers from. He remembered her joke about 'if they figured it out could he let her know'. *Maybe she really doesn't know where her powers came from,* he thought.

After dinner they headed to the nearby movie theater. He let her choose the movie and she picked some romantic comedy. Normally it would have been torture watching it, but Matt did not pay much attention to it. He was too busy going over her answers from dinner, making sure he remembered all of the information he had learned. After the movie, he made sure she got back to her car safely and then headed home himself. Thinking back on the night, he realized it had been fun, even though he had been trying to learn more about Jade.

CHAPTER 10

A couple of weeks later Matt and his team were redeployed to the Middle East. Before then, Julie saw Matt several more times. Mostly they went to dinner and the movies, but the last time she saw him they took a walk along the Oceanside Pier. The sun was setting and the ocean glowed orange and red as it reflected the last rays of the sun. The cool ocean breeze smelled like seaweed and salt water as it tore at her long hair. That was when he broke the news to her that they had their orders and were shipping out the next day.

"Nothing like a lot of notice," Julie quipped, but behind her sarcasm she was worried about him. She really liked spending time with him. "How long will you be gone?"

"I can't really say. I know that sounds like a cheesy line, but I really can't. I'll write or call when I can, but there will be times I just can't. So don't worry if you don't hear from me for a few days," he instructed her. What he wanted to say was *don't come and try to zap me out of combat just because you're worried about me*. But he had never talked to her about her abilities so he could not bring it up now. *I should not have dated her*, he berated himself. *She could get herself killed trying to save me.*

While he was gone, Julie did keep her 'eye' on them so to speak, but she did not just zap in every time he was in combat, even though she was tempted. She knew he would not want her to. The first time she had checked on him he had been souped-up on adrenaline. The others were nearby, and she checked on them quickly. She felt Demetrio, suddenly experience intense pain. Several of the men gathered around the lanky man. Soon they all started moving again, so she guessed they did not need her to save them. They were stressed in combat and there was fear, but not the same level of fear that she had felt while they were hostages. So she decided to leave them there, and just kept an eye on them until they were done.

Matt called her that night. He had been worried during the mission that she would pop in and take them out of there before they could finish. "Hey how's it going?" he asked casually.

"Great, how're you?" she asked innocently. Julie was dying to ask about Demetrio, but she knew she could not just blurt out that she knew he was injured.

"Oh, I'm fine. We had a mission today," Matt told her.

"Really? Who was hurt?" Julie asked, and then realized she had asked the question the wrong way.

"Why do you think someone was hurt?" Matt asked, hoping to get a clue to her powers.

"Um... doesn't that normally happen when people are in combat?" Julie pretended ignorance. She hated acting like a dunce, but she had to cover her blunder.

"We try not to," Matt said dryly. "Actually Demetrio was hit, but it wasn't serious. He'll be on light duty for a while until he heals."

Julie moved the conversation away from the topic, and the rest of the call was pretty mundane. They said goodbye a few minutes later. Matt sat thinking about it afterward. *Well, at least I found out that she knows when we're on a mission, and she didn't rush in when one of us got hit*, he thought thankfully.

A few weeks later, Julie was heading home from a day at the beach with her friends to escape the summer heat. She sat in her car, thinking about what she should do next. She had not checked on Matt in a few days, so she decided to use her powers to look in on him. As soon as she made contact with him she knew it was bad news. He was alive, but hurt. More than that though, he was scared and there was more than a little bit of panic in his emotions too.

Julie decided to leave her car there and zapped herself straight to the cave. Once she was there she wasted no time getting her disguise on, including the body armor vest he had given her when they rescued the students. It only took a few minutes before she was ready. Well as ready as she was going to be. With one last thought she decided to zap in from a crouched position. *I don't want to be too big of a target; I've learned that much from watching police dramas.*

Julie had never been in combat, and until recently had never even heard a gun fired. As she arrived the darkness was pierced with a sudden flash of light. Explosions were going off right outside of the small building that Matt's team had found shelter in. Glancing around, she saw in the dim glow of small fires, that it had once been made of concrete blocks, with wood beams supporting the upper levels. Now any upper stories that it might have had were being destroyed by artillery. There were large gaps in the remaining walls, and Matt's team was arranged in position just inside those gaps. Several more explosions went off within the first few seconds that Julie arrived. She felt the concussions reverberate through the very air around her and she cried out in fear. Her cry made several of the nearby men turn to look at her.

"WHAT THE HELL ARE YOU DOING HERE!" Matt screamed from his position behind the wall. Julie could see that the side of his face was covered in blood from a wound above his right eye.

"INCOMING!" another man yelled as Matt scrambled to reach her in time.

Julie felt the explosion first, and then it felt like someone punched her hard in the shoulder. She did not feel any pain, but she could feel sticky warmth spreading down her arm. Reflexively she fell to her side. She saw Matt belly crawling to her as she lay on the dusty ground stunned. *I can't leave them,* she thought. With all of her strength she concentrated on her powers and reached out to each one of the team. She could feel all of them, she did not know if it was going to work, but desperately she focused on being back at her cave.

They zapped into the center of the main room of her hideout, with a line of dust running along the ground connecting her and each of the men. The moment they arrived Julie fainted from shock and the effort of zapping them all.

Matt finished crawling over to her, and checked her shoulder. It looked like the shrapnel had not hit anything critical, but he wanted to be sure. "Doc! She's hit," he called over his shoulder. Doc had already started over to the fallen girl.

The rest of the team was taking stock of their surroundings. "Simmons… Demetrio, I want you to scout down that way," their lieutenant pointed down the rock tunnel that headed away from the room they were in. He seemed unaffected by the sudden shift in their location. "Chief, check those doors, I want a report on where the hell we are now." Then to Doc, "How is she?"

"She should be alright. She has a piece of shrapnel in her. I need to get it out before I can sew her up. Luckily she was wearing the vest, and the fragment got caught in the edge of it. It's cut into the muscle, but it doesn't look like it hit any major blood vessels," Doc reported. He had removed her cloak and hood and part of her shirt to expose the shoulder wound while he worked.

"So this is Jade, the one who saved us before. Damn, she's just a kid," Lieutenant Cooper said as he wiped his face with his rough hand. "Thank God she'll be alright. What was she thinking?"

"I think I know," Matt admitted. "I think she was coming to save us, me, again."

"Why?" Lieutenant Cooper asked suspiciously.

"I saw her a few times before we left the states," Matt admitted. Doc shot him a surprised look.

"And why didn't you report this to me?" Lieutenant Cooper asked with an edge to his voice.

"I think she deliberately searched me out the first time. I realized who she was only afterward," Matt said realizing it was best to explain everything now. "All I've learned is that she is a 20 year old college student going to Cal State San Marcos. She's in her second year of their nursing program. We went to the movies a few times, but I thought I should keep her identity secret for her safety. Remember that paranoid general, that had us tested for weeks? Imagine what he'd do to her."

Lieutenant Cooper nodded slowly. "I understand, but you should've reported it to me immediately. I'll want a full report of your actions when we get back." He noticed something else. "Wait. Where did she get one of our vests?" he asked angrily. He noticed the men around him suddenly turn to look anywhere else but at him. Shaking his head he said, "Never mind we'll discuss that later too."

Chief Nguyen came up to them at a trot. "LT, I've looked at the two other rooms. The first one is completely empty and has a heavy metal door that locks from the outside. I'm guessing it's probably some kind of cell. The second room is a store room. It's full of food and water supplies to last for weeks. There's even at least fifty pounds of MREs," Chief Nguyen shook his head at that thought. "All of the walls are solid rock; it looks like someone carved these rooms out of a mountain."

"Then where is the electricity coming from?"

Lieutenant Cooper asked, motioning to the light overhead.

"There is a small gas generator in the store room too. The fuel tank is full, and there is a five gallon gas can nearby. It looks like there's even a forced air ventilation system with in and out air shafts."

Simmons and Demetrio were returning from the tunnel. Simmons reported first. "LT you wouldn't believe the layout of this place. That tunnel leads about twenty yards to the east. At the end is a small hole just big enough for someone her size to crawl through. We'd have a hard time squeezing through it."

"Demetrio, can you blast it open?" Lieutenant Cooper asked.

"I could, but in this rock, any explosion would blow out our eardrums," Demetrio pointed out. They were all silent for a moment thinking. "Get this; there are two defensive positions along the tunnel where someone would have clear shots down the length of the tunnel through small rifle slits. They have grenade sumps and everything. This place was set up to hold off an army," Demetrio said, his voice held a touch of respect.

Simmons continued with their report. "We could hear artillery going off in the distance. We reset the GPS to get a lock on our location. It said we're someplace in the desert east of San Diego."

"Okay everyone, get yourselves patched up by Miller if you are injured and then settle in. It looks like we aren't going anywhere without her help." Lieutenant Cooper motioned at the girl Doc had just moved to a bed. In disbelief LT realized that it had also been carved out of the rock wall.

Julie woke up, starving, about an hour later. She opened her eyes, at first not remembering what had happened. Then it all came back to her in a rush of memory and she sat up with a gasp which turned to a whimper. Her sudden movement sent pain shooting down her arm from her wound and she clutched her shoulder.

Realizing she was not wearing her disguise any more she looked around panicked.

"Easy, you lost a lot of blood," Matt said reassuringly as he approached her from where he had been sitting, trying to keep her calm. He had a bandage wrapped around his head and he had been able to clean off most of the blood from his face. From the look of fear in her eyes he guessed what she was worried about. "Don't worry; I've known all along who you are," he admitted, as he helped her sit up. "Your secret is safe with us. I just told LT the little bit I know about you."

Julie considered this information for a moment before her stomach grumbled audibly. "I'm starving; could you get me one of the candy bars from that cabinet?" she asked.

As Matt went to get Julie the requested items she looked apprehensively around the room. With a sigh of relief she realized all of them were there. Some of them looked like they were sleeping, and they all had fresh bandaging on at least one injury, but they were all there. She had worried that she would not be able to zap them if she was not touching them. Then she noticed the lines of dust on the floor. *I used the dust as the way I touched them*, she thought surprised. After all, she could zap a person while touching them through their clothes. The dust was just an extended link between them.

Her train of thought was interrupted by a man in his late twenties who was coming over with an air of authority. He was the second man she had zapped out of the terrorist cell, the one that had been severely beaten. She had not seen him since, and had wondered about him. Matt came back to her bed and he gave her an open candy bar and a bottle of water. She eagerly accepted both. As she ate, the second man introduced himself.

"It's good to finally meet you ma'am. I understand your name is Julie? My name is Lieutenant Cooper, the guys just call me LT," he said with a smile, trying to reassure her as he offered to shake her hand.

"Yes, sir, I'm glad to see you are doing so well," Julie replied as she shook his hand and gave him a tentative smile.

"Yeah I guess I must've looked pretty awful the last time you saw me," he said and grimaced at the memory of his injuries.

"What do you think about my hideout?" she asked, trying to take the attention off of herself.

"Very nice, although I'm trying to figure out why you have what looks like a prison cell," he said and waved at the door to the empty room.

"Well I haven't figured out how to NOT take someone who has grabbed me, and I won't always have your men there to save me," Julie explained. She smiled shyly at the others. "Thanks by the way."

"Hey, no problem. It was the least we could do, all things considered," Simmons joked.

Julie smiled and turned back to Lieutenant Cooper, "So we figured I needed a place I could zap into, hopefully get away from them, and then zap away leaving them locked up."

"We? Who else is there?" Lieutenant Cooper asked intensely. "There isn't anyone else who can do this zapping thing is there?"

"No, just me, but I needed help. So I confided in my Uncle Mark, and he helped me design this place."

"Let me guess, he's a Marine?" Chief Nguyen asked, remembering the amount of MREs in the storage room.

"He used to be," Julie confirmed.

"How exactly did you make this place? How do you zap in and out? How long have you been able to do it?" Lieutenant Cooper finally let his curiosity and impatience show. "I have so many questions for you," he said shaking his head.

"Maybe you should tell us everything from the beginning," Matt suggested. By now all of the men had roused and were listening intently.

"I'm not sure where to start. I'm not exactly sure how I got my powers. I have a feeling it's from a head injury I had almost a year ago and complications from the meds they gave me." Julie said and paused, but seeing the looks on their faces she continued to explain. "I'd been riding on the back of a pedicab with some friends at a street party downtown. It jumped a curb, and I fell off backward hitting my head on the sidewalk."

"Did you have a concussion?" Doc asked.

"Yeah, a pretty bad one. They gave me Mannitol to reduce the swelling," she told them and saw Doc nodding his understanding, "but I had an allergic reaction to it. They don't know how, but I managed to pull through. I was in the hospital for weeks."

"When did you learn you could teleport places?" Lieutenant Cooper asked.

"It was a several months later that I zapped for the first time and it was purely by accident. You see, there was a puppy about to be burned in a brush fire and I zapped to it without thinking."

"Let me guess, your dog, Cinder?" Matt made the connection to the information he had learned on their dates.

Julie nodded. "I'd thought that maybe it was a fluke …that it'd never happen again. When I did it again by accident rushing to a test, and I figured out how to control it. Then I saved an old man that was lost in Oceanside, and then a little boy in Oregon."

"Hey I remember that one. The media was all over it, there was even a grainy video of you," Demetrio piped in from somewhere nearby. Julie couldn't see him, but she recognized his thick Chicago accent.

"Then there were you guys," Julie nodded as she continued. "That's when I went to my Uncle Mark for help, and we made this place. You know the rest from there."

"Not exactly. How do you find the people you are looking for? How did you know we were in trouble today?" This time it was Matt who asked her.

"All I need is a picture of a person or place. With you guys I used the terrorist video. I concentrate on the picture and then think about 'being there'. I know that sounds strange, but it's the best way to describe it."

"What about today? We've been in combat before and you didn't zap in," Doc asked from where he was sitting with his back against the wall to her right.

"Since you guys shipped out, I've been looking in on you," Julie admitted. She heard several of them complain they didn't understand, so she explained further. "Have you ever been able to feel that someone was close by, even though you couldn't see them?" They all nodded, they often relied on that sixth sense to save their lives. "Well, my powers are sort of like that. I can feel where a person is and what's around them, but if I concentrate on them I can also feel what they are feeling, physically, like if you're wounded, and some of your strongest emotions."

"That's how you knew one of us got hit that one time. I knew it! But you should've known who it was. Why did you ask?" Matt asked.

"I knew Demetrio had been hit, but not how bad," Julie explained.

"But then why did you come today?" Lieutenant Cooper asked.

"Today was different from other times you were in combat because there was panic under all of your feelings. You guys don't normally feel that kind of panic. What happened?"

Demetrio snorted. "Oh we were just pinned down by heavy mortar fire, quickly running out of ammunition, with no way out and no back up on the way for another hour at least. That's all," he said with a shrug.

"Speaking of which, how are we getting back? I don't want to get beamed back there," Simmons said, favoring his wounded leg. "And I definitely don't want to be zapped to Pendleton again, and face that crazy general."

"Crazy general? I heard on the news that there was a general that thought I needed to be 'controlled'," Julie laughed. "He's crazy alright. He can't make me do anything I don't want to; I'm not in the military."

"He may be crazy, but he's powerful. I wouldn't underestimate the power he has," Lieutenant Cooper disagreed with her. "Even with our CO pulling every string he had, he was still allowed to interrogate us for weeks," Lieutenant Cooper continued. He remembered their CO's expression when he had told him that the admiral had saved them from the worst of what the general had planned. Lieutenant Cooper had a feeling that they might not have survived it fully intact physically or mentally. He knew that certain interrogation drugs had some nasty side effects.

"You guys are as paranoid as my Uncle Mark," Julie said, trying to dismiss his warnings. She didn't want to think about this now, she was too tired. She decided to change the subject, "We have to think about getting you back before you get in trouble. Do you know where you want to go? Maybe some place we can get a picture of on-line?" Julie asked, thinking she could zap back to her room and get it, but she felt so tired still. Maybe she should ask Uncle Mark about getting satellite internet here.

"Hang on," Lieutenant Cooper interrupted. "Simmons, do you still have those recon pictures?" Simmons nodded and passed him a small camera. Lieutenant Cooper spent a moment studying the images on the small screen. Turning to Julie he clarified, "you need an open area, without lots of people and objects?"

"Yeah that's right, one that shows the area with enough details."

Lieutenant Cooper searched the camera's memory for a few minutes, regarding each picture critically. Finally he brought the camera over to Julie. "What about this place?"

he asked showing her the screen.

Julie looked at the picture. It was of an abandoned building. The dirt colored hovel stood alone beside a field of dried up crops. Its roof was caved in at one corner and its door was missing. "Where is it?" she asked curious.

"It's about a mile from where we were pinned down. It should be a safe enough place for us to wait for extraction. But its close enough to be a plausible place for us to have reached on our own," Lieutenant Cooper explained.

Julie nodded her understanding as she started focusing her powers on the desolate hut. "I can't feel anyone nearby, but I can only sense about twenty five yards in any direction."

"Alright, that'll have to work. How close can you get us to the wall?"

"I can put you within a foot or so of it," Julie assured him. "But can you wait a little while? I need to eat some more. I've found it helps when I've zapped too much."

"A few more minutes rest won't matter, and it gives us time to go over our cover story," Lieutenant Cooper said and turned to face the team. "We'll need to all have the same information when we're debriefed. After the official report, I'll approach our CO; I think he'll help us. You, however," and now he turned back to Julie, "need to start making another one or more of these hideouts. Now that we know about it, you can't count on it as your only one. Don't misunderstand; none of us would willingly give up information about you or this place. But there're ways to make anyone talk, especially if the interrogator isn't worried about the condition of the person when he is done. I think the general could get that desperate."

Julie rested and considered his warning, while the team agreed on their cover story. It didn't involve her in any way. They had decided to hide her involvement from the official record. Once the team had been officially debriefed Lieutenant Cooper would go to their CO and give him the real, but unofficial story. Julie concentrated on the picture; she watched the area while she rested. Still she could not sense any people. She put on what was left of her disguise just in case someone was watching, as the team gathered their gear. They had already decided what order she would zap them in. When they arrived at the abandoned building, it was dimly lit in pre-dawn light. The first two men quickly secured the dark building.

"Alright, bring the rest of the guys in here," Chief Nguyen instructed her.

She had to stop to take a break after the first four. It had been a long day and this was taking the last of the energy she had left.

Luckily the area remained empty the whole time she was transferring them. When she was finally done Julie was really tired, but she assured them that she could make it home. They waited until she was gone to call in their position for extraction.

CHAPTER 11

Julie had spent the last three days in bed. Once the pain meds that Doc had given her had worn off, her shoulder had started throbbing in pain. She took a large dose of ibuprofen and was able to tolerate the pain as long as she did not move it too much. Thankfully she was so tired she was able to sleep most of the time.

Julie told her parents that she was just really sick, and needed to rest. Her mom brought her chicken noodle soup in bed, which was wonderful, but it also made her feel even more guilty about lying to them. Her parents still did not know about her adventures, and she did not want them to find out while she was wounded. Luckily it was summer vacation so it didn't matter if she stayed in bed.

By the fourth day Julie could pretend she was not in any pain as long as she kept her hand in her pocket and didn't try to use her arm. The wound did not look infected, but it was hard to see her own shoulder. She knew she should have it checked out by someone. *I can't go to Urgent Care without having to answer a lot of hard questions*, she thought, *and I don't want to face Uncle Mark*. The only one she could go to was Matt. Doc would have been even better, but she did not feel comfortable zapping in on him unannounced.

After dinner Julie told her parents she was going to take a nap. Once she was in her room she locked her door. She zapped to her hideout for her disguise and then searched for Matt. When she found him she decided that he must be asleep because she could not sense any traces of emotion and he was so still. *Well if he's sleeping at least I know he isn't showering*, she chuckled again at that memory.

When Julie zapped to him she found that Matt was in a sort of tent. Actually it was part of a much larger tent. It had canvas walls separating his room from the rest of the tent, and a tarp for a floor. From the feel of the ground under the tent, it felt like there was sand under it. She turned from her examination of the room to find Matt. He was sleeping on a cot to one side of the room. She looked out of the window, which was made of clear plastic instead of glass. The sky was still very dark but it was graying on the horizon. Guessing that it would not be long until dawn, she settled in to wait for him to wake up. Not wanting to be seen even in her disguise, she sat down in a spot that would not be seen immediately from the door flap just in case someone walked in.

The sun was just breaking over the horizon when Matt's alarm clock startled her about half an hour later. He swatted at the offending clock and swung his legs over the edge of his cot as he rubbed his face. She noticed the cut above his eye had been cleaned and stitched.

Julie cleared her throat wanting to catch his attention without startling him. He looked up quickly at the sound and caught sight of her. "I guess I'm lucky you didn't pop in on me a few minutes from now, I would've been taking a leak," he said and shook his head ruefully. He looked up sharply, and asked earnestly "How's your shoulder?"

"I think it's Okay, but since I can't see a doctor to check it, I figured I'd see what you thought of it," Julie said. She got up and gingerly started taking off her hood.

"No, wait, this isn't the best place. Someone could see

you," he explained as he motioned toward the window. "Take us back to your cave for a minute."

Once they got back to her hideout, Julie carefully took off her cloak and mask. She had thought ahead and replaced the long sleeve shirt she normally wore with a tank top.

"Good idea," Matt nodded approval when he spotted her tank top. He also seemed relieved, and Julie wondered about that for a moment.

Matt had headed to her first aid cabinet when they had first arrived, and returned with fresh bandages for her shoulder. When he removed her bandage he noted the dry edges of the wound and that it was pink, but not the angry red color it would be if it was infected. "Actually, it looks really good, but I bet it still hurts like a mother."

"Yeah," Julie was at a loss for words with him standing so close to her. Luckily Matt did not seem to notice.

"I know you're doing this because of your friend who was killed, but getting yourself killed won't help anyone," he tried to reason with her. "You shouldn't have come to help us," Matt chastised her.

"Why not?" Julie asked.

"If you hadn't been able to zap us out of there you would've just made it harder for us to get out," Matt explained. "Don't ever do that again. I don't care how bad off we are, you don't belong in combat."

The lecture roused Julie out of her shyness. "I can't just sit there and let you guys get killed when I know I can do something about it!" she objected.

"You could have been killed!" Matt argued in frustration.

"So?" she demanded. "What do you think I should do with this power? Become a sideshow freak, or… I know, I could start my own business. 'Julie's Travel Service'. I can see it now, 'Need to be across the country for a meeting? Don't have time to fly? Just call me! I'll get you there in a jiffy!' " Julie snorted in derision. "I can help people!"

"But having you there could just make it harder for us. You could put us all in even more danger because you don't know what you are doing."

"Then teach me! I know I can help you, there is so much more I can do. If I had a radio link with someone, I could tell you if there is someone around the corner ahead of you. I could evacuate wounded and free up the others to keep fighting," Julie argued. She had given this a lot of thought. She did not just want to help when the situation had already gone to hell, and she could help other units if she had their pictures too.

"No way," Matt dismissed her arguments, even though her suggestions were tempting. *To have a way to know if someone was waiting to ambush you would be a big help*, but he refused to acknowledge the thought because it would mean putting her in danger.

"Why not?" Julie exclaimed angrily, she could be really stubborn. "You know I'll keep doing it anyway. I'll do it with or without your help. So you can choose to train me or not," Julie told him firmly. She decided to change tactics, "I'll do a better job if you teach me how, and it'll be safer for me too."

Matt was stuck, he believed her threat about helping whether he wanted her to or not. "I don't want you getting hurt," he tried one last argument.

"Then teach me so I won't."

Matt thought for a few minutes. "Combat's not like that. It's unpredictable. You could do everything right, and still end up dead. Remember your friend? A sniper would see your costume and wouldn't hesitate to put a bullet in your head."

"I want to help people, and I won't let another person die when I know I can save them," Julie stated simply.

Matt did not want to, he wanted to try to make her stop using her powers, but he knew that was futile. Maybe he could help her improve her skills enough to keep her from getting hurt. "Fine, but the first thing we need to work on is getting you to zap faster. You're a sitting duck while you sit there getting ready to go."

"That's a great idea! So when can we start?"

Matt groaned, and absently scratched at his stitches. "Well, we've been given light duty for three weeks while we get healed up," he said thinking out loud. "I'll make sure I'm ready for you at 10 am my time, here take my watch, I'll get another one," he said, handing it to her. "Make sure I'm alone and then try to zap me out of my room as fast as you can. That will be our starting exercise each day, and it will make it less likely that you're seen. Now get me back to my room before I'm missed."

Every day over the next week, Julie would retrieve Matt from his room and bring him back to the hideout. Then they would work on increasing her speed, by repeatedly zapping in and out of one room into the other, first by herself, then by 'rescuing' Matt. Some days she would bring Cinder along and she would zap back and forth between Matt and Cinder as Matt moved around the cave. She soon learned how to put two images in her mind, and string them together so that she could go from one to the next with increasing speed. After some more practice she learned to fine tune her position when she zapped in. Now she could choose exactly where she would arrive, either in front, behind, or even already practically touching the person.

Back at the base, Matt's buddies, other guys from his team that he hung out with, were starting to notice his absence. They teased him that he was becoming a lazy bum sleeping so much each day. He had turned down several of their invitations to join them for different activities that he would normally be interested in. One of his friends in particular, was getting worried about what he was really doing. So, one morning as Matt headed back to his tent to take a nap Martin followed him. He arrived just in time to see Matt suddenly blink out of existence. Stunned he entered Matt's now empty room and sat on his bunk. *What had just happened? I had seen an image of a green figure next to Matt right before he vanished, but it hadn't lasted more than a split second*, he thought bewildered. He decided to get a chair and sit outside Matt's quarters to wait. *I'm going to get to the bottom of this*. It took two hours for Matt to return. Suddenly he was striding out of the tent. "Hey Matt!" Martin sat up quickly as he called to his friend. "You've got some explaining to do."

Matt turned to see his friend sitting outside of his room. "What do you mean?" he said, trying to play innocent.

"You know what I mean… I saw you disappear two hours ago," Martin accused him.

"Shh!" Matt grabbed his arm and propelled him into his room. "You can't tell anyone what you saw. Swear!"

"Alright, alright, I won't tell anyone. Just tell me what's going on."

Matt hesitated. "Its top secret, I can't tell you," he stated, trying to evade the question.

"Bullshit, if it was part of a mission you wouldn't be using your quarters. Are you in some kind of trouble? Let me help," Martin offered sincerely.

Matt knew he could trust him. He had known him for years, so that wasn't the problem. "It's not my decision to make. Tell you what, tomorrow after I leave, come in and stand in the center of the room. If it's decided that I can tell you, you won't have long to wait, if not, I'll come back. And we'll just leave it at that."

The next morning Matt waited for Julie. She came at her regular time, this time she was fast enough that he did not even register her arrival before he was taken to her cave. "We've got to talk, there's a problem," Matt said, not waiting for their usual hellos.

"What's up? What's wrong?" Julie had been excited to see what he thought of how fast she had zapped him out, and was a little disappointed that he did not comment on it. But she got over it quickly hearing his serious tone.

"One of my friends saw me get zapped out yesterday. He wants to know what's going on."

"Do you trust him? Is he likely to turn you in if you don't tell him?" she asked nervously. Several possibilities flew through her thoughts and she started to worry.

"No, I trust him, he's a good friend and he won't do anything to hurt me," Matt assured her. "Actually, it might be handy to have someone else for you to train with too. But I haven't told him anything because it's your safety and your decision."

"I'd say that if you trust him, I'm fine with it," Julie decided, "and I agree I need to expand my training. So okay, let's tell him."

"Well, he's waiting to be picked up in my room right now," Matt explained. Before he could even finish his sentence she had gone and come back. Secretly Matt was really impressed with her speed.

"Holy crap! What just happened? Who are you?" Martin asked, turning to look at Julie who was standing next to him in her green costume. "Hey, you're that Jade woman! That was awesome! It was like going on a loop-de loop on a roller coaster."

After they made their introductions, they explained what they were doing and they made plans for the next day. Martin had been equally impressed with her hideout and had been eager to help them. So on the days that he was able to join them, Julie practiced stringing together multiple pickups and could now switch people. It really helped her develop her speed even more. Finally, it was time for her to work on a new skill.

"I've been thinking," Julie said one day as they rested at the cave's dining table.

"Uh, oh," Matt teased.

Ignoring him, Julie continued, "I think I need to be able to take a person without their weapons. What if I need to move a bad guy, I don't want him to be able to shoot you guys when I bring him back."

"Do you think you can? I mean can you do it without one of us losing a body part? I wouldn't mind if the target lost body parts but I'm kind of partial to all of mine," Matt commented from where he was sitting across from her at the table. Martin was getting a snack from her supply room.

"Let me try. I promise I won't zap you if I'm not sure I can do it."

"What are you trying?" Martin asked as he settled in his chair at the table too.

"I'm going to try to zap him without his weapon," Julie explained as Matt groaned in agreement.

Julie and Matt took position in the center of the room. Julie put a hand on his shoulder and concentrated. She focused on just Matt, feeling her powers outline his body. She held her concentration as she checked to make sure no part of him would be left behind, but that the rifle on his shoulder would stay. Then she zapped, not too far away, she only needed to go a few feet.

Martin spit the water he had been drinking out of his mouth. He was pointing at Matt and laughing hysterically. Bewildered, Julie looked at Matt. He was naked; completely and utterly naked. The only bit of cloth that was left on him was the piece that had been under Julie's hand. After a quick look at Matt and the realization that he was naked, Julie turned away and covered her eyes. She could feel her cheeks heating up and was thankful her mask hid her blush. Behind her she could hear Matt and Martin exchanging jibes as Matt started getting dressed.

"Well I guess I can be grateful I'm still in one piece," Matt said nonchalantly. "You can look now, I'm dressed."

"I think your hair cut got shorter too," Martin joked.

"I'm so sorry Matt, I didn't mean to," Julie apologized. She was so embarrassed she didn't know what to say. She couldn't even look him in the eye.

"It's Okay, not like it's the first time you've seen me naked," Matt teased her, remembering her appearance while he was in the shower.

"Oh really?" Martin asked, and the jibes began anew.

"But I don't think I want to volunteer for that again," Matt told her, ignoring Martin's comments.

They decided that they needed to think about how to have Julie practice that skill. Neither of the guys was willing to volunteer again, and Julie did not really blame them. That left them deciding what to work on next. Martin had an idea. "One thing you do need to practice is *not* taking someone who is holding you. That's why you have that cell right?" he asked, motioning to the door of her empty room.

"We would need to practice it by using something else, not one of us," Matt commented. "I don't want a repeat of the last time," he teased.

"Oh this is totally different, this time I'd just take off the hand if I did it wrong," Julie pointed out, grinning maliciously in rebuke. "I've an idea of what we can use. I'll bring it tomorrow."

The next day Julie presented them with a Halloween decoration she had dug out of their garage. It looked like an arm that had been torn off at the shoulder, complete with fake blood stains.

"That's lovely, and you had it just lying around at home?" Matt liked giving Julie a hard time.

"It was from a Halloween a few years back when we went all out decorating the front yard. But see, all we have to do is see if I can zap without it."

After a few attempts they figured out a way for the hand to be holding onto her. Her first try ended up with one of the mannequin's fingertips staying with Julie. "Oops, glad that wasn't you," she said mischievously and Matt made a face at her. "But seriously, it's harder because it's not alive," Julie tried to make her explanation not sound like an excuse. "Telling the difference between it and my clothes is rough. I think I'd actually do better with a real person."

"We'll just keep practicing with the mannequin hand for a while, thanks," Martin answered looking a bit pale, and rubbed his fingers unconsciously.

By the end of the week Julie was able to speed-zap an escape from the mannequin hand. "Look, it didn't even lose anything else," she said triumphantly. After her last run of speed zapping Julie held up the mannequin arm proudly. It was a bit worse for wear after the week's worth of practicing, but they all agreed that it didn't appear to be missing any more parts.

CHAPTER 12

A little over three weeks after they had started her training. Matt was back on regular duty, and Julie had only another week before her classes started again. She had been spending a lot of her free time making two new hideouts with her Uncle Mark's guidance. One was located in Mount Hesperus in the Revelation Mountains in Alaska. The second one was in a butte in the Badlands of South Dakota. Neither of them was as large as her main fortress in the Chocolate Mountains. They were different from her first one because they did not have access tunnels. After she reached an area in the mountain that was deep enough, she began backfilling the tunnel with the rock she was clearing from her living area. With a forced air ventilation system in place she did not need the tunnel and it made it nearly impossible for anyone to attack her hideouts. They also had one more addition: wells. A water source was critical for her to be able to live in them for any real length of time. Actually, Julie was planning on putting in a well or cistern in her first one also.

This morning she was taking a break and sat watching the news. Their foreign correspondent came on with the latest on a hostage situation in Baghdad. The British embassy had been attacked, and several embassy employees had been taken hostage. The terrorists were demanding the release of several of their comrades from Guantanamo Bay. The news was currently showing a clip of a hostage that the terrorists had paraded in front of a window. The video showed a terrified woman who was strapped with explosives. The terrorists had threatened that if they released the grip on the remote control the explosives would go off automatically. The news reporter was explaining that this made any rescue attempt almost impossible because they couldn't risk the hostages' lives. Julie knew that the pictures were of a scene from some time earlier, but the reporter said that the standoff was still going on. Julie concentrated on the picture of the hostage with the bomb strapped to her. Julie could feel the woman's terror, and that of the people surrounding her. Julie carefully focused on each person, but she didn't feel anyone who wasn't terrified so she guessed that there were no guards in the room. Next Julie concentrated on Matt. As she had hoped, he was with his team and they were alone.

Julie zapped to her hideout to retrieve her disguise. She double checked that the team was still alone and then decided to take the chance and zapped right next to them. Julie's entrance caused several of the men to reflexively grab their weapons. Most of them cursed at her unannounced arrival.

"Is this a bad time?" Julie asked innocently.

"What are you doing here?" Lieutenant Cooper demanded.

"You guys wouldn't happen to be close to the British Embassy in Bagdad, would you?" Julie asked.

"Yes," Lieutenant Cooper admitted reluctantly.

"Perfect, I have an idea on how to save the hostages without any of them getting killed," she said seriously. "But I need your help to pull it off."

"Is this another one of your plans where we all zap

in, and provide cover for you to zap out the hostages?" Matt guessed.

"Nope," she said cheerfully, "I've gotten fast enough they'll all be out before anyone notices. I just need a safe place to zap them to."

"And what do you plan to do with the explosives?" Lieutenant Cooper asked.

"I have an idea, but she has to be the last one out," Julie started to explain. Then she had caught the look from Matt so she refrained from explaining further. "Also it has to be a place that isn't connected to you guys. To protect you, it has to look like I did it alone again."

Lieutenant Cooper looked at Matt, "Is she always this way?"

Matt sighed and nodded, "Unfortunately, and if we don't help her she'll find a way to do it anyway."

"Well it's not like we have a lot of options. Let's work out the details," Lieutenant Cooper agreed, relenting. They discussed several options but ended up agreeing to send Julie alone. Teleporting any of them as backup would only increase the total number of zaps she would need to do. Demetrio was sent to find a location for Julie to use. He found a roof nearby that had been in the news footage that had run all day. There were British Special Forces positioned on it. They'd help confirm that Jade was working alone.

"Here, eat this," Matt said as he handed her a candy bar.

"You think I need this?" Julie asked between mouthfuls of candy.

"Yeah, I've noticed you can do around ten zaps depending on different things before getting too tired, and there are over twenty hostages," Matt explained with a shrug. "It can't hurt."

Then it was time for them to start. Matt, Doc and Demetrio had joined the British forces on the roof for the entirely legitimate logistical reasons of snipers and lookout.

Julie would use them to find the roof. Lieutenant Cooper and the rest joined the British forces gathering in front of the embassy, just in case they needed to make a direct assault on the building. Then they waited.

A few moments later, Julie zapped into the center of the room where the hostages were being held. It looked like a large meeting room. Several hostages cried out and scrambled away from her in fear. She tried to shush them, but it didn't help, and she started to worry that the terrorists would hear them.

"Who's in charge?" she asked urgently. When the ambassador himself stepped forward, Julie very briefly explained, "I'm here to get you all out of here."

"Alright, what can I do to help?" the ambassador offered.

"Just keep everyone quiet. This will just take a couple minutes and I don't want the terrorists coming in." Then, one by one Julie started zapping them out so quickly that it was almost impossible for them to see her. The entire time the ambassador kept his people quiet, as they grew excited to be rescued.

After about thirteen hostages had been rescued, Julie started feeling dizzy. On the roof top Matt noticed her sway after she deposited a hostage. The British forces were distracted escorting the latest hostages off of the rooftop and down to the waiting ambulances. "Stop, eat a candy bar now, while no one is looking," Matt said as he used his body to block any view of her face as she quickly ate the candy bar.

She was surprised at how quickly she felt better. "Okay, I feel better now," she said before long and she could continue the mission. She needed to stop one more time to refuel before she was done.

The ambassador was the next to last to go. "Take me last please, get her out of here."

"I have to take her last." Julie refused and with her head she indicated the bomb strapped to the woman.

"Don't worry, she'll be fine, but no one can be here after she leaves, just in case," Julie tried to reassure the man. Julie turned to the woman. "I promise you, I won't leave you, I will come back for you," she said. The woman nodded, but Julie could see that she was still terrified.

Julie returned a moment later next to the woman. She had obviously thought that she would be left behind, and when she caught sight of Jade she visibly relaxed.

"Okay. Just try to stay calm. I'm sorry, this will be a little embarrassing for you, but you'll be alive," Julie explained. She concentrated for a long moment and then she zapped them both out.

On the roof top Julie arrived with the now naked woman. Matt was ready with a blanket to cover her. In the distance they heard a hollow explosion. The woman, clutching the blanket around her turned back to Jade. She had a shy grin on her face as she spoke. "Embarrassing yes, but better than being blown up, thank you," she said as she turned to follow Doc, who was trying to get her to cover in the rooms below.

"You did it, that was risky, but I have to say you did it without leaving any part of her behind," Matt said shaking his head and grinning from the memory of his experience.

"I wouldn't have tried it if I didn't know I could," Julie said reproachfully.

"Are you always this self-confident?"

"Not always," Julie admitted, remembering the times when she had been unable to speak when he was close to her.

"That's hard for me to believe," Matt argued. "Alright, you had better get going. You've caused enough excitement here. Stay away for a while; this will make the 'general' watch us closely again."

"Alright, see ya later."

Julie's activities had attracted Mr. Smith's attention. He knew she was somehow communicating with the men of SEAL Team 3, but he wasn't sure how. The squad denied any prior knowledge of her plans, but it was all a little too coincidental that she kept showing up on their missions. If his superiors would let him, he could easily get the information he wanted. Smith snorted derisively. Unfortunately, his superiors weren't of his same mind… that the SEAL Team was expendable. This left him with only one option, wait and be ready the next time the Team needed her help.

CHAPTER 13

"Ow!" Julie complained as she rubbed her arm. "Take it easy Uncle Mark!" She was starting to regret joining him at his dojo for some hand to hand fighting practice.

"Why? A terrorist won't go easy on you if he gets a hold of you," Mark said seriously. He hated hurting her, but she needed to be ready for anything. "So are you still dating that guy?"

"You mean, Matt?" Julie asked. Matt was back from his deployment and they'd gone out a few times already. "Yeah, why do you ask?"

"Because he lied to you, he only started dating you because he was trying to get information about Jade," Mark said reasonably.

"Oh thanks!" Julie replied, mildly insulted.

"You know what I mean."

"Well, I didn't tell him the truth either. I totally played him that first date," she said proudly.

"Still, I don't trust him."

"My parents met him last week, and they like him," Julie tried to reassure him.

"No offense Julie, but your parents aren't the best judges of character."

"Why not?" Julie asked.

"They like everyone."

"No they don't!" she said defensively.

"They like me, don't they?" Mark said sardonically. Julie laughed at that. "Seriously, I want to meet him."

Julie groaned, "Promise me you won't try any macho bullshit with him."

"Me?" Mark feigned that his feelings were hurt. "Never!"

Julie considered for a moment. "Why don't you visit my parents the next time he picks me up on a date? You can meet him, and we can escape quickly if you're a jerk," she offered.

Mark shook his head in mock despair, "You don't have any faith in me."

The next week Julie told Mark when to be at her parents' house to meet Matt. She warned Matt ahead of time about her uncle wanting to meet him.

"Don't worry. I'll be fine," Matt reassured her for the third time. "I think I can handle one overprotective uncle," he joked.

Matt arrived about an hour later for the planned date. Julie opened the door and invited him in. Her Uncle Mark stepped up to introduce himself.

"So you're Matt. It's nice to finally meet you," Mark said as he offered to shake Matt's hand.

"And you're Uncle Mark that we've heard so much about," Matt replied.

"Why don't we step outside for a minute?" Mark asked.

"Uncle Mark…," Julie warned.

"It's Okay Julie. We'll be back in a minute," Matt reassured her as he followed Mark to the back door.

"Why are you dating Julie?" Mark asked, getting straight to the point once they were in the backyard. "Are you trying to control her?"

"Have you ever tried to make her do something?"

Matt laughed. "Let me tell you, she has a stubborn streak a mile wide."

"You could be trying to get her to like you just so she'll pull your butt out of danger," Mark accused him.

"I've been trying to prevent her from coming to get us!" Matt exclaimed. A sudden realization came to him. "She didn't tell you she was wounded, did she?"

"She was what!" Mark fumed. "What did you get her into?"

"Hold on, it's not like that. We were on a mission, and we got pinned down. We didn't call her, she just appeared, but she got hit by shrapnel," Matt quickly tried to explain. "Luckily she still got all of us out. That's when she took us to her hideout and my Team first found out who she was. Anyway, ever since then, I've been trying to convince her to not try to save us. But she's told me she'll do it with or without my help."

Mark looked away shaking his head. "Yeah, that sounds like Julie," he agreed, deep in thought for a moment. "Wait. You said 'Team'; you're with the SEAL Teams?"

Matt looked down for a moment, realizing his mistake. Finally he looked at Mark and nodded. "Yeah, I am, SEAL Team 3. So you can see why I really don't want her stepping in and pulling us out before we've finished a mission."

"So what can we do?" Mark asked. He had decided that he might be willing to give Matt the benefit of the doubt.

"She's forced me to train with her," Matt admitted, and Mark laughed at his predicament. "We've increased her speed. At least now she no longer stands there like a target when she's getting ready to teleport."

"Good," Mark agreed nodding. "That's one of the things I was worried about too. I've been working with her on self-defense."

"Like Karate?" Matt asked.

"Nothing that tame!" Mark exclaimed insulted. "No, I'm teaching her Hapkido with some nasty tricks tossed in. She'd get disqualified if she ever tried to compete, but it'll keep her alive longer." He paused then decided to explain more. "I'm teaching her to use punches, kicks and zapping together. If she does have to fight, the poor bastard won't see her strikes coming, literally."

"Good idea," Matt agreed. "I'd like to see that someday." Impressed, he decided he liked Mark despite his initial impression. They stood in silence, each one thinking about Julie. "Oh by the way, that hideout's got a sweet design."

"You like it huh? I think it needs a .50 caliber too, but Julie refused," Mark joked.

"I'm sure she'd have no trouble sneaking a PKM back the next time we are deployed. It's not like she goes through customs or anything," Matt offered. "I'll have the guys hang onto one the next time we find one."

"Hey Lisa," Julie called out to her friend who was sitting on a long board close to her. "I'm going to head in and take a break."

"Alright," Lisa said. "I'll be in a little later, I want to catch a few more waves first." Julie eyed the next wave coming in. "Oh, hey, I brought some sodas. You're welcome to have one if you want."

"Thanks," Julie said. "See you later," she added as she stroked to pick up enough speed to catch the wave. Standing up on her board she rode the five foot breaker into the shore. Carrying her board up the beach to their stuff she laid it down next to her towel and took the leash off her ankle. Digging into her friends cooler she fished out a soda and took a large swig before lying down to warm up in the late afternoon sun.

Julie heard her cell phone ring, and she squinted at the setting sun, as she opened her eyes. Rolling onto her stomach, she dug in her bag to look for her phone. Shading her phone so she could see the screen, Julie looked at the number of the incoming call. She did not recognize it but decided to answer it anyway, "Hello?"

"This time it's our turn to ask for help. Join us as soon as you can," she recognized Matt's voice. Before she could answer, she heard the other end of the line hang up.

She sat stunned for a minute. That was the first time he had asked for her help and it worried her. She took a moment to check on the team. They all seemed alright, so Julie relaxed a little. Still she knew he would not have called if they did not really need her. It took Julie a little while to get away from her friends with a plausible excuse, but finally she had said her goodbyes and was headed to her car. Luckily she had driven herself so she did not have to explain how she was leaving. As quickly as she could, she found an out of the way spot for her to park her car, where she could zap to get her disguise. While she was getting ready she thought about what she might be headed into. *Maybe they're bait for a trap*, she thought for a moment. *No, Matt would be worried if it was*, she reasoned, but she decided to be ready to zap out quickly just in case.

When Julie zapped to join the team they were waiting for her in an enormous plane hangar, but they were not alone. Julie was still prepared to zap out if there was any sign that this was a trap. The SEAL Team was standing at attention as their lieutenant came toward her. He was followed by a man with graying hair, in an officer's uniform with enough stars on his collar she guessed he was very important.

While the two approached her, Julie quickly looked around. There was a massive passenger jet at one end of the enormous building. The doors to let it out were closed, but through some windows along the ceiling she could see that it looked like early morning wherever she was. The whole place smelled like grease and fuel.

Julie had arrived in an area where another plane could

be parked, but instead of a passenger jet there were clusters of tables set up. One set of tables held communication equipment where two people dressed in uniforms sat with headphones on, taking notes while they listened. Julie drew her attention back to Lieutenant Cooper and the officer approaching her.

"My name is General Thompson," the man said as he drew closer. "I am the commander of the forces responsible for security at this facility. I understand that you may be able to help us with this situation."

"It's nice to meet you General Thompson, you can call me Jade," Julie introduced herself. "I'm sorry, sir, but what are you talking about? All I know is that I was asked to join them." Julie nodded toward the SEAL Team. "I don't know where I am, or what the situation is."

"I see… Lieutenant Cooper, brief her on the details," the general instructed and moved off to one side to give orders to several men who were waiting nearby.

"We are at the Baghdad Airport. A plane was hijacked late last night and is sitting on the runway," LT started to explain. "It is full of U.S, British, and Australian civilian contractors. As far as we can tell there are probably six hijackers, arranged throughout the plane. The President wants this to be done as quickly and as efficiently as possible. We are hoping you can help us."

"Okay, I'll need pictures of each person that boarded that plane. How many total passengers are there?" Julie asked, thinking about her options.

"Over a hundred."

"I won't be able to zap them all out. I'll pass out long before I get even half of them to safety."

The general had returned and overheard her comments. "Then what options do we have? I was led to believe that you could help us," he said and glanced at the lieutenant.

"Give us a minute, sir. I'm sure we can come up with something," Julie reassured him.

After the pictures had been gathered Julie sat and focused on each image. In a matter of minutes she had sorted the pictures by sensing the person's emotions and put them in stacks of scared and not scared.

"Okay. This is what I've found so far. These six aren't scared like the other passengers but they are so hyped on adrenaline that they are practically buzzing."

"These were the men that we had determined were most likely the hijackers," the general said, pointing at the six pictures. "We already knew that, how does that help us?"

"I need a diagram of the plane. I can tell you where each person is. Then you can plan from there," Julie suggested

"Over here," Matt called from a large metal table off to one side. He and his team had already been going over every detail of the plane's design. He waved at the diagrams in front of them. "Will these do?"

"Yep, just give me a few minutes," Julie told them as she began assigning numbers to each picture and writing the numbers on the diagram, based on where they were located on the plane. She wrote the numbers of the hijackers in red to distinguish them from the regular passengers. When she was done they could see that all of the passengers had been gathered in the main compartment of the plane. Two hijackers were standing at the rear of the plane, two in the cockpit, and "these two keep moving up and down these aisles," she explained pointing to the two numbers that she had written in the main compartment. All of them were standing bent over the table to see the diagram.

"How are they moving? Are they ever alone? Are they ever not able to see the two in the rear of the plane?" Lieutenant Cooper asked as he scanned the layout of the plane.

"One sec," Julie murmured and watched them for a few minutes. Her head was starting to pound, like she'd been staring at something too long. "Yeah, I think these two are supposed to be walking the opposite direction from the other, but one is walking faster than the other. Sometimes they are both walking away from the two in the rear of the plane."

"Okay. You'll zap us here," their Lieutenant told her pointing to the small kitchen at the rear of the plane. "We'll take out these two first, while those two are walking away." He pointed at the two standing guard at the back of the passenger compartment. "Then these two before they can see us and raise the alarm."

"Why don't I just zap out the hijackers?" Julie asked confused.

"It's too risky," Chief Nguyen told her. "They might notice before you got them all and then they'd start shooting," he explained.

"Well, that area is too small for me to zap you all in at once," Julie said considering the diagram. She doubted even three people could stand in that area comfortably. "How 'bout I zap you in by two's. Like this," Julie recommended standing between two of them with a hand on each of their shoulders. "That way we'll fit, and you won't have to hold onto me, so you can be ready to fire."

"That would work," Lieutenant Cooper liked the idea, nodding in agreement. Turning to the others he said, "We'll move down each aisle toward the cockpit. Use MP7s with frangible ammo. Get geared up," he told the team. Turning back to Jade he said, "You keep watch on the hijackers. Let us know if they change anything."

Julie took a seat off to one side of the area, trying to stay out of the way. She started watching the hijacker's movements with her powers. It only took a few minutes for the team to finish their final preparations.

"What are their positions now?" Lieutenant Cooper asked as he came up to her.

"The same," Julie assured him.

"We're ready when you are," LT told her.

"Okay. Can you guys stand in two rows?" Julie asked, and the guys looks at her questioningly "It'll make the zaps faster if you don't have to get in position before each jump," she explained. It took the team a few seconds to line up in the order they had decided to go in. Matt and Demetrio were the first two.

"Be careful," Julie urged him softly.

"Don't worry, this will be a breeze compared to what we would've had to do," Matt tried to reassure her. "Just get yourself out of there as soon as you've dropped the last ones off. We don't need you getting hurt."

"I promise. I'll be out of there so fast no one will even see me," she reassured him. But Julie secretly wondered if she'd be able to. Her head was really hurting from using her powers to watch so many different people.

"Ready?" Lieutenant Cooper asked everyone. "Let's go."

Julie zapped Matt and Demetrio in first with no problem. She was out of there even before they shot the first two hijackers. She returned a moment later with the next two in line, Chief Nguyen and Doc. She briefly caught sight of the bodies of the first two hijackers lying dead in the aisle. When she went back for Lieutenant Cooper and Simmons she was already feeling weak and her head was killing her, but she had to make the last jump into the plane. They needed everyone in to make the attack according to plan.

Julie let go of Cooper and Simmons. They were already moving down the aisles behind the others as she slumped to the floor. Julie could not focus her thoughts; the pain in her head was too intense. She knew she needed to get out of there, but could not concentrate long enough to zap.

One of the passengers spotted her through the curtain to the main cabin. "Look, its Jade!" he whispered loudly to his friend. "That's how they got on the plane." As the man got out of his seat, Julie could see he was a short, fat man with glasses. He looked like a computer nerd.

Another passenger spotted her. "Hey, can you get us out of here?" the man asked. He wore a large cowboy hat and had a heavy southern drawl.

Several passengers started moving toward Julie. They were pleading in louder and louder voices for her to get them to safety. Many of them were close to panicking. They got a grip on her as they crowded into the galley of the plane. She desperately tried to focus enough to zap out, but now she had to worry about not hurting them, and with more and more of them clutching her that would be hard. She managed to get a lock on the hangar, but she did not think she could concentrate enough to zap just herself out without hurting them. *I've got to take them all*, she decided and stretched her powers to take everyone who was touching her. Making sure she had all of the passengers that had crowded around her, she focused all of her will on zapping to the hangar.

In the hangar General Thompson and several Marines were waiting for Jade to reappear. It was taking much longer than it was supposed to. The mission controller was reporting that everything was going according to plan, so they could not understand where she had gone. A large mass of people suddenly appeared in the center of the hangar. From the middle of the group several men were calling out for help. The passengers spread apart, guilty looks on their faces. One of them, a man wearing a Stetson, lifted Jade from the floor.

"She just collapsed," the man said in explanation to the Marines that were rushing forward.

"Get a medic in here now!" General Thompson ordered to the communication desk. "Put her down over here," he directed the man carrying Jade. "What happened? Why did she bring all of you here?"

"We spotted her in the plane. We thought she could

get us to safety. She tried to push us away, but more and more of us grabbed her. We were all telling her to save us, and then... we were here," he explained in a rush. "We did this to her, didn't we?" he asked guiltily, realizing they were probably the reason Jade was hurt. "Will she be alright?"

"Who knows?" the general answered coarsely. "We'd have to know what was wrong with her in the first place."

On the other side of the hangar, doors were suddenly slammed open. A group of men advanced purposefully toward Jade, each one held a Glock pistol at the ready.

"I want her sedated and restrained quickly," the leader of the group started giving the rest directions. "We can't take any chances with her getting away. This may be our only opportunity to control her," he reminded them all. He turned to the only one of them carrying a briefcase, "You can start the treatment as soon as she's secured."

"Halt! This is a restricted area," one of the Marine MPs demanded of the group as they approached the command center.

"You will hand Jade over to us now," the man in the front of the group ordered the MP. The MP made no move to follow his order.

"Call for reinforcements," General Thompson said quickly to a radio man at the desk next to him as several Marines moved into defensive positions around Jade. The general himself moved to intercept the group's progress toward her. "I am General Thompson, the commander of this facility. Who are you?"

"You can call me Mr. Smith. We're from the Department of International Weapon Acquisition, and have been given the authority to take this *woman* into custody," the man said briskly, standing with his hands on his hips. The men behind him were all dressed the same as he was, in dark suits, ties and white shirts.

"Well, *Mr. Smith*," General Thompson said his name coldly. "Jade is here under my orders. No one will be taking her anywhere," the general stated. At that the

Marines standing around Jade raised their weapons to their shoulders. At the same moment a second squad of Marines arrived through a set of doors at the other end of the hangar. All of them advanced with their rifles at the ready and aimed at the intruders.

"Come now, general, you wouldn't want to put your career or the careers of your men on the line? From your record, I know you've never questioned orders. Why would you start now?" Mr. Smith said, his voice was cloyingly sweet. "She's not worth it," he added derisively.

General Thompson, aware of the hostages fidgeting uncomfortably, made a calculated decision. "So you want me to turn over a U.S. citizen, who just risked her life to save the lives of over a hundred people? And she did it all just because I asked her to?" General Thompson asked and paused for effect. He asked almost innocently, "What do you plan to do to her? Experiment on her?" Now his voice took a hard edge. "Not on my watch you won't!"

"Are you all mad!" this time Mr. Smith was talking to the Marines guarding Jade. "Don't you see what kind of threat she poses? She must be controlled and studied. Would you risk your careers to protect her?" The Marines ignored him, and Mr. Smith became even more upset. He glared around the hangar, and saw that none of the men wavered in their stance. "I WILL have her!" he yelled. Then he looked over at the passengers, and noticed several of them had their camera phones out. "They can't take pictures! This is a top secret operation. I want all of those cameras confiscated!"

General Thompson ignored his order. "Escort these men back to their vehicles. I want them out of this airport now!" General Thompson ordered several Marines who were standing guard. For a moment the tension built, as both sides weighed their options. The men following Mr. Smith evidently felt that the odds were against them and lowered their pistols, raising their hands in submission. "Make sure none of them get lost on their way out," the general added.

"What are you doing?" Mr. Smith yelled at his men. The Marines were starting to usher them out of the area. Smith broke away from the Marine holding his arm and turned back to General Thompson and yelled, "This isn't the last you'll see of me. She will be mine!"

General Thompson turned away from the agent. He motioned to another group of Marines. "You three escort these passengers to the medics outside to be checked out, and then get them back with the others."

"Do you want us to confiscate their cameras, sir?"

"What cameras, Marine? I didn't see any cameras, and we don't want to cause any more trauma to these hostages by searching them, do we?" General Thompson looked at the man meaningfully.

"No, sir!" the Marine answered with a knowing smile.

After the two groups had been ushered out, the general turned his attention back to Jade. A medic had arrived and was working over her. "How's she doing?" General Thompson asked the man checking her.

"Her heart rate's really weak and her breathing is slow," the medic reported. "But I have no idea why."

The general turned to the mission controller. "What's the status of the mission?"

"All of the hijackers have been neutralized, and the rest of the passengers are being evacuated from the plane right now," the mission controller reported.

"Where's SEAL Team 3?"

"On their way back here, sir."

A few minutes later the team arrived. They entered as a group, chatting about the mission, until they caught sight of Jade. Then all conversation ceased. In concerned silence, they trotted to where she was lying on the ground.

"What happened?" Doc asked the medic as he and Matt arrived at Jade's side.

"Almost a dozen passengers grabbed her and she was forced to bring them all here," the medic quickly summarized.

"What are her vitals?" Doc asked, and the medic reported everything he had found. "She was like this that other time," Doc said as he looked meaningfully at Matt. "I think she just needs a little time to recover."

Doc and Matt helped the medic get Jade settled onto a cot that had been hastily set up. A few minutes later Julie moaned.

"Jade," Matt called to her. "Jade can you hear me?"

She moaned again and opened her eyes. Matt helped her to sit up as she held her head.

"Was everyone all right?" she asked, looking around. "I was worried I'd hurt them."

"They're all fine. How are you feeling?" Doc asked.

"I've got the worst headache and I feel like I could sleep for a week," she admitted. "How many did I bring back?"

"Ten, you've been out for almost thirty minutes," Matt told her.

"Yeah, you missed all the fun," one of the Marine guards added.

"All the fun, what do you mean?" Matt asked.

"There was a group of men, one called himself Mr. Smith," the Marine filled them in. "They said they were from the Department of International Weapon Acquisition and were here to take Jade. The general stood his ground against orders and wouldn't let them take her."

"The Department of International Weapon Acquisition? I've never even heard of them," the medic piped in.

"I have, they're a branch of the Defense Intelligence Agency, real black ops work," Matt informed him. They were interrupted by the general's approach.

"That was the smoothest mission I've ever seen," General Thompson said, joining the group clustered around Jade. "Your skills definitely come in handy, young lady," he said with a large grin on his weathered face.

"Thank you, sir," Julie replied. "Thank you for protecting me. I don't want to think about what they would've done to me if they'd gotten me."

"It was my pleasure," General Thompson said warmly. "That Mr. Smith was asking for a kick in the teeth, barging in like that. Not to mention what he had planned for you."

"But what about you? You risked a lot defying him."

"It wasn't a big risk," the general assured her. "Thanks to you, we had a large crowd of civilian witnesses who, I hope, took pictures of the whole thing with their cell phones. After I report to the President I think it will work out just fine. In the meantime, though, I think you should get out of here as soon as you can."

"Yes sir, and sir... if you need me again, just give me a call."

Julie's headache lasted for several days, and every time she tried to focus her powers on anything it got worse. She forced herself to stop trying and finally her headache got better.

Just as General Thompson had hoped, it took less than a day for the photos that the contractors had taken to get to the internet. The civilian contractors had taken pictures of the whole thing. Several also took videos and had leaked them to the media. By the time the contractors returned home, many of them were asked to do interviews.

People from all over the world praised Jade's efforts in saving the hostages and angrily condemned the US government for wanting to imprison and control her. The major news stations started re-interviewing the families of people Jade had rescued in the past. All of them were outraged that their government was trying to hold her against her will. There was a general outcry from the public to protect Jade.

Meanwhile the President had received the report from General Thompson about the mission. It outlined how instrumental Jade was in rescuing the hijacked plane. Also, in the last few days he had received several phone calls from the British and Australian Prime ministers. They wanted to be able to reassure their people that nothing was going to happen to Jade, who had become something of a hero in their countries as well.

The President's term had already been plagued by scandals, and he did not need another controversy to turn the public even more against his administration. Within the week the President called a news conference. He vowed to investigate the reports of rogue agents acting outside of their authority. He also signed an executive order that would ensure that Jade would not be harmed in any way or held against her will. How enforceable that would be remained to be seen, but it was better than nothing.

CHAPTER 14

"Hey Julie, Ashley, look at this blouse, don't you just love it!" Tanya exclaimed, holding the blue frilly blouse up to herself.

Julie looked up from the pair of jeans that she was looking at. She tilted her friend as she considered her friend. The blue fabric looked good against her friend's dark skin.

"It looks good on you," Julie agreed smiling. She had known Tanya and Ashley since high school. They had been on the track team together. It was nice to spend time relaxing and hanging out with her friends. Matt and the guys were fun, but Julie thought that they would not have gone clothes shopping with her even if their lives depended on it.

Julie continued flipping through hangers on a rack of black jeans. Her last pair had been torn saving another kidnapped girl. She smiled at the memory of the bastard tied up on his living room floor. He had been shocked when she had appeared at the door of his house and demanded his surrender. Of course he had refused and attacked her. So she had happily used him as a practice dummy for some of the moves her Uncle Mark had taught her. Her jeans had ripped along a seam when she had tossed him. In the end she had hogtied him, and then released the kidnapped girl from the bedroom he had kept her in. When she called 911, Julie had told the girl to tell them that 'Jade had a present for them.' She had waited with the girl long enough to hear the sirens approaching.

Julie wished she could help more children who had been kidnapped. Whenever she was able to find them she would do whatever it took to save them. Sadly, more times than not, she wasn't able to. She discovered after one missing child, that she must not be able to find people who were already dead. The police report when the boy had been found had placed his time of death before she had tried to search for him

"I'm getting hungry," Ashley declared, distracting Julie from her dark thoughts. "When we're done here, let's go hit the food court for lunch."

The friends agreed and continued shopping the racks of trendy clothes. In the distance Julie heard several loud popping noises. *Those sounded like gun shots*, she thought stunned. Soon screams could be heard from the interior of the mall as people went running past the shop where Julie and her friends were browsing.

"What's going on?" Tanya asked confused, as she watched the people running by.

"Ashley, Tanya, we need to get out of here," Julie told them as she started ushering them out of the store. They joined the mob of people rushing to get out of the indoor mall. Julie heard more shots from behind them. "Keep going!" she ordered her friends. "I just have to help someone." Ashley and Tanya got caught up in the flow of people as Julie ducked into a kid's outlet store. She headed toward the back, hoping to find dressing rooms where she knew there would be no security cameras. Finding one, she ducked inside, then zapped to her hideout and quickly put on her disguise. Grabbing her shotgun she focused her powers on the mall.

Julie chose to zap back to the store they had just been shopping in. It was closer to the gun shots, but still out of direct sight of the rest of the mall. When she arrived she saw a few more people running past the store front. Another shot rang out and one of them fell to the floor. Julie ducked behind the wall by the entrance and focused her powers. She searched the area nearby and sensed people fleeing in all directions; they were terrified. Then she spotted two others who were different. They were moving slowly through the center of the mall and heading her way. As she watched the scene through her powers she heard the men shoot at another innocent shopper and saw the person vanish from her senses.

"No!" Julie screamed, raising her shotgun. Concentrating on the position of the attackers, she zapped herself behind them. They were walking casually through the mall, like they were window shopping. One was carrying a shotgun that he held loosely in his right hand. He was the shorter of the two and had short black hair. The other had a rifle that he held at an angle across his body, ready to take aim. His hair was longer and a bit shaggy, as if he had not brushed it in a long time. Suddenly she saw the one with the rifle aim at a large flower pot. Looking around it, Julie saw that he was aiming at a terrified woman who was huddled behind it.

"Freeze! You're under arrest!" Julie yelled at the top of her voice, hoping to get the man's attention before he fired. The two men turned around to look at her.

The rifleman who had been about to shoot the helpless woman swiveled his rifle to aim at Julie instead. She zapped several feet away as his shot blasted the spot where she had just been standing.

"This is your last chance…!" Julie yelled as she kept her shotgun aimed at a point between the two men, hoping they would listen. She was about five yards away from them.

Before she could finish speaking, the second man brought his shot gun up to aim at her. Julie zapped to their left as the pellets tore into the concrete column directly behind her previous position. She opened fire, aiming at their chests. Her first couple shots missed because of her hasty aiming, and the two men turned to aim at her new position. Zapping to the opposite side of the mall corridor, she arrived behind them as they turned to shoot at the last place they had seen her. This time she took a moment longer and carefully took aim. She hit the taller man in the back and he fell to the floor limply. His rifle skidded across the floor as it fell out of his grasp. The second man whirled around and took a wild shot at her before she could fire back. It hit the ceiling near her and she ducked reflexively. Standing up, she quickly fired two more shots. Several of the buckshot pellets from the first shot caught the second man in the shoulder, making him drop his shotgun. The second shot hit him squarely in the chest and he fell bonelessly to the ground.

Julie stood staring at the men on the floor, shocked. The first man was moaning, but he didn't try to get up. She was breathing heavily even though she had not been running. Realizing her hands were shaking, she slowly put her shotgun back on safe and lowered its muzzle. There were shouts coming from further down the building; and they were getting louder. She waited until the police were in sight, just to make sure the two men didn't try to leave, and then she zapped back to her hideout.

"Is she with you?" Mark asked Matt. He had called the young man as soon as he had heard the news that Jade had killed a man.

"No, I was hoping she was with you," Matt told him. He was worried about Julie too. "I saw the news footage of the security video. It was a good shoot; they were trying to kill her."

"I know, but that won't make her feel any better about it," Mark said angrily. He had heard the accounts from some of the survivors that had stated that Jade had tried to place the gunmen under arrest. "I'd have just shot the bastards from behind. She tried to arrest them," Mark said, astounded.

"That's just the way she is, you know that. She's probably at her hideout, too upset to think straight," Matt guessed. He wished he could get to her.

"Yeah, I've tried to call her, but there's no cell phone reception out there," Mark agreed. He was considering installing a satellite phone in her hideout the next time he had a chance.

"Call me if she comes to you," Matt directed.

"I will, but she'll come to you first," Mark said confidently.

About an hour later Julie zapped into the center of Matt's room. She was still in her disguise, but had removed her mask and hood. She sat in a rumpled pile. As she looked around she seemed surprised by her surroundings. "Well I guess that's what happens when I think about a place when I'm upset," she said to herself, sniffling.

Matt came up to her slowly, afraid she would zap out again if he startled her. "Are you alright?" he asked, sitting down next to her.

She looked up into his eyes. "I killed him," she stated as if that explained everything. "I've never killed anything before."

"It was the right thing to do," Matt tried to reassure her. He saw her eyes filling with more tears and he pulled her into his arms.. "He would've killed you… you had to kill him first."

"I could've…," she started.

"You did the only thing you could've," Matt reassured her again, and he gave her a hug. "You saved a lot of lives by shooting them. Remember that." He felt her nod against his chest as her tears soaked his shirt.

"Why did they do it?" Julie asked.

"They were part of the North American Islamic Jihad," Matt told her.

"Really?" Julie asked.

"Yeah, they haven't released the information to the press, but I checked one of my sources." Matt wiped tears from her cheek. "They would've kept killing innocent people until someone stopped them."

Chapter 15

"Julie, I need your help," Matt said without his usual greeting. His voice held a hint of desperation over the phone.

"What's wrong?" Julie asked as she used her powers to check on him. *I can't tell what it is, but something was definitely bothering him*, she thought. Going up to her room, she prepared to zap to get him.

"My sister is getting married next month and my mom wants me to bring someone," Matt explained in a rush.

"Wait... What?" Julie asked confused.

"My sister is getting married, and my mom wants me to bring someone," Matt said again more slowly.

"Okay, but what's so bad about that? Who does she want you to bring?"

"You," Matt said tensely.

"Me? Why me?"

"I've sort of told her that I've been dating a girl, and now she wants to meet you."

"Sure, no problem, I'd love to meet your family," Julie said cheerfully. "When's your sister's wedding?"

"This is funny. No, this is really funny. *I'm* taking a plane trip," Julie said and she couldn't help but laugh. The busy airline terminal was filled with people waiting to board their planes. "I'm taking a plane trip," she said, turning to Matt with a grin.

"I know, but it's the best way to hide your identity," Matt explained in a hushed voice. "If someone's watching me they might notice if you suddenly leave from a hotel room you never entered."

"I know why I'm flying, it's just really funny," Julie said again as she looked over at Matt. She noticed that he seemed really preoccupied. "What's wrong?" Suddenly she got an idea, "Don't worry about me, it's alright if your parents don't like me."

"No, that's not it," Matt said distracted. He sat uneasily for a while.

If he's not worried about his parents liking me then... Julie thought for a moment "Are you worried I won't like your parents? I'm sure they..."

"No, I'm worried you'll run screaming for the hills," Matt said seriously, cutting her off in his own nervousness.

Julie laughed, thinking that he was joking, but soon realized that he really was serious. No matter what she said, she could not convince him that everything was going to be alright.

Their flight to Texas was uneventful. Several times Matt tried to warn her about his family. "I'm sure they're not that bad, Matt. I'll be fine," was Julie's standard response. When they got to the Houston airport they made their way to the rental car agency. To Julie's surprise Matt had reserved a large pickup truck not a sports car like he normally drove. Soon after they started their drive to his family's home she understood why.

"Your parents live in the middle of nowhere?" Julie asked surprised as they bumped down a dirt road. They'd left driving west on 290, but after the first hour and several turns, she'd lost track where they were.

"Actually, this is part of their ranch," Matt said pointing to the fields to the right.

"Really?" Julie asked, impressed.

"My father runs the largest cattle ranch in the county," Matt explained.

"I never pictured you as a cowboy," Julie teased.

"That's because I'm not anymore," Matt stated flatly. "And if you tell the guys, so help me...," he trailed off with mock menace in his voice.

Julie laughed as Matt turned into a long driveway. Ahead she could see a two story farm house. Julie was surprised to see that it was made mostly of brick. *I guess they don't worry about earthquakes around here.* "It's a really pretty house Matt, I like it," Julie offered, trying to cheer him up.

Matt parked next to another large American truck. As Julie climbed down from the passenger seat she saw a small green-cloaked shape run head long into Matt. "Matt! Matt! You're home!" the small figure cheered.

"Bethany is that you?" Matt asked the small child as he picked her up.

"No, I'm Jade," the little girl said proudly. "And I'm here to rescue you!"

Julie was distracted by Matt's predicament and almost did not see the woman approaching her before she was enveloped in a large hug. "You must be Julie! My name's Martha, but you can call me Mom," the heavy set woman said. "You're even more beautiful than Matt said, but you're way too skinny. Doesn't he feed you enough? Well don't you worry; I'll take care of you. Let's go fix you something to eat."

"No that's alright, I'm fine for now," Julie sputtered trying to get a word in edgewise but the woman continued talking as she ushered Julie up the front steps and into the house.

"So Matt tells me you're a nurse? That'll be handy when you two have kids of your own, especially boys. Matt and his brother were constantly getting hurt as kids." Julie just mumbled her agreement as she got just a quick glance around the living room. It was decorated in classic ranch style, complete with a set of longhorns mounted on the wall above the fireplace. As they entered the kitchen Matt's mother continued their one-sided conversation. "Let's see, I'll grill up a quick hamburger for you. It's no trouble at all," she said as she saw Julie try to object. "Now, how do you like your hamburgers cooked?"

Now Matt's mom paused, waiting for an answer and Julie had a feeling she was being tested. "Medium well?" Julie asked tentatively.

Martha smiled, pleased by her answer, "That's just the way I like 'em too."

Suddenly the small green-cloaked child came running into the kitchen and grabbed Julie's hand. "I'm here to rescue you!" the small voice cried, and before she knew it Julie was being dragged from the room. She barely had a chance to wave an apology to Martha before she was pulled out a sliding glass door.

To her relief Julie was soon delivered to Matt's side. When the girl finally stopped pulling her Julie kneeled down to look at her. "Thank you very much for rescuing me Jade," Julie said seriously.

"You're welcome," the little girl said proudly as Julie noted that her long brown hair was barely being contained by the hood. But the most remarkable thing about the girl was her mischievous green eyes.

"How're you doing?" Matt asked from behind her, concerned.

"I'm not running for the hills," she told him reassuringly as she stood up to join him.

"Just give it time," the young woman standing next to Matt said with a smile. "I've lost a few boyfriends that way," she explained with a warm smile.

"They actually ran for the hills?" Julie asked with a grin.

"Well, not so much ran as got in their car. One even left in the middle of dinner," she admitted with a laugh. Now Julie had a chance to study her and she noticed that she was a grown version of the little girl. She was heavier set, tending toward her mother's build and her long brown hair was braided behind her in a ponytail, but her eyes were nearly a match to her little sisters.

"Julie, I'd like you to meet my big sister, Michelle," Matt said introducing her. "And this is Bethany, my eight year old little sister," he said indicating the child dressed up like Jade. Turning to Michelle, Matt asked, "So how long's this been going on?" he said, waving at the green, hooded cloak.

"She begged mom to make her that cloak after Jade saved you," Michelle explained. "But I've heard that Jade costumes are going to be the most popular girl's costume this Halloween."

"Really?" Julie asked surprised, not sure what to think about that.

"Sure, where've you been, the moon? Jade's one of the most popular celebrities with girls these days. She's right up there with the latest batch of Disney princesses."

"Oh... no, I didn't know." Julie looked over at Matt stunned at being called a celebrity.

Matt shrugged and smiled in answer. A deep rumbling sound announced the arrival of a large flatbed truck stacked high with hay. It pulled around the barn and parked out of sight. A few moments later an older man strode into sight, followed by a teenaged boy. The two were dressed in t-shirts and jeans, and wore classic leather cowboy hats. The man didn't pause on his way over to them, when he finally got there he enveloped Matt in a hug without a word. Holding Matt at arm's length he commented, "It's good to see you Son."

"Hey, Dad," Matt said with a relaxed smile. "It's good to see you too." Matt turned to the young man that had come up beside his dad. "Hey twerp, you've grown," Matt commented as he gave the young man a hug. "Dad, Steven, this is Julie," Matt said, turning back to Julie, "Julie this is my dad, Donald and my little brother Steven."

"It's a pleasure to meet you, sir," Julie said as she offered to shake his hand. The man used her outstretched hand to pull her into a big hug of her own. Julie practically disappeared in his embrace.

"Let her go, Dad," Michelle admonished her father. "You're going to smother her."

Matt's dad released his bear hug enough to allow him a chance to look at her. "You're a little thing aren't you?"

"Dad!" Michelle yelled at him again. "Leave her alone!" Michelle extricated Julie from her father's grasp. "You should be getting ready for tonight. You two stink!" she stated flatly.

Julie waved a quick hello to Steven as the father and son walked past them into the house. A few minutes later another young man came out onto the back porch. He was dressed in a tan sheriff's uniform, and had a thick mustache. Michelle moved to his side and gave him a quick kiss. "Matt, Julie, I'd like you to meet my fiancé, Bill. Bill this is my little brother, Matt, and his girlfriend, Julie."

Matt and Julie both said their hellos, and they stood and chatted for a bit. The rest of the evening went by in a blur. They had arrived just in time for the rehearsal dinner and it seemed like she was introduced to hundreds of Matt's relatives. The only recurring theme of the night was Matt's mom bringing her plate after plate of food.

"You know you don't have to eat it if you don't want to. We have a dog that'd be happy to take care of it for you," Matt offered, looking around for the dog he'd mentioned.

"No, it's fine. Actually I do need to gain some weight. I've been losing a lot with all the *things* I've been doing lately," Julie told him. "Even my mom is starting to get worried that I'm becoming anorexic or something."

An hour later the party started winding down, and Matt told his mom that it was time for them to check into the hotel. "I'm sorry all our bedrooms are taken by other guests, I'd love to have you stay here. How far is your hotel? You two have separate rooms now, don't you?" his mother admonished. "I want grandkids, but you need to get married first, you know. I'll tan your hide if you try anything before you're married."

"Yes, Mom," Matt agreed dutifully as Julie hid her smile.

Their hotel was just a couple miles away and Matt quickly checked them into their rooms. Julie's was directly across the hall from Matt's and they awkwardly said good night.

Julie was able to get a good night's sleep, but it looked like he had been up all night. "What are you so worried about now?" Julie asked when they sat down for breakfast. "I didn't run screaming for the hills. Actually I thought your family was really nice."

"Just wait, you'll see. Now that my sister is getting married, she'll turn her attention to me," Matt said forlornly.

"Who?" Julie asked. "Your mom?"

Matt nodded grimly as he finished his coffee, "We'd better start getting ready."

His sister's wedding was at ten that morning, so after breakfast they split up to get ready. Julie had picked one of her favorite dresses to wear. It was a bright blue that she thought complimented her eyes. She was just finishing her makeup when she heard Matt's knock on her door. When Julie opened it, she found him standing in his dress white's.

"You do look handsome in that uniform," Julie remarked as she reached for her purse. When she turned around he was still standing there looking at her stunned. "Matt, are you alright?"

"Huh?" Matt seemed to come out of a trance and smiled at her embarrassed. "So, are you ready to go?" he asked her. As they walked to the rental car, he blurted out, "You look really nice too."

"Thank you," Julie told him politely, secretly laughing at his behavior.

The wedding was held in their family's church. The ceremony was beautiful, and Julie enjoyed every minute of it. The bridesmaids were dressed in pink taffeta, and Julie felt a little sorry for them in the Texas heat, but she felt even worse for Michelle. She was wearing a gorgeous, elaborately lacy, gown with a train that was at least ten feet long. *She's probably so happy she doesn't even notice the heat*, Julie thought seeing Michelle's radiant smile. Afterward everyone left the chapel and walked to the community room next door. Julie used it as an excuse to wrap her arm around Matt's as they walked.

"That was such a wonderful ceremony," she said wistfully, resting her head on his shoulder for a moment.

"Oh no, not you too," Matt looked at her in fear.

"What are you talking about?" Julie asked surprised. A moment later, his mother was by their side.

"So, when are you going to ask her? You know I've always wanted another daughter," his mother teased Matt.

"I haven't thought about it, Mom," he said trying to dissuade her from the topic. "We just started dating. It's too soon."

Julie heard Michelle call to her mom. "Don't you worry sweetie, I'll keep after him," his mother said as she patted Julie's arm as she bustled toward the bride and groom.

When the matriarch was out of range, Julie burst out laughing. "Hey it's not funny!" Matt objected. "She's not going to let it go. You'll see," Matt said plaintively. "She's been pressuring me for years to find a wife." That just made Julie laugh even harder. Luckily his mother was too busy with Michelle's reception to get a chance to pester Matt again before it was time for them to leave for the airport.

"Now you make sure you keep eating. I expect you to look healthier the next time I see you," Martha admonished Julie as they said goodbye. Then she turned to Matt. "And you, don't let this one get away from you. I expect you to call me as soon as you've asked her."

"MOM!" Matt complained as he gave her a hug goodbye. "Enough already!"

Matt's father simply hugged them both. "You take care," he said, before he let Matt go. "Watch your back."

"I will, Dad," Matt reassured him.

"Don't worry, Dad," Matt's youngest sister leaped at her brother, "Jade will protect him."

"I'm sure she will," Matt agreed as he gave her a big hug.

CHAPTER 16

Julie only had one semester of nursing school left after the trip to Texas. *It went by so quickly*, she thought when she finished her Bachelor's in nursing. She had just sat for her boards when the military approached her officially. "What do you mean the Marines want me to work for them?" she asked Matt when he delivered the news.

"General Thompson was really impressed with your abilities. He wants to talk to you about becoming a civilian contractor, assisting the Marines in their missions in Afghanistan," Matt explained. He had been asked to arrange the meeting between General Thompson and Jade since there was not any other way for the general to get in touch with her.

"I don't know; I'll have to think about it," she answered. In the end she agreed, but she wanted to meet with the general herself before she would promise anything. Uncle Mark helped her decide where to meet him.

"Why are we meeting in a public library?" Matt asked Mark when he brought General Thompson to the meeting.

"A public library is private enough that they can talk without being overheard, but also public enough that I can make sure no one tries to grab her," Mark explained.

"That's ridiculous. The President himself promised her safety," Matt argued.

"No one knows who gave Mr. Smith the orders to capture Jade," Mark pointed out.

"You're just paranoid…," Matt started to argue.

"No, he's right," General Thompson interrupted him. "I've been arguing for months that Jade is an asset that needs to be protected, but I've been stonewalled at every turn. This administration views her as a threat, but I'm not sure why.

"Then why are they letting her become a contractor?" Matt asked.

"I think they believe it'll keep her out of the media spotlight," the general guessed. "The media's coverage of Jade and the government's treatment of her has been a problem for the President and his administration."

"Why are you doing it?" Mark asked, suspiciously.

"If she's officially under my command, I'll be able to protect her better," General Thompson explained. "It's not the best, but it's all I've been able to accomplish."

"Thank you general, I appreciate your help," Mark said after considering the man's answer. "She's over this way," he added as he led the two men to a table and chairs hidden between rows of books.

"Hi, General Thompson, my name's Julie." The general was surprised to see a young woman with shoulder length blonde hair. "Would you like to have a seat?" she asked.

"Thank you for agreeing to speak with me," the general answered formally, shaking the hand she offered.

The two spent the next hour discussing her contract

to work with the military. During their negotiation, she made sure he knew that she would not be an assassin for them. Morally she had problems with using her powers to kill people. Being able to appear without warning and shoot a person seemed too much like shooting fish in a barrel. She also described to him how she thought she could help them the most.

What General Thompson had in mind was very similar to what she wanted to do. She would work with the Marines and soldiers to help them evacuate wounded during large operations. Since her experience with the plane hijacking, they decided she could also supply logistical information during special ops missions.

In the end, Jade was given official standing as a civilian adviser attached to the Marines under General Thompson's command in Afghanistan. They also decided that the only ones who would know her true identity would still just be Matt's six man squad and General Thompson. But the guys decided they needed to make a few adjustments to her disguise.

"You stand out like a beacon that says, 'shoot me,'" Matt explained one day as she complained about her new outfit. "Every terrorist is on the lookout for Jade in a green cape. If you're wearing a uniform like ours, they won't be able to spot you as easily." So they decided to change her black mask to a balaclava, and everything else changed to standard combat uniform and body armor.

Julie zapped into the center of the command tent. Matt had called her a few minutes before and she had geared up as quickly as she could. This was only the second time she had been in the tent and she looked around, not sure what to do.

"One of the Australian's Remote Command Outposts is under attack," Lieutenant Cooper said coming over to brief her. "Over fifty men are about to be overrun, and reinforcements are too far away," he told her getting straight to the point.

"What can I do?" Julie asked.

"We're not sure, but at this point they need a miracle if they're going to survive," Lieutenant Cooper said grimly.

"Do we have any pictures of the area or the men?" Julie asked trying to think of her options.

"They have a Unmanned Arial Vehicle flying overhead; we might be able to patch into its video," Simmons offered.

"Yeah, let me see it," Julie hoped it had enough details for her to find them. A few minutes later Simmons called them over to the computer terminal.

"Here it is," Simmons said, pointing at the screen. "The drone is over ten thousand feet up, but I have the image zoomed in pretty close."

Julie studied the images. The angle was making it too hard for her to imagine the ground level view. "I can't get a lock on their location," she said, disappointed. She watched the insurgent fighters firing down on the isolated outpost from their positions on higher ground. *If only we could drop a bomb in their laps*, she thought bitterly. Then an idea hit her. Turning to Lieutenant Cooper she asked, "Can you get me a crate of grenades?" He nodded and ordered a man nearby to get one.

"Grenades? What for?" Matt asked, almost afraid to find out.

Julie asked a question in return, "How many seconds does it take a grenade to explode?"

"Between three to five," Matt answered. "Why?"

Julie ignored his question as she did some quick calculations. "It's thirty two feet per second, per second….So over a hundred feet, right?" she asked, thinking out loud.

"Right what!?" Matt asked, getting impatient.

"I could drop grenades on the insurgent's positions from above," Julie explained. "They'd land right in their laps." She turned to Simmons. "Can you ask them to fly that drone directly over each group of insurgents? And can you change the magnification to simulate a little over a hundred feet up?"

"Already working on it," Simmons replied.

Julie saw the drone begin flying over the enemy positions. A commotion at the entrance of the tent heralded the return of the man carrying the crate of grenades. Julie picked two of them up gingerly. "Okay, how do these things work?" she asked the men around her, as they all seemed to shrink away from her.

Lieutenant Cooper was the only one not fazed by her holding two live grenades. He came over and showed her the basics. "You hold down this part, called the spoon, then you pull this pin, and you throw it. Preferably at the enemy," he added with a grin.

"Okay, let's see if this works," Julie stated. She concentrated on an image from the drone. She thought she had it. "Can you pull the pins for me?" Lieutenant Cooper did and Julie vanished. Matt saw a flicker of desert camouflage in the drone's image. Almost instantly she returned to the tent without the grenades.

"One...two...three...fo--," Simmons was counting as she returned.

They saw the twin blasts as the grenades exploded above the insurgents. Her aim had not been perfect, but because they exploded in the air, they still wiped out the position. A cheer went up in the room.

"Nicely done," Matt complimented her.

"My aim was bad," Julie lamented, "and they exploded in the air."

"I don't think it mattered much to those bastards," Simmons said watching the screen. "Want to practice your aim with this bunch?" he asked, pointing to another clump of insurgents.

Julie picked up two more grenades; Matt pulled the pins this time. "It's better if they explode above them, they'll cause more damage," Matt explained. "So don't try to drop them lower." Julie nodded, and turned her attention to the video again. After a moment of concentration Julie zapped out again.

The moment she arrived back in the tent, Demetrio, their explosives expert, started counting as he watched the image, "One... two... three... four... f---." The blasts hit the target dead center. "Bulls-eye!" he yelled and another cheer went up.

"Wait, look at this! They're breaking through!" Matt interrupted their celebration. He had been watching over Simmons' shoulder and had noticed a different area of the battle.

"That's too close to for you to drop grenades. You'd wound the Australians too," Demetrio informed her.

Julie thought for a moment. "Alright, I'll be right back," she said.

"What…" Matt started to ask, but she had already disappeared. They all watched the screen. A moment later they saw Jade appear with a huge object, then disappear letting it fall on its own. "That looks like a boulder," Matt said amazed. Then as it started to come apart as it fell, he realized that it was a pile of small boulders. Julie appeared back in the tent and they all watched as the mass of rocks fell toward the ground.

"Will it work?" Julie asked as they watched. She was starting to worry that her idea would not be enough.

"We'll see," Matt said. The Australian troops caught sight of the falling rocks, and started scrambling to get further out of the way. It landed in the center of the insurgent assault. Bowling ball sized rocks flew dozens of feet in all directions, with smaller rocks flying even farther, spattering the defensive line of Australian troops. Julie gasped in fear. "No, it's alright. See, none of them seem to be hurt," Matt reassured her, as they watched all of the troops moving back to their positions.

"Where next?" Julie asked, sighing with relief.

Over the next few minutes they spotted three more targets for her. All of them were far enough away from friendly forces that the grenades would work. By the time those targets were destroyed, Julie was breathing hard.

"I need to rest for a minute," Julie said as she sank into an empty chair.

"I think you're done for now anyway. It looks like the insurgent attack is breaking. You've got five minutes to take a break and eat something," Lieutenant Cooper informed her.

Julie nodded and zapped back to her hideout to eat a candy bar or two. She knew if they needed her sooner they could call her on her satellite phone.

"Get a status report on their wounded. Find out if they have anyone really critical, otherwise Jade will be able to evac their wounded in five. Have them send us a picture of a secure area of their base," Lieutenant Cooper ordered, speaking to the communications personnel. Then he turned to the team, "Miller and Chief, you'll go in with her. Help secure the area until she's done evacuating their wounded."

CHAPTER 17

Julie shaded her eyes from the harsh sun as she looked around at the now familiar base. Orderly rows of tents lined the narrow streets of the tent city. She had been officially working as a contractor with the military now for a while. She had told her parents that she was working as a nurse in the VA hospital, which she told herself was not too far from the truth. Her primary role was providing logistical information during small group missions which were primarily with SEAL teams, like Matt's. She would focus on the point man and use her powers to watch his movements from the command center. If she spotted anyone besides the team around them, she would tell the radio man, who would pass the information on. It worked fairly well with one team at a time. She had tried to focus on more than one team during training one day, and it had given her a royal headache for several days.

The only way Julie could help on larger missions was as the Marine regiment's med-evac person. Each medic in the group was given a radio link to the base and could alert them if they had a man down. They would tell her which medic it was and then Jade would be able to find the wounded soldiers next to the medics and zap them out. To help her keep them straight, Julie would set up a board before each mission with the pictures of each of the medics. Then they would assign each medic a number. That way the communications officer could tell her medic's number and she could instantly look at his picture and find him.

To establish a safe area where Julie could bring the wounded back to, the Marines had created a landing zone. She liked to think of it as a 'zap landing pad'. It was basically a large flat concrete slab surrounded by a Hesco barrier. The earth and wire mesh blocks created a wall protecting the area that was right next to the main medical facility on the base. The area was designated so that it would always be clear of obstructions. As soon as she had zapped a wounded personnel in, the nurses and docs would rush in and move them into the hospital.

On days, when she was not needed, Julie was able to spend some time on base incognito. Her cover story was as one of the base's embedded reporters. *It's working pretty well too*, she thought. *It gives me a plausible reason for being on the base out of my disguise, and a room where she could zap back and forth from home.*

"Hey Julie, how're you doing?" a voice interrupted Julie's thoughts.

Julie turned to see Mariela and Susan, good friends of hers that she had met her first day on base. Of course they knew her as Julie, the embedded reporter. She had met them when she had gotten lost searching for her quarters. They had taken pity on her lack of knowledge of Marine lingo and had helped her follow the directions she had been given.

"I'm good thanks," Julie told the two women were walking toward her. "What've you been up to?"

"Nothing much, we've got a re-supply mission tomorrow, so today we're doing inventory and loading up,"

Mariela answered.

"Are you two headed to lunch?" Julie asked.

"Yeah, you want to join us?" Susan offered.

"Sure, that'd be great," Julie accepted as the three of them entered the mess hall together. She had to blink a few times as her eyes adjusted to the relative darkness inside the building.

As they got in line for food, Julie noticed Matt and some of his friends come in behind them. She knew he had spotted her too, but while she was on base as the reporter they pretended not to know each other in order to maintain her cover. and did not speak to each other. It was not the first time they had run into each other, but she noticed that he suddenly seemed really uncomfortable. Curious she let her friends get their trays first so she could eavesdrop on his conversation.

"Come on man, I'm not asking you to reveal secret information about her. I just want to know how 'you know who' is built under all that body armor," the guy with him asked. Matt's friend kept his voice low enough that Julie had to strain to hear him. Hiding her chuckle she kept listening.

"Honestly, I've never looked at her that way," Matt replied stoically.

"What! I know you're not blind or dead, and from what I've seen of her ass she's got a fine body," the man asserted. "Come on, just give me a hint. Are they about the size of oranges, or are we talking more like melons?" his friend asked making hand motions in front of his chest indicating the corresponding size comparisons.

Julie tried to hide her laughter by coughing, but it sounded more like choking.

"Knock it off jerk! There are women present!" Matt glanced apologetically toward Julie and her friends.

"That's never stopped *him* before," Mariela said as she rolled her eyes in disgust at Matt's friend.

"Come on Julie; let's go sit over there, *away* from

those guys," Susan agreed.

"See she's got a nice ass, how can you not look at it?" Matt's friend asked as he pointed to Julie's backside as she walked away. Matt slugged his friend in the arm. "Ow! What's your problem?" the man asked more shocked than hurt.

Matt turned to Julie and apologized. "Sorry ma'am, my friend was raised by cave men," Matt told her, then grabbing his friend by the arm he forcefully turned him around and took him out of the tent.

Later that day Julie came into Matt's tent and threw two oranges at him. He reacted quickly and managed to catch them before they hit him. "So, do you *like* oranges?" Julie asked with a wicked grin.

"Wait... hold on... it wasn't like that," Matt sputtered as he tried to come up with an excuse for his friend's comments. "Look I'm sorry, Mike just doesn't know how to behave around women. He's really a nice guy; he just can't keep his mouth shut."

Julie could not keep from laughing as Matt tried to apologize for his friend's comments. "So, you've never looked at me like that, huh?" she asked overly innocent.

"I had to tell him something to make him leave me alone," Matt explained.

"So you *do* look at me that way," Julie raised her eyebrows.

"No, I mean...well...," Matt tried to answer her without getting himself in more trouble.

Julie laughed and asked, "So how many guys do you think check out my ass?"

"All of them," Matt answered promptly.

"All of them!?" Julie exclaimed.

"We *are* talking about a base full of men who've only seen a few women for months," he teased her with his own evil grin. "Of course, they'd probably think any woman's ass is cute by now."

"Hey!" Julie exclaimed. "What's that supposed to

mean?"

"Nothing," Matt protested with a laugh. "Hey you better get out of here, we shouldn't be seen together. You know that."

"I know," Julie agreed. "I miss our dates."

"Maybe on my next day off you can take us somewhere," Matt offered. "I'll see you tomorrow."

The next evening, local time, Julie reported to the base in Afghanistan as Jade. The guys had a mission that night and she needed to get ready. Lieutenant Cooper was already waiting in the cramped briefing room.

"Hey LT, how's it going?" Julie greeted him.

"Good," he replied. "Here, start studying this picture. His name is Abdullah Osman al-Rashid. We'll need to know everything you can tell us about the area he's in."

Julie took the picture of a man with dark bushy eye brows, and a long, thick beard and mustache. His eyes were squinted slightly as he looked at something to the side. She closed her eyes to concentrate on his image. She found him quickly, but then she realized that she had also found him at two other places. Confused she used her powers to look at each place where she had found the man, wondering if she was somehow seeing the same place in a weird double vision. But each of the men she had found were in very different areas. Giving up, she opened her eyes. While she had been concentrating on finding the man in the picture the rest of the Team had arrived. They were all sitting quietly, giving her time to work. She spotted Lieutenant Cooper and waved at the picture in her hand. "Does this guy have twin brothers?"

"No, why?"

"I found three different men from this picture," Julie answered in explanation. "That's never happened before."

"We know that sometimes these guys have duplicates made of themselves as decoys," Chief Nguyen offered as a possible explanation.

"They make decoys? Like with plastic surgery?" Julie clarified.

"Yeah. They send their decoys into meetings or public appearances if they think they're in danger."

"Okay, hang on a sec," Julie said as she closed her eyes again and tried to distinguish one man from another. She found a slight difference in each of them, but one seemed to 'match' the picture she held better. "I think I've found the man in the picture," Julie reported. "But I've never done this before so I can't guarantee it."

Lieutenant Cooper had been thinking. "We also can't guarantee that the man in the picture is the one we want or one of the decoys," he said pointing out another problem. He paused in thought for a moment longer. "We need help if we're going to take all three of them at once. I want you to study each site and draw diagrams for each one."

"Yes, sir," Julie replied as he left the room.

Within two hours six more SEAL's had joined them in the briefing room. Julie recognized Martin from her speed training, but decided not to say anything. The other five men were new to her.

"Who are these guys?" Julie asked Matt who was sitting next to her.

"They're guys from SEAL Team 3," Matt told her.

"But I thought you guys were SEAL Team 3," Julie said confused.

"We're just one squad," Matt explained, shaking his head. "Each Team has over a hundred SEALs."

Julie studied the new men as she thought about what Matt had told her. She looked at each of the men in turn to familiarize herself with them and realized that one of them was Mike, the guy from lunch the day before. When she used her powers to get a lock on them she noticed that it took a little longer than it normally did with her Team.

"We will be hitting all three of these targets simultaneously tonight," Captain Lewis began, interrupting her thoughts as he started the meeting. "We will break up into teams of four."

"Sir, why don't I just go in and grab them?" Julie interrupted him. "It won't take me more than a minute to grab all three."

"We want to get any documents or information that could be found with the real Abdullah Osman al-Rashid, and we can't risk you being in theatre long enough to look for it," Captain Lewis answered her, then turning back to the group he continued to explain the mission. "Jade will take you in when she goes to retrieve the targets. Each group will secure their location and then search for intel. When you are done, radio back and Jade will extract you." He turned to Jade, "Do you have the diagrams?"

"Yes, here they are," Julie said. She double-checked each one before she handed them out. The men were still at each place. "I'll update them with final details right before we go."

"How big is this room?" Matt was pointing to the picture she had given his group.

"Figure they're all at a scale of about four feet per inch, give or take a foot or two," she shrugged apologetically and looked down. "That's the best I could do."

"That's better than we've had on some missions," one of the new guys piped in with an encouraging smile.

"Yeah, well, I hope it helps. Anyway, the targets are marked with a red X. Any other people in the area are marked with black circles," she continued to explain. She held up her copies of the sketches. "I'll be constantly checking on these while you plan, I'll let you know if anything major changes. You're welcome to look at my sketches as I work on them."

"Alright you all know what to do. I want you ready at 0300," Lieutenant Cooper ordered.

I'm so glad this isn't my time zone, Julie thought to herself when she heard the plan. The time difference from San

Diego to Afghanistan actually helped Julie. She was able to keep a normal sleep schedule and still do night missions with the Team.

As the men moved into groups to plan, Julie approached the captain. "Sir?"

"Yes, Jade?"

"I'd like to teleport individually with each of the new guys at least a couple times before we start the mission."

"Why?" Captain Lewis asked, looking at her quizzically.

"I seem to be able to find a person faster if I've teleported with them already," Julie tried to explain. She shrugged. "If I have to get them in a rush, I don't want to have to take extra time to find them. It'll only take me a couple minutes."

"Alright, let them plan for now. When they start gearing up you can work with them."

Julie nodded her thanks, and then headed back to her sketches. It did not take long for them to plan their entrances. The only thing different about these missions was they were not going to have to fight their way in. Julie alternated between each location and noted any changes. By midnight all of the people at each location had stopped moving. *They must all be asleep for the night,* Julie thought as she rubbed her neck to relax. Her work was interrupted when Lieutenant Cooper brought the six new SEALs over to her.

"Jade, I heard you requested to meet the new guys," Lieutenant Cooper stated as she turned toward them.

"Yeah, I want to make sure I have a fast link with each of them," she explained to him.

"This is Moore, Williams, Taylor, Martin, Gawaran, and Lujan," he pointed to each man in turn as he introduced them. "Men, this is Jade, you're all hers until she's done with you."

"Thanks LT," she said sarcastically. "Are you trying to scare them?" Julie asked reproachfully. Lieutenant Cooper just laughed and headed back to gathering his gear.

"Don't worry, you couldn't do anything that'd scare me." Julie turned to see who had spoken. It was the man who had been talking to Matt the other day in the mess hall. The name on his uniform read, 'Williams'. He was a lanky man, with an angular face. It looked like he had not shaved in a few days. The skin on his face was tanned, except for an area around his eyes, making him look a bit like a raccoon.

"Really?" Julie asked, looking up at him with a gleam in her eyes. "That's great! I've wanted to practice some things that the other guys won't try! When we get a chance I'll take you up on that offer," she said excitedly.

"Man, I think you just volunteered yourself for a whole bunch of trouble," Martin said and looked at Williams with pity.

"For now, I just need to be able to find you faster. So I need to zap around with you a couple times," she explained as she held out her gloved hand to Williams and he took it quickly. "Hang on tight!" she instructed him with a wicked look in her eye. As soon as he had taken her hand she teleported them instantly to half a dozen locations that she knew of.

When they arrived back at the base she stopped and released his hand. He stood swaying for a moment and looked like he was going to puke. "I'll be back in a minute," he mumbled as he stumbled out of the room.

Julie turned to Martin. "Martin, right? Are you ready?" she asked. He took her hand without hesitation and she zapped them to her hideout. "Hey, it's nice to see you again Martin. How've you been?" Julie asked him as they arrived.

"Good, but what are we doing here?" Martin asked as he settled into a familiar chair at her table.

"I just wanted to say 'hi'. I don't really need to practice zapping with you. I can find you about as fast as I can find my team," Julie admitted with a shrug. "But since

LT doesn't know about that training, we have to make it look good." Martin nodded in understanding. "Guess it's time to head back or they'll worry," she admitted. Julie took his hand again and got him back to the base.

When they arrived the others looked at him expectantly waiting to see how he handled it. He just smiled and asked, "Done?" When she nodded he replied, "Let me know if you need anything else." Then he headed off to get his gear ready.

Julie gave Martin a small wave goodbye, and then turned to the last four men. She stepped up to Taylor. He was a young black man, just a little taller than she was. "Ready?" she asked cheerfully, and offered him her hand. Looking over at Williams, who had come back in looking less green, Taylor paused only for a second before he took her hand. This time she zapped him to her hideout, and waited for him to get his bearings before she zapped him to the team's pool deck. He recovered faster this time. "How're you feeling?" she asked him,

"Not too bad," he admitted.

"Okay, we're going to speed zap two places in a row. Ready?" she asked. At his nod, she took him to both of her secondary hideouts almost instantly. She paused to check on him. "You alright?"

Taylor grinned at her, "You must've taken Williams on one wild ride, didn't you?"

"I couldn't help it. He needed it," Julie admitted. "Time to head back," she told him before they zapped back to base. Taylor gave her a cheesy salute and headed off to get ready. She took the last three men to the same series of stops. Each one took it in stride and headed back to their groups. When she was done, she noticed Williams was still sitting off to one side of the room watching them work. She walked over to him. Worried that she had gone too far, she decided that she should apologize. "Sorry," she said quietly.

Williams shook his head. "No, I asked for it," he

admitted as he ran his hand through his short haircut. "I was too cocky."

"Come on, let me show you how it'll normally feel," Julie said and offered him her hand again. She was impressed when it only took him a moment to consider before taking her hand. This time she zapped him to her hideout, and waited for him to look around. "Ready?" she asked and then took them back to the base. "How are you feeling this time?"

"Not bad," he admitted.

"Good, that's how it'll feel most of the time."

"Most of the time?" he asked with a touch of concern.

She chuckled, "Yeah, luckily, on most missions there's no need for me to speed zap a person around the world, with six stops, in only a few seconds." His eyes grew wide as he realized what she had just said. "I've got to get back to work, I'll see you later." As she walked away she called over her shoulder, "Oh by the way, they're more like oranges."

Williams stared at her puzzled for a moment, and then he must have realized what she was talking about and gave her an embarrassed smile.

CHAPTER 18

By 0300 they were gathered in a cleared area outside the command tent. Each man had his gear on and was ready to go. While she waited for the order to start the mission, Julie studied the men in each group. The first one had Lieutenant Cooper, Simmons, Williams and Gawaran. They were assigned to the first location, which was the one that Julie thought was the real man they were looking for. Matt, Demetrio, Moore and Anderson were in the second group. That left Chief Nguyen, Miller, Taylor and Martin to take the last location. Julie looked back down at the sketches she had made. She had checked them just a few minutes ago, but she checked them again just to be sure.

"Jade, let's get this started," Captain Lewis' order broke into her concentration. She stood up from where she had been sitting out of the way on the packed sand. Walking over to Lieutenant Cooper she took her position in the middle of the group. This first location had enough empty floor space for her to take them in all at once. "Ready?" she asked, looking around at each of them. At their nods she focused on the first target.

When they got there she waited just long enough for the men to let go of her before she zapped over to their target. He was asleep just like she had guessed, and she bent over his prone form. The instant she touched him, she took them back to the base. As they arrived she sensed him move, and instinctively she zapped backward just enough to dodge the blade he had tried to stab her with. Letting his arm swing past her she zapped in close enough to grab the back of his wrist with her left hand. Then she struck his elbow with a sudden jab of her right hand. She heard a loud crunch which was followed by his arm bending the wrong way. The target screamed in pain. Letting go of his wrist she stepped backward, a bit dazed by what had just happened. Several MPs stepped forward quickly to restrain him.

"Are you alright?" Matt asked as he ran up to her.

She realized in her fear that she had broken the man's arm without thinking. Matt was checking her for cuts even as she answered him. "Yeah, I'm fine," she said.

"That was nicely done," Matt congratulated her.

"I guess Mark's lessons *have* been worth it," she said embarrassed.

"If you're ready, take us in," Demetrio said, walking up them. "We don't want them getting any warning that we're coming."

Julie nodded and put a hand on Matt's and Demetrio's shoulders. This next room was too small for her to take all four at once, so she would need to take two trips to drop them off. By the time she had returned with the second target, the first 'al-Rashid' had already been taken away. The second target, who was probably a decoy had also been asleep and went without much of a fight. Julie just stepped out of the way as the Marines took him into custody. Quickly she took Moore and Lujan in to reinforce Matt and Demetrio. When she was done she headed straight over to Chief Nguyen's group with the sounds of the decoy's yelling coming from behind her.

"Ready?" she asked their chief and Doc.

"Let's get this done," Chief Nguyen nodded and she

took him and Doc in first.

She brought their last sleeping target back and without a thought, left him lying on the ground as she headed over to Martin and Taylor. Suddenly she heard urgent shouts of warning come from behind her and then a single voice shouted, "Allahu-Akbar!" Julie turned in time to see the second decoy throw something toward her. The object hit the ground and rolled to a stop at her feet. Behind her she could hear Martin and Taylor yelling at her to take cover, but instead she reached down and picked up the grenade. Frantically she tried to think of a safe place for her to take it. Thinking of a place, she zapped herself to the cell in her hideout and dropped the grenade. She arrived back at the base in the exact spot she had just left a moment earlier.

Martin ran up to her first. "Are you alright?" he asked stunned.

"Yeah, I'm fine," she answered. She shook herself trying to get back to the mission. She looked over at the man who had tried to kill her. He was staring at her in disbelief as he was dragged away, and she waved at him cheerfully. She turned back to Martin and Taylor "You two ready? Chief and Miller might need you." When they nodded she delivered them to the third location.

After she returned to the base she gathered her sketches and took a seat at an empty desk in the command tent. She tried to concentrate to check her diagrams, but around her she could hear muffled talking and she knew that some of the Marines were staring at her. Captain Lewis strode over to where she was sitting. "That was some show," he remarked. "Where *did* you take it?"

"The holding cell in my hideout," she answered. She continued almost distractedly, "I hope it didn't cause a cave in."

A shout rang out from the radio man, "The second assault group is ready to be extracted!"

Julie looked to Captain Lewis. "Go ahead. Get them

back here quickly," he ordered and Julie nodded in reply. Focusing on the four men at the second location she saw that they had clustered close together. She zapped into the center of their formation allowing them to easily reach out and touch her. Making sure she had all of them, she zapped them all back to base. Tired from zapping all four at once, she let herself sink to the ground in the sand of the cleared area where she had arrived.

"How are you holding up?" Matt asked as he knelt down next to her.

Julie looked up at him, "I'm just tired. I ate three candy bars before the mission started, so I should be fine." She pulled out her sketches of the first and third locations. "I'll just sit here and keep watch on them while I rest."

Matt squeezed her shoulder companionably and left her sitting there. Only a few minutes later, he came running out of the command tent. "Moore…Anderson… Demetrio… get ready. Lieutenant Cooper's assault group needs reinforcements." When he got to Julie he offered her a hand up. "You up to this?" he asked as he helped her to her feet.

"Sure," she stated as she dusted off her pants. "Where do you want to get dropped off?" she asked showing him her updated sketch. It showed the positions of Lieutenant Cooper and his men, and anyone else close to them.

"How far away can you sense? Is there a clear area nearby?" he asked, studying the diagram.

Julie concentrated on their lieutenant, and reached with her powers. "I think the area above them is empty. I can't tell if it's a roof or another floor."

"That'll work," he told her, nodding his thanks. He went to tell the others about the plan. When their gear was ready they gathered around her again. This time they all knelt, so they would arrive better covered. After dropping them off, Julie returned to base. From her kneeling position she lowered herself onto her back to rest.

"Medic!" Captain Lewis shouted as he ran up to her prone form. "What's wrong? Are you hit?" he asked when he got to her side.

"No, just exhausted," Julie kept her eyes closed as she answered him. The ground felt so comfortable just then.

The captain waved the corpsman away but searched for someone else. "You, Marine! Go to the mess hall and get her a glass of sugar water. Make it as concentrated as you can! Move it!" their captain yelled at someone over her. Then more gently he told her, "Rest while you can. They still need you to bring 'em back."

Julie nodded, she had not forgotten about the men. They were the only reason she had not given in to the urge to go to sleep. She kept a watch on them, even while she was laying there. Switching her focus between each of the them she could tell how the battle was going. A few minutes later she heard someone running up to her.

"Here, drink this. It might help," Captain Lewis said interrupting her concentration. She opened her eyes and started to sit up. The captain used his free arm to help her get the rest of the way up to sitting.

After accepting the metal cup, she lifted up her mask just enough to allow her to drink. As she chugged the super-sweet liquid she could feel the grit of undissolved sugar in her mouth. "Thanks, that was perfect," she said as she opened her eyes to look at Captain Lewis. "Any word from the third group?"

"They're ready for extraction whenever you're able."

"Okay, just give me a second," she said. She sat hunched forward for a little longer, and then taking a deep breath she sat up straighter and sent her powers out to find Chief Nguyen and the men with him. She did not bother standing up when she zapped to get them. They gathered around her and she brought them back without her needing to move a muscle. Once she was back at the base she went back to resting. Propping her head on her hand and bracing her elbow on her knee, she was able to let herself drift off. Around her she heard the guys talking, but their voices sounded far away and they did not bother her. She became aware of someone kneeling next to her. Opening her eyes she saw Doc looking at her worried. "Hey, someone got me a cup of sugar water earlier, can I get another one? But this time can he make it with coffee instead of water and put more sugar in it?"

She heard Doc ask around to find the Marine who had fetched the first cup. "And put more sugar in it this time," he instructed. A few minutes later running feet heralded the return of the young Marine. "This is more like sugar sludge!" Doc said as he looked at the cup of liquid.

Julie reached up and took it from him. "Perfect!" she exclaimed as she gulped down the thick, brown, sugary liquid. When she finished it, she sighed with satisfaction. "I'm watching the battle, they seem fine so far," she told Doc as she closed her eyes again.

"How are you holding up?" Doc asked concerned.

"I won't lie, I'm really tired, but that coffee seems to be helping," she admitted. She shifted her awareness back to her link with the Teams. After a little while, she felt a shift in their emotions. "Something's wrong," she told Doc.

Just then Captain Lewis came out of the command tent. "Get them out of there now!"

Extending her powers along her link, Julie found each man and speed zapped them out one by one. She was so fast that they seemed to pop into existence. A few of them had been in shooting positions propped against something and had to catch themselves to keep from falling. In less than a minute she had retrieved all eight men and sat panting heavily from the effort. Deciding she should lie down before she collapsed, she found a comfortable position on her back and closed her eyes. She must have drifted off to sleep for a minute, because she woke up as someone lifted her off the ground. "Hey! What's going on?" she exclaimed weakly, looking around.

"I'm just moving you out of the way. We don't want you getting stepped on," Matt explained with a smile as he carried her.

"I'm Okay. Really, I can walk," Julie said as she struggled to stand up. "Put me down, this is embarrassing!"

"Alright, alright, just give me a chance to put you down before you make me drop you," Matt objected to her struggling and quickly set her on her feet. "We thought you'd be out cold after all of that zapping."

"Actually I'm feeling alright," Julie admitted surprised. "That last cup of sugar coffee must've helped a lot."

"Sugar coffee?" Matt asked.

"Yeah, she asked a Marine to get her a cup of coffee with so much sugar in it that it looked like mud," Doc explained as he and Lieutenant Cooper met them by the command tent. "She practically had to chew it; there was so much undissolved sugar."

"It worked didn't it? It kept me going long enough to get them out. Actually that was my second cup, Captain Lewis got the first one for me, but it was just sugar water." Suddenly she remembered the end of the mission. "Why did I have to get you out so fast? What went wrong?"

"It was about to get messy. A group of insurgents had just brought in R.P.G.s and they were about to hit the mud brick building we were in from several sides at once," Matt said with a shrug. "We had already found everything we needed anyway." Turning to Lieutenant Cooper he asked, "So, where do you want us for our debriefing, Sir?"

Lieutenant Cooper looked at Doc and Matt, "You two head into the conference room. Jade, Captain Lewis says you can report in tomorrow for your debriefing. Head back home before you get so tired you can't get there."

CHAPTER 19

A week later Julie was headed to the briefing room for another mission. As she entered the command tent she realized that something was wrong. They were discussing an ambushed supply caravan that had left the base just an hour earlier. The caravan's mission had been to resupply the Combined Arms Battalion with fuel and ammunition. Julie realized she knew some of the troops in that resupply unit. *I hope they're okay*, she thought. The caravan had been ambushed just a few minutes ago and they were trying to figure out a way to reinforce the non-combat personnel that were currently pinned down.

Julie spotted Matt and his team off to one side; they had come to the meeting room for the same briefing that had brought her.

"Can I help?" Julie asked as she stepped up to their group.

"I'm not sure how," Matt told her.

"Yeah, not without you getting your head blown off," Demetrio agreed, always the optimist.

"There's a small group pinned down away from the rest of the convoy that are in the most danger," Matt continued as if he had not heard him. "The vehicle they're in isn't even armored, so bullets can go through it pretty easily."

"How many are there?" Julie asked, trying to come up with options.

"Ten, too many for you to safely take in one shot. The six of us are almost too much for you to all at once."

"I could do it in two trips."

"Just two? I thought you normally only took one at a time," the mission commander asked when he overheard their discussion.

"Taking more than one or two other people with me is like adding fifty pounds to your pack while you're running," Julie said. She tried to explain it in a way the commander would understand but she hated to admit she had limitations. "Each additional person is more weight. I can do it, but I burn out quickly."

The commander nodded his head thinking. "But you think you can do it in two trips? That seems like a reasonable amount of risk. Let's work on that plan. You, get me a picture of each of the personnel that are in that vehicle," he called to a Marine nearby. The commander walked off, already barking orders.

"I don't like this; I don't like this one bit," Matt grumbled to himself.

"That's just because you've got a crush on Jade," Doc teased him when he heard his grumbling. "You wouldn't be worried if it was one of us doing it."

"That's because none of us is as cute as she is," Simmons joined Doc in teasing Matt.

Julie was thankful for her mask; it hid her sudden blush.

Since Jade had started working at the base they kept a file of ID pics for every military member. It only took a few minutes for the commander to bring over a stack of pictures. Julie took them to look through. Her heart stopped. She recognized two of the women who were currently trapped in the ambush. Mariela had introduced her to them a few days ago.

The most time-consuming part of doing group rescues was getting all of them together at once. Julie made the first rescue with no problem. She zapped into the bed of the supply truck. Above her, she could see the canvas top that was the only thing protecting her. She had been able to teleport into a cluster of the trapped Marines and they quickly grabbed onto her. Her second attempt did not go as well. The two women were in the last group to be rescued. They were close to two of the guys and Julie decided to arrive next to them. One Marine was trying to provide cover fire. As he turned to join them Julie felt fire lance through her collar bone, and she passed out from the pain.

"Jade's been hit! I say again! Jade's been hit!" was the panicked report the command center received.

Matt's team had been listening to the rescue from the back of the room. When they heard the report Matt's gut clenched. *There isn't anything we can do to help*, he thought realizing that the reinforcements were still at least twenty minutes away.

"We're out of ammunition. Please advise," was the next communication from the Marines in the pinned down vehicle.

In desperation Lieutenant Cooper made a decision. "Tell them to remove her mask! If they are captured they are not to tell the terrorists who she is! She'll survive longer if they don't know her identity. Tell them to take off her disguise, damn it!" he yelled.

Matt was certain the group was about to be captured, and even though it would blow her cover, better that than the enemy know whom they had captured. The commander issued the orders to the trapped troops, and Matt prayed it would be enough.

Julie awoke, her right shoulder screaming with pain. She felt weak, and her mind was clouded by pain and exhaustion. The first thing she realized was that her mask had been removed. Fear gripped her. She knew she was wanted by several factions, dead or alive. Slowly she became aware of the scene around her.. She heard the screams and curses of the two women she had tried to save. One woman was pinned to the ground about two yards away from her. A man was holding down her arms as another man tore at her clothing. From somewhere behind Julie she could hear another woman cursing at them.

A sudden wave of horror and anger surged through Julie, giving her strength and helping to clear her mind. She struggled to her feet; the men were too involved to notice her. They were jeering at the first woman while they attacked her. That made Julie's anger even stronger. *Bastards!* Julie zapped to a place between them and managed to grab each of them by their shoulders. The pain she felt from her collar bone made her shriek, but she held on. The next thing the two men knew, they were falling several hundred feet to their deaths. Julie instantly zapped back to the cell before she had fallen more than a foot or two.

Matt was running between buildings when he heard the screams. He stopped and tried to pinpoint where they were coming from. They were getting closer, and the screams were of sheer terror. Looking up, he spotted two forms plummeting towards the ground. He watched as they impacted right in the middle of the 'zap landing pad.' He grimaced reflexively, but then cheered triumphantly. *They're Taliban*, he thought recognizing their outfits and knew that those two bodies meant only one thing. Julie was alive, and, from the looks of things, she was pissed. An instant later, two female personnel were speed zapped onto the landing pad one at a time. As the nurses hurried to their sides, Matt heard more screams coming from above them. "Clear the area! Move it!" Matt yelled not needing to look up to know what was coming down at them.

The medical personnel managed to clear the landing pad just in time as a third enemy body impacted the cement with a wet thud.

A split second later she brought back two Marines and Matt noticed Julie fall to her knee. She took a moment, before she zapped out again, and in that time Matt could see the wound at the base of her neck. She arrived back a moment later with the last captured Marine and collapsed limply to the ground.

Matt reached her even before the corpsmen could. He felt for a pulse, and found a very faint one. Two corpsmen rushed to the scene. "She is to be considered top secret. No one is to reveal her identity," he instructed them. The corpsmen nodded and Matt let them carry her into the hospital. He watched as they worked on her. From what he had seen, her injury had not looked too bad, but her pulse had been really weak. *Her blood sugar must be really low,* he thought. At that moment he heard the doctor order a bag of saline for her. Matt knew enough to know that would only make her blood sugar levels worse.

"No, listen doctor, you can't give her normal saline, it could kill her," Matt pleaded. He ran to catch up to the gurney as they rushed her into surgery.

"Who the hell are you and what are you talking about?"

"I'm Petty Officer Burke. You've got to listen. She's always weak after teleporting too many times. I think it lowers her blood sugar," Matt explained quickly then waited, hoping the doctor would listen.

The doctor nodded his understanding. "Change that order to lactated ringers, with a glucose drip, and also give Epinephrine IV push."

Matt watched as they hooked up the lactated ringers. After only a few minutes her vital signs improved. *She should make it now*, he thought with relief. As he left the ER he heard the doctor bark, "Where are those X-rays I ordered?"

Matt spotted two MP's outside the hospital. "You understand who that is, right?"

"Yes, sir," one of the guards replied.

"You won't let anyone but hospital personnel in," Matt checked.

"Don't worry, we've already sent for additional guards," the second guard explained. "We know she's a high security asset."

Relieved, Matt headed to the command center. He needed to report to his CO. When he got there he found three of the Marines that she had rescued. The other two, had been in the hospital being treated as he left. These three had just started their debriefings. Since his CO was in the room, Matt decided to wait and find out what had happened.

The first one to report was the woman. "We removed Jade's disguise as ordered. I don't think they had any idea who she was. We were separated from the men and were taken in a truck to a rundown building maybe a couple miles away." The woman paused for a moment then continued, "they chained us to the walls, then... Then they started pawing at us. They chose Bridgette to rape first." Again the woman stopped speaking, lost in the memory.

"What happened next?" the base commander asked to get her to continue.

"Then Jade woke up. She seemed really weak at first, and then she zapped the two bastards out first and came back for us," the woman finished.

That would explain the first two sky diving terrorists, Matt thought grimly to himself.

The next Marines to report were the two men. Their report was pretty much the same; they had also been left in a cell like the women, each of them chained to a wall. One terrorist had soon entered the room to begin beating their buddy. Matt unconsciously rubbed his arm that had been broken when he had been a prisoner. The two had been shackled so they were unable to help their friend. Jade had appeared and took the terrorist first, then had returned for them. *So that explained the third splattered terrorist. I'd better remember not to make her mad,* Matt thought with a silent laugh.

After they answered a few more questions they were reminded to keep what they knew of Jade secret. The three were then dismissed to report to the base hospital to get checked out.

CHAPTER 20

Julie woke the next day to the sound of someone entering her room. She tried to sit up to see who had come in, but her arm and shoulder were splinted to prevent her from moving them and it made sitting up a lot harder.

"Now you just lie back for right now. I'll help you sit up in a moment," a woman's gentle voice said from somewhere out of sight. Whoever had come in had noticed that Julie was awake, but she was still out of view. A moment later the nurse came to her bedside. She was an older woman with graying hairs sprinkled throughout her black hair. Her nametag read Kim Lorenzo, RN. Kim smiled warmly at Julie. "It's good to see you awake; you gave us all a scare for a bit yesterday. Thanks to your friend though, we were able to bring you around quick enough."

Julie looked around the room, wondering where Matt was. She was sure that was the friend the nurse had mentioned.

"He was called away for a mission, but he did spend the night watching over you," the woman explained. The observant nurse had seen Julie's searching glance around the room and had guessed the reason.

"A mission!" Julie exclaimed as she tried to sit up again.

"Don't even think about leaving this room! If you teleport out of here, you better hope the terrorists kill you this time or I'll have your hide!" the nurse scolded her, then smiled to take the sting out of her words, but Julie could tell she was serious.

"You know who I am?" Julie asked tentatively. She was suddenly self-conscious; she had liked the anonymity that her secret identity had given her.

"Yes, but don't worry, your secret is safe with us. Everyone in the ER when you came in has been sworn to secrecy. We'd have kept it secret anyway on our own. We know how many lives you've saved in the short amount of time you've been here," Kim explained as she worked. "There are guards posted outside your room who have strict orders to let no one in except your team, the doc and myself. They're not even allowed in," the nurse grinned at that thought.

"But what if Matt, or the others, need help?" Julie asked, still thinking about them.

"Believe it or not, they were doing this long before you came along, and they did just fine. They can do a mission without you watching over them," Kim said reassuringly. During the entire conversation the nurse had been busily performing her duties and charting her observations.

"Can I go to the bathroom?" Julie asked, suddenly aware of how badly she needed to go.

"I can imagine you probably need to. We put enough lactated ringers in you to fill a horse."

"Lactated ringers?" Julie asked as the nurse helped her to stand.

"Yes, your blood sugar levels must have been through the floor. You almost didn't make it. Luckily your friend filled us in on how teleporting affects your blood sugar."

Julie had to call her parents that day. There was no hiding the fact that she was not at home. Her nurse arranged for her to get a secure phone line. She started their conversation with "I'm all right, but I need to tell you something…" She could not tell them everything, she did not have enough time, but she told them as much as she could. She tried to reassure them that she would be home soon, and that she was all right.

"So what do you think of the food in this place?" Matt asked in a forced light-hearted way when he visited later that evening.

"Not bad. It's about as good as the other hospitals I've been in. Bland is the best way to describe it," Julie admitted finishing off the last bite. She was expecting another lecture from Matt, and was not looking forward to it. "How did your mission go?" she asked hoping to distract him.

"Good. We got a lead on the group that hit the caravan. They won't be attacking anyone ever again," he said with a smile. "We also found the room you were held in. We destroyed any evidence you were there."

Julie cursed silently to herself; she tried again to get him to think about anything but chewing her out. "I called my parents today. I told them as much as I could over the phone. My nurse won't let me zap anywhere."

"How did that go?" Matt asked as he sat on the chair next to her bed. "How'd they take it?"

"About as well as you'd expect… finding out their daughter's been wounded in combat halfway around the world when they thought she was at work at a nearby hospital," Julie said with a shrug. "Actually, I think they had already figured out that I was Jade."

Matt smiled at that thought. "Well it's not like there's a whole lot of people who can teleport," he pointed out. "How are you feeling?"

"Like a one-armed gimp," she said with a grimace.

Julie indicated her arm which was being held at her side and the bandage over a cut on her forehead. Then she remembered a question she had wanted to ask, but was dreading the answer. "I didn't hit anyone with the guys I dropped did I?"

"No, they screamed all the way down," Matt reassured her. "We heard them coming long before they could hit anyone. By the way, remind me not to make you mad."

"I woke up, and they were... I got so mad," Julie blushed. "Funny thing is that's probably the thing that saved us. It helped clear my head and gave me enough strength to get us out of there."

"I'm glad you're alright," Matt said in a subdued voice. "You really had us... me, worried."

"You mean you're not going to lecture me again?" Julie was relieved. This was so unlike Matt, she thought something must be wrong.

"No, I've been thinking about it," Matt admitted thoughtfully. "I can't stop you from doing what you do, any more than I could stop Doc or the others. I'd be hurt if they got killed too. I'll just have to deal with it."

They talked about other things until visiting hours were over.

Dawar was cleaning a table in the base mess hall. He had been looking for information about Jade's identity working as a spy for the Chinese military. He had been on the base for three months and still had not been able to find out anything useful. His superiors knew that Jade was operating out of this base for missions, but none of their spies had been able to find any information about her real identity.

Dawar was trying to overhear lunchtime conversations. He knew Jade was in the base hospital so one of the Marines might gossip about things they had seen or heard. A conversation at a table nearby caught his attention.

"Hey, have you seen Julie?" one of the women asked.

"No, I haven't seen her since yesterday," the other replied.

"She had an appointment with my division commander, but she never showed up," the first woman said.

"I bet she's working on the Jade story," her companion told her.

"She's going to get a reaming for missing her appointment," the first woman commented. "He might not agree to meet with her again."

"Yeah, but her newspaper will be more interested in Jade than any story about what a commander's doing."

"You're probably right. But she'll never get any information about Jade. There's so much security surrounding her room."

Dawar stopped listening. *Maybe there is a connection between the reporter's disappearance and Jade's injury*, he thought. Putting down his rag he left the mess hall to look into a few things. Before he reported to his superiors he needed to confirm his suspicions.

Julie was well enough to leave a few days later. Since it would be too hard to explain her injury, Julie could not use her cover story on the base until she was healed. She also could not stay hidden in her hospital room for weeks, so it was decided that she needed to return home while she recovered. The SEAL Team was also being rotated back to Coronado because their tour was over. They took Julie up on her offer to save them the long plane ride home and were waiting with her for the doc's final approval for her to be discharged. Simmons presented her with a box while they waited.

"We decided you needed this," Simmons said cryptically.

"What he's trying to say," Lieutenant Cooper started to explain after an annoyed glance at Simmons, "is that you're too valuable to us to risk losing you again. So we had your Uncle Mark make this bracelet for you."

"Why my Uncle Mark?" Julie asked, accepting the gift.

"So no one but us knows about its existence. You don't have to worry about anyone else using it to find you," Lieutenant Cooper answered.

"It has one of our smallest GPS beacons in it. If you ever go missing again, we'll be able to find you," Simmons explained. "It's also completely waterproof, so don't ever take it off," he added, proud of the new gadget.

It made her uncomfortable being called valuable, but she realized what they meant. "Thank you," Julie said as she studied the bracelet more closely. It looked like a fashionable leather-plaited bracelet with a decorative metallic bead at its center. It fit perfectly. "I hope I never need it."

"So do we," Matt admitted.

The nurse entered shortly after and gave Julie her discharge paperwork. She signed it, and then zapped them all home. They had arranged the use of a private meeting room on North Island. It was in a busy office building so no one would notice a few extra people leaving. They each left the room singly or in pairs a few minutes apart. Julie wore civilian clothes and left with Matt. She needed a ride home and if he rested his arm lightly over her shoulders it hid her injury. They looked like an ordinary dating couple as they made their way to the car they had arranged to use.

Matt had planned to just drop her off in front of her house, but Julie's mother saw their arrival and came out to the curb to greet them along with a very excited Cinder. Mary promptly invited Matt to stay for dinner to thank him for bringing their daughter home. None of them noticed the car parked across the street, or that the person watching them was making a phone call.

CHAPTER 21

"Hi Julie! How's your shoulder doing today?" Julie looked up to see Debbie. Dr. Emory's charge nurse greeting her with a smile.

"It's still a bit stiff, but it's feeling a lot better," Julie told her conversationally as she followed the nurse back to an exam room. She had been seeing Dr. Emory for her collar bone injury since she had returned with the guys.

As she followed the nurse, a man emerged from an exam room and nearly ran into Julie. "Pardon me, ma'am," the young man apologized.

"Corpsman Martinez! I thought I'd instructed you to leave early today," Debbie said sharply. She seemed upset by his presence.

"I'm sorry, Lt. Vinson. I was trying to catch up on my filing," the man explained quickly. The corpsman looked at Julie with a sneer, but then it changed to a normal smile and Julie wondered if she had just imagined it. He turned to Debbie as he explained, "I thought we were done seeing patients for the day, I can help if you need me."

Debbie seemed to realize she needed to explain Julie's presence. "Ensign Patterson called at the last minute and made an appointment with Dr. Emory. It's just a routine follow-up we won't need your assistance. Go home Martinez, you can finish your filing tomorrow."

Julie followed the nurse into an exam room, looking back down the hall she noticed that Martinez was still staring at her. He quickly turned away when he saw her looking at him. *It's nothing. Stop being paranoid*, she chided herself.

"Ah, Julie, how're you doing today?" Dr. Emory asked. The doctor was already waiting for her in the small exam room. "Well, everything is healing normally," he said as he examined her stitches. "I can't tell if your teleporting either hurts or helps your body heal, but I'd still try to limit how many times you do it until this wound is completely healed."

"Why's that?" Julie asked.

"Repairing damaged tissue is hard on a person's body. I can only theorize, but I suspect that teleporting also takes a lot of energy."

"Yeah, there're times I've passed out if I zap too much," Julie admitted.

"Really? How long are you unconscious for?"

"I don't know… it varies," Julie answered with a shrug.

"Julie, I think it would be good to study the effects teleporting has on you. We could do some simple tests whenever you have time away from working with the teams."

"I don't know, maybe…"

"Think about it. I can't promise anything, but it might help you."

Later that evening, Julie was struggling to hold the grocery bag with her good hand and open the door with her other hand. Her arm was still in the sling for her broken collar bone. It made it hard for her to manipulate the keys and turn the door knob, but she finally managed to open it. She set the bag of groceries down as she shut the door. "Mom… Dad… I'm home," she called as she picked up the groceries and turned to go in the kitchen. As she turned around she saw them. Her parents had been gagged and tied to some chairs. There was a man standing behind each of them with a pistol pointed at their heads. A third man lounged on their couch, with a welcoming smile on his face.

"It is so nice to finally meet you Julie. Or should I call you Jade?" he asked with a heavy Asian accent.

They're too far apart for me to take them at the same time, she thought grimly.

"If you teleport out of this room your parents will be shot," the man said confirming her fears.

"Who are you?" Julie asked coldly. "Why are you holding my parents?"

"I'm sorry, where are my manners? My name is General Jian. I am here with a business proposition for you, and your parents are here to ensure that you make the right choice. But we can discuss what we want later. We need to be leaving for a more private location."

Before Julie could answer or think of a plan, a fourth man came up behind her, and she felt the burn of an injection in her good arm. Then darkness enveloped her.

Matt sat waiting outside the movie theater they had chosen for their date. *Where could she be?* he asked himself. Julie was almost an hour late and he had not been able to reach her on her cell phone. He had not spoken to her since the day before when they had planned the date. *What could've happened?* he asked himself. Worried, he decided to stop by her house to see if her parents knew where she was.

As he drove up, Matt noticed that Julie's car was still in the driveway, but there were no lights on in the house. Knocking on the front door, he hoped his instincts were wrong. When no one answered he climbed through some bushes to look in a window. He could see bags of groceries and a gallon of milk sitting in the middle of the entry. Hearing a whimper from around the back of the house, Matt followed the sound and found Cinder. The dog was wounded, but he was still trying to crawl to Matt.

"It's okay boy," Matt tried to comfort the dog as he got out his phone. "Captain, Jade's missing."

"How do you know?" Captain Lewis asked and Matt filled him in on what he had found.

Within the hour their team had assembled in the briefing room. Simmons had already traced the GPS signal from Julie's bracelet.

"She's a hundred miles off the coast, traveling at about twenty-five knots," he reported.

"There's a P3 on its way to that location to find out what they're using. Let's hope she isn't on a sub. I've ordered a Seahawk to be scrambled. You'll use that to board whatever craft she is traveling on. We have to assume they're holding her parents as a way to control her, or she has somehow been rendered unconscious," their CO was explaining. "The rest of SEAL Team 3 is deployed overseas, but SEAL Team 1 is standing by if we need them. We'll know more once we have an identification of the vessel. We've also contacted the Ronald Reagan strike group. Several of their destroyers were on maneuvers up the coast and are now on an intercept course for Julie's coordinates. Get geared up. We need to get to her before the destroyers do. Whoever has her will probably kill her if they can't keep her."

Matt and his team geared up for an aerial drop. Whatever kind of ship they were using, short of a sub, they would use the chopper to approach the ship under their radar. Once they were in striking distance they would pop up over the fantail of the ship, just long enough for them to fast rope down to the deck.

In a short time the men were ready, and headed to the

helicopter. It would take over an hour to reach Julie's location.

Soon after takeoff the squad got the report that Julie was being held on a container ship. *That means that there will be a minimal crew*, Matt thought mentally preparing for the assault, *but we'll have a big area to search*. The men made last minute adjustments to their plans based on this new information. They had trained so often for this kind of mission there was very little that needed to be discussed. It was decided that an assault squad from SEAL Team 1 would join them to help secure such a large target.

During the flight Matt tried to be patient. It was normal for them to have to fly long distances to their insertion points, but this one was different. *I shouldn't have let myself get so close to her*, Matt silently cursed himself.

When they finally caught up with the container ship, the team boarded without much difficulty. SEAL Team 3's chopper approached first. Their door gunner took out the four guards that were positioned on the fan tail. He could easily make out the men with his infrared sights. Simmons and Demetrio fast-roped onto the deck. Matt and the rest of their Team joined them a moment later. Team 1 arrived less than thirty seconds later. They had planned on splitting into two groups to cover the ship's massive size better, with Team 1 taking the upper decks. Their goal was the control room. Team 3 followed the GPS signal below decks to find Julie.

Julie slipped in and out of consciousness. She fought to clear her mind, but she was unable to focus her thoughts enough to zap anywhere. If she really concentrated she could sense her parents in a room close by. She had no idea how long she had been out, but her mind was starting to clear. Julie felt a sudden prick on her arm as a man worked over her bed. Her confused thoughts turned to Matt, *Where's Matt? Does he know I'm missing?* She tried to focus on him, and found him. *That can't be right.; he feels close by*, she thought in disbelief. *They've found us!* She thought with sudden hope. Just before she sank back into unconsciousness, she saw the man hanging an IV bag above her, and the world went dark again.

The team entered the passageway into the lower levels of the ship, their footsteps echoed quietly on the steel bulkhead. A short way into the ship the corridor split. Chief Nguyen signaled for them to divide up to secure the entire level. Matt, Simmons and Doc were the group assigned to find and secure the hostages until they could be safely airlifted off the ship. Simmons had the GPS tracker and was second in their line. Matt took point and Doc took the rear guard.

Moving silently through the corridors, Matt spotted two guards ahead of them. His silenced rifle took them out before they were even aware that the SEALs were there. The three men continued to move down the passageway in a single file, hugging the bulkhead until they reached a narrow set of stairs leading down. Matt looked back at Simmons. He gave Matt a quick hand signal indicating that Julie's beacon was below them. Without warning, gun shots flew up at them from the stairs. Matt pressed himself against the bulkhead and returned fire. The gunman fell and rolled back down the steps. With a nod to the others, Matt surged down the steps. He knew he needed to move quickly getting past the narrow opening of the steps where he was an easy target. Not stopping until he was able to cover the passageway below. At his signal Simmons moved down the stairs past Matt to take a position at the bottom. When he nodded that it was all clear, Matt advanced the rest of the way down. Taking point again Matt continued in the direction that Simmons indicated.

Up ahead the corridor came to an end with two other

passageways continuing to the right and left. Before Matt reached the intersection a group of armed men turned the corner from the right. The targets had been running, their rifles at the ready when they spotted Matt and the assault group. Matt opened fire and took out two, but several of the men were able to get to safety back around the corner. The three SEALs opened fire on the men as the attackers tried to return fire.

General Jian listened to the report from his second in command. His men were under attack all over the ship. "I want all available men, everyone, down to the cells!" he yelled angrily. "They're trying to rescue Jade!" Instantly his lieutenant radioed more men. *Maybe, just maybe we'll be able to hold out until we meet the sub*, he thought. *If we can get her onto the sub we'll sink the cargo ship. Let them try to prove we took Jade then!*

Matt ducked as bullets ricocheted off the bulkhead next to him. Two more gunmen were attacking from the other direction. Simmons crossed to the opposite side of the passage to return fire as Matt tossed a grenade down the corridor to the right. Several men ran into the line of fire trying to avoid the explosion. After that it only took a few minutes for the Team to finish off the last of the armed men. As they approached the turn, Simmons tapped Matt on his shoulder and motioned for him to take the left corridor.

Matt approached the corner cautiously, and then quickly glanced both ways to make sure it was clear. Once he knew it was clear he continued down the left passage until Simmons tapped his shoulder to stop him. They were outside two doorways and Simmons checked his tracker before pointing to the one on the left.

The three took position around the door as Matt quietly tried the handle. It was locked. Simmons went back to the two men who had come from this passageway and searched the guards' pockets. When he found the keys he came back and silently unlocked the door. Matt took position to enter first as Simmons prepared to open it. Bracing himself, Matt signaled to Simmons to push the door open. Matt knew that if there were additional guards inside the rooms they would have heard the fire fight and would be ready. A few bullets ricocheted off the door frame confirming his suspicion.

With his back against the wall Matt looked deep into the corner on his right. Using the door frame as his pivot point, he began methodically searching the room. As he panned the room through the sight on his rifle he caught a glimpse of Julie lying on a cot. *I can't help her until I've cleared the room*, he reminded himself and continued to clear the room.

The first thing Matt spotted was the guard's elbow. Taking the shot, he heard a cry of pain and continued until he saw the man's head. His next round hit the guard in the center of his face. The guard slumped to the floor in a lifeless pile as Matt continued his sweep to make sure there wasn't any other threats. He finished checking the behind the wall on his right as he entered the room. Doc came in close behind him and went directly to the bunk set to one side of the compartment. Julie was lying there, unconscious and limp.

"How is she?" Matt asked as he came up to Doc.

"It looks like they have her on some heavy sedatives," Doc said, taking an IV out of her arm. "We'll have to carry her. Otherwise I think she'll be fine."

Matt nodded, "Let's find her parents and get back to the fantail and evac."

Commander Hicks stood on the bridge of the USS Decatur surveying the dark night outside. Around him his crew worked in stressed silence, the only sounds coming from the various displays. *They know we're on the brink of an international incident*, the commander thought recognizing the tension. His decisions in the next hour would be critical. *But we can't let a foreign nation take Jade.*

"Sir, I'm getting a sonar reading."

"What have you found, ensign?" Commander Hicks asked.

"It's reading as a MING III class sub."

So it was China that took her, Commander Hicks thought angrily. Walking toward the map of the California coastline Hicks asked, "What's their position?"

"It's 5,800 meters, sir. Bearing 32 degrees."

Hicks did some quick calculations. "The cargo ship is headed on a direct course to that sub. I hope the SEALs have had enough time. We're about to announce ourselves," he said grimly. "Get me a firing solution," he said turning to his torpedo man. "Go to active sonar." he ordered next. "We'll see how determined they are to keep their meeting with that cargo ship."

General Jian placed the radio back on its cradle. For a moment he stood slumped, looking like an old man. His tailored blue business suit seemed to hang on his frame. *They're leaving us*; the forlorn thought briefly caused him to panic. The sub he had arranged to meet them had reported that they were leaving. It was being actively pinged by three destroyers that were on an intercept course for the cargo ship. The sub commander knew he would never survive a run-in with three destroyers and had refused to come to the aid of the general and his men.

It doesn't matter, the general shoved his indecision to the back of his thoughts. As he stood at attention he returned to his usual stern but dignified appearance. If the destroyers knew the Americans were on board, he needed to make sure they were not able to take the girl back alive. *I'll die before I let them take her back*, he thought turning to his lieutenant, who was also dressed like a regular crew member to hide his identity. "Kill the girl and her parents," he commanded.

As Simmons guarded the doorway he heard men coming. With a quick warning to the others he prepared to take aim. There were only three of them and he was able to catch them by surprise. When Matt was ready, Simmons took the keys and silently unlocked the door to the next room along the passageway and prepared to open it. Again Matt took position to sweep the room, but this time there was no guards posted inside. Matt quickly untied Julie's parents and removed their gags. Motioning them to stay quiet, he urged them out into the hallway. Matt took the lead again, with Doc and the hostages in the center, while Simmons covered them from behind. As a group, they headed back the way they had entered, cautiously retracing their steps back to the fantail of the ship.

It was only a few moments before Matt heard the shouts from down the corridor. *Someone's discovered that Julie's gone*, he thought realizing what the shouts meant. Increasing their pace they continued back down the passage toward the rear of the ship. They would not signal the chopper until they were ready for pick-up.

The Chinese soldiers caught up with them quickly. Matt heard Simmons's warning moments before the first bullets were fired. They had just reached a bend in the passageway, and they all dove for cover around the corner. Simmons flattened his back against the bulkhead, just out of sight of their pursuers. After the first burst of fire ricocheted past his position, Matt saw Simmons pivot just enough to allow him to take aim. After a brief exchange of gun fire, Simmons signaled for Matt to continue on.

With any luck Simmons had wounded, perhaps killed, several of their pursuers, Matt thought with satisfaction. *That'll mean that they'll follow us more slowly.*

Soon they met up with the rest of their squad. Lieutenant Cooper indicated that they should continue on while he, Demetrio and Nguyen took positions along the passage. The ambush would provide Matt's group additional cover to evacuate the hostages.

It took only a few more moments to reach the fantail of the ship. Matt took position guarding the landing area while Simmons signaled the chopper for pickup. Once the chopper was in position, Doc, carrying Julie, and Julie's parents came out of cover to meet it. It hovered a few feet above the deck. Doc passed Julie's limp body up to the crew and then helped her parents get on board. Doc gave brief instructions to the medic on the chopper about Julie's condition. Once the civilians were well clear, the team set about ridding the ship of any further threats.

Matt and Julie walked along the beach of the Naval Base on Coronado. Julie had taken off her dress shoes. The feel of the sand sliding between her toes was relaxing. A subdued Cinder was limping along beside her. The vet had been able to save his life. Though it had taken several surgeries to repair the damage caused by the bullet ripping through his chest.

He'll need to take it easy for a few more weeks, Julie thought, *but he'd be fine.*

It had already been a week since Julie had been taken by General Jian, and a lot had happened. It had been decided that the only way to ensure her parents' safety was to change their identities. Word of Jade's kidnapping had reached the news by the day after her rescue. So they had reported to the news that both of Jade's parents, her only living family, had been killed in the kidnapping attempt.

In reality, her parents had been set up in Arizona with new identities. Her father had been close to retirement age anyway, so they had been moved to the mountain town of Flagstaff, near the Grand Canyon. Their new house was nestled on a wooded lot at the edge of town, which gave her mother plenty of room to garden. Her father could get a part time job as a professor at the university nearby to keep himself busy.

Meanwhile, Julie had been given a place to live on base. It was safer there than out in the community. She even had a new cover story complete with a new uniform. The khaki button-up shirt and trousers were so new the fabric felt stiff, and she fidgeted with its collar. Unconsciously she adjusted her garrison cap.

"It's weird having people salute me," Julie complained as they walked.

"Get used to it, Ensign Patterson. You need to act the part," Matt chided her.

She adjusted the sling around her neck. Her collar bone was still healing, but soon she would be back to work helping the SEAL teams. She thought about Dr. Emory's proposal to study the effects of teleporting on her body.

"What do you think about Dr. Emory's idea?" Julie asked.

"It would be good to know if it's doing any long term damage to you," Matt said, then shrugged. "Maybe we can figure out a better way to keep you from blacking out when you teleport too many times."

"What if someone gets hold of the information and finds out my weaknesses?" she asked, concerned.

"I wouldn't worry too much. 'Jade' has been given the highest security level, not just anyone will have access to your files," Matt reassured her.

They walked on in silence for a while thinking. "Speaking of weaknesses, now that my parents are safe I don't have to worry about them, but I'll never be able to have a normal life will I?" Julie asked. She turned to look at his face as they walked.

"What do you mean?"

"Well for one, I'll never be able to marry. Any man I fall in love with will be in danger," she said as she fingered the bracelet the team had given her. *If I didn't have this GPS beacon my parents and I would still be in the hands of General Jian*, the thought had been nagging at her over the last few days.

"You're right... you won't be able to marry *just any* man," Matt agreed. Julie caught the emphasis on the words '*just any*' and looked up at him in despair. "But if you found a man who was used to danger..." Matt let the sentence trail off.

Julie had been attracted to Matt since she had first seen him, but she had always doubted how interested he was in her. "Do you have anyone in mind?" she asked hesitantly, searching Matt's face for some indication of his real feelings.

"I might," he said with a grin as he bent over to kiss her.

Julie returned the kiss in a daze. During all of their missions together and their dates, Matt had never tried to kiss her, or take their relationship any further. She had often wondered if he really was not that interested in her. She had even considered that he had dated her just to control Jade, like her uncle thought. Julie closed her eyes as they kissed for the first time. *Maybe*, she thought, *I will have a normal life. Well, as normal as a person who teleports can have.*

Mr. Smith's eyes narrowed as he watched them kiss. *Am I the only one who can see how dangerous she is? Her very existence threatens the country!* The Chinese attempt to take her had justified all of his fears. He had tried to bring her under control, but he had been humiliated. *Imagine, humiliated for trying to protect his country!* His face turned into a mask of rage. He had lost everything because of her, his career, his reputation, and his prestige. With an effort he reined in his emotions; *I still have my connections,* and he smiled at the thought. They had been able to find out Julie's new alias and her whereabouts. He watched calmly now as the two continued walking. They were too distracted to notice him, a dark figure in a car parked along the street which followed the beach line.

For a moment Smith contemplated pulling out his Glock to shoot them where they stood, but he dismissed the thought quickly. He would almost surely be seen, and most likely he would be caught before he made it off base. He could not risk going to jail, besides he wanted revenge on the entire SEAL team. They had repeatedly snubbed his authority and sheltered the girl, proving they were as dangerous to the country as she was. He had time to make them pay, but he knew he had to plan. It would be very difficult; General Jian's failure proved that. He guessed that they were using a tracking signal, but he did not know which frequency it was. *It doesn't matter anyway, I don't need it*, he thought. Confident that he would have her one day, he started his car and drove away, leaving them behind. He knew the wait would just make his revenge all the more sweet.

CHAPTER 22

The phone rang again. Groggily Julie rolled over to look at her alarm clock. *It's not even 2 a.m*, she thought irritated. Reaching past the clock she grabbed her phone. "This is Julie," she answered.

"Get in here," Matt's voice said on the other end. It was tense and businesslike. His statement was short, but Julie knew what that meant... a mission. They never discussed what she was being called in for over the phone. There was always a chance someone might be listening in, and that would jeopardize her secret identity.

"Give me twenty," Julie answered just as abruptly.

"See ya," Matt acknowledged and hung up.

As Julie got out of bed Cinder looked up at her, and then put his head back down on his bed. He was used to her leaving at all hours. As she got ready Julie thought back over the last few months since China had attempted to kidnap 'Jade'. Once she had moved into this apartment her days had quickly fallen into a routine. She felt safe in her new apartment, with her new neighbors. Coincidentally, or perhaps not so coincidentally, most of the apartments surrounding hers had gradually become occupied by other Navy SEALs. They did not know her real identity, but she recognized them from her work with the teams, and felt reassured by their presence.

She had returned to her previous job of helping to retrieve wounded soldiers during missions, and providing remote reconnaissance during SEAL team operations. While she was in the States she was stationed at Coronado, under the command of Admiral Huntington. General Thompson was close friends with Admiral Huntington and trusted him with her safety. Occasionally she got calls like this one; it always meant there was some imminent threat that the teams had been called in for suddenly. But as she entered the two story, nondescript stucco building she was surprised by the number of people who filled the briefing room. *I don't even recognize most of them*, she realized a bit surprise. Scanning the room for a familiar face, she spotted Chief Nguyen looking at a map in one corner of the large room. She maneuvered over to him and looked over his shoulder. It was not a map as she expected, but a diagram of a submarine.

"Hey, what's going on?" Julie asked by way of a greeting.

"One of India's nuclear-powered subs has gone down off their coast," Chief Nguyen answered, startled out of his examination of the schematic.

At that moment Julie heard Matt's voice calling to them from across the room. "Julie, Chief, in here." His voice carried easily over the din of chatter. As Julie and Chief Nguyen entered the smaller conference room, they heard Admiral Huntington speaking just to SEAL Team 3. "We've made contact with the captain and received more details about how the Arihant class sub went down. It appears to have been a structural failure amidships, on the port side. Luckily it isn't in very deep water and they can confirm that most of the crew in the fore section of the boat was able to get to safe areas. They've been able to seal the bulkheads. Unfortunately, there is no way to know exactly how many survivors there might be in the other areas of the boat. The Indian Prime Minister has formally asked the international community to help wherever possible."

"Sir, I don't understand," Lieutenant Cooper interrupted. "This looks like a standard deep sea rescue mission. Why were we called in?"

"The Arihant was India's first nuclear powered sub and a real international political event. Several US Senators and International Diplomats were on a junket visiting India and are aboard the sub," the admiral explained. "The president has personally requested that Jade extract the Senators and the other international diplomats stranded on the disabled sub. We know they're with the survivors near the bridge. We've let them know you will be arriving soon."

Julie nodded in acknowledgment. "I'll need all of their pictures."

"We already anticipated your request," the admiral said as he handed a folder to Julie.

"I don't understand; there are only six pictures here. Where are the pictures of the sub's crew?"

"Your priority is the diplomats. The sub rescue team," and he motioned to the other room, "will work out a plan to rescue the trapped sailors." With that he turned away to brief the staff in the next room.

Most of SEAL Team 3 clumped together with Julie near a diagram of the Arihant. Lieutenant Cooper came to join them. "All right, you heard the admiral, what're our options?"

"I'll need a few minutes to pinpoint the diplomats and their condition," Julie stated. They all waited quietly while she marked the diagram with the numbers she had assigned to each photo. They had seen her do this many times before as they prepared for a rescue mission. There were two U.S senators, two British members of parliament, and two Indian government officials.

"I can't sense any water, actually the door is open

and the passageway is clear too," Julie reported with a puzzled look on her face.

L.T nodded. "That's what we had hoped. They're pretty far from the bulkhead that failed, so they had plenty of time," Lieutenant Cooper explained. "Alright, Burke secure the door. Miller, you're going in with Jade to assess any injuries they might have. Evac them in order of need. Julie get your disguise on. Do you have enough room to work?" Lieutenant Cooper asked. Each of them nodded in turn, and set to work getting ready.

A few minutes later they were ready. Julie had suited up as Jade in her usual combat uniform with her mask and gloves. Matt and Chief Nguyen were standing guard outside the door. The rest of the team had cleared the few pieces of furniture to the edges of the room. Julie took position just behind and to the right of Doc and put her left hand on his shoulder. This was her usual spot in a deployment. It would allow her to keep in contact with up to two team members while freeing up their arms to react to any threats on their arrival.

"Ready?" Julie asked. Doc nodded and she subconsciously held her breath as she zapped them to the disabled sub.

The officer's galley was a very small compartment so Julie had decided to zap them to the passageway just outside. Their arrival was greeted by shouts of surprise and excited cheers. Word spread quickly and soon the passage was filled with smiling sailors vying for a chance to see them. She tried counting how many sailors needed to be rescued, but lost count as they jostled each other in the narrow confines. Julie knew there were many others out of sight, but her attention was drawn back to Doc as he was formally greeted by one of the senators.

"Senator Torres, I'm Petty Officer Miller and this is Jade," Doc introduced her. "We are here to evacuate you and the other diplomats. But first, is anyone injured?"

"It is good to see you, Petty Officer Miller. No, none

of us is injured," the man answered, and then his attention turned to Jade. "You are a sight for sore eyes, Miss. It is a pleasure to finally meet you, even under these circumstances. Thank you for your assistance today."

The senator stood almost six foot tall, and he seemed to stoop under the low ceiling of the corridor. His short black hair showed signs of having once been well groomed, but now stuck out at odd angles, and his dark eyes seemed sunken from the stress of several hours stranded hundreds of feet under water.

"Glad to be of help, sir," Julie said in return, looking down self-consciously in acknowledgment of the compliment, her mask hiding her flush of embarrassment. She was saved from having to think of what else to say by the appearance of a short man dressed in a tan uniform.

"I am Captain Bhattacharya. Thank you so much for your assistance," the captain said in very clear English with a bit of a British accent. It only took a short time for Doc to evaluate the diplomats and for Julie to take them out in pairs. The whole thing was uneventful. As she arrived with each set of diplomats, EMT's would usher them onto gurneys and whisk them out to waiting ambulances for further evaluation. Before she left to retrieve Doc, Lieutenant Cooper brought a strange cylindrical device over to her.

"Take this to the sub," Lieutenant Cooper instructed her.

"What is it?" Julie asked.

"It's a carbon dioxide scrubber," he explained. "It'll help keep their air breathable while they wait for the rescue sub.

"Thanks LT," Julie replied before she focused on Doc. When she got there she took a moment to look at the sailors who had gathered to watch her work. *It's like I'm a huge celebrity,* she thought and they were excited to catch a glimpse of her. *I don't want to leave them here.*

Doc followed her gaze and seemed to sense her

feelings. "You wouldn't be able to take all of them anyway. There're way too many; you'd hurt yourself trying," he reminded her gently. When he saw that it did not seem to help, he added, "Don't worry, I overheard the captain. The rescue sub is less than an hour away and they have access to one of the ports. They'll all be out of here soon, and thanks to that carbon dioxide scrubber they'll be comfortable while they wait."

Julie nodded. She knew she could not have zapped them all back, but she still felt bad. "Let's go," she turned away as she said it, not wanting to see their faces any longer.

CHAPTER 23

An hour after the diplomats had left for the hospital, the rescue sub was in the process of retrieving the stranded sailors she had seen, but there were sections of the ship that they could not reach. Everyone in the briefing room was searching for a way to find the sailors who were still unaccounted for.

Julie had changed back into her regular uniform, so she would not attract attention. SEAL Team 3 was gathered once more around the diagram of the sub in the main meeting room. Julie turned away from the discussion. *I can't help them*, she thought. *I don't have the training*. So she headed around the room until she came to the admiral. She waited at a distance for him to finish talking to one of his aides. When he was done, she caught his eye. "Sir, can I have a moment?" she asked.

"Yes, Ensign?" the admiral waved a few of his waiting aides away to give them privacy. "You did a great job today. You can head home if you want."

"No, Sir, that's not it. I think I can help. I was wondering if I could get pictures of the missing crew," Julie asked. She was not sure what she would be able to do, but she had to try.

"I'm not sure I want to risk you like that, but if you can come up with safe options I'll consider it," the admiral mused. "Ensign Flores, contact the Indian liaison to request pictures of any crew that haven't been accounted for and give them to Ensign Patterson here. Tell them it is for identification purposes once we enter the ship."

"Thank you, sir," Julie said then followed the aide. Soon she was studying the first pictures to arrive off of the fax. She chose one picture of a sailor to start with because of his distinctive features. She concentrated on his narrow face, and his strangely crooked nose. *He must have broken it a few times*, was Julie's fleeting thought. She gave up when all she could sense was blackness, there wasn't even a flicker like she would sense if a person was at the limits of her perception. With a feeling of dread she chose another picture. This sailor had surprisingly green eyes. From his looks he could not have been much older than Julie herself. Again she concentrated. Again she saw only blackness and was about to give up when she sensed the flicker of light. She gasped, and opened her eyes. She needed to concentrate harder; *the Team needs to know more than just that they were alive*. Looking for a quiet area to sit, she went into the smaller meeting room. The furniture was still pushed to the side and the lights were off. Not bothering to turn the lights on, Julie sat on the floor and closed her eyes again and concentrated on the image of the young sailor. She found the spark again and followed it. With effort she was able to get a sense of his surroundings. Satisfied that she could provide the team with important information, she headed back out to the group.

"There is a group of sailors right here," Julie abruptly interrupted the team's speculation. Pointing to the diagram, she indicated a room midway down the length of the sub. "There are seven men there. I want to try to zap them out," she added the last part in a softer voice, not looking forward to their reactions.

Everyone stared at her in disbelief. "Are you crazy!?" "No way, you need more clearance!" "It's too dangerous!" "There's no telling what the conditions are like in there!" were only some of the shocked retorts.

"No, really. I think I can do this. You've got to let me at least try! They could be dead before we can get to them any other way," Julie implored. She got mixed reactions from them this time, several were still shaking their heads, but she could see a couple considering the option. She turned to the Lieutenant Cooper.

"Are those the only survivors?" Lieutenant Cooper asked.

"I don't know. They were the first ones I found."

"Wait, I thought you didn't want to zap into an area where there might be stuff in the way. Right?" Matt brought up the best argument he could think of.

"Yeah, I know.... What if I try to zap in above the water?" Julie suggested as she looked back to Lieutenant Cooper.

"All right. Figure out who is alive and where, and then tell me which ones you have enough room to SAFELY get yourself and one other person in."

"One other person! That will make it so much harder!" Julie objected.

"There is no way we're sending you in there alone. What if they overwhelm you in their panic while you're trying to save them?" he countered. The look on Lieutenant Cooper's face indicated Julie had better not try to argue again. He had made a good point. The memory of being overwhelmed by captives in a plane hijacking flashed through her thoughts. Julie nodded in understanding. "Let's take this to a private room. We'll attract too much attention if we do this here. Julie, go get the rest of the pictures and meet us there."

An hour and a massive headache later, Julie had finished marking the diagram to indicate where the survivors were throughout the sub. Thankfully, there were more sailors alive than anybody had hoped possible. They were clumped in three areas. The team was now surrounding the diagram with their heads bent, studying their options. Julie had also marked which areas she would have enough room to zap into and where she was not sure. There was only one compartment where the water level was high enough that she was worried, and there were several men trapped there. Admiral Huntington had decided that they would rescue the sailors in order based on the compartments that were the safest and that had the most men first.

"It's more important to save as many as possible before your strength run's out," the admiral pointed out. "They'll go fairly easily. If you pass out, any sailor still trapped will die."

While they planned, Julie changed back into her disguise, and then sat in a chair off to one side to rest. She sat with her eyes closed, rubbing her temples, willing her headache to pass.

She felt a light tap on her shoulder and opened her eyes. It was Doc holding a couple candy bars. "You'll need these. Eat a couple now to get powered up."

"Thanks," Julie said as she took the proffered candy bars and dutifully opened the first one. "I was thinking," Julie started, still chewing her first bite. She swallowed and continued. "We'll need a place that won't be damaged by large quantities of water." While she had been resting she had been thinking about the training they had done a few months back. They had practiced teleporting out of water. It had been a real mess the first time because of all the water she had brought back with them.

"We're already working on that," he assured her. "How's your head?"

"Better, this is helping. Thanks... I'll be ready when you are."

Doc nodded and headed back to the others.

They ended up moving into an empty warehouse,

down next to the dry docks. No one would see them; there was plenty of room, and water would not be an issue. Several of the Team's support staff had also joined them to help with any gear they might need. Lieutenant Cooper had selected Chief Nguyen to go with Jade. They were geared up in dry suits, masks and SCUBA gear just in case they ran into trouble. Lieutenant Cooper brought in a large duffel bag as they were gearing up.

"What's that?" Julie asked.

"Individual carbon dioxide scrubbers, enough for all of them," Lieutenant Cooper told her. "They'll help sustain those sailors while you're working."

Julie had never SCUBA dived before so Matt gave her a quick orientation to the gear. "The most important thing to remember is not to panic. Chief will help you if anything goes wrong. Just don't panic and make sure you don't let the regulator fall out of your mouth when the cold water hits you," he said sternly. That last comment made the butterflies in Julie's stomach speed up.

"Yeah, yeah, I know," she tried to seem nonchalant as she answered him. But Matt gave her a squeeze on her shoulder to reassure her anyway.

Chief Nguyen and Julie took their positions. Right before she zapped them, Julie checked on the water level in the compartment. *It's not any deeper*, she thought relieved. "Ready?" she asked, and with the chief's nod, she zapped them to the first group of trapped sailors.

In the damaged submarine sailors clung to pipes that ran along the ceiling of the galley for balance. The water was freezing cold and they had climbed onto the galley tables to get out of it. In the pale blue of the emergency lighting Aseem looked from one face to the next. Panic and terror were the most common emotions which met his gaze, but some already registered resignation and defeat. They had fought hard to save as many lives as they could when the sub had suddenly started taking on water. There were twenty men in this compartment alone, and they hoped there were others. But they all knew that they still faced the very real possibility of death. Aseem noticed one man had found a piece of Styrofoam plate and was struggling to find the words to write to his family.

Suddenly, there was a gust of wind in their terrible gloom, and a large splash of water. Aseem thought for a moment that it was another hull breach and braced for the water to hit him. But after a second he opened his eyes. In the near darkness he could make out two forms struggling to get out of the water onto an empty table. *How did they get in here*, Aseem looked at the sealed hatch and then back to the two people. They had climbed onto a table and removed their mouth pieces. One of them had hauled a large duffel bag out of the water and was activating a light.

Julie stiffened in fear as they plunged into the waist deep, icy water. She had brought them in a few feet up to clear the water level. Her teeth were locked around the regulator, so she did not lose it. She struggled to stand up in the waist deep water under the weight of the SCUBA tank. Chief Nguyen half pushed, half lifted her onto what appeared to be a table. *It's not as full of water as I feared*, Julie thought when they had arrived.

Chief Nguyen brought out a light stick and snapped it to activate the chemicals. Julie looked around in the gloom as she lowered her mask to cover her mouth again. The chemical light stick threw eerie yellow light that barely reached into the dark corners of the room, a mess hall, just as their diagram had indicated. The men had all climbed out onto the tables to stay out of the freezing water, just like she and Chief Nguyen. She studied their faces for their reaction. She had known that there were going to be twenty men, but seeing their shocked and terrified faces made her doubt her powers. *How am I going to get them all out in time?*

The sound of the chief's voice distracted her from her worries. She watched their faces, to gauge their emotions, ready to act if needed. They had planned before they left that if the men were panicked beyond reason and tried to mob them she was to zap them both out quickly. If that happened they would have to find some other way. Looking at them she realized that most of them had gone past panic to a kind of resignation to their fate. One in particular had not even raised his head at their arrival. Chief Nguyen asked a question in Hindi and paused. A moment later one of the sailors answered, "Yes, most of us speak English, but I can translate for the others. My name is Aseem."

"I'm Chief Nguyen, with the US Navy. I appreciate your help; that was about all the Hindi I know. If you can translate, it will go faster," the chief explained. He turned to the crewmen, "This," now he motioned to Julie, "is Jade." Julie waved shyly. "You've probably heard about her powers. We have a plan to get all of you out, but it will take almost an hour, so please stay calm."

Aseem translated for the few sailors that might not understand as Chief Nguyen spoke. A couple of sailors seemed to recognize Jade's name and were actively trying to encourage the most withdrawn of their shipmates.

Chief Nguyen continued, "Jade will take two of you at a time. I will stay here until the last two are retrieved. There may be times when it takes her a few minutes longer to come back. She will come back, so don't panic," he reassured them. Julie was nodding her head to agree with his last statement.

Julie thought about Chief Nguyen's last sentence as Aseem translated. The team had insisted that Julie only transport two sailors every five minutes. This would hopefully give her body a chance to recover some between jumps. She would not be any help to the rest of the trapped sailors if she passed out from exhaustion before she was done. Doc already had a case of Snickers and a twelve pack of Mountain Dew waiting for her back in the warehouse. *But what if it isn't enough? What if I blackout and leave them, even Chief Nguyen?* She shook off her doubt, it was time to get to work. *I'll just have to make sure that doesn't happen.*

"Try to group yourselves in pairs on the tables. That will make it easier and faster for her to get you. Don't be scared, you'll be in sunny San Diego soon. I've brought personal carbon dioxide scrubbers for you to use while we wait."

Julie waited for nods of understanding as Aseem finished translating. He had volunteered to be one of the last ones out so he could continue to help. Quickly the men tried to organize themselves. As soon as she saw two men standing next to each other she started. She zapped herself behind them on their table, then grabbing onto their shoulders, instantly zapped them to the warehouse. Medical personnel immediately moved in to evaluate them. As they were ushered away, Julie saw Matt and Doc standing next to a privacy curtain. She headed over to them. Matt already had one candy bar open and Doc checked his watch for the time.

"So what were the conditions down there?" Matt asked impatiently. She could tell the inaction was torturing him.

"It's Okay," she said after she finished the first mouthful of Snickers. "They're all standing on tables to stay out of the water. They didn't give us any trouble. I think they had already mostly given up on getting out alive." Julie finished her candy bar, "Okay, I'm ready."

"Oh no you're not, you've got two more minutes. Sit down," Doc ordered and pointed deliberately at a chair next to him.

Julie rolled her eyes with a hidden smirk but obediently sat in the chair. "Where's the foot stool? Then I'd be really comfy," she said with an impudent grin.

"If you pull this off without collapsing, I'll serve you drinks in a hammock for two days," Matt joked back, half seriously. He knew realistically that she probably would not be able to save over half of the sailors before she wore herself out. Matt noticed one of their support crew nearby, "Hey Corporal Campbell, can you go find Jade a foot rest?"

"Of course, Petty Officer Burke," the seaman responded dutifully, but Julie noticed the man's look of hatred as he glanced at them. *I wonder what that's all about.* Julie thought, but she was soon distracted from her worries by Doc.

"I'll bet she doesn't even make it to the end before she passes out," Doc agreed just to goad her.

"Well, you better start the blender because I'll be done by lunch," Julie said more confidently than she felt as she leaned back and closed her eyes to rest. She had found a total of fifty men still alive. These first twenty were in the easiest compartment because of its size. *Who know's what we'll find in the next compartments*.

"Okay, you're free to go," Doc said, intruding on her thoughts. Julie opened her eyes. "Take care," he added as she prepared to leave.

The next eighteen men went uneventfully. She brought Chief Nguyen back with the last two sailors, one of whom was Aseem. She sank into the now familiar chair, and found that someone had positioned a crate for her to use as a footrest. She smiled as she put her feet up with a sigh. She was already feeling the effects of zapping so many times, *but I'm not as tired as I expected to be at this point.*

Lieutenant Cooper and Chief Nguyen joined Matt, Simmons, Doc and Julie at her improvised lounge. "All right, we've studied your next compartment," Lieutenant Cooper said as he laid the sub's schematic on the table next to them and pointed to one set of Julie's notes. "This one is smaller than the mess hall, but it's farther from the hull breach so it should have less water."

Naveen was shivering badly. He and the other crewmen were huddled together for warmth, but the water level was up to their waists. There were seven of them total, including himself, in the engine room. They had waited as long as they could before they had closed the hatch. Still they knew they had locked out at least one of their shipmates to die. Naveen was starting to think he had been the lucky one dying quickly instead of slowly in this cold hell.

CHAPTER 24

Julie used her pictures to check on the sailors in their next compartment. Lieutenant Cooper was right… it would be tight but they seemed in good shape, all things considered. There were twenty-three sailors in this one. From the diagram it was a large sleeping compartment. What made it tight was there was only a narrow aisle between the bunks which were stacked three high. The sailors were spread out around the room so Lieutenant Cooper instructed her to zap into one end. That way Chief Nguyen would have a better defensive position if things went wrong. It had been over an hour since they had started the rescue mission, and ten minutes since they had brought the last set. Julie wanted to keep going. "I'm ready when you are," she said to Chief Nguyen.

"How are you feeling?" Doc checked her heart rate.

"I'm fine, they need out. Let's get moving," she said impatiently. Her impatience was growing because she had checked on the third group of sailors. Captain Lewis was joining them to check on their progress and she couldn't help asking. "Has anyone figured out how we'll get to them?" she pointed at the third group of numbers on the schematic that indicated the survivors she was worried about. Their condition had haunted her since she had first found the survivors trapped there.

"We're working on it. You just focus on your current mission. There are twenty-three men that need you first," Captain Lewis reminded her.

Julie nodded; she knew the engineers were trying to find a way to save those last seven men trapped in the engine room. She trusted that they would think of a way. She shifted her attention back to the twenty-three men waiting, without knowing they had any hope for survival.

Chief Nguyen finished checking his gear. "Ready."

Like the last room, Julie knew there was water covering the floor. So she concentrated on arriving above the water level. There was less than a foot of water so they did not need to wear their SCUBA gear and arrived with a splash as they dropped the last few inches. The first thing she noticed when they got there was that there was more light in this compartment. The emergency lights and flashlights the crew had, gave the compartment an eerie twilight effect.

This time when they arrived there was a bigger commotion. Several men jumped down from the upper bunks to confront them. Chief Nguyen took a defensive position in front of Julie with his weapon at the ready. He quickly explained who they were and their plan to get them out and the sailors began to relax and smile.

As he spoke he had also been lowering his weapon as tensions eased. Now he slung the M4 over his back as the men started pairing up. Julie walked up to the closest pair and offered them her hands. After that it went just like the first set of sailors.

Doc's plan of making Julie wait five minutes between each trip was working. She was nearly done with this second group when she realized she had been zapping for over two hours straight and she was not too tired yet. Julie was currently lounging at her now very familiar snack station, watching the group of rescued sailors. A couple of the sailors who had been rescued first were now helping the newest arrivals. She saw Matt and Aseem talking with a group of them. They were gesturing toward Julie so she knew they were talking about her. Matt saw her watching them and brought Aseem with him as he came to join her.

Julie went to stand up as they got closer, and Matt motioned her to sit back down. "I've been talking with the sailors. It's really interesting. They say every time you arrived they felt a gust of wind," Matt said, turning to Aseem for confirmation.

"It's true Jade," Aseem said with a thick accent. "The air smelled different too, like this place." He waved his hand at the warehouse.

"What do you think it means?" Julie asked.

"We think it means that not only do you take the air around you, you must also displace the air where you are arriving."

Julie nodded already considering the implications. "That's really interesting, especially if I am pushing the other air away. That might really be important for the last compartment," she agreed distracted. Julie had already thought of a few options. The trick would be getting proof so she could convince the admiral.

"What do you mean?" Matt asked suspiciously. He did not trust that look in her eyes.

"I'm not sure yet. I'll have to think about it. But it's time for me to get back to work," she said quickly. Before Matt could question her further, she had gone for the next pair of sailors.

"She's planning something, I just know it," Matt said to himself, but Aseem overheard.

"She wouldn't do anything that might get herself hurt, would she?"

Matt looked at him with a weak smile. "You don't know her very well…I've got to speak to LT."

Julie went through the next few rescues on autopilot. Her thoughts kept examining all of the possibilities if she was pushing the air. Several questions came to her. *What about pushing the water out of the way? Could I push a solid object? I don't think I want to try that*, she realized but she did want to try it with water. Her decision made, she deliberately aimed to arrive in the water on her next jump. As she zapped she watched her feet. Sure enough when she arrived in the crew quarters the floor was dry for a moment before the water came washing back around her.

"What was that?" Chief Nguyen asked, noticing the wave.

"Did you see that?" Julie asked in return. "I pushed the water away from my feet!"

"What are you talking about? I didn't see anything except a wave hitting us," Chief Nguyen told her.

"Next time watch my feet, and tell me what you see," she instructed him. Julie was excited as she went to the next two sailors. She could not wait to try that again. Before Chief Nguyen could answer, she was already gone.

Julie waited impatiently for the five minutes to pass. She was tempted to pace, but she knew that would make Matt suspicious. There was only one group of men left to rescue from the crew quarters. *I only have this last trip to test my idea.*

Finally it was time to zap and she stared at her feet as she went. "Yes!" Julie exclaimed as she saw the water washing back over her feet. Looking up at Chief Nguyen, "Did you see it that time? The water wasn't around my feet when I arrived."

"Yeah, that's what it looked like. But what does it mean?"

"It means that we can save the last group!" Julie gave Chief Nguyen a big hug in her excitement. "Quick, there's no time to waste." With that she grabbed hold of Chief Nguyen and the last sailor, zapping them out without further comment.

As they gathered in the warehouse, the team debated their next steps. Chief Nguyen was explaining "The space is fairly large. The problem is we think the water level is over three feet deep. There's no way for us to zap in above it."

"What if we were sitting down when we zapped?" Julie piped in.

"Yeah that might work," Chief Nguyen agreed.

"Jade, have you checked on them recently? Can you tell if the water level is rising?" Lieutenant Cooper wanted to double check.

"Hang on." Julie concentrated on one of the sailors in the engine room. Before, she had established the water level by sensing the feeling of cold on their bodies. Then it had been up to their waists, but now it was closer to their shoulders. Leaving contact with the sailors, she focused on the team. "It's gotten worse."

CHAPTER 25

Naveen was still conscious, but just barely. Already a few others had succumbed to the cold and were being held up by shipmates who were still standing. "Saresh! Stay awake!" Naveen said to jar the other man back from the edge of hypothermia. He looked over at the pipes running the length of the engine room. The leak had not grown any bigger, but the steady spray of water was slowly filling their tomb.

"Then there's no way," Chief Nguyen said shaking his head. "If the water level is up to their shoulders, that means there's only a couple feet of clearance above the water. That's not enough room."

"I can do it," Julie argued. "The water will get pushed away; we'll be fine."

"That MIGHT have worked in only a couple inches of water, but with the increased pressure of five feet of water it MIGHT NOT," Matt said, skeptical that she had just imagined the water moving in her previous experiments.

"We'll try it some time when you're fully rested," a

deep voice cut off their argument from behind them. "You won't be zapping into the water for this mission," Admiral Huntington said. "I want to try another way. Can you zap while lying down? And stay flat?"

"Sure, that's no problem," Julie answered, understanding his plan.

"Miller, check her out. Report back to me when you're done. I want to know if she is in any condition to try to bring nine people back in one trip," the admiral instructed him, then turned his attention back to Julie. "My plan is for you to zap yourself and Chief in from a prone position, wearing full SCUBA gear. Get those seven sailors together quickly and get all of you back in one trip. But I don't want you to try this if you are not ABSOLUTELY sure you're ready. You will be of no help to anyone if you are too weak to get everyone back safely."

Julie was on a cot Doc had forced her to lie on. The rest of the team stood around waiting for him and the other medics to finish. She felt a bit silly with all of them towering above her. They had hooked her up to various contraptions to test her blood oxygen levels, her blood pressure and her heart rate. There was only one test left and Doc was bringing it over.

"Ugh, I hate that thing," Julie said with disgust. She looked at the blood glucose monitor in disdain. "I jump every time you stick me," Julie said, whining more than she meant to and she realized she must really be getting tired.

Doc ignored her grumbling, and sat down next to her cot. "Dr. Emory thinks this can give us an idea of how run down you are," Doc reminded her. "Which finger do you want me to use?" he asked, a sadistic grin turned up the corners of his mouth.

Julie could not resist giving him her middle finger. Doc ignored that too as he quickly jabbed her finger to get blood. Julie jumped as she always did. He dabbed the blood up with the test strip and inserted it into the device. Julie tried to look over his shoulder to see the display. The glucose monitor chirped and Doc looked up at Admiral Huntington. "All her levels are in the normal range, but she's got to be tired," Doc reported.

The admiral turned to Julie. "I don't want two of my team stranded down in that sub. Tell me honestly, can you do it?"

Julie took a deep breath. Now serious, she considered how she felt. She was definitely tired, she felt like she could have taken a nap right then. Then she thought of those seven men freezing to death in that cold dark sub. She let out her breath, "Yes, sir, I can do it."

It took Chief Nguyen and her only a few minutes to suit up in their dry suits and SCUBA gear. This time he snapped a chemical light stick before they zapped and secured it to his BC. Because of the tanks, it was decided that they would lay face down when they zapped. Matt doubled checked all of her gear, while Chief Nguyen finished checking his own. "The water down there will be freezing cold, the shock of it might make you scream or open your mouth to gasp, so concentrate on keeping your lips tightly clamped around the regulator. Just breathe steadily and stay calm. Remember, Chief Nguyen will help you," Matt reminded her.

It was impossible to speak with the regulator in her mouth, so she gave Matt a thumbs up and turned to look at Chief Nguyen as he settled down next to her. This time he held onto her elbow so he would already have a good hold on her to help her when they arrived. When he gave her a thumbs up, she zapped them into total darkness.

They hit the water the moment after they arrived. The cold water stung the exposed skin of Julie's face and hands. She clenched her teeth, and took a breath, using all of her will power to keep from panicking. She felt herself being lifted upright by her arm and she tried to help Chief Nguyen. Once they both had their heads out of the water, he held up the chemical light stick and the greenish yellow light reached the sailors.

Julie nearly cried out at the sight of the sailors. Only three of them were still standing, clinging desperately to each other and the four sailors who had succumbed to the cold. She half swam, half walked over to the men. Chief Nguyen helped her maneuver through the water in the bulky equipment. They were squinting from the light and barely seemed able to focus. The Chief was talking to them as they approached, explaining that they were here to help. *I don't care if they panic or not*, she thought planning on zapping them out as soon as she got to them. Julie needed to take as little water with them as possible. She was already at her limit and any extra weight would tire her out even more. There was no time to lose; Julie grabbed the nearest man, concentrated on her link to them all. Making sure she had everyone, she zapped them home.

Matt kept looking at his watch. It seemed like it had been an eternity, but his watch said it had only been two minutes when a pile of limp bodies arrived, heralded by a wave of water spreading across the warehouse floor. Matt rushed forward with Doc and the medics. He saw Chief Nguyen struggling to free himself from the tangle of bodies as he tried to support Julie's limp weight. Matt grabbed Julie's other arm and the two of them dragged her back from the rescued crewmen. Doc removed her SCUBA gear while they supported her, then they lowered her onto the same cot she had just recently used.

Doc checked her pulse and respiration first, then her blood sugar. Matt waited impatiently.

"What's her condition?" Admiral Huntington asked.

"I think she's just exhausted. All of her levels are low, but not too bad. She probably won't wake up for a while," Doc reported.

Ten minutes later an ambulance crew rolled in a

gurney. Matt watched as they lifted Julie's still body. Doc gave them specific instructions. Matt told himself that she would be fine, he always worried when she overextended herself like this and debated joining her in the ambulance.

"Burke!" Matt heard his lieutenant summoning him to the debriefing. He knew from their uniforms that this was a specially designated medical response team that had authorization to care for Jade. *I'll have to catch up with her later*, he thought sighing. As he joined his team, he glanced over his shoulder and saw the medics rolling her gurney out the door.

CHAPTER 26

The debriefing was fairly short compared to a usual one, since most of the team had not been actively involved in the mission. Matt waited impatiently, watching the clock, anxious to check with the medical team on Julie's condition. It had already been half an hour, and they should have had time to assess her condition fully. At that moment one of the admiral's aides came into the debriefing room. *That's unusual*, Matt thought. He and Doc exchanged puzzled looks, and then turned back to Admiral Huntington.

Admiral Huntington's face turned grave. "Jade never reached the hospital and the ambulance can't be found," he said in explanation to their curious gazes. "Simmons, do you still have a tracking device on her?" Simmons gave a nod. "Then call it up; we need to find her."

Simmons headed toward the team's gear to get the tracking device he always kept handy. Next the admiral turned to Lieutenant Cooper, "Get your team ready. We may not be able to help, but I want them ready."

Matt cursed under his breath. He knew it was unlikely they would see action, and he felt helpless knowing it would be up to the FBI and local law enforcement's responsibility to get her back. Unless she was out of the country they would have no authorization to take out her kidnappers. He cursed again, and waited for Simmons to locate her signal. Since the last attempt on Jade they had increased the range, and changed the frequency on her transmitter. It only took a moment for Simmons to get a lock on her position. Surprisingly she was off the coast, headed to international waters. *What are the odds?* Matt thought as they prepped the helicopters. *There are so many other ways to transport a captive and anyone in the spy business would know the SEAL teams would be the most likely asset to handle a situation at sea.* He adjusted his gear as he continued to get ready. *It could be a trap,* he thought a moment later, but he also knew that there was no other option but to go after her.

While the team got ready Admiral Huntington had ordered a Poseidon reconnaissance plane to locate her. Matt was surprised when he heard what type of ship she was on. Unlike last time, she was being held on a commercial fishing boat.

We'll only need one squad to cover the whole ship, he thought. *Any more than that and we'll get in each other's way.* They might even get caught in friendly cross fire. The biggest disadvantage of a small ship was there would be no way to conceal their arrival if they used a helicopter. Instead they would need to use a high speed intercept ship to catch up with them and then approach the ship silently after dark in a combat rubber raiding craft.

Matt checked his watch; it had been nearly four hours since Jade's abduction. Before they had left the base, the MPs had reported finding the ambulance. It had been in a warehouse close to where the Team had been working to rescue the sub crew.

She'd practically been taken out from under our noses. Matt ground his teeth at the thought.

One of the ambulance medics had been found dead with a bullet wound to the back of the head. San Diego police officers had gone to search the other medic's apartment, where they found the second medic dead, also killed by a gunshot wound to the head. He had been killed several hours before the abduction happened. That meant that whoever had abducted Jade had known about their operation and had been ready to strike the moment Jade was to be transported.

Someone on our team's been spying on us. The thought made Matt cold with fury. He pushed the emotions down. He would deal with the traitor later; right now he needed to focus on getting Julie back.

The team transferred onto the nearly silent raiding craft once they were close enough to the fishing vessel. It was now completely dark and they should be able to overtake the small ship and board it without detection. Matt's eyes strained to see every detail of the ship using his night vision goggles as they approached. No one was on deck or in the pilot's cabin above. *That's odd*, he thought, searching again for any signs of concealed gunmen.

Chief Nguyen piloted the zodiac up alongside the port side of the ship. The raiding craft was several feet lower than the fishing ship and Simmons had to pull himself up over the railing before he dropped in a defensive crouch as he scanned the deck. Behind him, Matt followed him over the rail. Simmons and Matt moved off to a spot where they could watch the deck and cover the rest of the team as they boarded. There was no resistance as the team assembled on the deck and prepared to search the ship.

Lieutenant Cooper looked at Simmons, who had been watching his tracker. Simmons pointed toward the hold of the ship. The team moved forward, spreading out to cover the area better. They approached the edge of the dark hole that marked the cargo hold. Like most fishing vessels the hold was meant to hold large quantities of ice and fish.

This one was empty except for Julie, who was tied up, lying limply in a few inches of water. Her mask had been removed but otherwise she seemed untouched. From the edge of the hatch, the only way to see the walls of the hold was to hang slightly over the edge. Doc held Matt's legs as he lowered his upper body over to search the hold, his MP7 held at the ready with the beam of its light searching into the darkness below.

"All clear," he reported as they pulled him up.

"This doesn't make sense," Lieutenant Cooper stated, looking around, considering the possibilities. "Where are the bastards? All right, let's…" but he was unable to finish his order as the Team was hit by a burst of sound.

Matt felt like his head was going to explode as he dropped to the deck in pain and confusion. In the last moment he had of consciousness he saw other members of the team lying next to him. Then everything went dark.

CHAPTER 27

Matt startled awake. His arms hurt and he realized he had been hanging from handcuffs attached to a wall. He got his legs under him and took the weight of his body off his wrists as he looked around. The other members of his team were hanging from their wrists from smooth, white plastic walls. *We're in the cargo hold*, he realized, recognizing his surroundings. The men were spaced along the wall about every eight feet. Julie still lay in the center of the hold, motionless. All of their gear had been stripped off, including their communication headsets.

"LT! Demetrio!" Matt called urgently to the nearest of his team. "LT!" Matt called a little louder. Lieutenant Cooper's head started to lift in response. As he raised his head Matt saw dried blood coming out of his left ear.

Matt looked around the hold again and saw a few of the others waking up. All had dried blood coming either from their noses or ears. *What hit us? How long were we out?* Matt wondered.

"Ah, you're awake. I was worried you wouldn't wake up in time. I hope I didn't hurt you too badly with my new toy," a voice tinged with sickly sweet sarcasm sounded from above them. The man was out of sight from Matt, but he thought he recognized the voice. Lieutenant Cooper was straining to see him from his position.

"Smith, you bastard! What did you do to us?" Lieutenant Cooper yelled at the figure above.

"Oh, I just used one of the research boys' newest toys. It's called a Sonic Enforcement Device or S.E.D for short. It's meant to blast crowds of rioters or attackers with a sonic wave that normally knocks them out for a few moments with no side effects. Today I turned it up to full blast just to see what would happen. You've been out for a good forty minutes," he said cheerily. Matt could tell Smith was enjoying their helplessness.

"Why are you doing this?" Lieutenant Cooper demanded.

"I'm protecting my country!" Smith snarled as his anger flared. He paused, gaining control of his temper. When he spoke again it was in a conversational tone. "I swore to protect my country, even if my country doesn't know it's in danger."

"What are you talking about? What danger? Jade? She's more than proved her loyalty to the county," Lieutenant Cooper said trying to reason with Smith. Matt knew he was also trying to buy time. Smith was a loon, but if the lieutenant had enough time, he might trick Smith into making a mistake. They needed a chance to come up with options.

"Her very existence threatens our country! Even the most loyal, trained spy can be turned with torture or coercion. You know that, but still you protected her. You, all of you, were given commendations for your work with her," he said in disbelief. Smith started walking around the edge of the hatch, coming into Matt's view. He was still dressed in the medic uniform, but now he held one of their MP7s, which he aimed at each of them in turn. His gaze fell on Matt. "And you! You LOVE her!" His voice was filled with disgust and spittle flecked his lips. His gaze went back to the lieutenant. "You think you can control her, you think she'll always follow your orders. Ha! She'll get bored with playing soldier and then she'll start rebelling. You won't even know it until it is too late." he said as he continued walking around the opening of the hold. He came to a control panel. "But I plan to put an end to this stupidity. I'll stop her now before she can hurt anyone. I just wish General Thompson was here too. Ah well, I still have time to kill him. There's no rush," he said dismissively. With that he pushed a few buttons and water began pouring into the hold. "It's a shame she won't know who stopped her, but it's probably better this way," Smith said to no one in particular, then turned his back and walked out of sight.

The team waited a few moments to see if Smith would come back to watch them die. Lieutenant Cooper was the first to say anything. "Can anyone free themselves?" he asked. The question set each of the men to action trying to break loose.

Matt turned to brace his feet on the wall and grabbed the chains of his hand cuffs. He pushed with his legs trying to break the links, but it was no use. Next, he tried to wiggle his hands loose from the cuffs, straining to pull them off. Blood welled from scrapes around his wrist. He looked down at the rising water. It was already up to his ankles. From behind him he heard sputtering, and spun around to check on Julie. The water level had reached her mouth and she had breathed in some water. "Julie! Wake up!" Matt yelled.

Julie sputtered again, and struggled to sit up. Her arms were tied behind her back and her legs were tied together making it hard for her to lever herself upright in her weakened state. She fell back into the water which was now close to covering her head. Fighting down panic, Julie rolled onto her stomach and got her knees under her. Finally clear of the water, Julie was able to take a deep breath of air. She coughed a few more times to clear her lungs of the water she had breathed in.

"Julie, can you zap us out?" Lieutenant Cooper asked hopefully.

"I... I don't know," Julie said; her voice was weak from exhaustion. "What's happening? Where are we?"

"There's no time for an explanation right now. Can you zap us back?" Lieutenant Cooper asked again.

Julie sat slumped forward, resting on her knees. She was silent for a long moment and Matt thought she might have passed out again. "Julie! Wake up!" Matt called to her trying to get her to respond.

Julie shook her head, as if trying to clear her thoughts, and looked around the hold. She spotted Matt and Lieutenant Cooper just behind her on her right. She shifted her position so she could look at them more easily. "I don't know how many times I'd be able to zap. I'm so tired," she said weakly. Again there was a long pause. "I could go get help maybe. Who should I get?"

Lieutenant Cooper shook his head. "No, there's a traitor back at base. We don't know who it is. You could end up captured again and we'd die here anyway," he explained.

The water continued to rise slowly, as they all thought about their limited options. It had reached Julie's waist as she knelt on the floor of the hold. She was so tired; it was almost all she could do not to lie back down.

"Julie, what about your Uncle Mark?" Matt had been considering her hideout and remembered that her Uncle Mark had been the one who planned it. *Hadn't she said he had served in the Marines?*

"Yeah, I... I think I could get him. I'll try," she said looking up at Matt. Hope gave Julie more energy. "I'll be back, I promise."

Julie arrived on the floor of her Uncle Mark's apartment. The water she had brought with her was spreading across his carpet. From somewhere above her she heard noises, and within moments Mark was advancing down his stairs. In one hand he held a flashlight, and in the other he held his Glock balanced over the wrist of the hand holding the flashlight. The light traveled around the room. Julie tried to call out to him, and the noise drew his light down to her form. She had fallen on her side when she had zapped in, no longer strong enough to sit up. Seeing her, Mark dropped his pistol, flipped on a light and rushed to her side. He was dressed in a black robe, but from somewhere he drew a large switchblade and started to cut the ropes holding her arms.

"What happened? Are you alright?" Mark asked as he continued to free her.

"It's a long story, Uncle Mark. We don't have much time. The team is in danger and we need your help." she explained in a whisper. "I barely have enough energy to zap one more time," she added. Julie rubbed at her aching wrists as she lay flat on her back now that her arms were free.

"How are they being held? Are there any guards?" Mark quickly tried to assess the situation.

Julie answered his questions as well as she could. It did not take long. "Rest here while I get my gear," Mark said standing up. He headed out to his garage. Julie woke with a start as he returned to her side. He was carrying a black duffel bag and had changed into a wet suit and SCUBA gear. A rifle was slung over his shoulder.

"How long was I out?" Julie asked, worried that she had slept too long and the others would be dead by the time they reached them.

Sensing her concern, Mark reassured her, "Not long, about ten minutes maybe. Are you ready?"

"Yeah, I think so. That nap helped a little."

"Can you take us to the deck of the ship just outside of the hold?"

Julie nodded in answer.

"Okay, let's go."

Matt was struggling with his handcuffs again. He had no idea how long it had been since Julie left. They all knew there was a good chance she had passed out again, but at least she should be safe. The water level was up to Matt's shoulders, he would have to start treading water soon. He knew that the odds of them escaping were getting pretty slim.

Suddenly a knotted rope was thrown into the hold and a man in a black wet suit and SCUBA gear jumped down from the deck above. He sent up a wave that swamped the team as he hit the water. Surfacing, he removed his mask and regulator. "Looks like you boys could use a hand," Mark teased.

"Hey Mark," Matt said in sudden relief.

"It's good to see you still above water," Mark said with a grin as he swam toward Matt.

"Got something for these?" Matt asked indicating his cuffs.

When Mark got close enough, he raised a pair of bolt cutters out of the water. "I think these might work," he said with a mischievous grin. Mark's bolt cutters snipped through the handcuffs easily. Next he swam toward their lieutenant. In only a few moments Mark had cut all of the team free. As each man was released, he moved to climb the rope.

Matt had gone up first. When he got to the deck he looked for Julie. He found her lying on the deck a few feet away from the edge of the hold. He checked her pulse. It was really weak, but it was there. Relieved, he looked around for anything he could use as a weapon in case Smith came back to check on them. He found a black duffel bag that had not been there before with a rifle lying on top. *Mark must have brought it*, he thought opening the bag. Inside he found a sawed off shot gun, a Glock, a second rope, a small first aid kit, and a Mac-11. There were a few spare magazines preloaded for the Glock and Mac-11. He also found a set of handcuff keys. Matt shook his head as he started undoing the cuffs still attached to his wrists. *I like the way this guy thinks*, Matt commented to himself. He picked up the Mac-11 and chambered a round.

A noise caught Matt's attention. He turned to see Lieutenant Cooper hauling himself onto the deck. Matt grabbed the Glock and handed it over to him along with the set of keys. "Check our raiding craft," Lieutenant Cooper instructed him. "I'll help the others."

Matt knew what he was going to find, but he followed Lieutenant Cooper's order. He reached the side of the ship where they had boarded. Checking once again for any sign of Smith, he glanced over the railing. Their raiding craft was gone, just as he had expected. Matt continued along the railing, headed toward the ladder up to the pilot house. He was hoping to use the radio to call for help, but it was smashed to bits just like the control panel that operated the fish hold. He headed back down to report.

When he got back to the hold, the rest of the team was already assembled on deck and a couple of them were helping Mark climb the last few feet. Matt reported to Lieutenant Cooper what he had found. "It looks like the lifeboat might work, it has an outboard engine, but it'll be too slow to catch up with Smith."

Lieutenant Cooper shook his head, "Right now our main objective is to lie low and stay hidden. As long as Smith thinks we're dead he won't try to run. That'll give us a chance to find the other traitors in the unit."

"So are we going to head back to the ship?" Simmons asked.

"No, we don't know who the traitor is, so no one can know we're still alive. Once we're safe, I'll contact General Thompson. We have to warn him about Smith, and I'd trust him with my life. He'll find the traitors and get Smith," Lieutenant Cooper said looking around at the assembled men. "Gather up any useful tools and weapons you can find. Also search for ANY fuel, we'll need it if we stand a chance to make it back to shore."

The men went to work. Mark found an extra can of fuel for the lifeboat. About ten minutes later they had lowered the lifeboat into the water. The fishing boat was threatening to capsize by the time they were loading it with the supplies they had gathered. It was taking on more water on its starboard side and was now listing sideways. Julie had been loaded on the lifeboat as soon as it was secure. Once the scavenged gear was aboard, they all boarded the small craft. Starting the lifeboat's motor, they watched the fishing vessel roll over. It took only a few more minutes for it to completely submerge beneath the dark water. Simmons checked a compass he had found on the bridge and headed the lifeboat due east back to the San Diego shoreline.

CHAPTER 28

They approached the Torrey Pines State Beach before dawn. The familiar landmarks were barely visible in the low-lying fog along the shore. The tide was coming in, and they were able to bring the small boat far up onto the beach. The men worked quickly and in silence to unload the gear they had scavenged. Doc carried Julie onto a dry section of beach and continued to monitor her condition. She had remained unconsciousness through all of the commotion.

"We can't leave the lifeboat for anyone to find," Mark said. Chief Nguyen nodded his agreement. Together they shoved the boat back out to sea. Once it was free of the beach, Mark jumped in and used the last of the fuel to take it past the underwater shelf where the land dropped into a deep ocean trench. Once there, he took the fire ax that was mounted to the side of the lifeboat and swung it over and over, demolishing the bottom of the boat. Soon water was flowing freely into the hole he had made. Dropping the ax, Mark jumped out of the doomed lifeboat and swam back to shore.

Now that the boat was gone, their next step was to find a ride. "We can't call a taxi… that would just draw attention to us," Lieutenant Cooper stated what they all knew.

"Don't worry, I've got it covered," Mark told them. He seemed ready for this as well. Fishing in the duffel bag he brought out his cell phone. He hit one button; it must have been a preset speed dial, because a moment later someone answered. "I have a pick-up." There was a pause. "No, it's for me this time. I need a plain cargo van, the fewer windows the better." Again there was a pause. "Right... Meet me at the Torrey Pines State Beach. Yep.... Usual deal, what's your ETA? ... Right, twenty minutes. I'll be ready."

All of them were staring at him. "We probably don't want to know why you have a private car delivery service on speed dial, do we?" Lieutenant Cooper asked.

"Let's just say I have clients that want to be able to do business without any interruptions," Mark said with a straight face. Then he added, "They'll be here in twenty and they'll meet me up along the road. I trust them, to a point, but it would probably be best if they didn't see you."

"Right, everyone, gather your gear. Miller, you have Julie. We'll stay hidden down here under the bridge until Mark signals," Lieutenant Cooper directed them. He kept an eye along the beach as the men followed his orders. It was unlikely for surfers to be out this early, but you never knew. He glanced toward the road and for a moment could not spot Mark for a moment. When he finally did spot him, he was standing in plain sight. He was doing a good job of looking like he belonged there. Mark was fussing with his SCUBA gear as if he did this every day and was innocently waiting for his ride. Lieutenant Cooper shook his head again. *I don't want to know about Mark's business*, he thought, *but he's a handy man to have on your side.*

The van arrived on time, followed by a smaller transport car. The driver of the van confirmed delivery with Mark, handed over the keys and then climbed into the passenger side of the car. A moment later the car drove off, leaving Mark and the van alone on the road. Mark waited; making sure no one was close before he signaled to the team.

At the signal they swarmed up the sandy embankment. Mark had the rear doors of the van open and the team settled into the cargo area. Doc arranged Julie between himself and Matt so they could support her nearly lifeless form as the van jostled and bounced along the road. Mark drove while the entire team stayed hidden. It took them over an hour to reach their destination and they all dozed off to different degrees during the ride. Matt roused himself as he sensed the van slowing. It turned sharply up a driveway and entered a cool, dark garage. They waited until after the garage door was completely down before Mark opened the side of the van.

"We're here. Make yourselves at home," Mark said inviting them in. "It's small, but it's private and secure."

"Where are we?" Chief Nguyen asked.

"My place. I'm not a blood relative of Julie, so no one will even know to look for me. This should be a good base of operations… at least until Julie can zap you to her hideout."

They all piled out. Mark motioned to Doc. "Let me take her," he offered. Lifting her out of Doc's care, Mark carried her like he would a small child. Matt and Doc followed him into the building. They passed the small utilitarian kitchen to their left, and then they turned away from the kitchen and entered a living room, where the beige carpet under their feet squelched with water. Matt noticed the ropes that had been used to tie up Julie still lying on the floor. He forced his eyes to look away. Around the room he saw a common theme to Mark's décor: a black leather couch, a black coffee table, black blinds, and a black entertainment center. The rest of the team were securing their position and taking note of the exits and possible defensive positions. They all felt the specter of the traitor looming over them. Matt turned to follow Mark and Doc up the narrow stairs.

There were two bedrooms upstairs. Matt glanced into the first one as they passed it and saw that it was filled with a massive computer desk with four monitors arranged on it. Then they came to the master bedroom. This room had a queen-sized bed with, of course, black sheets and comforter. Mark gently placed Julie on the bed and covered her with a blanket. Doc checked her pulse again. "What do you need?" Mark asked as he watched Doc assess Julie's condition.

"What she really needs is a bag of IV fluids with a dextrose push. But even a few packets of sugar would help," Doc explained.

"I have a few emergency supplies. Let me see what I can find," Mark said and headed out of the room and into the hall bathroom. Doc and Matt heard rummaging sounds and banging from drawers and cabinets being opened and closed. Two minutes later Mark returned carrying a bag of lactated ringers, an infusion kit, and a dose of oral glucose like diabetics sometimes needed.

"What do you have, a whole trauma suite in your bathroom?" Doc asked surprised. Mark simply raised his eyebrow with a smile and a shrug in answer. Doc turned his attention back to Julie and quickly had the IV in and flowing. With Matt's help he squirted the glucose paste under Julie's tongue. "There, that should help. Now she just needs to rest."

"I'll take the first watch," Mark volunteered. "You guys need a chance to refuel too. You look almost as bad as she does. Go get yourselves some chow and take a nap."

The two men did not argue and gratefully headed down the stairs. Most of the team was already raiding the cabinets for food, and the microwave was buzzing as it heated up something. Matt noticed with relief that someone had moved the ropes out of sight. After they had all eaten, stuff ranging from ramen noodles to mac & cheese, they found comfortable spots around the living room and crashed.

Matt woke to the sound of a weapon being cycled through its action. He glanced around the dark room warily. The only light was coming from the kitchen and he got up to investigate. As he approached he saw that Mark had a towel, a black towel of course, spread across the surface of the table and his Glock lay in pieces on it. The Glock's slide was in one hand and a cleaning cloth in the other.

Matt glanced up the stairs.

"She's doing alright," Mark said. He had seen Matt's glance and knew what he was thinking. "She's still asleep, but her pulse is stronger." He paused as he finished cleaning the piece in his hand and reached for the next one. "What happened yesterday? Why can't you report back to base?"

Matt sat down on one of the kitchen chairs, and watched Mark clean his Glock. He told Mark the basics of their day, rescuing the downed sub crew, finding out that Jade was missing. He paused when he got to the part where the MPs had found the ambulance in the warehouse close by.

"It wasn't your fault," Mark told him, reading Matt's mind again. "If you had gone with her you'd have died with a bullet to the back of your head just like the other two. She wouldn't have been able to live with that." Matt did not respond to that, so Mark switched to another subject. "So who's this Mr. Smith? Is he a SEAL?"

At that Matt gave a harsh laugh. "No, none of us would ever turn against her. She's saved all of our lives at least once."

"Someone betrayed us," Lieutenant Cooper said darkly. He had come up behind Matt. "Until we know who, no one outside this house can be trusted."

"So what's the plan LT?" this came from Chief Nguyen who had sat up on the couch.

"I have an idea, but I'll need your help, Mark."

Mark rode his black Harley through the quiet streets of Carlsbad. The sun had gone down a few hours ago and the pale orange street lights lit patches of the road as he went. He came to the address on his GPS. It was a large stucco house with a red tile roof. Immaculate landscaping of palm trees and tropical flowers wrapped around the house on both sides as far as he could see. A huge shade tree could be seen towering over the back of the house.

Parking his bike, Mark put his helmet on the back of the seat. His black riding leathers made little noise as he walked up to the front door. It was dark on the front step, but the doorbell button glowed to the left of the door. Mark rang the bell and stepped back to wait. A few moments later he heard confused voices from farther in the house. He heard a man and a woman talking. The porch light was turned on, and there was a pause. Mark knew he was being considered through the door's peep hole and he stood still waiting. The man's decision made, Mark heard the dead bolt of the door slide back. The heavy door opened enough for Mark to see an older man standing in a bathrobe and slippers. But it wasn't the slippers that made Mark pause before he spoke. The man had a shotgun leveled at Mark's chest. *At this range he can't miss*, Mark thought as he cleared his throat. "Sir, I have a note for you," and as non-threateningly as possible Mark held out the folded piece of paper.

"Who are you?" the man demanded.

"A friend of a friend," Mark said cryptically.

General Thompson finally seemed to remember him. "It's you, but she's…" he said in disbelief. The general took the note and opened it. His gaze intensified as he read. By the time he had reached the end of the note the man had set his shotgun aside. He looked up at Mark, shock and relief plain on his face. "Do you know what this note says?"

The general's feeling of relief reassured Mark that Lieutenant Cooper had made the right decision. "Yes, sir."

"Is it true? Don't lie to me," the general said. His gaze held an implied threat.

In reply Mark brought out his phone and dialed his house number. He handed the phone over to the general. "It's a secure line," Mark reassured him.

The general looked skeptical, "No cell phone is secure."

Mark smiled ruefully. "This one is."

Someone must have answered, because the general's attention was drawn back to the phone. "Yes, I read the note… Yes, I know… No, I don't want to know where you are. Stay hidden… I'll take care of it… Thanks for the warning, I'll be careful. He won't be able to hurt us…Oh you'll know when I'm done," the general said as he disconnected the call and handed it back to Mark. "Thank you."

CHAPTER 29

Julie woke to the painful pressure of her bladder about to burst. *I have to pee so bad,* she thought desperately as she tried to sit up, but a wave of dizziness hit her and she sank back onto her pillow. She looked around the room. She recognized the black decor and smiled. She was at Mark's. *But, where's the Team?* she thought worriedly. She heard steps coming up the stairs and turned her head to see Matt coming to the bedroom door. "Hey," she said relieved, as she waved a greeting. She was rewarded by a huge smile that erased the lines of concern from his face. "You're just in time to save me."

"What do you mean?" he asked, a shade of concern came back to his face.

"I've got to go to the bathroom!" Julie said with a grin and a laugh. "Can you help me stumble over there?"

Matt laughed in return and lifted her right arm over his shoulder and wrapped his left arm around her waist to support her weight. "I was so worried about you," Matt admitted once she was in his arms.

"I was worried about you too," Julie agreed. "I don't know what I'd do if I lost you," she admitted as he helped her walk. She was so light he practically carried her across the hall. At the bathroom door, Julie stopped him. She pulled away from him and leaned heavily on the vanity. "Shoo, you don't get to come in here," she scolded him. Matt started to protest. "I'll be fine. Can you start some mac & cheese for me?" she asked to distract him.

"How'd you know he had mac & cheese?"

"Mark always has mac & cheese. I think college students take cooking lessons from my uncle," she explained.

A few minutes later Julie made it down the stairs with Matt's help. Tired again, she sank onto the black leather couch with a sigh and closed her eyes. Around her she felt the members of the team gather close to her, but she kept her eyes shut, relaxed. She opened them again when she felt someone pick up her left wrist.

"Oh come on, Doc, can't a tired person just close their eyes without a medic taking their pulse?" Julie tried to joke.

Doc looked at her skeptically. "Do you know how long you've been asleep?"

"No idea," Julie said smugly. "But my generation is rather proud of our ability to sleep all day."

"You've been unconscious for two days," Matt supplied the answer as he set the bowl of Mac & Cheese on a tray on her lap.

"Two days?" Julie asked stunned, looking from Matt back to Doc for confirmation. Doc nodded. "What's happened while I was out? Who took us?" Now that she was more awake questions popped through her mind. Suddenly she was filled with doubt. "Did everyone get out safely?" She searched the faces of the men around her. They were all there except for one. "Where's Simmons?" Julie asked close to tears as she looked for the blond man.

"He's fine. He's upstairs on my computer. He's a bigger geek than I am," her Uncle Mark laughed from the door to the garage. "You eat and we'll fill you in on everything you missed." As he entered the room she could see that he was carrying a small bag.

Doc seemed interested in what he was carrying. "Were you able to get them?" he asked as he took the bag that Mark offered him in response. He came back to Julie's side and started unloading the bag. Julie groaned at the sight of its contents.

"Not more torture devices. How could you, Uncle Mark?" Julie whined in mock despair, watching with dread as Doc removed the glucose monitor from the bag along with a blood pressure cuff. But she offered no resistance as Doc continued his assessment. She used her other hand to shovel food into her mouth. "So, tell me. What happened?" she asked a few mouthfuls later.

Before anyone could answer her, they were cut off by a thunder of footsteps on the stairs. Simmons entered the living room in a burst of energy. "You HAVE to see this!" he exclaimed as he turned on the TV. He flipped through the channels until he found what he was looking for.

Everyone watched expectantly. As the commercial ended, the news broadcast began with, Breaking News blazoned across the screen in red. The commentator looked at the camera with serious intensity. "We have more details on the raid at the Defense Intelligence Agency. It appears that the FBI has led a raid in conjunction with the DIA to apprehend one of their operatives."

The feed changed to a video of a man, locked in handcuffs being dragged between several men. They could see Mr. Smith's face as he swore at the camera. "I did it to protect you! She was dangerous! How dare you touch me! Take your hands off me!" His wild eyes revealed his insanity. The camera came back to the news commentator. "We've been unable to get an official statement from the FBI, but unofficial sources have reported that the agent known as Mr. Smith, is charged with the murder of Jade and several other military personnel. We have learned that Mr. Smith's real name is Special Agent Richard Strickland. Strickland has worked for the DIA for twenty years and is considered a high level field operative. As of yet the Navy has been unable to comment on Jade's current condition, and will not confirm or deny her death. We will continue to report on any further developments as they become available."

Simmons turned off the TV, as they all sat in stunned silence. "Well, he said we'd know when he was done," Lieutenant Cooper commented dryly. "We should probably stay hidden a few more days, until he finds the traitors."

"So *is* Jade dead?" Julie asked.

"That's up to you," Matt replied.

For Julie, the next few days went by in a blur of sleeping, eating (and blood tests) and watching the news. The news reported the arrests of two other men believed to be Agent Strickland's accomplices. One had been an assistant working in Dr. Emory's office, Corpsman Martinez. She vaguely remembered meeting him at one of her appointments. The other one had been one of the support staff for the SEAL teams. His name was Corporal Max Campbell, but Julie was not sure if she had ever really met him. With their capture, it was safe for the team to return to base. Mark wanted to stay anonymous so he dropped the team, including Julie, at a seldom-used scenic overlook on the way to San Diego. There they called General Thompson to report on their location. He sent a convoy of Humvees from Pendleton to pick them up.

Four days after waking up she felt strong enough to try to zap. "All right, let's just try a short jump. Go from here to over there," Doc instructed her. They were in the team's ready room. Doc pointed from the white board at the front of the room to a space at the back of the room. Most of the team was gathered to watch.

Julie concentrated, and then tried to zap herself across the room. She made it, but stumbled in exhaustion as she appeared. "Why am I still so tired?" Julie asked plaintively. She had not realized how much she had grown accustomed to being able to zap to anywhere at any time. Now she felt vulnerable, knowing that if she was attacked again she might not be able save herself. She looked at Matt, fear in her eyes.

"It's Okay, maybe you just ran your zapping batteries too low. Give yourself more time to rest," Matt said as he came over to give her a comforting hug. *But what if...* Even in her thoughts she could not complete the sentence. She felt as helpless as when she had been tied up at the bottom of that ship's cargo hold, waiting to die.

Chapter 30

Julie sat stretching, tired from running laps. Her muscles were burning but it felt good to be out of her apartment. She was sitting on a patch of grass across from her housing area thinking about the last few weeks. The news had been buzzing with rumors about Jade's whereabouts. There were whispers circulating on both sides of the debate. Some people claimed to have seen her; others claimed that they had seen her body in the morgue. The Navy continued to maintain a lockdown on her true condition.

"Hey, kiddo!" the familiar call drew her attention to the other side of the road. Her uncle was walking toward her, a big grin on his face. "How's it going?" her Uncle Mark asked cheerfully.

"Good, how've you been?" Julie asked getting to her feet.

"Pretty good… I was wondering, how's your special skill coming along?" Mark asked a bit tentatively.

"It's coming along well, don't worry. I'll be back globetrotting in no time."

"That's great!" he exclaimed relieved. He had known how much she wanted to get her powers back.

"So what brings you here?" Julie asked.

"Your parents asked me to get in touch with you," he admitted after a moment of silence.

"You know I'd love to see my parents," Julie said with a frown. "But I'm the reason they had to change their identities. If I visit them, I could just be putting them in danger again."

"I figured that was what was keeping you away," Mark told her, as he nodded understanding. "But what if I went ahead and secured their house ahead of time? You could just pop in. As long as you didn't go outside, no one would even know you'd been there."

"Really?" Julie asked excited. "Do you think it'd be safe?"

"Check with the guys and see what they think," Mark suggested. "Oh, your mom would like to invite you and Matt over for Thanksgiving."

"That's only a month away, Mark! I'll have to find out if I can get leave by then."

"Well I would've asked you earlier, but you were busy getting yourself killed," Mark pointed out. "Besides, they probably won't have you back in the field by then," he reasoned.

It turned out that Jade was declared dead before Thanksgiving. The Navy still had not found a way for her to continue to work with the military and ensure her safety. There was no way to know how many people in the government shared Strickland's and the traitors' views. *On the bright side that means I have plenty of time to visit my parents*, Julie thought as she packed her suitcase. The admiral had granted Ensign Patterson's and Matt's requests for leave. Julie heard a knock at the door as she put the last item in her suitcase. When she answered the door she saw Matt grinning at her.

"Aren't you done yet?" he teased her. Then he saw the suitcase she was pulling behind her. "How long did you say this vacation was? It looks like you have enough stuff to last for a month."

Julie swatted at him playfully in response. "Why don't you be useful and carry that to the car for me," she teased him back. "I have to get Cinder."

"Women and their packing," Matt grumbled cheerfully as he hauled her large suitcase down the stairs to the parking lot. Behind him he could hear Julie lock her apartment. Soon enough, they were headed off base.

"Where are we going?" Julie asked. When she had invited Matt he said he would deal with security at this end of the trip.

"We're headed over to Simmons's place. He has an enclosed garage, and he doesn't mind us using it to store my car when we zap out," he explained as he turned on the radio.

It came on in the middle of a news report. "Special Agent Strickland, who is charged in connection with Jade's disappearance was arraigned today. His arraignment was held quickly, in part to satisfy the public outrage. He has been charged with six counts of kidnapping, and two counts of murder and treason. It is expected that Smith's attorneys will ask for a continuance so they can prepare his defense," the commentator paused. "Meanwhile he will be held without bail in a maximum security prison awaiting trial."

Matt quickly changed the station. "Sorry about that." He looked over at her. "Have you decided if you still want to help us with missions?" Matt asked in as casual a tone as he could.

Julie thought for a moment. "I'm not sure. I feel like all I've done is endanger you and the others."

"You didn't attack us, Strickland did. You need to get that straight in your head," Matt told her. When he glanced over he saw Julie's frown and knew she did not get it yet. He tried a different angle. "Do you remember those girls you saved from their kidnappers? Would you blame them for being kidnapped, just because those sickos couldn't resist taking them?"

"No, of course not," Julie objected immediately.

"It's the same with General Jian and Strickland. It's not your fault they want to control your powers. You're only responsible for what you do," he pointed out. "The guys and I are big boys; we can make decisions about our own safety. We aren't your responsibility either."

"I guess I see what you mean," Julie admitted grudgingly, deep in thought. "That doesn't mean I'm not going to worry about you," Julie said at last.

"Don't worry, I know I can't break you of that habit," Matt said in mock surrender. He pulled his blue Dodge Charger up to Simmons's house. They could see that the garage door was already open and Matt pulled straight into the open space. As soon as they were in, the door started rolling down behind them.

Julie spotted Simmons at the door to the house. He was dressed in board shorts and a T-shirt and looked even more like a surfer. "Hey, thanks again for the use of your garage."

"No problem," Simmons told her. "You deserve a break."

Matt unloaded their suitcases and Julie stepped up beside him with Cinder. She was impatient to leave. It had been months since she had seen her parents and she had never seen their new house. Focusing her powers on her parents she found them easily. "See ya," she called as they disappeared. The next instant they were standing in her parents' living room. Julie had to endure her mother's tearful fussing for nearly ten minutes before she was finally able to extricate herself. As soon as she could, she went to join Matt and Mark who had taken refuge in the kitchen.

"Hey Mark, thanks for setting this up. I really appreciate it," Julie told him as she joined them.

"Like I told you before, it's no problem," Mark admonished her. "I was just showing Matt the new toy I bought just for this occasion." In his hand he held a small box with a wand connected to it by a cord.

"Yeah, Simmons will be jealous when he finds out," Matt agreed appreciatively. "He'll have to update his own equipment."

"What is it?" Julie asked.

"It's the latest in bug detectors," Mark said proudly.

"It's a 'bug detector,' like for termites?" Julie teased him.

"You laugh, but this baby can find even the most sophisticated surveillance equipment," Mark defended his new toy. "I've wanted to get this thing for a while, and securing your parents' house was a great excuse."

The next day was Thanksgiving and her mother went all out cooking. She was up before dawn getting the turkey ready. Julie slept in, and when she came out of the guest bedroom she found everyone already in the kitchen. Matt and Mark were drinking coffee.

"Did you guys sleep well?" Julie asked as she poured herself a cup.

"I did, but the old man here is complaining about the couch being uncomfortable," Matt joked.

"Old man!" Mark scoffed in mock anger. "Kids these days have no respect for their elders!" Mark returned the jibe.

Julie laughed. "Hey mom, do you need any help?" she offered.

"Not yet sweetie, you just help yourself to some breakfast and keep me company while I get this ready," her mom encouraged her.

Mark tapped Matt on the shoulder and motioned for them to head out to the living room. "We're just going to clean up our beds," Mark told Julie when she noticed them leaving.

Her dad kept reading his morning paper and Julie's

mom prepared the stuffing. "So I've heard that 'Jade' might be dead," she finally said after a few minutes of silence. "What will that mean for you?"

Julie tried to swallow the mouthful of coffee she had just taken, but her throat seemed to close off from emotions. "I'm not sure yet," she admitted when she finally managed to swallow the coffee without choking on it.

"Do you like what you're doing with Matt and the Team?" her mom asked. Julie looked up, surprised by the question.

"Mark has been explaining some of the things you've been up to," her dad explained.

"I don't know. I really like helping to retrieve wounded men, getting them to a hospital quicker than anyone else could… and I like helping the Team on missions, trying to keep them from getting hurt," Julie said thoughtfully. "Yeah, I guess I do really enjoy what I've been doing," Julie replied, surprised by her own answer.

"Well then, why would you stop doing it?" her mom asked matter of factually.

"What do you mean?"

"Well, if Jade dies, are you going to keep working with the Team?" her dad asked, as he took another drink from his coffee cup, looking up from his paper.

Julie had not thought of it that way before. *To stop working with Matt and the others…* Julie suddenly came to a decision she had been debating for weeks. "Yeah, I'll keep working with the Team, one way or another."

"Good," her mother told her with a smile. "I'm glad to hear it. I was worried that that bastard Strickland had broken your spirit."

Julie was shocked by her mom's cussing, but also that she was encouraging her to keep risking her life. "Aren't you worried that I'll be killed?" Julie asked a bit hurt.

"Of course we are, but we also want you to do what you think is right for you," her mom said and smiled at

Matt as the two men came back into the kitchen. "Besides, this handsome young man has been doing a fine job keeping you safe."

Matt blushed at her comments. "We've been trying to ma'am, but to be honest she's pulled us out of some bad situations too."

"Good, then that's settled, Julie will keep working with the SEALs because it sounds like you all need each other to keep yourselves safe," her mom stated firmly. Stunned, Julie and Matt looked at each other and laughed.

The rest of the day went by quickly with a combination of chatting and lots of eating. They ended up staying up past midnight as Julie's dad and Mark exchanged embarrassing stories about each other from before Julie was born. The next morning they spent one last breakfast with her parents before Julie zapped them home.

"That was a fun trip," Matt told her as he drove Julie home. "Thanks for letting me tag along,".

"Yeah, my parents are one of a kind," Julie commented. She was still stunned her parents had helped her make the decision to keep working with the Team. "So I guess the question now is not *if* but *how* am I going to keep helping the Team?"

"We can let the admiral worry about that," Matt said dismissively.

CHAPTER 31

The next Monday Julie got ready for work early. She had finally convinced Captain Lewis into letting her zap into water. Ever since the sub rescue she had been thinking about how the water had moved away from her when she zapped in. Her nervousness and excitement had kept her from sleeping.

"Are you ready for this?" Lieutenant Cooper asked when she joined the team in the briefing room.

"I think so, sir," Julie told him.

"I want you to test it here, in the pool, first," Lieutenant Cooper explained the plan. "Teleport in up to your neck. If something goes wrong here, we have a chance to save you."

"Okay," Julie agreed.

"Miller, I want you to have your med kit ready just in case," the lieutenant directed.

"I always do when she's anywhere close to water," Doc agreed.

When they were done planning, Julie quickly changed into her spring suit. She wore the lightweight wetsuit during training to keep from getting chilled. Its short sleeves and legs did not interfere with her movements like a regular wetsuit would. When she was ready she headed to the Team's pool. The rest of the guys stood on the deck watching.

Standing on the edge of the pool, Julie was suddenly nervous. *What would happen if she was wrong?*

"You don't have to do this," Matt said next to her, mirroring her own thoughts.

Before she could lose her nerve, she zapped herself into the water. From the pool deck it appeared to Matt as if a crater, over ten feet across and at least ten feet deep, had appeared in the surface of the water. Julie was suspended in the air for a moment before she fell into the depression. Then the water rushed back into place enveloping her, and she disappeared from view. Matt dove in after her with Doc close behind.

Even with Matt's advanced swimming skills, it took him a few precious moments to find her under the waves. He grabbed her over her shoulder. With her body pinned tightly to his chest, he propelled them both to the surface. Doc joined him and helped support Julie as she sputtered for breath. Several moments later, they had her to the edge of the pool. The men on the deck lifted Julie out as the others climbed out on their own.

As they sat on the deck, Julie continued to cough, clearing her lungs. "It worked! I told you I could do it!" Julie announced triumphantly between coughs.

"You've got to be kidding!" Matt said in disbelief. "You almost drowned! No way, you're not doing that on a mission!"

"Alright, listen up," Lieutenant Cooper got their attention. "Today I want you to check your gear, after that you have a free training day. Julie, get checked out by Dr. Emory."

After she got the all clear from Dr. Emory, Julie went to join the team. The guys were bicycling up Palomar Mountain this time. About halfway up the steep incline, they got the call from Captain Lewis. A plane had been hijacked on its way to Florida.

Chief Nguyen finished attaching the canister of knockout gas to the air hose. With a final twist, it was secured. He turned the valve that would release the gas into the passenger compartment of the plane above him. *They won't know what hit them*, he thought with a smile. The gas was colorless and odorless. Activating his comm he sent a brief message, "It's a go."

Miles away in a cargo plane, the rest of the team got his message. Immediately Julie focused her powers on the hijackers and pilots of the threatened 747 and watched. With her powers she could feel them slowly going to sleep. They needed to time this perfectly. If she zapped the team in too soon they might be in danger. If they went in too late the airliner could crash. *There, one hijacker down*, she thought and waited. Soon the rest of the hijackers fell asleep, as well as the pilots. Julie opened her eyes and nodded as she reported to the rest of SEAL Team 3, "It's time."

"Let's go… you all know the plan," Lieutenant Cooper gave the command to begin. All of them put on their gas masks, and Julie started zapping the team into the hijacked passenger plane. The first two, Simmons and Demetrio, went to the cockpit. Simmons's job was to secure the flight deck and keep the plane flying. Demetrio was to do a thorough sweep of the plane starting in the cockpit to check for explosives.

Then she zapped in Matt and Doc. Matt would be in charge of securing the terrorists in the main cabin, while Doc monitored the condition of the passengers. Finally, she took Lieutenant Cooper to the rear of the plane. From there he could look for additional threats and help Matt secure any hostiles there. They needed to get all of the hijackers disarmed and tied up quickly so they could discontinue the knockout gas as soon as possible. The plan was for the team to be gone without anyone seeing how the hijacking was ended.

Jade waited in the main section of the cabin, watching SEAL Team 3. The entire mission went quickly and without a hitch. As they were finishing Simmons put the plane on autopilot to give the pilots enough time to regain control of the plane. Then they radioed to Chief Nguyen to disconnect the canister.

Julie zapped the team out in reverse order. That left Simmons able to monitor the plane's instruments as long as possible. The effects of the gas wore off quickly and as Julie speed zapped Simmons out of the cockpit, the pilot was already starting to come to.

"That was a close one," Simmons exclaimed as they arrived back on the cargo plane.

"You weren't seen, were you?" Lieutenant Cooper checked.

"No way, he was still too out of it, and Julie definitely wasn't spotted," Simmons reported. He turned to Julie, "That was some quick pick-up. Good job."

"Good, remember, no one can know how or who rescued that plane," Lieutenant Cooper reminded them of something they all knew. It had been decided that it was too risky having people know Jade was alive and well. So the official story had been that Jade had died on that sinking fishing vessel and her body had never been recovered. Very few people knew that Jade was still alive. *Even the new President doesn't know yet*, Julie thought with a grin. That meant that any missions they went on with Jade had to be done in complete secrecy. They made sure that no one saw them appear or disappear.

Matt returned from talking to the pilots of their C130 cargo plane. "I told them we've scrapped the training jump. They'll get us back to base within the hour."

Julie thought about the plane. Over the last few months Julie had continued to train with the Team. During that time they had discovered that she could not teleport from a moving vehicle to solid ground or vice-versa without serious consequences. *What was that old sci-fi quote,* she thought to herself, *'You canna change the laws of physics, Captain.'* Namely, an object in motion tends to stay in motion. The first time she had zapped herself from a moving zodiac onto a beach; her momentum had thrown her ten feet through the air to crash head first into a sand dune. If she was moving when she zapped, she would be moving at the same speed wherever she arrived, and her momentum would keep her moving until she ran into something. Conversely, if she was standing still when she zapped, the rear wall of the vehicle she was zapping to would hit her. So, in order for them to reach the hijacked plane, they had to be traveling at the same speed, hence the cargo plane.

The team rested or chatted companionably for the rest of the flight. Doc was telling them about his wife's pregnancy. They were expecting another boy.

"Have you picked a name yet?" Simmons asked.

"I want to name him Thomas, but Susan wants to call him Patrick," Doc answered.

"How old are your other two sons?" Demetrio asked. "I can't remember."

"My oldest, Ethan, is six now, and Ricky is already three," Doc answered.

Julie just sat back and listened. It felt good to be with them. Over the past few months, the only times she had really felt safe were when she was with them. She spent as little time as possible in her apartment alone. If she was away from the team she would startle at any little sound. Her hideout was the only place she felt safe alone; but if she stayed there too long, she started feeling isolated and depressed.

Too quickly, the flight was over. When the plane came to a stop Julie zapped back to her apartment. From there she drove to Matt's house off base. Officially Matt lived there, but unofficially it was more like Jade's secret headquarters. That was where the rest of the team would meet her for their debriefing. Within an hour they all started arriving.

"Hey Julie, how've you been?" Chief Nguyen greeted her. Whenever any of the Team saw her in public they always acted like they hardly ever saw her, in case they were under surveillance.

"Not bad. How're Tracy and the kids?" Julie asked about his family, continuing the charade. Each of the members of the Team arrived separately, and greeted her as if they missed her. Together they entered the house and they all fell silent as Matt turned on blaring music and a sound track of their voices. That was another thing they had worked on over the last month; they had made a dozen different sound tracks of them talking. This one was of them drinking and hanging out. There were also recordings of them playing poker or watching sports games. Together they entered a small room that they had built in the center of the house.

The room had no windows and the sound of the party faded as the door was closed behind them. They had created the Mission Room as a spy-proof chamber where they could prepare for and carry out missions in secrecy. It was soundproof, bulletproof, and essentially impregnable if they locked the massive door from the inside. One wall held a large white board; another wall sported a massive gun rack. Julie spotted her Beretta pistol and shotgun that she had added to the guys' arsenal. *Not that I ever use them*, she thought thankfully. This is where they zapped in and out from for most of their missions.

Lieutenant Cooper was the first to speak. "Did anyone have any security breaks?" he asked. Everyone shook their heads. Lieutenant Cooper nodded his approval, "Good job everyone. I'll want a full report from each of you tomorrow. Remember, our cover story is the skydiving exercise that was scrapped." Turning to Julie he continued, "What's your cover story for the last three hours?"

"I was seen entering my apartment three hours ago

by several neighbors. Then when I left to come here I stopped to chat with two people. I told them I was taking a break from doing some online course work to go to a party."

"That's good," Lieutenant Cooper stated, nodding his approval. Looking around at the team, he continued, "I'll report to Captain Lewis in the morning. For now you're dismissed."

"Well then, let's get back to the party," Simmons said with a grin as he opened the Mission Room door. Music which had been held at bay by the room's soundproofing blared around them. "Got any beer, Matt?"

Together Julie and the Team headed into the main part of Matt's new house. "Hang on a sec," Matt answered as he headed to the sound system and waited for a pause in the recording. All of the recordings had built in pauses in the dialog, and they all waited quietly until one of those breaks. Then Matt shut off the recording. "Who wants a beer?" Matt asked loudly over the still blaring music, as the team settled in for an evening of relaxation.

The party lasted another couple hours before they started to leave. Before anyone stepped outside, Matt checked the security cameras. If nothing looked suspicious then they could leave singly or in pairs. As the team members headed out, they would covertly double check that the area was safe.

Julie watched Chief Nguyen leave and saw his guarded stance. She sighed. "I'm sorry you guys have to live like this," she said to Matt, who was also watching, monitoring the area.

"What do you mean?" Matt asked keeping his eyes on the screens. "Like what?"

"You're back in the States; you should be able to relax and let down your guard, but because of me you can't," she said motioning to the image of Chief Nguyen glancing around the street as he got into his car.

"We're always checking our surroundings. It's no big

deal that we have to be a little more careful leaving after a mission," Matt said with a shrug. "Besides, we all want to do this," He looked over at her and noticed the sadness in her eyes. Matt pulled her into a hug. "You're the one who has paid the biggest price."

"Ah, it's not so bad sleeping in my hideout," she said with a smile trying to reassure him. She looked up into his eyes. He worried about her living alone in her cave, but she thought it was a small price to pay to feel safe each night.

"Hey, Julie, almost ready?" Simmons asked, interrupting them. "I've got to get going soon. Jenny's waiting for me."

"Sure, just a sec," Julie answered pulling away from Matt's embrace.

"Another hot date with Jenny huh? You two must be getting pretty serious," Matt teased him.

"Might be," Simmons agreed. "She is *amazing*."

"She'd have to be to put up with you," Matt called as Simmons headed to the living room. Then Matt looked down at Julie frowning, "You be careful."

"I'll be fine… " Julie said giving him a quick kiss. "I always am. Simmons will wait to watch me get in my door." Every time she drove home, one of the guys would follow her. "I'm safe once I'm in my apartment, especially since Admiral Huntington put out the news alert about an increase in burglaries in the area. Now my neighbors really keep an eye out for trouble."

"See I told you SEALs are always watching their surroundings." Matt silently thanked Captain Lewis again for arranging it that most of the apartments around Julie's were occupied by other SEAL Team members. Even if they were unaware of who she really was, they would keep anyone from breaking into her apartment.

CHAPTER 32

When Julie woke up the next morning she zapped herself and Cinder to her apartment from her hideout. She turned the news on in the background as she got ready for work. The news was reporting on the miraculous rescue of the hijacked plane. Their plan had worked. No one had any clue to what had happened. Some passengers were even crediting divine intervention. For the most part she ignored the TV, until she heard the commentator give the lead-in to the upcoming story. They had information on the believed identity of the hijackers and she turned up the volume.

"The FBI has identified the group as a fringe, militant group with ties to Islamic extremists," the gorgeous blonde reporter stated as she checked her notes. "Here is some video from a news conference held earlier at the FBI headquarters." The reporter's gaze went off camera as the feed shifted to the pre-recorded news conference.

A man with gray-streaked blonde hair was shown standing behind a podium with the FBI emblem emblazoned on the front. On the screen in front of him the caption read Special Agent-in-Charge Joseph Kettner. "The individuals who were detained from the hijacked plane have claimed to belong to a group called the North American Islamic Jihad. We believe that this group's total numbers are actually fairly small. Over the last five years they have tried to claim responsibility for acts of terror, and random accidents across the country. In fact, we believe that these acts were done by isolated perpetrators in 'lone-wolf' scenarios. However, there is an ongoing investigation into this domestic terrorist group. They do have ties to the Palestinian Islamic Jihad terrorist organization. Anyone with knowledge pertaining to this group, or evidence in any of their attacks, is urged to contact the FBI…" Julie listened for a little while longer as the reporters at the news conference asked questions. It was soon clear that the FBI would not release any further information regarding what they knew about the North American Islamic Jihad.

Julie thought about what she had learned about the group from the guys. The homegrown terrorist group was actually pretty well equipped and surprisingly well organized. It was a loose-knit group of Islamic extremists and others with a grudge against the country. The FBI was monitoring their key members. Occasionally they were able to thwart an attack, but information about those operations never reached the news. In reality, the number of their attacks had been growing over the last few years. The government had decided that it would be better if the country was kept in the dark about how strong the N.A.I.J. was becoming and had hidden information on some of their attacks behind reports of accidents. *They don't want anyone to panic by finding out how many actual attacks were being carried out*, Julie thought

Julie decided to take Cinder on a shorter run than usual this morning so she could get to work earlier. When they got back, she finished getting ready. Giving Cinder one last petting, she told him, "See you later buddy," and headed off to work.

Heading to work was not like a typical commute. It

started off normally enough; she would drive to Admiral Huntington's offices where she was listed as an executive assistant. She would show up and say hi to everyone on her way into her office. Then she would close her door and zap to a woman's restroom in the SEAL Team 3's headquarters.

Since Jade had died, her team had been on a shoestring budget. They did not even have their own building, which is why they had to use Matt's house. That meant that they were forced to get training days in whenever they could. Captain Lewis would make sure the other members of the Team and their support staff were at other locations on the days she was scheduled to work. None of them could know about her being alive. It was the best way to hide her involvement with the Team's missions and protect them from groups trying to get to her.

When she arrived at the Team's headquarters she realized that she was early. *I really need to practice swimming*, she thought regretfully. She changed into her swimsuit and headed out to the pool. She had been swimming for several laps when suddenly someone swam up to her and grabbed her arm.

"Don't worry, I've got you," Matt said as he helped her to the side of the pool.

"Hey," Julie exclaimed surprised. "What are you doing?"

"I came out on deck and it looked like you were drowning," Matt said confused.

"Jerk! I'm not drowning! I was just swimming laps!" Julie fumed as she started swimming again.

A few minutes later Matt sat at the side of their practice pool, a towel draped over his wet shoulders. He continued to watch Julie as she swam laps, still not sure if she needed his help.

"Aren't you going to save her?" Doc asked as he came up beside Matt.

"No, she's just swimming laps," Matt replied.

"You call that swimming?" Doc asked with a grin.

"No, but she does," Matt told him. "I already went in for her once and she got mad at me."

Julie finished her lap and heard Matt's last comment. "I don't want to hear it from you two. I can swim well enough to get around. People weren't meant to swim. If we were, we'd have flippers." When they laughed at her comment she got annoyed and exclaimed, "Darn it, I could beat any of you at a hundred yard sprint! Make me run a marathon any day, but this swimming thing sucks."

"Don't worry, we can teach you," Matt offered.

"Oh no way, I'm not going to let you guys try to teach me to swim. I've already signed up for lessons at the base pool," Julie explained as she climbed out onto the deck.

"We'd better get to the briefing room," Doc reminded them.

"Any idea what the plan is for the day?" Julie asked.

"Water-based drop zones," Doc explained. "We need to find a way to eliminate the cannon ball effect."

"Yeah, sounds like fun," Julie said with little enthusiasm remembering the last time she had zapped into water. "You'll have your resuscitation gear nearby, right?"

Matt and Julie followed Doc to the briefing room, and took their seats. Once everyone was seated, Lieutenant Cooper started. "We know the effect Jade's zapping causes to water entries. We need to find a way for Jade to deliver a team for swimming or Combat Rubberized Raiding Craft incursions. I want us to find the optimum distance above the water that won't cause a significant disturbance in the surface." Next he focused on Julie, "I want you to start about four feet above the water. You are to zap in with the CRRC and then get yourself back to the deck." He turned to the rest of the team. "We'll do the first tests with no one on board. Once we've found the right height above the water we'll practice some more, fully loaded. Gear up and meet back on the pool deck."

Julie headed back to the women's restroom. It also served as her locker room. There was a sink and counter top along one wall with a toilet stall next to it. She had added a landscape painting to the wall across from the sink to give it a feminine touch. But tucked in the far corner from the door was a single gym locker. Julie kept some of the gear she might need for training in it. After opening the lock, she grabbed her spring wetsuit. It was mostly black with pink stripes along the arms and legs.

Since Julie had started training with the team, their pool had been fully enclosed for privacy. As she opened the door to the pool, warm humid air enveloped her. The smell of chlorine was a familiar reminder of the months of training she had gone through with the team. Ahead of her she saw a Zodiac sitting on the deck with Lieutenant Cooper standing next to it. The rest of the guys were stationed around the edge of the pool. Simmons was standing between her and the craft.

"What's up?" Julie asked as she passed him. "Why are you guys all spread out?"

"We're playing lifeguard. Don't want you drowning like last time," he said with a wicked grin.

"I didn't drown last time!" Julie exclaimed with mock indignation, and a big grin. "I *almost* drowned," she corrected. She had kept walking as they had talked and now she turned to their lieutenant as she got closer. "Where do you want me to take the Zodiac?"

"It's not a Zodiac, it's called a Combat Rubber Raiding Craft," Lieutenant Cooper corrected her.

"Oh, sorry, it looks like a Zodiac," Julie apologized with a grin. "Where should I sit?"

"I want you in the center. In a mission the squad will be arranged around the edge," Lieutenant Cooper explained.

"Alright, let's give this a try," Julie said nervously and took her position in the center of the boat.

"Remember, teleport it over the water, and then get yourself right back here. We don't know what will happen."

"Got it," Julie answered with a nod. She paused for a moment as she put the locations in her thoughts for the zaps. An instant later she appeared above the pool, and then in a flash she was sitting next to Lieutenant Cooper on the deck. She looked back at the pool to see what happened. The boat had fallen into the crater created by her zapping and, as the wall of water rushed in to fill the space it had left, it swamped the craft, tipping it over violently. A few moments later, as the water calmed down, several of the team dove in to retrieve it. Gripping the ropes that ran along its sides with one hand, they swam it back to Julie.

"That crater looked about four feet deep still. This time zap it eight feet up," Lieutenant Cooper directed her.

Julie took her position again. This time she appeared even higher above the water. Back on the pool deck she watched what happened this time. The craft landed with a smack on the calm surface of the pool.

"Alright, this time lower it a little. Let's try to get it as close to the surface as you can."

It took a couple more tries for her to find the perfect height. Then, while the team geared up and loaded into the raiding craft, she snacked on a protein bar and a soda. She was not tired yet, but they had found if she kept refueling throughout missions or training, she could zap many more times than if she went until she was exhausted and then ate something. As she finished her soda she saw the guys were ready and she took her position. "Ready?" she asked them; at their nods she zapped them over the pool.

Like before, she brought herself back to the pool deck as fast as she could. From her position she watched their first attempt. They dropped about six feet to the water's surface. The port side of the craft hit first, tossing the men on the other side across the raft. Then the starboard side smacked the water jarring them again.

Watching, Julie cringed at the scene and stepped forward preparing to jump in. She was not sure what she could really do, but she was certain that some of them would be hurt. Lieutenant Cooper stopped her with a hand on her arm. "They're fine, look," he reassured her. Sure enough, with only a few choice curses the team was settling back into their positions and then paddled back to the deck.

As they hauled the raiding craft out Lieutenant Cooper advised them, "Weigh your gear, and yourselves. Make sure both sides are even. Let's try this again."

Several minutes later, after adjusting their positions on the raft and rearranging their gear they were ready to try again. Julie took her place.

"Ready?" she asked, again they nodded. "Hang on."

Julie delivered them like she had before, then anxiously watched from the deck. This time their landing was much more level and the whole craft landed with a belly-flop like smack. All of the men were able to keep their seat through the jolt.

"Good work. Take a break. I want you to practice again this afternoon."

Matt finished stowing his gear and came over to Julie. "Hey, we're headed to the Pizza Parlor for lunch. Want to join us?"

"Sure, I'll meet you there," Julie agreed and headed back to change, then zapped to her office. On her way out she made sure she spoke to several of the staff. Then she spotted Admiral Huntington in a conversation and gave him a quick wave.

"How is that report coming?" he asked across the office.

"Really well, I got a lot done. I'm just headed out for a quick lunch, sir." Julie knew Admiral Huntington was aware of their training. Their conversation was mostly a cover.

"Good. I expect it on my desk before you leave tonight."

"Yes, sir," Julie replied and headed out to her car. The place the guys had chosen was just off base and it would not take her long to get there. She drove through the gate on McCain Boulevard and turned right on South O Street. A quick turn to her left and she was pulling into the parking lot.

Juli spotted Matt's car and out of habit she used her powers to look at him. The guys were trained to observe their surroundings and gauge any potential dangers. She had never learned, so she used her ability to sense others to check that it was safe. As she focused on Matt she was hit by was a glaring spot of energy. It was like a spotlight to her powers. She focused closer on him, fearing something was wrong, but as far as she could tell he was not worried at all.

Julie got out of her car and hesitantly entered the familiar restaurant. She paused just inside the door as she looked around. It looked the same as it always did with its grey and white mottled floor tile, the square wooden tables arranged around the room and the glaring blue neon lights above the doors to the kitchen. It was early for the lunch hour crowds and there were only a few other people eating. *I can't see anything out of the ordinary*, she thought.

"Hey, over here," Matt called when he noticed her, as if he thought she could not find them.

Julie used her powers again to look at the area around Matt. The bright flare of energy was right next to him. She opened her eyes. Simmons was sitting at the table right where it was coming from. Julie approached the group, staring at the thing in Simmons's hand. The flare of energy was coming from a device with knobs and dials that he was fiddling with.

"What's wrong, Julie?" Matt asked noticing her odd behavior.

"That thing... That thing is putting out some sort of

energy I can see..." she told them and glanced around. No one was close enough to overhear her. "With my powers," she added more quietly just in case.

"Really?" Simmons looked up at her in surprise. Now the rest of the group had stopped their conversations to see what was going on.

"What is it?" Julie asked.

"It's a transmitter. I was experimenting with new locator signals with longer ranges for your bracelet," Simmons explained quietly.

"What do you mean, you can sense it?" Matt asked confused.

"You know how I can kind of sense things around you when I look at you with my powers. Well it looks like a really bright light," Julie tried to explain.

"That's great!" Simmons exclaimed, excited.

"Yeah, I guess," Julie said halfheartedly. She was not sure why it was so great.

"The possibilities are endless!" Simmons asserted. "There are so many things we could use it for!"

"Like what?" Chief Nguyen asked.

"Well..." Simmons thought for a moment. "We could use it to tag something so Jade could zap to it without a picture."

"Could we use it to tag wounded?" she asked hopefully getting an idea. The one thing that really bothered her about Jade's persona being dead was it meant she was not allowed to rescue wounded personnel any more.

The team started scheming and they batted around ideas through lunch on how they could pull it off. The discussion was still going when they headed back to base. By the time she arrived back at the team's headquarters she found them discussing it with Lieutenant Cooper.

"Let me speak with Captain Lewis. Maybe he'll know of a way."

Julie walked, carrying her groceries in from her car. It had been a long day of training with the Team and she was getting home late. It was already dark and the shadows loomed around her. She looked around, suddenly nervous as she closed her trunk. There was no one around, at least not that she could sense. Uncertainly she headed down the sidewalk to her apartment. She was juggling her keys as she finally reached her door when the memory hit her. *It'd been dark just like this; she'd been struggling to open the door… She could almost feel the sting of the injection that General Jian's man had given her before she blacked out.* Julie was really scared now, but she tried to reason with herself, *Cinder's waiting for me right inside*, but the memory kept nagging at her and she couldn't bring herself to open her door.

"Hey Julie!"

"Oh," Julie jumped in surprise at the sudden appearance of her neighbor. "Hey, Brad."

"Sorry, I didn't mean to scare you…" Brad looked at her with concern. "You alright?"

"Yeah, I'm fine. I'm just having a hard time opening my door," Julie told him lamely.

"Here, let me help you," Brad said as he held out his hand.

Julie gave him the key to her apartment. In a moment he had opened the door and was holding it for her. In front of her Cinder sat wiggling excitedly at her arrival, still Julie stared into the dark apartment, hesitant. They stood for a moment neither one moving.

"Let me get those for you," Brad offered as he took the heavy bags from her and carried them into her kitchen.

Julie followed him in and turned on as many lights as she could, looking around her apartment like something was about to jump out at her.

"There you go, need anything else?" Brad asked as he stood smiling at her.

"Oh, no thanks, you've done enough already," Julie said embarrassed. Berating herself for being so silly, she tried to come up with an excuse to explain her behavior. "I've had a hard day; I must be more tired than I thought." Brad was heading out, and she followed him to her door. "Thanks again for the help."

"No problem. Take care," Brad said companionably.

"Matt! Hang on a second."

Matt turned to see a buddy of his from the Teams. He was on his way in to command for the day. "Hey Brad, what's up?"

"Remember my neighbor, the friend of yours that you asked me to keep an eye on? Julie?"

"Yeah, what about her?" Matt asked worried.

"Is she in trouble or something? I know it's none of my business, but she's really scared."

"What do you mean?"

"Well, remember a while back I told you about how jumpy she was when I came up behind her?" Brad reminded him. "It's getting worse. Like last night, I found her standing outside her apartment door, just staring at the lock. When I said hello I thought she'd jump out of her skin she was so scared. Do you know what's got her so rattled?"

Matt considered what he could tell his friend, and decided to tell him a portion of the truth. "Julie had a stalker who attacked her almost a year ago. He'd been waiting for her inside her old apartment. He even shot her dog. Then he tried again a few months ago when she was leaving work."

"He attacked her on base!" Brad exclaimed. "Did they ever catch the guy?"

"No," Matt said half truthfully. General Jian would never be a threat to her ever again, but they all understood that there was no way to find out how much the Chinese military still knew about Jade. *Strickland's attack four months ago would've just made her fears worse.*

"Crap. No wonder she's so nervous," Brad said sympathetically. "At least her nightmares have stopped."

"What nightmares?"

"Well about four months ago I'd hear her yelling in the middle of the night. The first few times it happened I went over and knocked on her door to see what was wrong. She'd answered the door with a terrified look in her eyes, all sweaty. She told me it was just a bad dream and that she was fine," Brad explained. "But honestly she looked really spooked. Then all of a sudden she stopped having them."

"What makes you think that?"

Brad shrugged, "I didn't hear her yelling anymore."

"Hey, thanks for letting me know," Matt said. Saying goodbye to his friend, Matt tried to think of a way to help Julie. He had known that she had started sleeping in her hideout, but she had never told him why. Now he knew.

CHAPTER 33

Nidal sat in the coffee shop, an untouched cup of coffee was on the table in front of him. *I hate this place,* he thought looking around. It was a hub for infidels with their immorality and feminism. The woman who had taken his order had worn lip and nose piercings and had no regard for a woman's proper place in society. It represented everything he hated about his country, but it was a safe place to meet Hassan without arousing suspicion. He fidgeted in his seat. Realizing he should be drinking his coffee, he took a sip of the terrible drink. *Ugh,* unconsciously he made a face at the taste. *I can't wait to get out of this place.* To brighten his mood he began imagining the ways he could blow up the building. The image of the people around him, lying dead in the rubble, made him smile.

"You look like you're enjoying yourself," Hassan said as he sat in the chair opposite Nidal.

Immediately Nidal hid his smile. He disliked Hassan, but he represented a foreign organization that was willing to fund his freedom movement so Nidal tolerated him.

"What took you so long? I've had to wait *here* for nearly an hour," Nidal said in disgust.

"I had a meeting that went late," Hassan said with a shrug. "You seem to have survived the torture," he grinned patronizingly.

Nidal knew that Hassan thought his network of American terrorist cells was amateurish. He wanted to smack the grin off the man's pompous face, but he restrained himself and waited.

"Have you decided on the day?" Hassan continued, not noticing Nidal's anger.

"We'll do it on September 11th, but I need another million dollars to make sure all of our associates have the supplies they need."

"Another million!" Hassan growled. The grin had vanished from his face. "We've already given you enough!"

"We want to send a message that will show the world we are not to be dismissed. They've blamed some of our attacks on accidents," Nidal hissed angrily under his breath.. "I want to make sure that this time they can't explain away our attacks."

Fool! Hassan thought disdainfully, but after a moment he shrugged, *another million wasn't that much to pay to accomplish his mission.* "Fine, I'll have it wired to your account by tonight," he agreed reluctantly.

"There's been another Somali pirate attack on an oil tanker. This time they took five US citizens hostage," Lieutenant Cooper placed the five photos on the folding card table in front of where Julie sat with the Team in their Mission Room. "Admiral Huntington has asked us to find them."

"How do we evac them without them seeing us?" Demetrio asked.

"We're not going to evacuate the hostages. Our mission will just be to take out the pirates holding them," Lieutenant Cooper explained. "After we've removed any threats, I'll make an anonymous tip to the local authorities."

Julie had been looking at the pictures, and had already started a sketch. "The Americans are being held in a room with lots of other people."

"The pirates have been busy lately. Those are probably other hostages that they're holding for ransom," Chief Nguyen told her.

"Is there an area outside of the room that's clear?" Matt asked.

Julie switched to a different picture and stretched her powers. This hostage was closer to a wall, and Julie could sense a clear area on the other side. "Here," she drew what she could sense on her sketch. She switched to another hostage; this one was farther down the wall. When she used her powers she could sense three people that did not feel like hostages. "There're three pirates here," again she made notes on her diagram.

"I wish you could tell us the coordinates of that building. We'd be able to get a satellite view of the whole place," Simmons brought up an old gripe.

"Sorry, no can do," Julie apologized again. "I wish I could."

"Wait, if I was back at headquarters I could patch into the satellites and locate the place if there was a beacon," Simmons suggested eagerly.

"How big would it be? I could drop it off quick, no problem," Julie offered.

"Good idea Simmons, why didn't you think of it before?" Chief Nguyen harassed him.

"Alright, Simmons get that beacon ready. Meet Julie here tomorrow morning. You'll have all day to locate that building and get us a visual," Lieutenant Cooper told him. "We'll hit them tomorrow afternoon."

"This is it?" Julie held the beacon in her hand. "It looks like a cockroach."

"Yep, that's all I'll need to find them," Simmons answered her.

"Do I need to put it near a window, or something?" Julie looked up from the small device.

"Nope, just put it in a dark corner, or along a wall. No one will notice it," Simmons said proudly.

Julie focused her powers on the hostages, looking for one close enough to a wall for her to get a lock on a clear space. "Okay, I think I've found a good spot."

"Make sure you're not seen," Matt warned her, "and get back in one piece."

Later that day the whole Team gathered over a satellite view of a building. It looked like a small warehouse. "The beacon is here," Simmons pointed to a red dot on the printout.

"This is where it is on my sketch," Julie pointed to a red dot she had added to her sketch. It was almost in the center of the large building.

"This group of pirates is much better organized than they've been in the past," Chief Nguyen commented.

"What do you mean?" Julie asked.

"Most of the time they have much smaller operations," the chief explained. "Keeping this kind of location secure and funded would take a large coordinated group."

"Alright, you all know what to do. Get geared up, we'll be hitting the target at 1500 hours, which will be 0300 local time," Lieutenant Cooper instructed them.

Within the hour the Team was ready to go. They had cleared the table and chairs from the Mission Room, giving them plenty of room to teleport. Matt handed Julie a headset and motioned for her to put it on. As she put it over her ears she could hear Simmons, "Testing... Testing."

"I can hear you," Julie confirmed.

"This will be just like the missions you helped us on

back in Afghanistan. Keep an eye out, and let us know if someone is nearby. We'll hear you, but we probably won't say anything to you because we don't want to be overheard," Matt explained.

Julie took a deep breath. Unlike the missions she helped them with before, she would be the one talking to them, telling them what she was 'seeing' around them. "I don't know your strange combat lingo. I hope I don't confuse you by speaking English," she joked, trying to hide her worry.

"We'll figure it out, I'm sure," Matt reassured her.

"Let's go!" Lieutenant Cooper called out, interrupting their conversation.

Julie had taken a moment to get a good look at the area where she had dropped the beacon. The hallway had been about twenty feet long before it turned, and about eight feet wide. She zapped them in as pairs; Matt and Simmons were the first two. They had already moved down the hall toward the turn by the time she brought in Lieutenant Cooper and Doc. Finally she brought in Demetrio and Chief Nguyen. Back in the Mission Room she sat on the floor with her back to the wall, and watched their progress. The group had split up to go both ways down the hall. She found Matt leading the larger group, and as she shifted through each man, she found that it was Demetrio and Chief Nguyen who had taken the other way.

Damn, Julie cursed to herself. *That'll mean I'll have to shift my focus between both groups.* She knew focusing on more than one group during a mission could give her a headache. Shifting back to the first group she spotted a potential danger. "Matt, there're two people ahead of you and to your right at 2 o'clock," Julie advised them. She 'saw' his group stop. She guessed that the people she had sensed were coming down a hallway that intersected theirs. As the two came in line with the Team, they vanished from her awareness. *Two down*, she thought nervously.

She continued to shift between Matt and Demetrio.

Letting each man know what she could sense around them. She did not want to distract them too much, so she tried to keep her descriptions short, but informative. After what seemed like an eternity of watching their progress, she noticed two of Matt's group move away.

Ah Hell, they're splitting up again, she thought frustrated. *Now I'll need to shift my focus between Matt, Chief Nguyen and LT!*

Looking at Chief Nguyen's group she saw two men coming up quickly from behind them. "Chief, there're two men coming up fast from your 5 o'clock," she told him. She watched as he and Doc changed their positions to meet the oncoming threat. In moments two more pirates to disappear from her senses.

Now she checked on Lieutenant Cooper. *Crap!* "LT, I don't know if you can see this, but there are six people right in front of you, and two smaller groups are coming at you from your 2 o'clock and your 8 o'clock."

"What are the six in front of us doing?" She could barely hear the lieutenant's whispered question.

"I can't tell, but they're not moving," she tried to give him a little more information. "They are in two rows, evenly spaced apart." She 'watched' as Lieutenant Cooper and Doc moved closer to the six pirates. They barely moved as they disappeared from her senses.

"How big are the next two groups?" Lieutenant Cooper whispered.

"The group that's closer and coming from your current 2 o'clock has eight people. The other one has four," she tried to describe them. She heard gun shots over the headset. They were much louder than the Team's suppressed weapons had been. *It must be the pirates! That noise will wake everyone up!* Sure enough, when she focused her powers around Lieutenant Cooper's position again she could see more figures coming toward them. "Now there's four more joining that first group, and a couple more coming from the other way."

Julie opened her eyes, desperately looking for something to help them. *If only there was someone who could give them some back-up,* she thought. Then her eyes landed on her shotgun. Quickly she got to her weapon and grabbed a box of shells. Loading six shots into the tube under its barrel, she put a seventh shell in the chamber and racked the round with a satisfying ca-chunk. She checked the position of the second group heading for Lieutenant Cooper and Doc. There were still only six men. *Can I really do this?*

The thought of shooting six men made her pause, but then she thought about losing Doc or the lieutenant. Her mind made up, she focused her powers on the pirates and zapped herself as far behind them as she could, then opened fire. At that range her pellets were spread really wide. If she had been trap shooting it would have been an issue, but the men were much larger than the clay pigeons she had practiced on. With them packed next to each other filling the hall, it just meant that each shot hit several targets. She emptied her semi-auto shotgun as fast as she could, aiming at the center of their backs. Then she zapped herself back to the Mission Room. Checking on Lieutenant Cooper and Doc she saw that they were taking care of the pirates that had attacked them. Shifting her attention to Matt, she saw that his group was approaching Chief Nguyen and Demetrio.

"Burke, Chief, you're coming up on each other," she warned them. Julie saw the four men regroup together and continue on. Soon it was obvious that they were headed toward the pirates attacking Lieutenant Cooper and Doc. Caught in the crossfire, the pirates died quickly.

"Where's the second group you reported?" Lieutenant Cooper asked breathing heavily.

"They're gone," Julie said vaguely.

"What do you mean they're gone? Did they leave?"

"No, I took care of them," Julie said, dreading the yelling at she was going get.

There was silence on the comm for a little while. She used her powers to watch them as they headed to the group she took out.

"I thought I heard a shotgun," Doc said flatly.

"We'll discuss that later," Lieutenant Cooper said seriously. "Right now I need to call in the locals."

It took less than an hour for the local police to respond to Lieutenant Cooper's anonymous tip. "Jade, it's time for us to come home," he signaled her as the six men gathered. Julie zapped behind each pair and zapped them back to the Mission Room.

"What were you thinking?" Matt asked, confronted her first.

"I was wishing there was another Team of SEALs that I could zap in to back you guys up. But the only thing I could find was my shotgun," Julie said stubbornly, glaring back at him. Then she gave in and said more softly. "It wasn't what I wanted to do, but I was worried about LT and Doc."

"At least it was well done," Demetrio gave his opinion from where he was taking off his gear. "They didn't even get a chance to see what hit them."

"You were what, ten, maybe fifteen yards away from them?" Chief Nguyen asked from his side of the room.

"Yeah about that," Julie nodded. "I figured at that range each shot would hit a couple targets. I just emptied my gun as fast as I could and zapped out."

"The problem wasn't your technique, it did the job alright," Lieutenant Cooper interrupted their conversation. Now his expression became grim as he said quietly, "Don't ever go in theatre again without letting us know. If we had engaged those targets while you were there we could've hit you."

"Yes, sir," Julie promised, hanging her head. His quiet seriousness hit her harder than if he had yelled at her. "I wasn't thinking. I won't do it again."

"Make sure you don't," Lieutenant Cooper said

seriously.

"For the record, we could've handled them," Doc said with a wink as he followed the lieutenant out of the room.

"Come on, the first round is on me," Simmons joked, giving Julie a pat on the shoulder as he passed her. Demetrio and Chief Nguyen followed the others out, each one giving her a companionable swat on the back or shove, leaving Julie and Matt alone.

"I guess you're going to yell at me some more, huh?" Julie grumped.

"It *was* a pretty stupid thing to do," he reminded her.

"This team is the only thing I have left in my life," Julie explained quietly. "If anything ever happened to *any* of you I don't know what I'd do."

Matt pulled her into a hug, and kissed her forehead. Seeing his chance to find out about her nightmares he asked, "Julie, how're you doing, really? Strickland's attack must've really scared you."

She shrugged against his embrace. "I'm Okay," she lied.

"I'm serious. Most people who've been through what you have over the last year, would at least have nightmares," Matt said gently.

"I had some nightmares a few months ago, but I'm fine now," Julie told him. She did not want to admit to him that she was jumping at shadows too.

"Really? You haven't had any more nightmares since then?" Matt wanted to be sure.

"Yeah, that's why I sleep in my hideout now. I feel safe there."

Satisfied that she at least had her nightmares under control he decided to stop prying. "Come on, let's get changed quick and head out for something to eat. We can see if any of the other guys want to come too if you want."

Julie sniffled a little and then chuckled. "Yeah, that'd

be fun."

A week later, Lieutenant Cooper called the Team back to Matt's house for another mission. "Admiral Huntington has asked that we take out this man," he said, placing the picture on the table. "His name is Raul Diaz. He's the head of a major drug cartel."

Julie was studying the man's picture preparing to look for him.

"Julie, look for a place we can put another transmitter. This is going to be another mission where surveillance satellites will be a huge advantage," Lieutenant Cooper instructed her.

Julie nodded. She had already found Raul, but there were too many people around him. "I can't. There're people all around him."

"Take your time, but keep trying. Let us know if you find a safe area. These guys are cold blooded and well trained, so we'll be going in with you to drop off the transmitter," Lieutenant Cooper explained. He looked at his watch. "It's 0800, head back to your cover job in the admiral's office. Give us a call if you find an opening. Otherwise we'll all meet back here at 2200 hours. Our best chance will be sometime during the night."

Julie' headache had grown through the day as she had watched the target, but it had paid off. Because she had been watching him for so long she had been able to map out much of the building as he had moved around all day. By 2200 hours Julie had already found an area near their target that they could use to drop off the transmitter. She pointed to her sketch. "This is what I've found so far. He's been asleep for the last hour, so I can only sense about this far," she explained, circling a portion of her map. "There're two other people with him, most likely women."

"You're probably right, but why do you think that?" Chief Nguyen asked.

Julie blushed with the memory of what she had

sensed from the guy, "About an hour ago he was.... Let's just say he was busy," Julie said blushing even more. Glancing up she saw that they were all staring at her with various expressions on their faces. "I didn't watch, you pervs!" she exclaimed, making them all laugh at her discomfort. She wadded up one of her pieces of paper and threw it at them.

"Okay, Okay," Lieutenant Cooper broke into the commotion. "Chief and Simmons, you'll go in with Julie. Get that transmitter hidden well."

A few minutes later they were ready and Julie zapped the three of them to the area she had found. They had made her kneel on the floor as they crouched around her before she teleported them in. As they moved away from her, Julie could see that they were on a large balcony. Simmons quietly moved toward a potted plant in the corner, while Chief Nguyen brought a tiny camera out of one of his pouches. Surprised, she watched as he began taking pictures of the surrounding area. Julie stayed exactly where they had left her, but through the railing of the balcony she could see that the balcony they were on overlooked a compound of buildings. In the distance she could see one guard tower with two men walking around. As soon as Simmons finished hiding the transmitter he came back to Julie and stood guard over her. Chief Nguyen took another moment to take more pictures before he came back to her. Taking her shoulder he nodded for her to take them back.

"So what's with the pictures Chief?" Julie asked when they were back in the Mission Room. "Are you looking for other places for me to zap you?"

"No," he said shaking his head. "That'd be too dangerous. I was getting intel on their defenses for when we hit them."

After that the group headed home. It would take at least a day for the satellite to move into position. The Team would plan their attack without her, so they decided to wait to meet again until the next night. Julie arrived at Matt's house around 7 o'clock. They had planned on having dinner together before the mission.

"What do you mean we're not going in tonight?" Julie asked surprised.

"Admiral Huntington has ordered a missile strike, using the transmitter's coordinates for targeting," Matt explained. "There's nothing there that we need to recover, and this way we don't have to go in." Julie sighed with relief; that meant she would not have to worry about them tonight. "We just need you to check that our target is still there."

Julie used her powers to find Raul. She found him sitting on the same balcony they had visited the night before. "Yep, he's practically sitting on the transmitter."

"Good," Matt said, and pulled out his cell phone. After punching in a number he listened for a moment. "It's a go," he said briefly, then hung up.

"So that's it?" Julie asked.

"Yep, the bomber was already on its way," Matt agreed.

Julie thought about all of the people she had sensed in the compound the day before. *They're all going to die because of me*, she thought. "What kind of bomb are they using?" she asked, dreading the answer.

"Probably just a five hundred pound JDAM. Enough to take out the building he's in," Matt answered with a shrug. It took a moment for Julie to remember what JDAM stood for, joint direct attack munition. It was a very complicated name for a guided bomb. Matt must have read her expression when she realized how much damage a five hundred pound explosion would cause. "Hey, don't think about it," he ordered her. "It's not your fault. That decision was made by someone a lot higher than us on the food chain."

Julie nodded, Matt was right. *I don't want to think about it too much.*

CHAPTER 34

"Julie!" Brad called out. "Hey, don't go up to your apartment right now," he said as he came up to her.

"Why not?" she asked perplexed, as she got out of her car.

"I'm not sure, but there's a delivery vehicle parked nearby that's been there all day," Brad explained.

Julie looked around, suddenly nervous. Brad caught a flash of light across her face. She must have seen it too, because they both looked up at a nearby roof. He saw the sun glint off of a scope. Brad felt Julie grab his arm and then he was ten feet away from her car. Behind them her windshield shattered in a star pattern from the impact of the sniper's bullet. Julie looked back at the shooter, at the same time Brad saw her bring her leg back like she was about to kick something, then she was gone. Instinctively he dove for cover just as another bullet hit the ground where he had just been standing. Looking up, he was just in time to see Julie appear above the sniper. She kicked the sniper in the head and blinked out again. Brad spotted a second figure running along the roof away from the sniper's position, as Julie appeared back on the sidewalk.

"Hey, take cover!" Brad yelled at her from behind a

concrete support.

Brad noticed that her eyes were closed, as she brought her right arm back like she was about to hit something. Then she vanished again. Brad looked back up at the roof and saw her arrive in front of the fleeing man. She landed a solid blow to the oncoming man's face which stopped him in his tracks. When she disappeared again, she instantly reappeared above him and kicked the sniper in the back of the head. The man went down like dead weight. Julie reappeared on the sidewalk next to Brad breathing a little faster.

She turned to him and smiled a bit shyly. "Um... Hi...," she said hesitantly.

"What the hell just happened?" Brad asked her as he came up beside her. People had started to emerge from their apartments and a crowd was gathering in the parking lot. He noticed that she was cradling her right hand.

"Hang on, I should probably call this in," Julie got out her cell phone awkwardly and dialed a number.

"I already called the MPs," Brad told her, thinking that's what she was talking about. To his surprise she called someone else.

"I was attacked again," she said briefly, keeping her voice low so no one could overhear her. "A couple snipers," she explained. "They're not going anywhere," she paused to listen. "No, I didn't shoot them with my shotgun!" she said irritated. "Let me check," she said as she closed her eyes. "They're still alive, but they're out cold." She listened for another moment, "Yeah, Brad Binuya's here. He's the reason they didn't get the jump on me." There was another pause as she listened again. "He called them already, before I got here." She nodded unconsciously as she answered, "Okay." Then Julie handed the phone to him. "It's Lieutenant Cooper. He wants to talk to you," Julie explained.

"Lieutenant?" Brad said into the phone.

"Petty Officer Binuya, I know you've got a lot of

questions, I'll explain everything later. Right now I need your help again. First, were there any other witnesses?"

"No, sir" he said quickly.

"Perfect. I need you to talk to the MPs."

"What do you want me to say?"

"Tell them you were alone when the snipers shot at you, and that you saw someone fight them, but you don't know where the third person went."

"I understand," Brad said.

"Good, and thanks for saving her. We owe you."

"No problem... She's who I think she is, isn't she?" Brad asked.

"Yes," Lieutenant Cooper confirmed what Brad had already guessed. "I've got to call the admiral. As soon as you can get away from the MPs, help her get to the briefing room safely."

"Yes, sir," Brad agreed and hung up. He could already hear sirens approaching. He noticed her favoring her right hand still. "How's that hand of yours?" he asked. Brad used his body to help hide her hand as he took it gently. "That guy's face hit it pretty hard," he joked.

"I think it's just bruised."

"Can you move it?" Brad asked as he watched her flex her fingers. She was able to move all of them without too much pain. "It's probably okay, but you might want to get it x-rayed."

"I'll keep an eye on it," she agreed. "Thanks for saving my life," Julie added quietly.

By then a large number of people had assembled in groups around them. "It's my pleasure, Jade," he whispered her name into her ear, and then winked at her.

Julie smiled shyly and looked at her feet. Brad wondered what she was thinking. "Stay close by. I'll take care of the MPs," he told her.

Julie nodded, "LT told me to say I didn't see anything."

"Good, that's best," Brad agreed. If he was the only

witness they would not have to worry about their stories matching.

Brad made a point of meeting the patrol car when it arrived. Julie mingled with the crowd, trying to be inconspicuous as she put her hand in her pocket to hide her swollen knuckles. Quickly he explained what had happened. The officers called in reinforcements as they evacuated the building that the sniper's had used. Then they secured the access to the roof and waited for the additional officers to arrive. When they did, they stormed the roof. Brad watched as the MPs searched the area. It was not long before they reached the downed snipers. Afterward an officer approached Brad again.

"Are you the one who called this in?"

"Yes sir, I'd noticed a strange vehicle parked nearby."

The officer looked through his notes. "I see that, I have its license plate number here. What made you think it was suspicious?" the officer asked.

"It's a delivery vehicle that'd been sitting in the same spot all day," Brad said in explanation.

"What happened after you called it in?"

"I was standing over here by the parking lot when they started shooting at me," Brad said as he pointed to Julie's windshield and the sidewalk. "I took cover behind this column. That's when I saw a fight break out on the roof."

"Did you see where the third person went?"

"No, sir."

Julie watched as Brad was interviewed by the MP for a while longer. "Alright, I have your information. I'll contact you later if I have any more questions," the MP informed him.

"Yes, sir. Is it alright if I take my girlfriend out to dinner?" When the officer nodded, Brad headed back to Julie's side. "Let's go," he said as he put a protective arm over her shoulders. He scanned the crowd critically as they moved through the parking lot, and led her to his car. He put her in the passenger seat of his yellow Mustang, before going around to the driver's side.

"Sorry you have to go through all this trouble," Julie said embarrassed.

"It's no problem; I didn't have any plans tonight anyway," Brad smiled encouragingly. "So I guess this is why you're always so jumpy."

"Yeah, we'd hoped Jade's death would keep them off my trail, but I guess someone's still looking for me."

It was a short drive to Team 3's building. Brad made Julie wait in the car while he scanned the area. When he let her get out of the car he stood protectively over her as he escorted her into the building. Matt opened the door for them. Brad thought it was odd how quiet it was. He would have thought the whole Team would be mobilized after an attack on Jade, but when he got her to the briefing room, only Captain Lewis and Lieutenant Cooper were there to meet them. *I bet most of Team 3 doesn't know that Jade is still alive*, he realized.

"It's good to see you in one piece," Lieutenant Cooper greeted Julie. "What happened?"

Julie gave them a quick rundown of the attack, starting from when Brad met her at her car.

"Wait, why did you think to warn her, Petty Officer Binuya?" Captain Lewis asked Brad.

"Matt had told me that Julie had been having trouble with a stalker. So I wanted to warn her about a suspicious vehicle I'd seen," Brad explained.

"I think Julie needs to be moved to more secure housing," Lieutenant Cooper said and turned to Captain Lewis for agreement.

"LT, please, I know there's a risk, but can't I stay where I'm living now?" Julie begged. She turned to Captain Lewis. "I'm tired of hiding. I'm tired of being scared all the time. If they've found me so be it!" she said determined.

Captain Lewis thought for a moment. "You're sure no

one witnessed Julie taking out the snipers?" he asked turning to Brad.

"Yes, sir."

"And you reported to the MPs that they were shooting at you?"

Again Brad answered, "Yes, sir."

"Alright, I'll have to clear it with Admiral Huntington, but I think he'll agree. We're going to make it public knowledge that you were the target of the attack. If I remember right, those living quarters were assigned to mostly Team members. They'll naturally keep a closer eye on the area. If they alert you to anything, get Julie to safety and alert us."

"So can I stay at my place tonight?" Julie asked.

"No," Captain Lewis said sternly. "Until we're sure that these two acted alone I want you to lay low. Stay in your hideout until further notice," he instructed her.

"Can I stop by my apartment before I go?"

"Yes, Chief Nguyen is there already. Then zap straight from there to your cave."

"Thank you, sir," Julie headed out of the briefing room, with Matt and Brad following her.

"Julie, I'm just curious, why didn't you just teleport to safety when they started shooting?" Brad asked as he followed her out.

Julie looked surprised by the question. "I couldn't leave you to face those guys on your own," she answered simply. Turning to Matt she said, "I guess I'll see you later. Let me know what happens with those two, will you? Oh, what should I do with my car? The windshield has a bullet hole through it."

"I'll take care of it," Matt reassured her. "See ya later."

Then Julie just disappeared. Brad shook his head, "I just don't get her."

"Join the rest of us," Matt agreed with a grin.

"No, really, she attacked those two because she

thought I was in danger?" Brad asked confused. "She seems so timid most of the time, but the way she took out those two she looked like some sort of anime ninja."

"Yeah, if someone else is in danger she goes on the offensive," he agreed again. Shaking his head he added, "I wish I could've seen it. Her uncle's been training her in self-defense. So we don't really know what she's capable of."

Julie spent the next three days in her hideout. *Luckily I grabbed stuff to do when I stopped by my apartment*, Julie thought in dismay. She was lounging on her bed, playing yet another video game on her tablet, bored out of her mind. Matt had called a few times to check on her and to update her on the investigation. The last she had heard, the two men were still being interrogated.

She jumped as the phone rang, shattering the silence of her hideout. Cinder raised his head from where he was lying to watch her cross the room to answer the satellite phone. "Hello?"

"Hey, we've got some answers. Ready to come back?"

"Yes!" Julie nearly yelled in her excitement of getting out of the cave.

Matt laughed, "Why don't you zap to me, we're…"

Before he could finish Julie was standing in front of him. "It's so nice to see another person!" she said, and nearly embraced him, but she restrained herself when she noticed they were not alone. "Hey guys," she said cheerfully to the team. She noticed that Brad was also there and she glanced curiously at Lieutenant Cooper.

"We've decided Petty Officer Binuya will be a better asset if he knows the details of your security," Lieutenant Cooper explained.

"Especially, since you've already revealed your secret identity to him," Matt could not resist teasing her.

"Hey Brad," Julie greeted him with a smile, ignoring Matt's jibe. Then she turned to the lieutenant. "So, what've they found out?" she asked. Matt waved her to sit down as Lieutenant Cooper started the meeting.

"From the little the intelligence guys could uncover, the two men were spies from China. Based on their phone records, it appears that their last contact with their superiors had been that morning. The agents found where they've been staying. When they searched the place they discovered that the snipers didn't know exactly which apartment was yours. They only suspected that you lived in the area. We're attributing their capture to a fictitious off duty MP who saw them and interfered with their operation."

"What's going to happen to them?" Julie asked. "They won't get a chance to tell anyone about me will they?"

Lieutenant Cooper smiled reassuringly. "No, they're going to disappear somewhere no one will find them," he told her.

CHAPTER 35

It had taken nearly six months to make it possible for Jade to start retrieving wounded personnel again, but finally they had presented the idea to the three major bases in Afghanistan. Julie would be taking the wounded to a custom built structure outside Bethesda for treatment. As far as the hospital staff knew it was a new high-tech facility. It had a massive antenna mounted on the roof, along with a large radar dish, both of which were not connected to anything. While the inside of the building was mostly comprised of movie props. The highly technical control panels and monitors looked impressive, but in reality did nothing except generate random noises and flashes.

The bases in Afghanistan had been told that this new technology would be able to retrieve any wounded military personnel who have been tagged by a transmitter. The device was a small box with a switch on one side and Velcro on the other. Each medic in the combat units would be issued the transmitters. When they got to a critically wounded soldier, they could activate it and attach it to the soldier's uniform. The top secret facility would sense the transmitter and use its signal to find and teleport the individual instantly. After it was done, it would activate an alarm to alert hospital staff to the presence of the wounded personnel.

Julie silently laughed to herself when she heard their explanation. *Whatever it takes*, she had thought. In reality she would be seeing the transmitter beacon and then speed-zap the wounded person into the new building. A motion sensor in the room would sense her arrival and activate the siren, before she zapped back to their Mission Room. The signal was bright enough she would have no trouble finding it even from back in San Diego.

Julie's routine changed after that. Now that she was back to doing retrieval missions, she needed to be available at a moment's notice. During a briefing the next day they presented her with a new device.

"What in the world is this? Some sort of high tech, ultra-classified new gizmo?" Julie asked as she looked at the small black box. The only distinguishable features on it were a tiny LED screen and a clip to attach it to your clothes.

"Actually, it's a piece of old technology. It's called a pager. When the command gets word that a unit is under attack they will call a number. The unit commanders think it is to turn on the device, but really it calls the pager," Simmons explained eagerly. His geek side was enjoying the new toy.

"But why would we want to use such old technology? My dad used to have one of these when he was a kid," Julie said. She was looking at the tiny LED screen with doubt.

"Because it's completely untraceable," Simmons beamed with pride. "If we used a modern phone for instance, someone would be able to track where it was received. Pagers only receive the information that the number has been called; they don't respond back to the system."

Simmons also handed a pager out to Matt and Doc.

"What's the plan?" Matt looked to Lieutenant Cooper as he held the tiny device.

"All three of you will get the alerts. Julie will be using the Mission Room at the house as her primary base to teleport in and out. Julie, you'll gear up and head there to watch for the beacons. Matt, when you get an alert, you're responsible for securing the house. No one is to gain access to Jade at any cost. Miller, you are to get to the house and provide additional security and, in the case of Jade becoming wounded, to provide medical care."

"No problem," Doc agreed.

They received their first alert the next day. Julie and Matt were out to dinner at Friday's Sports Bar and Grill. It was the same one they had gone to for their first date. Since then it had become one of their favorite places.

Julie's pager beeped first, right as the waitress arrived with their food. The sizzling plate of fajitas smelled amazing. Matt's pager went off only a few seconds later. They looked at each other and laughed at their luck.

"Excuse me miss, we have to leave, will this cover our bill?" Matt asked the waitress as she finished placing their plates on the table, and handed her $40.

Surprised the waitress stood stunned for a moment, "Oh, sure, no problem. I'll just box these up for you," she offered, confused. She started to gather up the plates.

"We don't have time. Thank you anyway," Matt said as they stood up from their seats.

Outside the restaurant they climbed into Matt's car. Instead of driving out to the street right away, Matt drove around to the back of the restaurant. He checked for security cameras. After making sure no one was watching, he nodded to Julie, who zapped back to her apartment to put on her gear. It was very similar to the uniform she had used when she worked out of the base in Afghanistan: combat fatigues with the same bulletproof vest she had been given by the team so long ago. Then she put her long blonde hair up into a bun at the base of her neck and pulled on her full face mask and then her helmet. Just in case someone was able to spot her, they wanted her identity protected. Once she was ready, she called to Cinder, and zapped them both to the Mission Room. Opening the armored, soundproof door she sent Cinder out into the house. He would provide some protection while she worked until Matt was able to get there. Sitting in the center of the room, she focused her powers out, looking for a beacon, and waited.

Julie was not sure how long she had been waiting before the first beacon was activated. She saw it flare up at the edge of her awareness. They had practiced this many times, but this was the first time she was doing it for real and she was nervous as she focused on it. Taking a deep breath she zapped to the beacon and then to the trailer as fast as she could. Without thinking, she looked down at her hand which she had placed on the beacon as she zapped to the device. It was stuck to the MOLLE webbing of the man's camouflaged vest. She looked at his wounds; he had burns and deep gouges along one side of his body. He moaned in pain. Around her she heard the siren suddenly kick on, and she zapped back the house.

Stupid, don't wait there, he could have seen you! Julie berated herself. She sat down again to watch for another beacon. Matt poked his head in the room a few minutes later, "All's secure out here. How's it going?"

"Only one so far," Julie reported, deciding not to mention her stupidity.

"I hear Doc…we'll be here if you need us," Matt said before closing the door again.

Julie rescued four more personnel before her pager beeped again, signaling the end of the battle. She rubbed her temple as she opened the door. Concentrating for that long gave her headaches. Matt and Doc's pagers had also beeped and they met her outside the room. Matt handed her a soda. "How'd it go?" he asked.

"Good, I think," Julie answered after swallowing her

first gulp of soda. "It's nice to be back helping retrieve wounded."

CHAPTER 36

Julie sat on her couch relaxing. She had been up all night evacuating wounded from a battle that had lasted for hours. Her head was killing her and she was exhausted from zapping so many people. Sipping the orange juice she had poured for herself, she reached for the TV remote. Cinder came over and rested his head on her leg, a subtle cue for her to pet him. She smiled and rubbed his ears. She had been picking up wounded for a few months and for the most part it had not been too much for her. But the last week she had been busy. With the insurgents making a power grab, she had been needed nearly every day to evacuate wounded, and so Admiral Huntington had given her the day off. Unfortunately Matt had to report to base, that meant she would be alone most of the day. Raising the TV's remote control she started flipping through the channels. She turned it to the local news station hoping to see the weather report. *Maybe I could go surfing*, she thought lazily.

She started watching the news in the middle of a story about a local elementary school whose students were donating their hair to Locks of Love. The reporter explained that the adults who were doing the cutting were either cancer survivors themselves or had family members affected by cancer.

The story was interrupted as the words "News Alert" blazed across the screen in lurid colors. The lead anchor for the channel was gripping papers in front of him - his usual calm demeanor gone.

"We have reports coming in from all over the country. Several important bridges have been blown up at major freeway intersections. Also, the power grids in dozens of east coast cities have gone down, including New York and Washington D.C." The reporter paused for a moment as he studied the computer screen in front of him. "This just in from the AP: several explosions have been reported in the Mall of the Americas. No word is available yet on possible casualties. We have...." The TV shut off in the middle of the report. The room fell silent as all of the electrical devices in her apartment lost power. Beside her on the couch, her cell phone rang. She saw the number identified on its screen. She answered it quickly. "Hello."

"Julie, are you alright?" Matt's voice was tight with concern.

"Yeah, I'm fine. What's going on?"

"Just get in here now, it'll be safer for you until we figure this out."

Julie dressed and packed a bag with a few personal items in case she was not able to return to her apartment for a few days. "Come here, boy," she called, grabbing dog food and Cinder's leash. "You get to spend the day in Matt's back yard." She zapped herself and Cinder to the Mission Room and then went through the house to let the dog go in the backyard. There she set her supplies on the table. Next she zapped herself directly into the women's restroom at Headquarters. Quickly she headed out to the briefing room and almost ran into Matt, who had been pacing right outside the door.

"What took you so long?" he snapped at her.

"I grabbed a few things in case I couldn't go back," Julie answered lamely. "What's wrong?"

"The cell towers are down now too. I couldn't reach you... and we need you," he told her. Matt had grabbed her arm and was propelling her down the hallway. He handed her a mask. "Put this on. Jade is officially alive as of this moment."

"I don't understand. Why?" Julie asked. She pulled on her mask just as they reached the briefing room. Matt opened the door for her and half pushed her in. The room was full of people. Julie knew the Seal Teams had hundreds of support personnel. She had seen them before, but not all stuffed into the small meeting room at once. Even though the room was standing room only, it was eerily silent except for Captain Lewis, their direct commanding officer, was standing in front of the room giving orders.

At their entrance he stopped mid-sentence. "Everyone, you probably all remember Jade," he remarked. At his introduction the room was filled with quiet exclamations and whispering. "Her death was a security measure, but with the current situation we can't keep her hidden any longer."

"What's going on?" Julie asked.

Captain Lewis turned to Jade. "The President's decoy plane just exploded in mid-air, and we have information that Air Force One has several gunmen trying to assassinate the President," he told her.

Julie pushed her shock aside. "What are my orders, sir?"

"You and SEAL Team 3 are to board the President's plane. Rescue the President and as many of his staff as possible," the captain instructed her.

"Where should I take them?"

"The team will brief you further once you are moving," Captain Lewis said avoiding the question. Julie got the feeling that he wanted to keep the location secret even from his own personnel. She understood his decision. After all, they had found spies in their support staff last year, helping the rogue DIA agent capture her and the guys. "Right now zap yourself and Burke to the rest of your team. They're getting geared up as we speak."

Julie turned to Matt. "Ready?" she asked. Matt nodded and she zapped them to Lieutenant Cooper.

When Julie and Matt arrived, the rest of the squad was waiting in the hold of another cargo plane. Chief Nguyen opened the cockpit door and told the pilot to take off. Matt started gathering his gear as Julie went to Lieutenant Cooper. "What's the plan, Sir?"

"We are in communication with the President's secret service agents. They have fallen back to a defensible position in Air Force One. The President is uninjured, but several of his security detail have been wounded," Lieutenant Cooper's explanation was interrupted as Doc handed Julie an orange drink.

"What's this?"

"Just drink it, I'll explain later," Doc said cryptically as he walked back to their gear.

Lieutenant Cooper continued. "You'll zap all of us into that compartment. Then as we help hold the position, you will zap the President out first, then his security detail. Sketch the layout on here," Lieutenant Cooper instructed her, handing her a pad of paper and a pencil. "Don't take too much time to get an idea of the layout of their position," Lieutenant Cooper cautioned her.

Julie pushed her headache out of her thoughts as she set to work. Over the past year the last President had lost his bid for re-election when his administration had been plagued with controversies. President McIntire had only been in office for a few months. She had voted for him; he seemed to be different from the last President. *I hope he's alright*, she thought as she used her powers to check on him. He was a tall, slim man, and she pictured his dark red hair, with grey at the temples. It only took her a moment to find him. Quickly she mapped out the layout of the area he was in and the location of his men. It looked like two men were positioned around the President, basically on top of him. Two more personnel were off to one side, and there were four more about ten feet away in a line.

Lieutenant Cooper and some of the members of the team looked over her shoulder as she put in the last details. "Looks like the best spot would be in the middle," Lieutenant Cooper gave his assessment.

Julie thought of a new concern, "Do they know we're coming? What if they shoot us?" Julie didn't like zapping into the middle of a fire fight.

"We can't tell them we're coming because we don't know if the terrorists are monitoring communications," Lieutenant Cooper told her. "We'll go in surrounding you. If they fire, you should still be able to complete the mission."

"You mean the Team is going to be taking the bullets to protect me?" Julie asked shocked. "There has to be a better way!"

"We're not just protecting you; we're covering the President's only way out of danger. If you get hit, we'll all be trapped there and we can't risk the President being assassinated," Chief Nguyen piped in from where he sat against the plane's wall. Next to him the cockpit door opened and Julie heard a voice shout. When the door closed Chief Nguyen shouted to the Team, "We're up to speed."

Lieutenant Cooper motioned for Julie to get in the center of the space. "Tuck up in a ball… less of you will be exposed," he explained as he threw a ballistic blanket over her. "Stay tucked until we tell you it's all clear."

"For the record, I don't like this plan," Julie complained as the Team arranged themselves around her hunched form. She could feel them all wrapping their arms protectively over her shoulders and head. "Ready?" Julie asked with dread. They all answered back, "Ready" and she zapped them onto Air Force One.

The next moment the air was filled with gun shots and shouting. "Hold your fire! US Navy, hold your fire! Hold your fire!" After what seemed like an eternity the shouting died down and she heard Lieutenant Cooper state more calmly, "We're here to evac the President."

"How did you get here?" asked a man somewhere in front of Julie. "How do we know you're friendlies?"

"We are part of SEAL Team 3 and this is Jade," at that Lieutenant Cooper tapped Julie on the shoulder and she came out from under the ballistic blanket. "We'll stay to help cover your evac. She'll teleport you to our plane, and then return for the wounded and the rest of the personnel." As they continued to talk, Julie took the time to check on the team. They were all still positioned around her, hands raised to show they were not a threat. She gasped silently to herself; she spotted blood on Chief Nguyen's hand as he held it over his shoulder, putting pressure on a wound. Then she saw that Demetrio's lanky form seemed to be crouched awkwardly. She could not see it, but using her powers she could tell he was hit in his leg. *Damn terrorists*, inwardly she cursed the people who had made it necessary for them to be here.

"Jade? She was supposed to be killed a year ago," the statement came from a different voice. "Why wasn't I informed of her existence?" Jade returned her attention back to the speakers.

"Mr. President, the Secretary of Defense was planning on briefing you soon in private. We had to report her death to protect her. Before today only a handful of people knew she was still alive," Lieutenant Cooper admitted, and then a burst of gun fire interrupted their conversation.

"Alright, get President McIntire out of here. We can

discuss this later," the first voice spoke again. Now that Julie was not covered by the team she saw that the man who had originally spoken was a lean, gray-haired man. His eyes were intense slits as he scowled at the situation.

"Miller, you and Jade take Demetrio, the President and those two," he waved at the secret service agents beside the President. "Chief, Burke, hold the door. Simmons, you and I will position ourselves back here." Demetrio had to lean heavily on Doc for support as Doc helped the shorter man to his feet. The difference in height between the two men would have been comical if the situation was not so serious. Julie followed the two men as they approached the President. She could feel the slit-eyed man assessing her as they got closer.

"Take us out of here," he commanded, "but if you endanger the President I'll kill you myself."

Doc moved around behind her and she felt him and Demetrio place their hands on her shoulders. Their presence gave her courage, and she took a deep breath. "Just hang onto my arms," was all she could say. She focused her thoughts onto their transport plane. "Ready?" she asked. When they nodded, she zapped them out.

Once they arrived, one of the secret service agents shoved Julie violently backward into Doc. Demetrio cried out in pain as they struggled to stay on their feet. The two secret service agents drew their weapons. "Land this plane immediately!"

"We can't; if we do Jade won't be able to retrieve the rest of the men, sir." Doc spoke calmly but firmly as he shifted Julie behind his large frame. Demetrio was trying to move to a better position.

"They aren't important. We need to get the President to a secure location. This plane is a sitting duck for an attack," the secret service agent said as he motioned with his pistol. "You three will just stay over there while we talk to the pilot."

Anger surged through Julie. *He wants them to leave the*

team behind! "You can't be serious!" she yelled. "Not important! They're more important than you are! They've saved my life too many times to count!" Julie yelled advancing toward the man, she was not sure what she would really do, but she had an urge to hit the bastard.

Doc placed a restraining hand on Julie, as the secret service agents raised their weapons. "It won't even take her a minute to bring all of them back. There's really no reason why you shouldn't let her," Doc tried to reason with the man.

"I'll give you six good reasons, those six terrorists onboard Air Force One," the lead agent said coldly. "The only way they could've infiltrated our security is if we had traitors in the Secret Service. How do I know I can trust your team?"

"Enough! Matheson, stand down," the President said gruffly. He had listened to the whole exchange and had made up his mind. "They didn't have to come and get us. Besides, if they wanted me dead I'm sure she could've done it already," President McIntire pointed out. He nodded to Jade. "No offense meant, miss," he said pleasantly. Turning to Matheson he said more sternly, "I don't want our men or SEAL Team 3 left to die. You *will* let Jade continue her mission as planned." Matheson, started to argue with the President, but quickly changed his mind. The President addressed Jade, "Go on, bring as many as you can back without getting yourself hurt." Julie had zapped herself out before he finished speaking.

Julie arrived next to Lieutenant Cooper and Simmons. "What took you so long?" their lieutenant demanded.

"That jerk of an agent tried to stop me from coming back. Doc tried to reason with him," she told them, then ducked reflexively as gunshots rang out. "The President had to order him to let me continue the mission," she continued to report.

"What was he thinking?" Simmons exclaimed.

"That he couldn't trust even his own men because of

the traitors that snuck these terrorists on board. He was willing to leave you all to die to guarantee the President's safety," Julie explained. She could almost see his point of view. *Hadn't they mistrusted all of the SEAL Team's support staff after one of them had helped the rogue DIA agent try to kill them?* she thought. *But we didn't leave them to die because of it.*

"We'll deal with him later," Lieutenant Cooper said. "Jade, start the evac, wounded first, then everyone else, as fast as you can."

"Yes, sir!" Julie was more than happy to get this mission over with. As promised, she was able to retrieve the six remaining Secret Service agents and the Team in less than a minute. Once they were all back on the cargo jet, she allowed herself a moment to rest. She sank to the floor as far away from the wounded Secret Service agents as she could get. She saw Doc bandaging Demetrio's thigh as Simmons helped Chief Nguyen. Matt brought her another orange soda-like drink. "How are they doing?" Julie nodded toward Chief Nguyen and Demetrio as she took the plastic bottle and dutifully started drinking the super sweet liquid.

"They'll be alright," Matt reassured her.

"Was anyone else hit?" Julie asked worried.

"Most of the shots hit our body armor. We'll have bruises, but that's all," he told her.

After a few gulps she asked, "So what's this stuff anyway? It's almost too sweet," she said with a grimace.

Matt chuckled. "Doc got the idea a few days ago. We were just waiting for the shipment to arrive. We'd planned on having you try it first during training."

"So what's in it?"

"It's normally given to pregnant women to test their glucose tolerance," Matt admitted.

"Why am I drinking it?" Julie asked.

"It has fifty grams of pure glucose," Matt told her. "You can drink it faster than you could eat a candy bar. Your body should be able to absorb it faster than the sugar from a candy bar, and the glucose is even easier for your body to use," Matt said ticking off the sickly sweet drink's benefits on his fingers as he listed them.

"So, does it work as well as Doc expected?" Lieutenant Cooper asked. He had joined them while Matt was explaining.

"Well, I was able to zap more people without needing to refuel, so I guess it does help," Julie admitted. She was actually impressed with how well it worked now that she thought about it. "So what's the plan now?"

"Think you can stand?" Lieutenant Cooper asked, offering her his hand to help her up. "I think we should have this conversation with the President and Matheson."

"Can't I just drop Matheson in the ocean, sir?" Julie grumbled as she followed him over to the President and his escort.

"Don't tempt me," Lieutenant Cooper replied under his breath to keep the others from hearing. In a louder voice he spoke to the group they were approaching. "Mr. President, I would like to discuss our next steps with you."

Matheson took a step forward to block them from coming any closer to the President. "*Our* next steps don't concern you. We will decide where and how the President will be secured."

"Just a minute, Matheson, I want to hear what this officer has planned," President McIntire told the agent, stepping forward to meet Lieutenant Cooper. "First I'd like to thank you for getting us out of that mess." He offered his hand for the lieutenant to shake, and then Jade. "That was some fine work you did."

"Our pleasure, sir, but we aren't out of the woods yet," Lieutenant Cooper said guardedly. He looked at the two men. "Are you aware of the attacks that have happened around the country?"

The President nodded. "We had reports of several cities blacking out, and bridges being blown up. That's why it was decided I should board Air Force One."

"I'm afraid it's much worse than that, sir. Before we left to get you, there were already reports of dozens of bombings at large public areas like malls. Cell phone communications were down, and nearly eighty percent of the nation had been blacked out. I hate to think about what else might've happened while we've been up here," Lieutenant Cooper stated.

"Good Lord. The entire country will be in chaos!" The President was shocked by the implications of that many attacks. "There would have to be dozens of people involved in this attack, all of them being coordinated together."

"Exactly, sir. We won't know for a day or two the extent of the damage they've caused. It may take even longer to find out if they had help from the inside. At this point we can't really trust anyone. For that reason I advise relocating you to a secret facility that *no one* knows about," Lieutenant Cooper recommended. He paused to let the Secret Service agents absorb what he had just said. He knew the Team had probably already guessed the location. At his side he heard Julie's groan of understanding.

"You're suggesting my hideout aren't you?" she asked glumly.

"It's the only place that'll be secure," Lieutenant Cooper confirmed. "We're the only ones who even know it exists, and we're not sure where it is exactly."

Julie knew Lieutenant Cooper was right. She nodded her agreement. "And you don't even know the best part about its location," she admitted.

"Wait, what's this hideout? How do we know it'll be safe enough for the President?" Matheson turned to Jade. "What makes this place so wonderful?"

Julie waited for Lieutenant Cooper's nod to explain. With a sigh of resignation she explained her hideout's location. "It's in the Chocolate Mountains, in Southern California. And when I say 'in' I literally mean it is in one of the mountains, about a hundred feet into the bedrock.

The entire area around the mountain is an active artillery range. There're so many unexploded shells littering the plain around my hideout, no one will be able to get in without blowing themselves up." Around her, she heard whistles of appreciation; even the team was impressed. She glanced at Matt and saw his look of sadness. He seemed to realize how much she was sacrificing.

They finished their planning quickly after that. Even Matheson was unable to argue with her choice of locations. When they landed she was to zap the President and the six unwounded agents to her hideout. The team would make sure the wounded agents got medical attention at the base hospital. Jade was to stay at the hideout, as well, in case it was attacked and they needed to move the President quickly.

"How will I contact you?" Julie asked Matt as the plane taxied to a halt on the runway.

"The President will need to call Washington to let the world know that he's alive and well, but we don't want anyone tracing his transmission back to your hideout. So in two hours, plan on zapping him to me. We'll have secured a position by then. Also, we'll know more about the condition of the country too. Maybe we'll even have a new location for you to move the President to," Matt said optimistically. He paused. "I'm sorry you're losing your place. That was a sweet location."

Julie nodded in agreement. "You'll just have to help me set up a better one to repay me," she told him and managed a weak smile.

"That's a deal," Matt said happily. "Hey, remember, if Matheson gives you a hard time you can always zap him to the Arctic for a second or two," Matt joked, trying to cheer her up. He knew it would not be easy for her to spend the next day stuck in a small area with that blowhard.

Julie chuckled at that image. Then another dark thought seemed to come to her. "Will it be safe for me to sleep? What if he does something to me? Tries to drug me?" she asked as her darkest fears from her last brushes with death roared up from where she had buried them.

"I promise he won't," Matt said putting his arms around her.

"How do you know?"

Lieutenant Cooper's voice broke into their conversation. "Time to move people, Jade you're up."

Matt held her at arm's length for a moment longer, "If they do, where are they going to go? You're the only one who can get people in or out of there," Matt pointed out with a grin. Julie nodded halfheartedly as she pulled away from him and gathered some supplies Doc had selected for her.

Matt walked next to Matheson with a companionable smile on his face. "If anything happens to her while she's with you, there's nowhere you'll be able to hide from us," he warned the agent under his breath. Noticing the President's approach, Matt smiled broadly at both men and patted Matheson on the back. More loudly he said, "I'm glad we agree."

CHAPTER 37

Julie sat at the opening to her hideout, staring out into the desert. She was petting Cinder absently, deep in thought. It had been several hours since she had teleported the President to the prearranged meeting so he could contact the government and reassure the world that he was still alive. They were only to use the satellite phone to call out in an extreme emergency to prevent the enemy from tracing the signal back to them.

Too soon it had been time for her to return the President to the hideout. She had given the President and his men a quick tour of the cave. Immediately, Matheson had ordered a full assessment of their location from his men, completely ignoring Julie's input. After that final snub she retreated with Cinder to the entrance of the cave. It was the farthest she could get from Matheson. She sighed. Her mask was bothering her and she scratched at the fabric absently. She had never had to wear it this long before. A sound from the tunnel behind her made her zap several feet away. Taking a defensive stance, she turned to face whoever was approaching her. Cinder stepped between her and the man.

President McIntire stood with a slight look of

bewilderment on his face. His dark business suit was smudged with dirt and dust from her hideout. His tie was gone and his shirt was unbuttoned a little. "I'm sorry. I didn't mean to startle you," he said apologetically. "Can we talk?" Julie glanced down the tunnel. The President saw the motion and seemed to understand her concern. "I ordered them to stay behind. They won't bother us." After a moment Julie relaxed. "May I sit?" he asked politely.

Julie nodded uncertainly. "I'm sorry I don't have a chair."

"That's alright, the ground is fine. You know I served in the Army years ago. I spent many days and nights sitting on the ground. I doubt it will hurt me now," he said cheerfully as he took a spot close to where Julie had been. He sat down a little stiffly but without complaint as he studied the desert beyond. "This is a wonderful facility you have. Thank you for letting us use it for a time."

Julie nodded again. "No problem, you can have it for as long as you like," she answered him glumly. She sat down on the floor near him, leaning back against the cave wall.

"Oh, don't worry. I'm sure we'll be out of your way soon and it'll be all yours again."

"No, no it won't," she said sadly. "As soon as this is all over I'll have to find another location."

"Why? We won't damage this one," the President said, surprised by her response.

"Do you know the details of the attack on SEAL Team 3 and myself last year?" Julie asked, staring out at the darkening desert. The late summer sun was setting over a distant ridge.

"I seem to remember there was a rogue DIA agent who managed to kidnap you and entrap the Team."

"His name was Strickland, but it wasn't just him. He had a spy at my doctor's office, and one in the support staff of the Teams," Julie told him as she looked over at him. "We still aren't sure we found all of his accomplices.

The only way I can sleep safely, without one of the guys from SEAL Team 3 standing guard over me, is to come here. No one could find me here; it's been my refuge, my safe haven, each night since Strickland took me." She stopped speaking and concentrated on scratching Cinder's ears.

"And now we know where it is. You won't feel safe here ever again," he said guessing at the rest of her thought and paused for a moment. "I'm sorry. I hadn't realized what our arrival here would mean for you. I'd offer you my resources to make another one, but I know you'd have to refuse."

Shaking her head she replied, "No, no one can help me. Worse yet, my existence puts the team in danger, as well. They could've died that night all because they tried to save me. Ever since, we've been doing missions with hardly any support. Now they'll be targets again for anyone trying to get to me," Julie said sadly. Cinder seemed to sense her sadness and whined. Julie looked away. "Can I have some time alone?" she asked.

"Of course," the President said as he rose quietly and headed back down the tunnel. He paused and looked back; behind him he could hear the soft sounds of her crying.

"She's been out of sight too long." Matheson grumbled, as he paced across the living quarters of the hideout. "Davis, go search the tunnel. See if she's still there. If she's gone we're going to have to call for help." At that moment Jade stepped into the room from the tunnel, Cinder at her side. "You! Where have you been?" he fumed, pointing at Jade accusingly.

Jade took a step back as if she would leave again, and Cinder blocked Matheson's approach with a low growl. "That's enough, Matheson! Leave her alone!" President McIntire ordered his agent. He walked over to Jade and put his arm around her shoulders. "From now on you'll treat her as if she outranks you, Matheson. If you don't, as soon as we're out of here, I'll have you reassigned." With a comforting squeeze of her shoulder the President released her, ignoring Matheson's sputtering. "Come on, I saved you some dinner. I hope you don't mind we just helped ourselves to your pantry while you were busy."

Stunned, Julie followed the President over to the dining table at the side of the main living area. "That's alright. I'm sorry I needed to be alone for so long. I just needed to..." she paused, trying to think of an excuse besides crying her eyes out for nearly an hour. Luckily her mask hid her blotchy cheeks. She hoped her eyes weren't too blood shot. "...think," she finished her sentence lamely. When she got to the table and sat down she realized with dismay that she would not be able to eat anything while they were around. The thought made her start laughing uncontrollably. The seven men around her looked at her as if she had gone mad. She realized she must be really tired for her emotions to be so out of control. Trying to gain control of her laughter, she said haltingly, "I'm sorry.... I just realized I can't.... eat here... have to take off....my mask." She stood and picked up the plastic utensils and paper plate full of heated MRE rations. Now under control, she continued more calmly. "I'll just go eat down the tunnel." Turning to Matheson as he started to object, she said, "Don't worry, I won't leave, no matter how obnoxious you are."

The next morning they received a call. The Secret Service had done a full security check of the President's Emergency Command Center. Jade was to bring the President and his six agents to SEAL Team 3's building. Then they would be able to provide her with a picture of a room inside the secret bunker.

When Julie arrived she staggered a bit, unbalanced. Doc was closer to her and offered her his arm for support. "What's wrong?" he asked concerned. He started to bring out the dreaded blood glucose monitor.

Julie shook her head. "I'm just tired. I couldn't sleep at all last night," she explained as Doc tested her anyway.

Chief Nguyen came to her side next. "Why not? That bastard Matheson snore too much?" he asked. His arm was in a sling, but other than that he looked none the worse for the bullet wound in his arm.

Matt arrived carrying a cup of coffee as she answered. "No, he stared at me all night, with that look in his eyes," Julie told them and shivered at the memory. "He reminds me of Strickland," she admitted to them.

Chief Nguyen turned to consider Matheson, but Doc was already nodding his agreement. "You guys didn't hear him rant when we first got them off of Air Force One. It sounded like he had taken it straight out of Strickland's book of insanity."

The coffee had started to kick in and Julie paid more attention to the other people in the room. "Hey, is that General Thompson? He's the new Secretary of Defense, isn't he?"

"Yeah, he's been in a meeting with Admiral Huntington and Captain Lewis for the past hour," Chief Nguyen explained.

"It looks like they've been waiting to speak with the President," Simmons noted as they watched the three men follow President McIntire and Matheson into a meeting room. Two Secret Service agents took position outside the door.

Lieutenant Cooper came over to join the rest of the squad. Julie realized that she had not seen Demetrio yet. "Hey, where's Demetrio? Is he okay?"

"He'll be fine," Lieutenant Cooper reassured her. "Captain Lewis ordered him to report to the base hospital for his leg."

"What're our orders, LT?" Chief Nguyen asked first.

"We've been ordered to wait here until further notice."

"How's the rest of the country doing?" Julie asked.

She had worried all night about the chaos that could have been raging while she was stuck in her hideout.

"After the first hour there were no new attacks. Local law enforcement and emergency responders were able to get things mostly under control by late last night. They're still digging people out of buildings that were bombed, and most cities have put curfews in place. People are being encouraged to stay in their homes unless they are emergency personnel," Lieutenant Cooper described the situation. He rubbed his temples as he thought about all of the damage. The team stood in silence, deep in their own thoughts.

"What about the rest of the staff on Air Force One?" Julie asked, remembering the other people she had sensed being held hostage on the plane.

"They landed Air Force One and a strike team cleared the last of the hijackers," Chief Nguyen said. "Most of the President's staff survived by holing up in locked compartments," he reassured her.

They only had to wait a few minutes before they saw Matheson emerge from the meeting room. "Lieutenant Cooper, the President would like to speak with Jade and your men."

They all filed into the room and stood at ease in a line. Julie stood at the end, waiting to see what happened next. With a sigh of relief, she noticed that Matheson stayed out in the hallway. President McIntire, Admiral Hutchinson and Secretary of Defense Thompson all approached them. The team snapped to attention and saluted at their approach. Julie stood still, uncertain what she should do.

"At ease, men," Admiral Huntington said after returning their salute.

"We've been discussing what should be done with Jade," Secretary of Defense Thompson started. The team stiffened at his wording. "Let me explain. Ever since she helped us rescue that plane full of civilian contractors in

Bagdad I've argued that she is one of this nation's greatest assets and should be treated as such." The general paused for a moment studying each of them. "Until now, my arguments have been pushed aside. Thankfully, President McIntire has just agreed with my assessment. We've decided that during the next few weeks, at least until the present situation is stabilized, she will be reassigned to the President's security detail."

Julie's heart sank. She hung her head in a mixture of exhaustion, sadness and fear. *That means I'll have to endure Matheson for weeks, maybe even months*, she thought dismayed. *How am I going to be able to sleep or take off my mask until this was over?*

"We've also decided to reassign this squad.... as her personal security detachment until further notice," Thompson continued.

Julie looked up in shock. Matt bumped her with his elbow to get her attention. She looked down the line at her friends and saw them all grinning encouragement.

"So what do you have to say, Jade?" President McIntire asked expectantly. "I won't force you to serve alongside my security agents, but I'd feel a lot better with you close by to pull my butt out of danger again, if needed. It's also the safest place for you and your squad until things get back to normal."

"I'd be honored, sir," Julie replied with enthusiasm.

"Lieutenant Cooper, you and your men are responsible for protecting Jade until further notice. That includes making sure no one learns top secret information about Jade's true identity or the extent of her powers. Is that clear?" the President asked firmly.

"Yes, sir!" Lieutenant Cooper replied.

"Can I ask one favor?" the President asked, looking around the assembled men. "I think I'm the only one in the room who hasn't really met you yet," he asserted turning back to Julie.

Julie looked to the others, they all nodded their

approval. She turned to Secretary of Defense Thompson. He had protected her so long ago in that airplane hangar. Then he had found the spies that had helped Strickland. When he nodded his approval she knew it would be alright. Taking off her mask she ran her fingers through her bedraggled hair to try to get it in order. Then she shook the hand the President offered her. "Hi, my name's Julie."

"It's nice to finally meet you, Julie." President McIntire said warmly.

"How've you been, little lady?" Secretary of Defense Thompson asked cheerfully, all formality gone. "Has the Navy been treating you well?" he joked, glancing at his friend Admiral Huntington with a smile.

"Yes, sir," Julie answered with a shy grin.

"So what do you think? I've finally found someone who agrees with me about how important you are," Thompson said smugly.

"Thank you," Julie said giving him a hug. "It's good to see you again, sir." she whispered. She had not seen him since the sub rescue and had not realized how much she missed him until now.

"We should start preparing for the President's transfer," Admiral Huntington interrupted their reunion. "Lieutenant Cooper, your men can have a few hours to get in contact with their families. After today they won't be able to call them for the foreseeable future."

"Thank you, sir," Lieutenant Cooper replied grateful his men were being given the chance.

"Dismissed," the admiral said, releasing them to their work. Julie hurriedly put on her mask as she joined the others to leave.

"Lieutenant Cooper, Petty Officer Burke, can you stay behind for a moment?" Secretary of Defense Thompson asked. Matt stood aside while his team left. Once they were gone the general asked them, "How's she been, really? She seems worn out, and I don't just mean tired. Her spunk seems to be gone."

"It's been a hard year for her, sir," Lieutenant Cooper told them. "Finding out that there were spies in the staff she counted on really shook her confidence. I'm not sure which was worse, the doctor's assistant or our support staff," he explained, then stopped and looked at Matt.

"Go on, we won't hold it against her," Admiral Huntington said.

"Honestly, she's really nervous whenever she's not with at least one of us," Matt admitted reluctantly. "She's constantly looking over her shoulder looking for threats."

"That's not surprising after what she's been through," the Secretary of Defense said. "It has to be hard not knowing who you can trust. She probably imagines danger around every corner and rightfully so," he remarked shaking his head. "I'm sorry it took so long for me to get your team the support it should've had all along."

"I know you can't say it," the President said, looking at the other men. "But I can. The former President was an idiot for not giving this team the support it needed." Turning back to the SEALs he reassured them, "Jade and your squad aren't going to be left out in the cold any longer, Lieutenant Cooper."

"Thank you, sir," the lieutenant replied sincerely.

CHAPTER 38

It took about half the day for the Team to prepare for their new assignment. Of course Julie had immediately taken the President and his Secret Service agents ahead to the secure bunker. Julie made an extra trip to take Cinder to her parents' house.

"Mom…Dad…," she called when she arrived in their dark living room. She noticed that all of their blinds were closed. When her parents came out of the next room she saw her dad was holding a shotgun. "When did you get that?" she asked, relieved that they had a way to protect themselves.

"Mark got it for us a while back," her father explained with a shrug.

"You look exhausted, come sit down," her mother offered, coming over to her.

"No, I can't stay, I just wanted to stop by and check on you," Julie told them. She looked back at her dad. "How bad is it here? Do you guys need anything?"

"The power's out all over town, but other than that, we haven't been affected. We have enough food and water to last us for a while," her father said to reassured her.

"We're planning on just staying inside and keeping the

doors locked until this thing blows over," her mother explained.

"Good," Julie said, relieved she would not have to worry about them. "Can you take care of Cinder for me? I'm going to be busy with the team for a while."

"We understand dear, take care of yourself," her mom and dad gave her hugs goodbye.

"Don't worry if you don't hear from me," she reminded them before she left. Then she zapped back to her apartment to pack extra clothes.

By the time she zapped back to the Team, she found them ready to go. To her surprise, Petty Officer Binuya was also there. "Hey Brad, what's up?" Julie asked as she approached the group.

"It seems your team was down a man. They asked me to fill in for a while," he explained.

"Jade, we need to head out as soon as possible." Lieutenant Cooper interrupted them.

"Right," Julie nodded. "Is everyone ready?"

After they arrived at the President's bunker it took them another few hours to find quarters that met the guy's requirements. They were taking her security very seriously. Simmons had packed one of his favorite toys, a device that could detect hidden cameras and listening devices.

"You'd think we were in some sort of high security bunker or something," Simmons complained as he removed yet another device from the ceiling.

"I want nightly sweeps of the room for surveillance equipment. The Secret Service may have promised that they wouldn't try to identify Jade, but we need to guarantee they can't," Lieutenant Cooper directed. He scanned the layout of the room. "Jade, you'll sleep in the bunk farthest from the door along the back wall. We'll set up a screen covering that end. That way you'll have a little privacy, and a shooter won't have a clear shot at you from the door. The rest of us will bunk along both walls. We'll set up the area closest to the door as a work space." He glanced around to where Julie was sitting. She had fallen asleep with her head resting against the wall behind her.

"You failed me!" Hassan struck the man standing in front of him with a pistol, knocking him to the ground. "How could you put the bomb on the wrong plane?"

"Our intelligence said that was the plane he would use. We don't know why they changed planes last minute," the man said without daring to stand up.

Hassan continued to fume. "We spent millions funding those idiots the North American Islamic Jihad to ensure the President would board Air Force One. Then we failed to accomplish the mission!"

"Our operatives on the ground crew did manage to board Air Force One," the man on the floor offered.

"Yes, and then they still failed to kill him," Hassan pointed out.

"Our spies say that Jade evacuated the President from the plane. There was no way for our people to follow them."

"Jade? That can't be, she died a year ago," Hassan said, remembering the day fondly. "Find out if Jade is really still alive."

Julie woke up to find herself lying on a simple metal framed bed. Her mask had been removed as well as her armored vest. Nervous, she looked around confused. On three sides of her there were plain white walls; the fourth wall was created by what looked like a sheet that had been attached to the ceiling. She heard low voices coming from the rest of the room. She sighed with relief when she recognized the guys. As she approached the curtain wall she realized that it was actually two sheets that had been hung overlapping to create a self-closing door. She lifted one flap to the side and emerged from her 'room'.

"Hey, look who decided to join us," Simmons joked from where he sat on his bunk.

Lieutenant Cooper, Brad Binuya, Doc and Chief Nguyen sat around a table that had been positioned in front of the door. Knowing the guys, who did not do anything without a reason, she figured it had been put there for some defensive purpose.

"How long have I been out?" she asked as she joined them at the table. They moved over to make room for her.

"Since yesterday at 1500 hours," Doc supplied her. She looked at her watch. It was about ten in the morning now.

"Yeah, you crashed so hard you didn't even wake up when we carried you to bed," Simmons teased her again.

Julie grinned to help hide her embarrassment. "Like I've said before, my generation prides itself on how well we can sleep in," Julie joked back. Julie's stomach growled, reminding her that she had been neglecting it. "How does a person get food in this place?"

"What would you like?" Binuya asked getting to his feet.

"I can just go get it myself," Julie objected.
"Just tell me where to go."

"No, you can't 'just go' and get it yourself," Lieutenant Cooper reminded her. "When you're ready, we'll go over the safety procedures we've put in place."

"You're right, sorry LT," Julie apologized. She turned back to Binuya. "Anything that doesn't move fast enough and lots of it, I'm starving," she told him. "And thanks."

"Make sure her coffee has extra sugar in it," Doc called after him as Binuya headed out.

Julie slugged Doc in the shoulder, and then she looked back to Lieutenant Cooper. "I'm hesitant to ask, but what's the procedure for me to use the girl's room? A shower would be great too," she added wistfully.

Julie felt silly as they mobilized to take her to a nearby bathroom. The facility they were in was designed to support the President and a full staff including women so she would not have to use a men's locker room. After she gathered her fresh clothes, she put on her mask. Simmons had gone ahead to secure the location. Then Chief Nguyen escorted her down the hall. As she left the room she spotted Matt stationed outside the door; he gave her a knowing smile. When they got to the bathroom Simmons came out to report it was all clear. The two of them took position outside the door, as she went in.

The room was set up just like a women's locker room at any gym: an area with toilet stalls and sinks, and a separate area that had shower stalls along one wall with benches along the opposite side. After relieving herself, she stripped for a shower. Nothing had felt so good in her life. It had been days since she had washed her hair and it felt wonderful to get clean. When they arrived back at their room she found her food already on the table. It was a variety of items including fruit, bagels and some danishes. As soon as the door was closed she took off her mask and started chowing down.

"Slow down, you'll choke. Didn't your mother ever teach you to chew your food?" Doc teased.

Taking the time to swallow what was in her mouth, she paused long enough to explain. "Sorry, I couldn't really eat while we were in the hideout either," she said, nodding toward the mask she had placed beside her on the table. "I couldn't take it off in front of Matheson, and he freaked anytime I tried to leave the room." Gulping down another couple mouthfuls, she paused again. "Speaking of Matheson, how is he handling our reassignments?"

"He's learning to deal with it," Simmons said as he tinkered with a pile of electrical instruments that he had laid out on the table in front of him.

"What are those?" Julie asked as she continued eating more slowly.

"They're the surveillance devices that I found around the room," he explained and waved to a few holes dug in the ceiling and wall nearby. "Some of them are pretty high tech. The Secret Service always gets the best gadgets first," he added a bit jealously. "I think a few of them will accidentally land in my bag," he said nonchalantly as he examined what looked like a miniature camera.

Lieutenant Cooper came in as Julie finished the last of her late breakfast. "Ready?" he asked her.

"Yeah, what's the plan?" Julie took a sip of her coffee; it had plenty of sugar and cream in it, *just the way I like it*.

"This entire facility is basically a fortress. It's currently in lockdown mode. No one is able to go in or out. That means the only threat to the President, or you, would be someone who is already inside. You and the Secret Service can handle the President's security. We've been concentrating on keeping you and your identity safe. This room is as secure as we can make it. You should be completely safe and you can remove your mask freely while you're in here. One of us will be standing guard outside the door at all times, to ensure no one enters the room without our permission. Matheson has assured us that none of his personnel will try to identify you, but we will be doing surveillance sweeps at least once a day to make sure no one's tried to install cameras or listening devices. You aren't to leave this room without at least one of us escorting you at any time. If there's a traitor in their personnel you could be on their target list along with the President. Do you understand? Let us decide when it's safe and how many escorts you need. You are not to go off on your own," Lieutenant Cooper said firmly.

"Okay, okay. I'll behave, I promise," Julie said and raised her hands in a gesture of surrender. "What I don't understand is why I'm here. What am I supposed to be doing?"

"We are scheduled to meet Matheson at 1200 hours. He'll give us instructions so we can all coordinate in case of an attack on the President. Meanwhile, make yourself at home."

Julie sat in the President's advisory meeting that afternoon. She was in a position off to the side and out of the way, but with a clear view of President McIntire. Her entrance into the room had caused quite a stir before the meeting started. She had followed the President into the room and taken her seat amid a low murmur of whispers and not too concealed pointing. She felt like a sideshow freak on parade. Luckily the commotion had died down as the President called the meeting to order.

Now she mentally reviewed the meeting they had held earlier with Matheson. Her instructions had been fairly straight forward. Stay within view of the President at all times during his meetings through the day. If anything threatened the President she was to take him somewhere safe. If she was able to grab one of them at the same time that was fine, but she was not to try to evac everyone. Matheson had accepted that Jade 'probably' had other safe locations in addition to the one hideout he had seen. Evidently that one had impressed him enough that he believed her when she assured him that any other ones she 'probably' had would be equally secure.

"What about you guys?" she had asked Lieutenant Cooper.

"Stay in the secondary hideout until you are sure we are out of danger. You can tell what we are feeling, right? So you'll know when the action is over?" he asked, and then waited for Julie's nod of agreement. "Then you are to stay with the President, *no matter what* is happening with us. Do you understand? If you've stashed the President somewhere where no one can find him and then you zap into combat, you could be killed and the President would die where you left him. Do I make myself clear?"

Julie hated the idea, but she knew that she would have to obey him. Lieutenant Cooper was even more right than he knew; both of her secondary hideouts had no tunnel to the outside. They were completely sealed except for the ventilation shafts. She could not leave the President in one of her other hideouts and risk not being able to return.

Julie noticed Matheson staring at her. She stiffened, nervous. "What! Is there something bothering you?" Julie said sarcastically, cutting off Lieutenant Cooper.

Matheson looked towards Lieutenant Cooper and answered her question. "You're going to have to change her outfit. Even that mask, it doesn't work to hide her identity."

Lieutenant Cooper looked at Julie appraisingly. "You're right," he agreed.

"What do you mean?" Julie self-consciously shifted in her chair. Now the whole team was appraising her. "Could you guys stop staring at me, please?"

"Sorry, Jade," Lieutenant Cooper addressed her finally. "Matheson has a point. We switched you to fatigues and just your mask when you started working in the field."

"Yeah, you said my green cloak was a 'come shoot me sign'," Julie reminded him.

"I'm sure that worked fine for combat situations where people didn't have time to study you. But you're going to be sitting for long periods of time. If you are in that uniform any spy that's in the room will have plenty of time to learn a lot about what you look like," Matheson said reasonably. "For instance, I already know you are about five feet six inches tall; you have blue eyes, and pale skin. You probably weigh about 120 lbs., and by your voice I can tell you are in your early twenties," he said and turned to Lieutenant Cooper. "That's about right isn't it?" Turning back to Julie, "and I've only been studying you for the last five minutes."

The entire Team was on edge now and Julie was starting to back away from Matheson. He noticed their nervousness and raised his hands palms out. "Hang on, don't get all defensive, I'm only telling you this to illustrate my point," he told them and sighed. "I think I need to say something to you all. I read up about you Jade, what little there is anyways." He glanced around the group, but his gaze landed on Julie. "I know about General Jian and Strickland. I can understand Strickland's concerns about your powers." Now some of the Team shifted their weight, ready to grab their weapons. Matheson continued, deliberately ignoring their movements. "I know they could be used against us if you fell into the wrong hands, but I can see no evidence that you've gone rogue or are likely to do so of your own free will. So, I agree with the President, your powers are a huge asset to our country. You need to be protected, not persecuted."

So now she was sitting in the middle of a meeting where everyone else was wearing their best business attire and she was wearing her old disguise, the Ren-faire costume. She had the sides of the cloak draped completely around her body hiding its contours. The hood was pulled low over her eyes, allowing her to still see out, but hiding the color of her eyes and the skin around her eyes. *Don't mind me everyone, I'm just your friendly neighborhood superhero*, Julie thought ruefully as she wished for invisibility. She glanced around the room; most of the staff had stopped gawking at her as they paid attention to what the President was saying. By the door she saw Chief Nguyen and one of Matheson's men standing guard. Matheson himself was standing to the side and slightly behind the President's chair. Behind her she could just sense Matt standing to the side of her chair. Sighing, she resigned herself to her new situation.

CHAPTER 39

The next few days went by in never-ending boredom. She sat in the President's meetings at all hours of the day and night. Most of them had been interesting at first because they gave her information about how the country was recovering from the attacks. The effects of some of the attacks were still being felt: like the chemical spills that had poisoned the water to several major population centers, or the major highway interchanges that had been blown up in many of the large cities around the county. In a few days the meetings turned to talks about what to tell the media and international politics. She had been in that conference room so many times she would probably dream about it for years.

When she was not helping to guard the President she hung out in their quarters with the rest of the team. *Why didn't I bringing a book to read*, she thought after the first day. The facility was on full lock down, which meant no one was allowed to enter or leave for any reason. The good news was that it gave Chief Nguyen time to recover from his wound.

Now, as she entered the same meeting room again, she noticed with surprise that there were different people in the room. Most of the meetings had been attended by the President's personal advisory committee. They reported back to him on the issues he had assigned them. This time the room was filled with a group of men in police uniforms mixed in with other men in suits, whom she had never seen in the bunker before today.

"Where did these guys come from?" she whispered to Simmons, who had been assigned to guard her.

"They've started allowing outside personnel to enter the bunker," he answered her. "Keep your eyes peeled, but don't worry too much... they should be safe enough."

Again, her entrance sparked a bit of a commotion, since this was the first time they had seen her. Interested in what she might learn today, she ignored their whispers and took her usual spot in a chair in the corner to watch.

"Special Agent Kettner, I hope you've made progress on the identities of the terrorists," President McIntire addressed a man at his right.

"He's from the FBI," Simmons whispered into her ear, but Julie had already recognized the blond man as the same man who had given the press conference after the plane hijacking where they had gassed the entire plane.

"Yes, sir. We've gathered surveillance videos from most of the locations that were attacked. Unfortunately we've only been able to isolate photos of approximately forty individuals of interest. Our staff is working around the clock, trying to identify them. So far we have been able to confirm the identities of about a dozen known N.A.I.J. members. I'm hopeful that it won't take us much longer to confirm the identities of the rest."

"What plans are there for their arrests?" the President asked.

"We will have to assess dangers to the public and possible collateral damage before we plan any arrests," Kettner stated.

"How long could it take to apprehend them all?"

"Weeks, even months, sir. This group has a network

that could keep these individuals hidden from us indefinitely," the FBI agent admitted grudgingly.

Julie shifted in her seat, gathering the courage to speak, but Simmons placed a hand on her shoulder. He wanted her to wait. The rest of the meeting went by, providing more detailed information about how the terrorists had infiltrated so many secure locations. Julie paid little attention to it; her thoughts were on those photos. As the meeting was adjourned Julie turned to Simmons.

"I know, let's talk to LT first," Simmons said before she could speak. He must have guessed her thoughts.

Julie stood in front of the President's desk, waiting her turn. President McIntire was looking at a chart. An advisor stood over his shoulder, pointing to details on the paper as he explained his information. Lieutenant Cooper stood at her side as other members of the Team took their usual positions by the door, duplicating the presence of the Secret Service agents standing there. Finally, the assistant was dismissed and President McIntire turned his attention to them.

"Can I help you Lieutenant Cooper, Jade?" he asked. The President nodded to the chairs in front of his desk. "Would you like to sit?"

Lieutenant Cooper glanced around the room at the various staff members working at make-shift desks. "Could we have a moment alone with you, Mr. President?" he asked. The Secret Service agents by the door automatically moved to object.

"Send for Agent Matheson," President McIntire instructed the agents by the door and one of them went to get Matheson. It only took a moment before the man was entering the room. Matheson dismissed the other Secret Service agents to wait outside. Simmons used his toy to search the room for bugs; he nodded that it was all clear.

"Mr. President, how much do you know about my powers?" Julie started by asking.

"Only that you can teleport anywhere in the world," President McIntire admitted.

"Actually I can't zap to any place without either knowing the place already or seeing a picture of it," Julie corrected.

"She can *also* locate a person anywhere in the world and teleport to them just from their photo," Lieutenant Cooper explained, revealing her other ability.

"Why are you telling us this?" Matheson asked suspiciously.

"The terrorists!" President McIntire guessed. He leaned forward eagerly.

"I think I could help you catch the terrorists who attacked the country," Julie agreed, nodding.

"If the picture has enough detail she can locate the person and take them wherever you want," Lieutenant Cooper explained their plan.

"Can I see the photos that the FBI has gathered?" Julie asked. The President handed her one of the many files that was laying on his desk. She opened the folder and looked at the first photo. Concentrating on the man's features, it only took her a moment before she found him. "I found this one," she said as she set him in one pile on the President's desk in front of her. She concentrated on the next one. All she found was emptiness; shaking her head she placed his photo in another pile.

"What's different about that one?" President McIntire asked. "It looks like it's a pretty good picture."

"That's not the problem," Julie shook her head as she answered. "He's dead."

Lieutenant Cooper immediately turned to Matheson who was about to ask a question. "Don't bother asking; you already know too much about her powers," he said matter-of-factly. Matheson sat back in his chair, a look of disappointment on his face, rather than anger.

Julie continued to sort the pictures into piles of found and dead. Then she came across one that was different. She spent several minutes concentrating on it. The picture was good enough; she could see his thick mustache, his shaggy black eyebrows, and his short business-like haircut. *Why can't I get a lock on him*, she wondered, *he isn't dead.*

"What's wrong?" Lieutenant Cooper asked, realizing that it was taking her too long.

"I don't know. He isn't dead, but something is blocking me from locking onto him," she said and looked up puzzled. "This has never happened before."

A few days later, Jade and the Team had assembled at the FBI headquarters. The FBI had just apprehended the individual that Julie was unable to get a lock on. The team was there hoping to find out why. The man was sitting at a table in an interrogation room, and Julie was studying him from the other side of a one-way mirror. He had been strip-searched and given a set of prison type clothes to wear.

"We're sure he isn't holding or wearing anything that could block her powers," Agent Kettner said.

"I don't get it," Julie said turning back toward the team. Even with him ten feet away, she couldn't find him with her powers. "What could be blocking me?"

"It must be something inside his body," Simmons said.

"Can you x-ray him?" Lieutenant Cooper asked the lead FBI agent in charge of apprehending the terrorist group.

"We already have," Agent Kettner replied. "He had a pacemaker put in a few months ago."

"That must be it, since she still can't sense him," Lieutenant Cooper mused.

"Alright, I'll have our tech guys look into this. We'll

find out if there's something about this thing that could be blocking Jade," Agent Kettner agreed.

Simmons came into their quarters as everyone was enjoying some down time. "Hey Julie, try to find me," he told her. From her seat at the table she concentrated on finding him with her powers. Normally she could find any of the team in an instant, but this time there was something blocking her.

"What's going on?" she asked confused. "I can't find you."

Simmons tossed an object to Doc. "Now, try," Simmons continued. Now she could find Simmons without any problems, but when she tried Doc, he was blocked.

"What is this thing?" Lieutenant Cooper asked as he took the device from Doc.

"It's just something the FBI's techs made to mimic the electromagnetic field that is generated by that guy's pacemaker," Simmons explained.

"How'd they figure that out?" Doc asked, impressed.

"They found that the pacemaker emitted a slight electromagnetic field and they reproduced it," Simmons explained with a shrug. "They asked me to have Jade check it out to make sure they'd identified what was blocking her. The good news is that the pacemaker he had installed is one of the newest models and not many people have it yet."

CHAPTER 40

"This is risky," Chief Nguyen commented to Lieutenant Cooper. They stood in a group which included Matheson.

"She knows that," Lieutenant Cooper agreed.

"I don't get it," Matheson admitted. "Why would she risk herself like this?"

"She knows the longer it takes for the FBI to catch these guys, the longer it'll take the country to recover," Matt said walking up to their group. He turned to Lieutenant Cooper. "We're ready."

The three men followed Matt back to Jade. She had already chugged one of the sweet orange drinks back in their room before they had gathered at the FBI headquarters. In front of them was a steel door, and they could see through a one-way mirror beside it into the drab concrete interrogation room beyond. She was standing in her green cloak, focusing on the first picture in the stack. She set the photo down and instantly she was gone. Almost as quickly a figure arrived in the cell, and then she was back outside the room with them. The man inside the room looked stunned. He had evidently been about to open a door because he was holding a set of keys out in front of him. An FBI agent by the window spoke into a box on the wall. "You are under arrest. Drop the keys, and place your hands on the wall in front of you," the agent ordered the suspect. The man stood bewildered for a moment longer, and the agent gave him the instructions again. This time the man followed the orders.

Lieutenant Cooper approached Special Agent Kettner. "We need to hurry this up. The more time we spend at this, the more likely someone will alert the others. We have no idea how sophisticated their communications network is and the element of surprise is the only thing keeping her safe."

The agent looked toward Jade, and nodded in understanding. He moved toward his men. "We need to clear this room as fast as we can, people!" he yelled at them, spurring them to work faster.

Jade retrieved nine more terrorist suspects for questioning. She was averaging about one every two minutes or so, depending on how cooperative they were about being arrested. She stood for a moment breathing heavily.

Doc put a hand on her arm. "Take a break. We need you to keep going at a steady pace and there are twenty photos left," he reminded her. He caught her hand and took off one of her gloves so he could stick one of her fingers to get a blood sample. She was so used to it now that she barely flinched. "You're a little low, drink some more juice."

Julie took the bottle of orange stuff from him. "Does this come in any other flavors? This one is getting old really fast," she complained. He agreed to order some as she looked for a place to sit. She spotted the rest of the guys. They were standing around two chairs. Matt saw her and motioned for her to sit. "Is anyone else going to sit with me?" she asked, looking at the other chair.

"No, that one is for you to prop your feet up on," he told her.

Julie sank into the chair with a sigh. She was really

starting to get tired, but she refused to admit it. "Hey, this is kind of familiar," Julie said with a grin. "I seem to remember last time we did this you promised me a day of being served daiquiris in a hammock. I never did collect on that one."

"Well, as soon as we have a day off, I will." Matt promised her.

"It's time to get back to work Jade," Lieutenant Cooper instructed her.

Julie picked up two more without a hitch. Then as she concentrated on the next one, who was in a room with five other people, she noticed something. Digging through the pile of photos, she checked on her hunch. The others had seen her, and had come to check on her.

"What's the problem, Jade?" Chief Nguyen asked

"These four men," and she laid the photos out in a row, "are all in the same room together, and that's not all. There are two other men we don't have pictures of."

"How does she know that?" Matheson asked. "Never mind; forget I even asked," he added.

"How do you want me to get them?" Julie checked the group again. "These two are close enough together I could take them at the same time," she suggested pointing at two of the suspects she had found in the room.

"Kettner!" Lieutenant Cooper called to the FBI agent. "Are you sure that room is bulletproof?"

"Yes, sir, even the glass."

"Alright, Jade. I want you to take the two first, but bring them out here. We'll subdue them. Then take the other two and put them in the cell together. Try to point the last one away from the other, just in case."

Julie nodded. "What about the two we don't have pictures of?" she asked.

"We don't have arrest warrants for them; you'll have to leave them," Kettner informed them. "If we were there we could verify that they were with the suspects. Any lawyer would be able to argue that there's no proof they were in the same room."

Brad cursed. "That means they'll be able to warn the others!"

"Do we keep going?" Matheson asked the Team.

"I think I can do it. I'll know if they're expecting me," Julie said.

"I won't even ask," Matheson said with a shake of his head, but he noticed that the Team seemed to accept what she was saying.

Agent Kettner instructed his men to get into position. "Assume that they are armed and dangerous," he advised them. Then he turned to Jade and the SEALs, "Stay back and let us take them, unless things get out of control. Jade, you get yourself behind your squad when you're done."

Julie looked at the pictures in front of her, stringing their images together in her mind. She retrieved the first two a moment later and then she teleported out of the area. Instantly she speed-zapped to the next target. Making sure she arrived behind them, she brought the last two, one at a time, into the holding room. Then she zapped herself to an area behind SEAL Team 3. She arrived to the sound of muffled gun fire. Looking around, she saw the first two men were already handcuffed. The gun shots had come from inside the cell. She walked up behind the team, "I saw that coming," she said quietly. They all jumped at the sound of her voice.

"Could you do me a favor? Don't sneak up on us like that!" Binuya complained.

"You alright?" Matt asked as she followed them up to look into the room.

"Yep, no problem," Julie said more calmly than she felt. Adrenaline was coursing through her giving her a slight buzz of intoxication.

"We need to move faster now, people. The two she left behind will be notifying the rest," Lieutenant Cooper warned everyone in the room.

Julie took a deep breath to steady her nerves, and

then got back to work. The next four went uneventfully, but then she had to skip one because he was moving too fast. As she looked at the next photo in the pile she realized that he was in a space that was too small for her to zap into. "Hey guys, I can't get this one. He's hiding in a closet or something. I can only get to the room outside of it."

"But he'll have a clear shot at you as you open the door," Chief Nguyen completed her sentence.

Lieutenant Cooper called to one of the nearby FBI agents. "Get your men ready, you'll need to take this one yourselves." Quickly he explained what Julie had found and Agent Kettner agreed that it would be better for them to apprehend the suspect.

It took a few minutes for the agents to plan their attack. While she waited, Julie had a chance to have another glucose drink as she rested. When they were ready, Julie zapped the group of six FBI agents, in pairs, into the room outside of the closet. Then she zapped back to the Team. They waited for the call to come and get them.

It only took a few minutes before the phone rang. Lieutenant Cooper answered, "All clear? Great, stand in pairs around the room. She'll come and get you." Julie did as he had promised, taking the suspect and one agent first, and then retrieving the rest in quick succession.

The next five suspects tried various ways to keep from getting caught. Julie was impressed with their communication network to have been able to warn so many of them. It had only been about half an hour and already several of them were armed and started firing as they arrived in the room. Luckily Kettner was right. The room was taking a beating, but none of the bullets had breached the walls yet. It was proof however that she needed to keep going no matter how tired she was getting. The longer they had to prepare the more dangerous it would be.

Julie sat studying the picture of the man who had

been moving when she had found him earlier. He was no longer moving too fast for her to get to him, but there was something different about him.

"He's headed toward a crowd of people!" Julie hollered as she used her powers to sense his emotions. They were a mess, full of fear, but also excitement and resignation. "I think this one is a suicide bomber," she called to Lieutenant Cooper. "Call Command, make sure the pool is clear! I have to get this guy out of there now!" she yelled. She realized they were running out of time as she felt the man's emotions rising. The suspect was surrounded by people. *I can't wait any longer.* She looked at the Team's pool with her senses. As far as she could tell it was empty.

Without waiting for them to give her a ready signal she zapped the man from his location to the Team's pool. This time she deliberately aimed to put him below the water's surface. She zapped back to the FBI Headquarters a moment later.

Lieutenant Cooper was on the phone as she arrived near him. "That's an order!" he yelled, then hung up the call. "The bomb detonated seconds after you dropped him off. The pool was empty, and the explosion was completely contained under water," he reported. "That was quick thinking! Our pool will need some major repairs, but no one was hurt."

"What just happened?" Agent Kettner asked, stalking up to the group. "Where's the suspect?"

"I'm sorry, sir, I'm afraid you'll have to collect the remaining bits of your suspect from our pool's filter," Simmons said with mock seriousness.

Giving Simmons a stern look, Lieutenant Cooper clarified, "What he means is that Jade just prevented another suicide bombing. Your suspect was on his way to blow up a populated area." He turned to Julie, "Five more to go. Do you think you can do it?"

Julie felt the rush of adrenaline surging through her

veins. She felt like she could zap a whole platoon. "I'm fine, let's get this done," she stated, and walked back to the table where the photos of the suspects were sitting. Looking at the next one on the pile she concentrated on it. As soon as she found him she zapped him to the holding cell, but as she zapped herself out she began to feel really tired. *There's only four left, I can do this,* she told herself. Her hands were shaking as she looked at the next suspect in the pile. As soon as the room was empty she went for the next one.

The Team and the FBI agents watched as she brought in another suspect. They were almost done. *There's only three more after this one,* Matt thought as he watched Julie work. It could not be over soon enough in his opinion; this mission was almost as bad as the convoy rescue mission she had gone on. *We should've made the FBI do their jobs and not risk her like this,* he thought. They waited for her to return with the next suspect. It only took a couple moments longer than usual, but it was still unusual. *Something's wrong,* Matt thought. He was about to tell Simmons to activate her locating signal when they arrived in the cell. For a split second he thought everything was going to be alright, but then Julie slumped where she stood.

The suspect was standing bewildered a few feet away from her. Matt heard the FBI agent ordering the man to step forward and place his hands on the wall. He started to comply, *maybe it'll be alright after all,* Matt thought hopefully, but then a sound must have drawn the man's attention. He turned around to find Jade where she sat slumped on the floor. Seeing a chance to escape, the man drew a knife and grabbed her. He held her with one arm around her neck and the other clutched the knife jammed into her side. With the arm around her neck he forced her to her feet.

Agent Kettner and their lieutenant were the first ones into the room. They had their guns drawn, aimed at the suspects head. "Drop the knife!" Agent Kettner shouted.

"No way, she's my ticket out of here. Aren't you, bitch?" the man said as he gave Jade a shake by the arm around her neck. "Get me out of here! Take me to…" the man paused thinking. "Take me to Syria, NOW!" he yelled, pressing the knife further into her side and she flinched.

"She can't take you anywhere right now. She's too tired. Why do you think she was still in there with you in the first place?" Lieutenant Cooper spoke calmly, trying to buy them some time.

The suspect looked at Lieutenant Cooper suspiciously. "Fine! I want a car," the man said thinking quickly. "Yeah, bring me a car, and let me walk out of here. I'll let her go as soon as I'm gone."

"Okay, we'll get you a car. Just give us a minute," Agent Kettner said soothingly. He nodded to the remaining agents outside the room. A couple of them ran off down the hallway. "See? It'll just take a few minutes while they get your car," Agent Kettner continued to try to placate the suspect.

Matt looked at Julie, trying to gauge her condition. Her body was limp; the man was supporting most of her weight with his hold around her neck. Then Matt noticed her raise her hand cautiously, and hold up two fingers before she relaxed her hand again. He realized she was trying to tell them she would need just a couple minutes to recuperate. Matt saw Lieutenant Cooper nod imperceptibly, to acknowledge the information. "Why don't you start walking down the hall? They won't be able to drive the car into the building. We can meet it out front."

"Okay, but no tricks! All of you back off! I mean it. If I think you're going to try something I'll kill her!" the man warned them and viciously jabbed the blade into Julie's side making her gasp in pain.

Lieutenant Cooper put a restraining hand out to prevent anyone from rushing forward. Everyone backed out of the room as the man half dragged Jade out by her neck. Matt had to hand it to Julie. She was staying calm enough to pretend to be mostly unconscious while she was actually fully conscious and probably terrified. She was forcing the suspect to carry her. It made him move slower and it was taking a lot of his attention to maneuver them down the hall. The man kept trying to turn around to watch the FBI agents behind him and the SEAL Team in front of him at the same time. They were almost to the elevator when Julie made her move. She vanished from the man's grasp. With Jade's disappearance the FBI agents swarmed over the suspect. Matt could hear a commotion coming from behind him and knew it must be Julie. He let the Team take care of her. He advanced on the suspect, gun raised to cover the FBI agents who were forcing him to the floor. Once the suspect was being dragged down the hall, Matt turned to check on Julie. She was lying flat on the floor, with one of their packs tucked under her head as a pillow. Doc had removed one of her gloves and was testing her blood sugar levels.

"Her heart rate is slow, but steady, and her blood sugar levels are really low," Doc reported to their lieutenant. "She must be exhausted. I have what I need to hook her up to a glucose drip but, we need to get her to bed."

Lieutenant Cooper turned to Kettner and Matheson as they approached. "We'll need a vehicle, one that can hold at least four people," he said to Kettner first. Agent Kettner agreed and left to arrange one. Then Lieutenant Cooper turned to Matheson, "Can you get us into the bunker? She needs someplace secure to rest."

"Of course, I'll drive," Matheson offered then moved away to make a phone call.

Matt noticed a hole in her body armor and unfastened it enough to check for any injuries. He spotted blood on her shirt under the body armor. "Shit!" Matt exclaimed. "Hey Doc where's your first aid kit? It looks like that bastard actually did get her."

Binuya saw a small piece of metal protruding from a gash over her ribs. "When did he break his knife?" Brad asked.

"He didn't, it must've been in her when she zapped out and she cut it off with her powers," Matt explained as he pulled the tip of a knife out of the oozing wound. Binuya watched as Doc and Matt quickly bandaged Julie's side.

In the end, the FBI was able to get a large passenger van and the entire Team was able to travel together. They put Julie on the middle row, propped between Matt and Doc. Even with Matheson driving, it took some time to get through security to get close to the bunker. Matt carried her into the facility and placed her in bed. After the room was secure, he started to remove her cloak.

"I don't get it, why's she still out cold?" Binuya asked Matt as he helped get Julie out of her body armor.

"Teleporting takes a ton of energy. We joke about her sleeping so much, but from what Dr. Emory found every time she zaps it uses as much energy as us running a mile. If she takes a person with her, it uses even more energy."

"That's why you guys give her those sugar drinks? Right?"

Matt nodded. "Those sugar drinks are pure energy in a bottle for her," he answered the question as he worked. "Still, what she did this morning is the same as running close to forty miles in less than an hour." Binuya looked down at the sleeping girl with more respect. Matt checked her bandage quickly, when he was done Matt covered her up with a blanket. "She can do even more if she paces herself," he added, gently brushing her hair away from her face.

"You love her don't you," Binuya commented watching Matt.

"Yeah, we try to keep it under wraps, but the guys know," Matt agreed. "It's just so hard to have a relationship when shit keeps hitting the fan."

CHAPTER 41

Julie sat enduring her third lecture of the morning. The guys had ganged up on her when she had first gotten up. The main gist of their lecture had concentrated on her intelligence, or lack thereof, for continuing to zap after she knew she was getting too tired. Then Lieutenant Cooper had really dressed her down about jeopardizing her safety. Now she sat in front of the President's desk alone except for Lieutenant Cooper. They had even made her remove her hood for the lecture, so she could not hide behind it. It felt like she was back in elementary school in the principal's office.

"Yes, sir. I understand. I will stop teleporting before I get to the end of my strength," she agreed solemnly. "Honestly, I had felt just fine when I went for that last suspect, actually I felt like I could run a marathon. I just suddenly felt drained. I don't know what happened," she tried to explain.

"We're guessing she had an adrenaline rush and then when that passed, her exhaustion hit her," Lieutenant Cooper volunteered.

"Lieutenant, I expect you to find a more accurate way to gauge her ability to keep working," President McIntire said shifting his attention to Lieutenant Cooper. "It's obvious that she can deplete her resources past the point of exhaustion without warning."

"Yes, sir," Lieutenant Cooper agreed. "There had been a physician, Dr. Emory, who was studying the effects of teleporting on her body. Unfortunately we had to abandon the study after one of his assistant's revealed classified information about her to Agent Strickland."

"I understand," the President said considering the situation. "I'll speak to General Thompson about possible solutions." There was a knock at the door interrupting the President. He looked at his watch. "You're dismissed for now, but I don't want to find out that you have teleported to the point of passing out again. You may not have been treated like one before, but you are now officially an asset of the United States and I won't have you endangering yourself needlessly," he admonished Julie again.

After Julie put her hood and mask back on, the two of them left the President's office. "I'm sorry, sir. I really didn't know I'd crash like that," Julie apologized again to Lieutenant Cooper.

Outside the office Matt and Doc overheard her as they fell in behind them. Matt put his arm around her shoulders. "We know. Really we're the ones who need to get used to the fact that you go from a little tired to out cold in seconds. For most people it takes some time to work themselves to the point of passing out," he said with a look of tolerance on his face.

"Hey, that makes it sound like I'm a wimp!" Julie objected. She hit him in the chest, laughing. He pretended that her blows hurt and yelped an apology. Doc hit Matt on his other side. This time he did not need to pretend as much that it hurt. They had arrived at their room in the bunker, and the three stopped goofing around as they entered their quarters.

"The President has ordered us to find a more accurate way to gauge her condition than just blood sugar," Lieutenant Cooper informed the entire team, as he settled in a chair at the table.

Doc nodded, "Good, I agree."

"But first, we need to get you re-charged," Lieutenant Cooper said turning toward Julie. "Matheson told me he doesn't need you today, but he wants you at full strength by Friday." To the rest of the Team he added, "We have work to do too, and very little time."

"Why?" Julie asked. "What's Friday?"

"Sir, we've just received word from the N.A.I.J. One of their informants has obtained information about Jade," the man said and then waited nervously.

"Go ahead, what is it?" Hassan asked impatiently.

"They've found something that can block Jade."

"What do you mean, 'block' Jade?" Hassan asked in disbelief. There was no way a group as unsophisticated at the N.A.I.J. could have found out anything that important. *After all, hadn't they just had most of their members captured a few days ago?*

"The informant overheard that Jade couldn't find one of their members. The guy has a pacemaker that puts out a signal that blocks her powers," the man reported.

"How did their informant find out about this?" Hassan asked doubtfully.

"She's the girlfriend of one of the FBI agents who was in charge of figuring it out," Hassan's assistant explained. "Evidently he likes to talk about work after they've had sex."

"That's good... maybe we can use that," Hassan remarked. He seemed pleased for the first time in the assistant's memory. "Have your men figure out what signal it is as soon as possible. It could give us another chance to kill the President."

On Friday, the President had his first public speech since the terrorist attacks. It had been nearly three weeks, and this was to be an unannounced appearance at the New York Convention Center. They were hosting a conference on worldwide terrorism. The President was not a scheduled speaker on the conference's agenda, but he had secretly arranged with the conference coordinators to make an appearance.

"So why is he going if it's so dangerous?" Julie asked Matheson after their security briefing. She had learned that the conference was considered a highly dangerous location for the President to appear. With so many representatives from all over the world in attendance, it was impossible to completely eliminate threats.

"The President needs to make a strong appearance on the world stage to reassure our allies, and keep our enemies at bay. If they think that the U.S. has been weakened by a homegrown terrorist group, it would put many of our current negotiations at risk," Matheson was giving her the same explanation that the President had given him when he had argued with the President about his decision.

"And you guys think *I'm* reckless with my safety," she teased him as they arrived at the President's office. She became more serious as she turned her attention to Chief Nguyen. "Is everything ready?"

Chief Nguyen spoke into his comm device and nodded.

"Are you ready, Mr. President?" Matheson checked with President McIntire.

"As ready as I'll ever be," the President admitted.

The men took their predetermined positions around Jade. Chief Nguyen and Matheson were in front, Jade held onto their shoulders as usual. Behind her, the President rested his hands on her shoulders while two Secret Service agents kept one hand on her and one on the President. When they were all in position Jade teleported them to a secure location at the conference hall. As they arrived, Julie saw most of the rest of the team and more of Matheson's men.

"Where's Simmons?" Julie asked Matt in a whisper as she joined him at his position by the door.

"He's positioned outside, on the roof of a building nearby," Matt whispered back.

"Jade," Lieutenant Cooper called to get her attention and waved her over to him. "I want to be clear. You are to stay in this room with us, unless there is an active threat against the President. Hopefully all will go well and you'll be our ride back to the bunker. *If* a threat is identified, you are to get to President McIntire and take him back to his office in the bunker directly. You *are not* to try to come get us for any reason. Do I make myself clear?"

"Yes, sir," she agreed. Julie watched as the President and his Secret Service agents left the room. The room was very close to the main conference hall, and they could hear the roar of applause as the President took the stage. Julie listened as the President addressed the attendees and the commotion of his arrival faded. Ignoring his speech, Julie listened and waited for danger. She knew that Lieutenant Cooper was in the hallway beyond, where he could see the President clearly. Her powers told her that Matheson was standing just out of view from the crowd, scanning the attendees, looking for threats.

It was almost ten minutes into the President's speech when the first shot rang out. It sounded like a door slamming and it took Julie by surprise. "GO!" Lieutenant Cooper yelled at her. "The President is under fire!"

Instantly Julie was at the President's side, along with Matheson who had come out to cover the President with his own body. She grabbed onto both of their shoulders and focused on the bunker... but it was not there. Shocked, she tried again. It was like something was blocking her. Frantic she tried to get to her hideout... Still nothing.

"What's wrong? Get him out of here!" Matheson was

yelling at her as bullets hit the stage around them.

Suddenly pain lanced through her lower back, she almost blacked out from the shock of it, but she held onto her consciousness. Desperately she tried to get back to the team. As soon as she focused on it she shifted them to the small room just outside of the hall. Lieutenant Cooper arrived back in the room and stared in shock at the President. "Binuya, Chief help Matheson cover the President! Miller, Burke hold the door!" Lieutenant Cooper ordered. He approached Julie where she sat on the floor clutching her side. "What went wrong?" he asked her over the sound of screaming and gunfire.

"I tried to get him out," she paused as she flinched in pain, "but something is blocking me. I can't get us anywhere outside of the building."

"Where are you hit?" Lieutenant Cooper asked when he noticed her pain.

"My back," Julie said moving her hand away from the wound. She stared absently at her blood-covered glove.

"Miller! She's hit!" Lieutenant Cooper yelled as he took Doc's position by the door.

"Let me see," Doc instructed her as he came up. "Lie down."

"There's no time. I have to find a way out," Julie tried to object.

"Lie down, or I'll make you lie down," Doc said with deceptive calm. Julie decided to obey his order.

"You said something is blocking you?" Matheson asked as Doc inspected her wound.

"Yeah, it feels the same as that terrorist I couldn't get," she agreed. Then she was unable to continue for a moment as she clenched her teeth in pain. "Damn it, Doc! That hurts!" Julie objected to his care.

"Do you want the good news or the bad news first?" he asked in answer to her curses.

Julie paled a little at his words. "The bad," she said in a whisper.

"You've still got the bullet inside, and I can't tell if it hit any organs. The good news is it didn't hit any arteries or you'd be dead already," he said lightheartedly, trying to distract her from the pain. More seriously he said, "Don't worry; we'll get you patched up at a hospital."

"You have a strange idea of good news," Julie said and grimaced in pain as she tried to move. "I'd gladly zap myself to a hospital if you can find a way for me to get through the wall."

"I have it!" Chief Nguyen suddenly yelled from his position over the President. "The beacon! You said you'd 'zap to a hospital' and I remembered the beacons you used to spot wounded!"

Lieutenant Cooper spoke into his radio. "Simmons! We need you to turn on a beacon!" He paused to listen. "Yes, like the one to tag wounded... Do it quickly!" he ordered. He turned to Julie. "He'll set it up as soon as he can. Keep a look out for it."

"Yes, sir," Julie said weakly. She could feel herself getting tired and she wanted to go to sleep.

Doc was working on her wound. He looked up as Julie lost consciousness and turned to the closest team member. "Chief, I need your help. Hold this," he said, indicating the bandage he had pressed against Julie's wound. As Chief Nguyen applied pressure to the wound, Doc dug through his bag. He pulled out a preloaded syringe, and injected it into her arm. After what seemed like an eternity her eyes opened.

"How... how long was I out?" Julie asked weakly.

"Not long. Try to find the beacon," Doc instructed her.

Julie closed her eyes to concentrate, she opened them quickly. "Got it!" she said.

"Get the President, Matheson and Miller to that beacon. That's an order!" Lieutenant Cooper commanded from his position by the door.

Julie nodded as the three men arranged themselves

next to her prone form. Matheson was speaking into his headset even as Julie zapped them to Simmons's location. *That's odd*, she thought when they arrived. *It's so dark*, and then even the sounds around her faded away.

It only took a few moments for the helicopters that had been circling the area on standby to arrive on the roof. Matheson was ushering the President toward the first Nighthawk. He yelled over his shoulder at Doc and Simmons. "I've instructed the other chopper to take you to New York Presbyterian Hospital." With that, he climbed up into the first helicopter behind President McIntire.

Simmons picked up Julie as the second Nighthawk landed on the spot that the President's helicopter had just vacated. Doc grabbed his gear and climbed in first, then reached down to help Simmons lift Julie's still form up beside him. They were airborne in seconds and headed east.

The team had taken over Julie's hospital room. They had no real authority in a civilian facility, but they had remained as close as possible to her during her surgery. Then they had escorted her gurney through the hospital. Packing into the private recovery suite they had set up to protect her. Lieutenant Cooper turned on the TV and was searching for a news station. He raised the volume once he found one.

"This is Channel 13 News with the latest information on the attempted assassination of President McIntire. We now know that the President was airlifted away from the scene by helicopter from the roof top of a neighboring building. It's still unclear how he got to that rooftop. The rescue can be seen in this amateur video, which shows a second helicopter landing on the roof. We have been told that one of the President's security personnel was wounded during the attack. That person was airlifted by the second helicopter to New York Presbyterian Hospital.

Hospital staff have declined to comment on the condition or identity of the wounded agent."

Lieutenant Cooper sighed, "Good, at least so far the hospital is keeping a tight lid on this."

"Hold it," Binuya commanded from the other side of the privacy curtain blocking the door. The rest of the team readied their weapons, as Binuya spoke to the person at the door quietly. "LT, the police commissioner would like to speak to you," Binuya said without moving the curtain.

Lieutenant Cooper joined Binuya by the door, careful to block any view into the room as he came around the curtain. He shook hands with a man who stood about six feet tall, with salt and pepper gray hair that matched his mustache. "I'm Commissioner O'Malley. Lieutenant," the man paused, "I'm sorry I don't know your name."

"Lieutenant or just LT will work," Lieutenant Cooper refrained from giving the man his name even though the commissioner had been fishing for it.

From inside the room Lieutenant Cooper heard movement and a moment later a single statement, "All clear." Lieutenant Cooper moved the privacy curtain back to allow the police commissioner access into the room. He saw that the men had erected a screen over Julie's bed to hide her identity while they spoke.

After a nod to the men in the room and a quick glance toward the figure now hidden in the bed, Commissioner O'Malley turned back to Lieutenant Cooper. The police commissioner cleared his throat to continue. "I received a phone call from the *President* today," he said, emphasizing the title, obviously still a bit shocked. "He informed me that I am to provide you with anything you need to protect Jade," he told them. Again he unconsciously glanced toward the bed.

"Your help will be greatly appreciated. We can secure this room, but we could use help with the rest of the facility," Lieutenant Cooper suggested.

"I've already taken care it," the commissioner said. Is

there anything else I can do for you?"

"We need any security footage of her destroyed," Lieutenant Cooper stated immediately. That was one thing he had been worrying about since they had arrived at the hospital. *If a news station got ahold of that video*, Lieutenant Cooper considered the possibilities with dread.

"No problem, I'll take care of it myself," the commissioner assured him.

"As soon as she is stable, we will be transporting her to Bethesda, so hopefully we won't be in your hair for very long," Lieutenant Cooper told him.

"No, don't worry about it. Keep her here as long as she needs. It's an honor to be able to help her," the commissioner explained. "I'll do background checks on the staff and I'll also ask that the hospital to clear this floor if possible," the commissioner offered.

Lieutenant Cooper nodded. "Thanks, but we'd like to keep her presence here hidden," he cautioned.

"I understand, I'll just confirm what the news already believes...that one of the President's Secret Service agents was wounded. I'll come up with some excuse to explain the tight security," he stated. He turned again to the gathered men. "Let me know if you need anything else. Just ask my men. I've already posted two of them outside your door."

Julie woke up later that night. "Hey guys. Anyone get the license of the truck that hit me?" she asked with a weak smile. Matt was sitting next to her, holding her hand.

"Glad to see you back in the land of the living," he teased. The rest of the team came over to her bed.

Julie looked around. "Hey Doc, do you have any better news for me?" she asked.

"You'll live, but you're going to be out of commission for a while," he informed her.

"Cool, I've needed a vacation," she joked. "Where's my tropical drink with an umbrella? You owe me, remember?" Looking around the room she asked, "How long are we here for? Where are we anyway?"

"You're in New York Presbyterian. It was the closest hospital to the convention center. We'll head to Bethesda as soon as you're stable."

"I'm fine," Julie argued. She tried to sit up, but fell back. All of the color had drained from her face.

"No, you're not fine," Matt told her as he brushed her cheek. "That bullet tore through your abdominal muscles, nicked your intestines and you lost a lot of blood."

"Oh," Julie said weakly, still pale from pain. "Is that all?"

"The doctor thinks you'll be strong enough to transport tomorrow," Lieutenant Cooper said. "We've already arranged the chopper."

"Has anyone figured out what happened today? Why couldn't I get us out?" Julie asked.

"Matheson says they found transmitters throughout the convention hall. They must've activated them right before they attacked," Lieutenant Cooper explained. "He still hasn't figured out how they found out about that signal. The only possibility is someone inside the FBI."

CHAPTER 42

Julie felt a little stronger the next day, but it still hurt like hell to try to move. She lay there helpless as the nurse took care of her, while the guys hung out in the hallway. Finally she was done getting her dressing changed and other, more embarrassing things done for her. They had let her dress in a pair of scrub pants and a shirt. *I won't have to ride in a chopper knowing my butt was hanging out of a hospital gown*, she thought thankfully.

When the nurse left, the team came back in. "Ready?" Matt asked with a sardonic grin.

"Hey, that's my line!" Julie said indignantly.

"Not today it's not," Matt said as he lifted the sheet over her head. "You okay?" he asked once she was covered and strapped securely to the stretcher.

"I feel like a dead body," she complained.

"Sorry, but it's the easiest way to get you loaded without anyone seeing you. There's no way we could sweep the whole hospital for bugs," he apologized.

"Let's go," Lieutenant Cooper ordered as they wheeled her gurney out of the room. There were only four of them; Chief Nguyen and Binuya had gone ahead to Bethesda to arrange security there. Doc, the lieutenant,

Simmons and Matt each took a corner of her rolling bed and guided it through the empty halls. The police commissioner's men had cleared them of all staff while she was being moved. New York City police officers were stationed at strategic locations along their route for added security. It was an uneventful trip to the elevator and up to the roof to the waiting Seahawk.

"Miller, Burke, you in first," Lieutenant Cooper commanded as they approached. After Julie was lifted in on her stretcher, Lieutenant Cooper and Simmons climbed in as well. Lieutenant Cooper signaled the pilots and the Seahawk rose above the hospital roof, and then headed out over the city. They had only been flying for a few seconds when the team heard the familiar staccato of bullets hitting fuselage.

"We're hit!" the pilot yelled into their headsets. The chopper was sliding sideways through the air, and then it started to spin wildly. The guys clung to her stretcher to keep it from moving. "We're going down!" the pilot yelled again.

"Matt! What's happening?" Julie screamed. The team all had headsets except for her.

"Someone's shooting at us!" Matt answered her. "Oh, and the chopper's going down!" he added with a false sense of calm.

"Can you reach the pilots?" Julie asked.

"Yes," Matt admitted then realized what she was thinking. "You can't! You're too weak, you could die!"

"We'll all die for sure if we crash," she reminded him. She looked at the others. "LT, it's our only chance!"

Suddenly the chopper tipped on its side. "Burke, Simmons, grab the pilots. Everyone hold onto Julie!" Lieutenant Cooper ordered.

Julie focused, it was so hard to think through her pain and the spinning of the chopper. *There!* She had it, the perfect spot. A moment later they were falling through midair. It was only about eight feet before they hit the water with a sudden jolt. Pain flared through her midsection and she almost blacked out. Then she started to sink. Julie tried to stay calm as she struggled to get out of the restraints that held her to the stretcher, but as she felt herself sinking further down she panicked. She felt hands at the straps that held her securely. One by one they were released. Suddenly she felt an arm wrap around her torso and she was dragged upward. She sputtered for breath when they got to the surface. She tried to help whoever was rescuing her; she tried to swim.

"Just relax," Matt ordered in her ear. Gladly, she let her body go limp. He swam both of them to the side of the team's practice pool. Her side hurt so badly she did not even try to help them lift her out of the pool. Doc examined her side as Matt went to get towels to dry her off. She was shivering violently.

"Why am I so cold?" she asked Doc while Matt was gone.

"Probably shock. Just hang on. We'll take care of you," Doc reassured her. He had removed her bandaging. Doc looked around and yelled to someone outside of Julie's vision, "You! Go get me a med kit! Now!" She could sense a crowd gathering at the end of the pool.

"That doesn't sound good," Julie said trying to stay calm.

"You've just torn out some of your sutures. No problem," Doc said in a convincing tone.

Matt had just returned and saw the wound. He looked at Doc, worry in his eyes. Then he smiled calmly at Julie, "Yeah, no worries. You just rest. We've already called for an ambulance to take you to Balboa."

While Matt was talking he had been gently drying her off, and now he wrapped her in dry towels trying to warm her up. Someone else was propping her feet up as she slowly drifted away. Julie felt a prick of pain in her arm as Doc started an IV. In the distance she heard Lieutenant Cooper yelling, "Keep those people back! Clear the way for the medics!"

Julie woke up, confused about where she was. She did not recognize the room, but as she looked around she could tell she was in another hospital. There was an IV running into one arm, and a thing clamped to one of her fingers with a cord running to a machine. On her arm a blood pressure cuff started inflating automatically. She kept looking around, feeling very alone. She had been living with the whole team for weeks in a fairly small room. She had gotten used to never being alone. Now, with everyone gone she felt isolated and afraid. A second later she heard a door open quietly, somewhere out of her eyesight. She heard footsteps coming closer to her bed. She was starting to get nervous, images of kidnappers flitted through her imagination until Matt finally came into view.

"Oh, you're awake… I just left for a minute," he said apologetically.

"Hey," Julie said weakly. Her voice cracked and she tried clearing her throat. Matt offered her a drink. After a few sips she tried speaking again. "How is everyone? Did I get everyone back?"

"Yeah, we're all fine. It was a bit of a shock being dropped in the pool, but it makes sense. It would've hurt a lot worse hitting the ground."

"Where's everyone?" Julie wondered again, this time out loud. Then another thought came to her. "Is it safe here?"

"We've been taking shifts sitting with you since you got here. The others are rotating through guard duty, but we've had some help with that," he said as he grinned cryptically.

"Help? Who would you guys trust enough to help?"

"When word got out that Jade was here, Navy and Marine commands have been vying for the privilege of guarding you. There are so many personnel guarding this hospital inside and out I wouldn't have believed it if I didn't see it for myself," he explained with a disbelieving shake of his head. "They aren't allowed in here, but it's really nice having their help securing the area. Besides, these volunteers are zealots about protecting you."

"How long have I been out?" she asked. He made it sound like she had been there for a long time.

"For a few days. You tore out several of your sutures internally and some of the ones holding the incision closed," Matt summed up her injuries.

Julie looked up at the bag of whole blood attached to the IV line. "I guess I must've lost more blood too."

"You could say that, yes," Matt tried to joke. Then he said quietly, "Your blood pressure wouldn't stabilize. We weren't sure you'd make it there for a couple days. They decided to do another exploratory surgery yesterday and found more internal bleeding."

Julie was silent for a moment, shocked. *I'd almost died*, she thought is disbelief. Then she saw the look on Matt's face as he stared down at her hand. "Well, I guess I won't be able to wear a bikini ever again," she said, trying to cheer him up.

Matt looked up and smiled. "What do you mean? Scars are sexy," he told her.

Julie laughed, and then groaned in pain. "Maybe on guys," she agreed.

Admiral Huntington answered his phone on the third ring. "Yes?"

"Admiral. I have the secretary of defense on the line," his clerk's voice was stiff with formality.

"Put him through," the admiral ordered. When he heard the phone click to the new line he greeted his old friend. "Hello Charles, what can I do for you?"

"Actually I'm calling to report to you," Secretary of

Defense Thompson said sincerely. "I wanted to make sure you heard the news as soon as possible."

"What is it?" Admiral Huntington asked interested.

"They've caught the man responsible for the attacks on the President and on Jade's chopper," Thompson said getting right to the point.

"Who is he?"

"His name's Hassan Abdula. He worked for the Arabic Oil Council."

"That's that organized crime syndicate isn't it?"

"Yeah, we've found evidence that they've been funding the N.A.I.J. for the past year just so they would get a chance to assassinate the President," the defense secretary explained.

"But why? President McIntire was just elected," Admiral Huntington asked surprised.

"Evidently they were worried his policies would cut into their profits."

"Why was the A.O.C. after Jade?"

"They weren't; Hassan was acting alone when he shot at her transport helicopter," the secretary of defense explained. "He was hoping her death would help save his life with the Arabic Oil Council. With Hassan in custody she's not in their sights for now. But they certainly don't like her after she ruined their assassination attempts."

"They're just one more terrorist group with a grudge to add to the list. Don't worry, we've got her covered now," Admiral Huntington assured his friend.

"Speaking of which, the President wanted to know how the project was going."

"It's ahead of schedule. I've never seen a project get done so fast," the admiral admitted.

"Good, the President will be happy to hear it."

CHAPTER 43

A few weeks later Julie was about to be released from the hospital. She was under strict orders not to teleport for at least another month. "So how are we going to leave?" Julie asked.

"We've got a surprise for you," Matt answered with a grin.

"Don't tell me we're going by helicopter again," Julie groaned.

"No, your Uncle Mark has been helping to get this set up," he told her mysteriously.

"Mark? Oh, this could be interesting," she said dramatically. After a few minutes she had a thought, "Where am I going to stay while I'm on bed rest? I can't zap to my hideout."

"My house. I owe you those tropical drinks, remember," Matt joked. "Seriously, we've been ordered to guard you and keep you on strict bed rest for the next few weeks. We didn't want you to feel like you were in prison so we picked my place. It has a security system already installed, and enough room for us to bunk."

"Sounds great. I look forward to being a couch potato for a change," Julie remarked happily.

"It's almost time to go, put on your disguise," Matt said as he tossed her clothes and her green cloak and mask. It took Julie several minutes to get dressed and put on the familiar outfit. She had to go slowly because of the pain. Matt waited by the door, behind the privacy curtain, for her to finish. Once she was done he waved theatrically at the wheelchair he had waiting for her. "Your chariot awaits," he intoned.

Julie rolled her eyes with a chuckle at his antics, but dutifully sat in the proffered chair. Her little bit of exertion had already tired her out. Matt opened the hall door and pushed her out of her room. As she emerged she gasped in surprise. Posted along the hallway, about every ten feet was a member of the military standing at attention in their dress uniforms. They were from several different branches, but they were all saluting her.

"What do I do?" Julie asked nervously, under her breath.

"Salute them back," Matt suggested with a chuckle.

Julie did as she was told and they all dropped their salutes. From their posts by her door Lieutenant Cooper and Chief Nguyen fell in behind her wheelchair. "At ease!" Lieutenant Cooper called out, as they continued down the hall.

As they passed, each person came forward to shake her hand. A camera man seemed to come out of nowhere and started taking their pictures. "This is okay?" Julie asked, surprised.

"Yeah, they won't be able to get anything from the pictures. You have your disguise on," Matt reassured her. "The President wanted to release controlled photos of you. The world wants to see you, and if we give them a little controlled access, people will be less likely to go nuts trying to find you. Besides, the country needs something good to think about these days."

"What about your identities?" Julie knew if a terrorist got information on them, they would be a way to get to her.

"That's easy to take care of with a good photo editing program. They'll edit us out. Just relax and enjoy your fans," Matt advised. Each service member there wanted to thank her personally for saving their life or someone they cared about. Julie lost count of how many men and women shook her hand. They got to the elevator and Julie sighed with relief as the door closed.

"It's not over yet," Matt warned.

"You're enjoying this too much," Julie complained.

"You've saved a lot of personnel and they've never had a chance to thank you," Lieutenant Cooper said reasonably. "These men and women were the lucky ones whose names were chosen out of the hundreds who asked to meet you."

"Hundreds?" Julie gulped. She had never thought about how many people she had helped.

The elevator door opened onto what looked like a back service hallway. "Are we at the right floor?" Julie asked as they started to get off the elevator.

"There are too many reporters and onlookers waiting out front. Don't worry, we've planned for this," Chief Nguyen answered her.

"Yeah, it was actually your uncle who thought of it first," Matt added.

"Ah, we're sneaking out the back door, huh," Julie remarked with a chuckle. "That sounds like one of Uncle Mark's usual escapes."

As they emerged from the elevator they were met by more service personnel and another photographer. But this hallway was fairly short, and Julie could see that there were only about ten of them. These men she recognized from her work with the Teams. They were just some of the men that she had used her powers to watch during missions to warn them about ambushes or other threats. Again each one wanted to shake her hand and thank her. This time she was able to comment on her memories of them too, so the trip down the hall took longer.

Just inside the service exit she was met by Secretary of Defense Thompson and Admiral Huntington.

"Jade, on behalf of the President of the United States, I am honored to present you with the Navy Cross for services for your country," Admiral Huntington said formally, as he placed a medal around her neck. The photographer snapped pictures commemorating the event.

"Thank you, sir, but I don't deserve this, I just wanted to help," Julie stammered, shocked. She heard laughter come from the men down the hall.

"You've 'just helped' hundreds of wounded soldiers, sailors, and Marines. You've 'just helped' prevent more wounded by spotting possible threats, and you 'just helped' save the life of President McIntire... twice," Admiral Huntington said, listing off her accomplishments.

"But I wasn't the only one, sir," Julie objected again, embarrassed. "I had help; I couldn't have done it alone." She thought about Chief Nguyen and Demetrio taking bullets to protect her when they boarded Air Force One.

Admiral Huntington chuckled. "I've never had such a hard time giving out a medal," he chided her. "But don't worry; the men of your Team will be getting medals in an even more secret meeting."

"Just accept it already," Matt ordered her teasingly. "We've got to keep moving."

"Thank you, sir. It's an honor helping our troops," Julie said, as cheers and applause started down the hall in answer.

Secretary of Defense Thompson stepped up next and shook her hand. "You've done some really amazing things these last few months," he told her with a smile

"Thank you, sir," Julie said sincerely. She looked at both men. "I hope my coming here wasn't too much trouble."

"Nonsense!" the admiral quickly argued. "Balboa was more than happy to take that honor away from Bethesda.

They always get the high profile cases. This time Balboa will have the bragging rights."

"Enough of this sappy stuff," Mark interrupted them. He had opened the service door from the outside. "We need to get moving before someone notices we're back here."

"He's right," Lieutenant Cooper ordered. "Let's go."

"Think you can walk a little ways?" Matt asked.

"Sure, just give me a hand up."

Matt helped her to stand and then kept a hand on her elbow as they went through the door. Outside she spotted Simmons, Doc and Binuya guarding the two black sedans with dark tinted rear windows. Her Uncle Mark was holding the back door of the second car open for her.

Once Matt and Julie were settled, Mark slid into the driver's seat. "We're moving out," he said into a hand set.

"Who are you talking to?" Julie asked curious.

"The decoy cars," Mark answered as he started the car. She watched as the lead car pulled out in front of them. Together the cars drove around the side of the hospital and met up with a third black car that had been waiting by the lobby doors. Julie saw a mob of people and cameras swarming around the third car as it joined them.

"Why so many decoys?" Julie asked.

"I'm betting that there're at least one or two news helicopters following us overhead. We need to lose them before you can be safe," Mark explained.

The three cars shifted position around each other as they merged onto the freeway.

"Who's driving the other cars?" Julie asked, fascinated by the idea. She watched the three cars randomly change lanes around each other as they drove down the freeway.

"We had plenty of volunteers, but we chose mostly Team members," Matt explained this time. "Mark arranged the cars. Oh, you'd better start taking off your costume."

She noticed that the three cars were exiting the freeway. Ahead, Julie recognized the Mission Valley Mall.

Quickly she took off her mask and cloak. "We're going shopping?" Julie joked.

"Nope. We just need cover for a moment. In a minute we'll pull up next to my car. We'll have to get out pretty quickly," Matt warned her to be ready.

Once the three cars pulled into the parking area under the mall itself, each took a different direction. Mark continued on until he pulled up to Matt's blue Charger. "Here's your stop you two," her uncle called from the front seat.

Matt got out first and surveyed the area. "Okay, all clear," he said and offered Julie a hand out of the car as she slid over to his side.

"Thanks, Mark," Matt said.

"No problem," Mark replied. "Just keep her safe."

"Thanks, Uncle Mark," Julie added, and then followed Matt to his car's passenger door carrying her mask and cloak wadded up into a ball.

Mark had already continued through the parking garage as Matt pulled out. Julie looked around trying to spot all three black sedans, but now she counted six identical cars. Each black car was poised by a different exit. Apparently on a signal, all six cars left simultaneously. Matt waited a few minutes, driving casually through the parking garage before he left the covered area. They did not spot any of the decoy cars again during the entire drive to Matt's.

CHAPTER 44

That night Julie sat relaxing on Matt's couch watching a movie the guys had dug out for her. Her incisions hurt, and she was tired, but she was not ready to head for bed yet. Matt had been on duty all day watching the security cameras and checking the perimeter as he put it. He had only spoken to her briefly through the day, taking his guard duty very seriously.

She heard the four men from her team talking in the next room. From what she could over hear, the day shift was reporting over to the night shift. *Is this the way the rest of my life will be? Someone always standing guard over me,* she thought miserably, tears welling up in her eyes. The briefing must have ended because the four men came out of the room. Julie wiped away a tear that had run down her cheek as Matt joined her on the couch.

"How are you feeling?" he asked sitting down next to her.

"I'm a bit sore, but I'm okay," Julie told him.

Matt reached over and tucked her hair behind her ear. "Come here," he said as he motioned for her to snuggle next to him. As she gingerly settled against his side he rested his arm around her. They sat like that for a while watching the movie, enjoying being close to each other. After a while Julie noticed that Matt was not really paying attention to the movie anymore. He had taken her hand as they had snuggled, and now he was staring at it absently stroking an old bruise where an IV line had been.

"What's wrong?" Julie asked, sensing that something was bothering him.

"When you were lying in the hospital, and the doctors couldn't figure out why your blood pressure was so low…" he paused, obviously upset. "I thought I was really going to lose you this time."

"I'm going to be fine," Julie tried to comfort him. "Besides, I'm too stubborn to die," she joked, trying to cheer him up.

"If I had lost you…I don't know how I would have kept going," Matt continued. "I love you so much."

"I love you too," Julie said, surprised he had actually said the words. She had known that he loved her for a while now, but he was not the kind of guy who said things like that often. "Matt, what's my life going to be like now?" she asked a few minutes later.

"Don't worry about that," Matt told her. "We'll figure it out together when the time comes."

Julie sat on the couch flipping through the channels. There was nothing on and she had already watched every movie in the house at least a dozen times. She had spent the last two weeks on bed rest and was going stir crazy. If she did not find something else to do soon she would go nuts. The guys were not much help either. They were constantly monitoring the security cameras or something. Just then a perimeter alarm sounded. Someone was in the yard. Suddenly nervous, Julie looked around for one of the guys. She knew Doc and Binuya were in their room sleeping since they had been on the night shift. A second later Matt came striding out of the monitor room. He headed straight to the front door. Simmons entered the room from another part of the house, rifle in hand.

"Who is it?" Julie asked as Matt opened the door.

"Hey guys," Matt said as he waved in Lieutenant Cooper and Chief Nguyen.

"Please tell me you've come to rescue me from my boredom," Julie begged when she saw them come in.

"We thought you'd be looking for something to do," Chief Nguyen said with a grin. "These guys are always boring."

"Ha, ha, very funny," Matt retorted.

"We're here to help you design your new hideout," Lieutenant Cooper explained ignoring their exchange.

"Yeah, I'll have to work on that when I get a chance," Julie agreed. She had been wondering how much time she would have on her days off to work on expanding one of her hideouts.

"You'll have plenty of time. The President has ordered that as soon as you're allowed to teleport, your top priority is to create your new hideout," Lieutenant Cooper explained. "Also, we're to supply you with any equipment you need."

"I have two secondary hideouts already started. Which one should I pick to expand?" Julie asked. She had chosen both of them for their remoteness. "One is located in Mount Hesperus in Alaska. The second one is in a butte in the badlands of North Dakota. Which one is better?"

They spent the next hour debating which location would be better as her main facility. In the end, they all agreed on the one in Mount Hesperus. It had the better water supply and the harsh weather made it more inaccessible. Over the next two weeks Matt, Simons, Doc and Binuya helped her plan the hideout's new layout. Chief Nguyen or Lieutenant Cooper would stop by periodically to check on their progress and give their opinions. When her hideout was finished it would have a separate bedroom, living room and a study along with the weapons cache and enough emergency food and medical stores to last a month.

"Is it ready?" Matt asked the person on the other end of the phone. "Right," he nodded unconsciously as he answered a question. "We'll be right there," he added before he hung up.

Julie had been eavesdropping. "What's ready?" she asked when he hung up.

"Take us to LT," Matt said in answer. "He has something to show you."

"Wait, let me get my mask and cloak," Julie said and she turned to leave, headed for her bedroom.

"Don't worry about it," he told her. "You won't need it where we're going."

Surprised, she took his hand. Focusing on Lieutenant Cooper, she shifted them to a room she had never been to before. On three sides it had plain walls. The fourth side was open to a hallway that led off to either side. The rest of the team were there, including Demetrio and Binuya. Then she noticed that several other men were standing off to one side. Worried, she turned to Matt, "But you said…"

"It's alright," Matt reassured her, "they've been chosen to join the team. There'll be missions when we need more men, and this way we can rest if we get wounded."

Julie looked at them again, and recognized Martin from the days she first started training with Matt. She walked up to him, smiling. "Hey Martin, it's good to see you again," she offered to shake his hand.

"Hi, Jade. Yeah, it's nice to finally SEE you," he joked, shaking her hand.

"You can call me Julie if you want," she introduced herself. She turned to the next man. "Williams, nice to see you too. I'd have thought you'd had enough of me after that prank I played on you before."

"My first name's Jason," Williams said and smiled for the first time since she had met him. "You can't scare me off that easy," he reminded her.

"That's great! There's this one rescue I've wanted to try. You'll go sky diving and I'll try to zap to you while you're falling. I haven't decided if it'd be better if I try to give you a parachute, or drop you in the pool," Julie explained excitedly. She paused trying to think of other things she had been wanting to try.

Martin looked at his friend with pity, "I told you, you volunteered yourself for all sorts of trouble."

"What are you complaining about? You never got hurt when you were helping to train me," Julie objected, feigning insult.

Then Matt introduced her to each of the new men. She recognized a few of them from her time helping the Teams, but she had never learned their names. The first one saluted her, and she blushed. "Please don't salute me," she begged.

"Yes, ma'am," he replied, dropping his salute.

"And please don't call me ma'am. You can call me Julie, or Jade if you really want to be formal," Julie told him with a wry grin.

"Yes m... I mean... sure.... Jade," the man seemed to struggle with the words.

"See, you can do it," Julie joked. "Besides, I don't outrank you, so why're you saluting me anyway?"

"They've never met a top secret person before," Matt teased her. "Things and places yes, but not a person."

The rest of the men Matt introduced her to tried their best to refrain from saluting or calling her ma'am. When they were done with the introductions they all seemed more relaxed. Finally Julie noticed a yellow line painted on the rough concrete floor. She looked at the rest of the floor in the large open area. She saw 'LZ Keep Clear' written in large red letters. On the far wall she saw a new SEAL Team emblem with the letters RRDT.

Confused she looked at Lieutenant Cooper.

"Welcome to the new SEAL Remote Reconnaissance and Delivery Team," Lieutenant Cooper answered the questioning look in her eyes.

"Why is it called the Remote Reconnaissance and Delivery Team?" Julie asked still confused.

"We needed to call it something, but we still needed to keep you secret. Calling it SEAL Team Jade would be a big give away that we were connected to you. This is the Landing Zone, LZ for short," Lieutenant Cooper continued to explain. "This is where you will teleport us in and out of for most of our missions. The rest of the facility has everything we might need," he told her. "Feel free to look around. This place is completely secure."

"Really?" Julie asked doubtfully. She realized that she was becoming as paranoid as her Uncle Mark.

"It has metal shielded walls to prevent any signals from being transmitted out, along with multiple security perimeters including a retinal scanner," Lieutenant Cooper explained proudly. "That's just a few of the security measures they've built into this place. No one will be able to fight or fake their way in here, or get information about you out."

Julie had started to head down one of the hallways, when she noticed a room that was directly across from the LZ. "What's in there?" she asked, and then froze in fear as several people came out of the room. She recognized Dr. Emory and his nurse Debbie. Behind them some more people she did not know followed them out of the room.

"It's alright. They've all been cleared to know your identity," Matt reassured her. She looked like she might zap out of there any second, she was so scared.

"I'm sorry, Julie," Dr. Emory said. "The corpsman who revealed your information was new to my office. He didn't have clearance to see your file, but he knew what he was looking for and he found a way to bypass our security. We never wanted to put you, or your team at risk. I hope you'll be able to trust us again."

"This facility is completely isolated from any other area, including the computer system. Your information will be entirely contained here, and steps have been taken to ensure that none of it can leave the building," Simmons explained to ease her fears.

Doc tried next. "Julie, we need a real doctor who is cleared to care for you, just in case you're wounded again. I know I'm good, but I can't do everything by myself," he joked, trying to reassure her. "This is a fully equipped ER in case any of us need it. The staff will be available 24/7 right here. We won't have to risk transporting you to another hospital."

"Also, we need to continue to research how teleporting affects you," Lieutenant Cooper pointed out trying to reason with her. "We need to find a better way to tell when you are about to crash. It could be doing permanent damage to your body when your blood sugar drops too low."

"I know, but..." Julie was still uncertain.

"Come on. Let's show you the rest of the place," Matt suggested. "You're going to love it."

The team took her on a tour of the entire building. They had thought of everything they might need to do missions or training. Besides a briefing room, it had a full sized pool, a wrestling mat, an indoor shooting range, and a weight training room.

"What's this room?" Julie looked into a room about twelve feet by twelve feet with stark concrete walls, floor and ceiling and a heavy steel door. Covering the walls and ceiling was a thick, gray material. "What's that for?"

"Those are Kevlar blankets to help absorb shrapnel," Demetrio explained. "This is the room where you can take anything that goes boom. We don't want to have to fix our pool again."

"Seriously?" Julie asked impressed. "Nice." Then she grimaced at a thought, "I'd hate to be the one responsible for cleaning it afterward."

"That's what the floor drain is for," Simmons said with a smirk, pointing to a huge drain set into the floor.

"Why do I need a bedroom here?" Julie asked confused. The final room they showed her looked like a college dorm room. "I just finished my new hideout."

"It's just in case you can't go home at night," Simmons teased her. "You'll have a comfortable bed for us to dump you in while you sleep it off."

Julie shoved him in response. "This place is perfect guys," she said honestly. Then she saw something lying on the bed. She went to pick it up and found that it was a camouflage version of her hooded cloak.

"Your old one was looking a bit tattered, and this one won't scream 'shoot me' either," Lieutenant Cooper explained.

Julie was at a loss for words. All she could say was, "Thank you."

"There's one more thing," Matt said from behind her. She turned around and saw him kneeling, holding up something in his hand. "Will you marry me?" he asked.

Julie stepped forward and saw the ring he held. It sparkled like blue fireworks. She looked down into his hopeful eyes. "Yes," she said with a huge smile, and then kissed him as around them the team started cheering.

ABOUT THE AUTHOR

Janet Racciato graduated from Washington State University with a bachelor's degree in Natural Resource Sciences. Later she went back to school at California State University San Marcos and earned her Multiple Subject Teacher's Credential and a Moderate to Severe Special Education Credential. She worked for many years as a special education teacher and then later as a director of a school for children with special medical needs. Recently Janet put aside her special education career to be a stay-at-home mom to be able to spend more time with her family and pursue her writing.

Made in the USA
San Bernardino, CA
22 August 2017